The Glass Madonna

The Glass Madonna

Donna Meredith

Wild Women Writers
An independent publishing company

The Glass Madonna

ISBN: 978-0-9829015-0-2

Published by Wild Women Writers, P.O. Box 3426
Tallahassee, FL 32315-3426
www.wildwomenwriters.com

Logo design by E'Layne Koenigsberg of 3 Hip Chics, Tallahassee, FL
www.3HipChics.com

Cover Art by DeDe Harter, who creates drawings, paintings, and sculpture from her home-based studio in Tallahassee, Florida. She teaches art at Florida State University and Valdosta State University.

Printed in the United States of America

Dedication

This book is dedicated to the elves, fairies, and squirrels that populate the woods on Lowndes Hill and my great aunt Olivia Marie Heitz who brought them to life with her amazing stories, and to my mother, Patricia Heitz Stanley, who read to me every night with love and devotion. Every child should be so lucky.

Acknowledgements

I thank the many early readers of this novel: Laura Garrison Codgill, Jo Folsome, Kristel Heil, Liz Jameson, Shirley Jones, Noreen Lieb-Beattie, Harriet McDonald, Pat Murphy, Leslie Patterson, Mary Jane Ryals, Karen Schneider, Jean Sleeman, Michael Whitehead and Charlie Wilkerson. Their suggestions improved the novel immensely.

I also want to thank the glass artists and factory workers who took the time to talk to me about their craft: my uncle James Heitz, Katie Lannan, Leslie Nolan, and Warner Whitfield.

Thanks to my colleague Lesa Cannon for providing the background on asthma.

Thanks to Rhett DeVane, Peggy Kassees, Hannah Mahler, and Susan Womble for their encouragment to get this book into print. And I'm grateful for the careful attention given to the manuscript by editor Paula Kiger.

I appreciate the support of the Tallahassee Writers Association and the many fine writers and friends I've met through the organization.

Thanks to Ron Franscell, author of *Angel Fire*, for helping me see that I needed to throw my protagonist "over the cliff."

A special thanks to now-retired Florida State University professor Sheila Ortiz-Taylor for admitting me to her creative writing workshops, where I benefited from the gentle nurturing she gives to all new writers.

Thanks, also, to the Leon County Library reference staff and to David Houchin of the Harrison County Library, who was extremely helpful, particularly in locating an obscure thesis on the Socialist party victories in Adamston, West Virginia, which inspired a whole thread in this novel. My apologies to descendants of Walter Boyles, who really was the Socialist mayor of Adamston, but all other details about this character were purely fiction.

Above all, I am grateful for the support of my family, which enabled me to write this book. My husband gifted me with a laptop to start the book and he put up with all the time it consumed. I can't remember a day since I was born that my mother, Patricia Heitz Stanley, hasn't insisted I could do anything I set my mind to. And the joy my daughter Tamara Huston, her husband John, and my grandson Julian bring to me makes every day a blessing.

Prologue

June 1963

Pale morning light sliced through the Venetian blinds and laddered the top of the black enamel chest of drawers with silver stripes, pooling at last inside the object of Sarah's desire. Inside the one object in her aunt's bedroom that always commanded her eye. The glass Madonna. Every Saturday, Aunt Livvie parted with some small treasure squirreled away inside the drawers, but so far, she had refused to hand over what Sarah wanted most.

"If it broke, you could get hurt," Livvie said one weekend. The most crushing excuse of all—"You're too young"—tumbled from Livvie's lips another Saturday, and it wasn't the kind of blunder her aunt was prone to make. If anything, at eleven, Sarah considered herself too old for dolls, but the Madonna wasn't exactly a doll. More like what Sarah's mother would call a figurine.

Sarah sucked the last muffin crumbs from her fingers and traipsed behind her aunt toward the chest of drawers. Pain shot through Sarah's big toe as her sandal rammed the bedpost. It was her legs again. Her gross, spindly legs. They sent her elbows on a collision course with door frames and banged her knees into tables, causing purple splotches to bloom days later. By the time her mother asked what happened, Sarah couldn't remember. Her legs had stretched three inches taller since Christmas, making her the tallest kid in the sixth grade. A freak, except on the basketball court where having the longest reach was a good thing.

As they approached the Madonna, Sarah forgot the throbbing toe. She sensed rather than saw the celery walls, the slim stack of Aunt Katherine's books on the bedside table, the closet bottomed by Katherine's shoe collection and topped with Livvie's hat boxes, the shiny bottle of Estée Lauder cologne to the right of the comb and brush on the vanity.

Sarah offered a subtle hint. "Look how pretty Mary is. Doesn't she just shine with love?"

No reaction from Livvie.

Wispy curtains on either side of the black chest stirred with a breeze already beginning to warm though it was not yet ten o'clock. Instead of reaching for the Madonna, Livvie opened the middle drawer. The scent of lavender floated out. Anything might be inside those drawers: hand-painted fans, pink-beribboned sachet bags, beaded coin purses with scarab bracelets tucked inside. Treasures all, but not what Sarah wanted.

She twisted her torso from side to side, scratching the back of one calf with the sandal on her other foot. Her toe remembered the bang into the bedpost and protested this further abuse. A black and white photograph of Sarah's four aunts—old maids, her father called them—was propped on the right edge of the chest in a silver frame. Though Sarah had seen the photo a million times, this morning the resemblance struck her smack between the eyes.

"The Madonna looks an awful lot like you."

Livvie's laughter tinkled into the room. "Honey, this old lady could play the Wicked Witch of the West without make-up."

"No, I mean when you were young. The way you looked in that picture."

"Believe me, I wasn't much better looking then."

Despite her aunt's denials, certain similarities stood out. Narrow faces. Pronounced cheekbones. Barely upturned lips saying without words, *I am content just as I am.* Only the noses differed significantly. To Sarah, Livvie Heimbach had always seemed beautiful as she plucked the green umbel of a mayapple and offered it as an elf's umbrella along with a story. A double-cupped acorn became a fairy telephone. A found arrowhead, the tale of an Indian princess. Sarah studied her aunt, really seeing her for the first time, comforted, that yes, she was wearing a cherry-print apron with the ever-present tissue tucked behind the bib. Yet it was a bit of a surprise to discover Livvie was pointy-nosed and so tall and thin the kids in school must have called her names, too. Toothpick. Spider legs. Bag of bones. Stand sideways and stick out your tongue and you'd look like a zipper. Sarah had heard every joke.

Livvie closed the first drawer and opened another. "Now, where did I put your little something? I'd have sworn—"

A cloud veiled the sun, and the Madonna's translucence faded to pearly gray. Sarah picked the figurine up and tried to change her aunt's focus. "What kind of glass is this?"

Livvie's eyes flicked up. She went back to rummaging in the drawer. "Satin glass. Some call it frosted."

Sarah set the statue down and traced an imaginary neckline under her collarbone. "I love satin. I'm going to have a satin wedding dress with gazillions of pearls sewn all over the top and a train so long it will take three bridesmaids to carry it."

"Here it is." Livvie held out a yellow-striped box with Bonne Bell lip glosses and cologne. "You're too young to be talking weddings, but you're about the right age for this, I expect."

Sarah whooped and hugged the package close to her chest, the Madonna forgotten momentarily. She remembered her mother's rule, and her smile collapsed. No lipstick. Not even pink. Eleven was either too young or too old for almost everything. Eleven stunk.

Her aunt seemed to know what she was thinking. "I already asked your mother and it's okay."

Sarah threw one arm around Livvie's waist, the other still clasping the cosmetics. "Thanks."

Livvie patted Sarah's springy curls. "Anything for you, honey."

Sarah loosened her hold on her aunt and tilted her head to one side, eyes cast upward. "Would you let me have the Madonna someday?"

She waited for Livvie to say, *Of course, honey, what's mine is yours.* Instead, wrinkles plowed her aunt's forehead. "The Madonna is passed to the woman in the family who needs her most."

No one could want her more, but how could you need a nine-inch tall figurine? "Hope it's me."

To Sarah's surprise, Livvie's face crumpled. Her bony fingers worried their way inside her apron bodice and fidgeted with the tissue. "Please don't wish for that. I'm going to pray right now you won't be the one." Livvie's eyes squeezed shut and her lips moved silently.

Sarah sucked in her lower lip. Holy cow, what had she done now? The injustice of the whole scene weighed upon her. She hadn't asked for anything outrageous. Only a figurine, for crying out loud.

A sour belligerence took hold in her stomach. "It's okay, I don't really want it anyway. I have lots of dolls."

When Livvie's eyes opened, her expression once again mirrored the Madonna's.

Sarah was still a little mad, but Livvie's loving smile drove the last anger away. She hopped down the stairs and waited at the bottom for her aunt, who proceeded slowly, advancing only when certain her shoe was planted firmly on a step, one hand braced against the oak banister, button-front dress fluttering against her calves. Sensing Livvie would not deny her two things in a row, Sarah asked to hold her uncle's glass design of trees. Sarah didn't know why she loved glass. She just did. Her mother said it ran in Sarah's veins, the Heimbach side. Livvie lifted the picture from the living room wall and released it into Sarah's hands with a warning not to break it. A moment later, the basement door whined open and Livvie's footsteps tapped down the stairs, growing less distinct until they faded into the electric hum of the house.

Sarah angled the glass in her lap so that it captured the light slanting through the window. Colors shimmered to life. Emerald and lime leaves. Walnut and milk chocolate bark. One tree, probably a dogwood, was sprinkled with white flowers. Itsy bitsy pieces of glass, none outstanding by itself, created a forest so magical she half expected to see elves and fairies winking at her from the foliage. She traced her fingers across the slick surface, wondering how the colors flowed seamlessly into each other without blending or smearing. She shifted the picture to her left hand and scratched her thigh where the shag carpet devilled the bare skin below her shorts.

"What in the Sam Hill are you doing?"

She nearly dropped the picture at the sound of Uncle Mahlon's gravelly voice. "I washed my hands before I touched it." Aunt Livvie's lemon muffins lingered on Sarah's sticky hands as surely as their fragrance remained in the air, but the lie was out before she could stop it. Uncle Mahlon's eyes sought fault. She was sure if she poked her finger into her uncle's heart it would be as hard as the glass he made, unlike her aunts, who proved all softness under angles and old bones. Not quite as tall as Livvie, Mahlon was so thin his belly and chest seemed hollowed out. Pale streaks of scalp peeped through dark hair he wore slicked back.

Her uncle scowled. "How'd you get it off the wall in the first place?"

"Aunt Livvie—"

"Never mind, none of your aunts have learned to say no. Spoil you kids rotten. Give it here before you break it."

Sarah raised the picture over her head. When certain the glass was secure, she rose from the floor. "It's so beautiful—did you really make it?"

He grunted an answer, but the corners of his mouth wiggled slightly, enough Sarah knew she was no longer in trouble. She risked another question.

"How?"

Mahlon snapped an answer. "Glass isn't something you can explain in a few minutes."

"I want to learn, even if it takes all summer."

"Girls can't apprentice."

"Why?"

A book clutched between her hands, Aunt Katherine crossed the living room, her stooped shoulders serving to exaggerate the contrast between her short stature and her sister Livvie's height. Katherine settled into her favorite green brocade chair. "Really, Mahlon, why is that?"

Mahlon flicked his head toward her aunt's book. "Don't know why you read such trash." Sarah took a closer look. *The Feminine Mystique.* She wasn't sure exactly what "mystique" meant, but figured it must relate to mystery. If you asked her, men were the mystery. She never knew what to say when her aunts sent her into the den to greet her uncle. He never praised report cards or complimented new clothes. He hid out in that cubbyhole behind the *Clarksburg Exponent-Telegram.* Neither did she understand her father, why he drank so much pop when it made him so mean.

Mahlon re-hung the picture and addressed Katherine without bothering to look at her. "That book's revived all your foolish notions. Thought you'd laid them to rest a long time ago when you got the right to vote. You know only boys apprentice. Union rules."

Now her uncle was talking nonsense. Sarah's neighbor, Rita Watson, worked in the glass factory, had ever since Sarah had known her. But with a sudden queasiness, Sarah realized she'd never heard Rita talk about making glass. She talked about pulling finished pieces off a conveyor belt and wiping them down with a rag. About packing ash-trays into tiny compartments of large corrugated boxes. Never about actually making anything. In a dizzying flash of certainty, Sarah knew her uncle spoke the truth.

Katherine's reading glasses slid even further down the bridge of her nose. "Fiddlesticks. It's not like the union has any real power these days."

"Never heard of a girl doing glass," Mahlon said.

"Soon, the way the world's going, no one will be making glass the old way. Pete's certainly not going to be the one to carry on."

Mahlon's lips thinned, and Sarah could see her aunt had scored a point in a battle she didn't entirely grasp. Who was Pete? Sarah felt her uncle's eyes on her again, measuring, and finding her wanting in some way. She rolled all the anguish she felt into a basketball. Then she pictured the ball getting smaller and smaller, until it was like the hard red ball she used for jacks, rolled up hard, tight, and not a single tear would slide out, not a single crack would show on her face. She had perfected this trick at home around her father.

Her uncle suggested her brother Garrett might want to apprentice and her control evaporated. Words blew out of her mouth so fast they stumbled over each other.

"Don't bother to ask him he only cares about baseball because he thinks he's going to be the next Stan Musial and all he ever does is practice pitching and when he's not outside he's collecting those stupid cards and memorizing batting averages, so he wouldn't be the least bit interested and besides he's a stupid jerk." Hadn't he ruined her science project, a volcano, by setting fire to it? Said he wanted to see the lava flow. Moron. She took a breath. "I really, really want to make pictures and vases like you do." The glass-front cabinet in the dining room shone with vases in rose, brilliant blue, emerald with gold swirls, iridescent glass that seemed to change colors as you looked at it. Each one a marvel—and not to be touched.

Her uncle's face didn't soften one bit as his eyes flicked between her and Katherine. "If you're that interested, you can come to the studio today." To Katherine: "Ten to one, the brat'll get bored and I'll have to quit early to bring her home."

Sarah hardened her face again so he couldn't see how the remark cut. Going with him didn't seem like such a hot idea now, but no way would she give him the satisfaction of backing out.

Katherine sniffed. "Unlike you, I don't gamble, and especially I'm not going to gamble on anything as precious as my niece, but I think she'll prove you wrong."

Mahlon didn't speak to Sarah as she trotted behind him down the steep concrete sidewalk leading away from her aunts' house. Some distance away, smoke stacks poked above the tree-line, belching a continuous stream of gray pollution into the air. When Sarah was little, she thought they sent out messages like Indian smoke signals. Today their message seemed to be "No girls allowed." Her uncle used to work in the factory before he retired. For three blocks, she trailed him through a neighborhood typical to Clarksburg, past two-story homes, some freshly painted, some shedding their skins like onions, all bunched together, defying gravity as they tried to find a level perch. If the first home on top of the hill gave in, the whole line would go down like dominoes. They passed a father doing Saturday chores, scenting the air with the green smell of clipped hedges and fresh-mown grass. They cut through an alley lined with metal trash cans that smelled of chicken bones and rotted produce, passed by backyards with webbed lawn chairs and laundry flying like flags in assorted shapes and colors. At last they arrived at the workshop her uncle shared with two fellow hobbyists. A converted garage. Nothing special.

The inside was surprisingly cheerful with cabinets painted royal blue trimmed in butterscotch.

"Pretty colors," Sarah said.

Mahlon humphed. "Your Aunt Maggie's idea. She painted everything the year before she died. Plain varnish would have been fine."

True, but without color the room would look ordinary. The three kilns along one wall reminded Sarah of the bears story: an extra large kiln, a wee one the size of a Legos box, and a medium kiln perfect for Mahlon's project. It was round and lined, so he said, with special bricks. Her uncle turned a knob and set the heat to 1,400 degrees.

At that moment Sarah saw the picture on the back wall. She couldn't look away even though she knew she should. Movie-star gorgeous, the woman was composed of tiny pieces of glass. Long tendrils of hair waved softly over mounded breasts with petal pink nipples.

Chest—the word her mother half-swallowed when forced to refer to that body part—wouldn't begin to describe those swellings. Sarah crossed her arms over her own buttons. They showed no inclination to grow, despite the bust exercises she did daily. Her best friend Rachel already wore a training bra.

"Did you make that picture?"

She pointed and his eyes followed her motion to the wall. He took out a white cotton handkerchief and tucked a corner behind the frame, letting the rest drape over the picture like a bib. "Told your aunt girls have no business in a glass studio. Better forget you saw that."

"Did you make her?"

"Yeah."

"Who is she?"

He picked up a piece of clear glass as large as the countertop. "My wife."

"Where is she? Did she die?"

"She—" He coughed, lightly at first, then deep in his chest, fist pressed over his mouth. The coughing deepened until he bent over double at the waist. When the spasms faded, her uncle's face looked pasty and pinched. "If you ever want to come back here, you better not say anything to your aunts about that picture."

"What are you making now?"

With a razor knife, he scored the glass and split off a ten-by-fourteen inch rectangle. "Another picture with trees. This will be the base."

From a bottom cabinet her uncle grabbed a large wooden frame with fabric stretched over it. A silk screen, he said. He laid it on top of the plate glass. "What colors do you want?"

She leaned over the work table, her feet nearly dancing. "Fall trees. Orange, gold, red and brown."

Uncle Mahlon took four jars of dust from a cabinet and sprinkled a spoonful of one over the silk screen.

"What's that stuff?"

"Frit. Ground up glass."

The jars held what looked like slightly different shades of dirt. Not orange or gold at all.

He anticipated her question. "The colors change when they're heated."

Pinholes punched in the screen formed trees of different types and sizes. Mahlon sprinkled the frit over several of them, each time removing the screen from the plate glass to show her the design where the dust fell through. He turned the silk screen over to reverse the designs, then let Sarah sprinkle two trees along with brown frit for trunks. Mahlon scratched a match and a ruler-sized torch whooshed out a flame. He motioned to a jar filled with what looked like pick-up sticks of all colors and told her to choose one for foreground grass.

She handed him a stick the color of canned peas, and he held it, a little at a time, in the flame. As the glass became pliable, he stretched it into a very thin thread and broke off tiny pieces. He scattered them across the bottom third of the picture. With a tiny brush, he whisked away a few stray specks of frit, and the piece was ready for the first firing. He placed it on a fireproof paper inside the kiln. This layer wouldn't be ready until the next day, when he would add a second layer of clear glass with another tree or two screened on to create the illusion of dimension. Finally the picture would be re-fired and cooled again.

"Can I come back and help?"

He glanced at his wife's picture on the wall and frowned. "Guess so. Don't forget you're not to mention my wife to your aunts."

"I promise." She put the jars of frit back in the cabinet. "I want to make vases like the ones in Livvie's china cupboard."

"Don't hold your breath. You won't be making a vase, not for a long time."

"Can I watch you make one?"

"You ask too many questions."

Her aunts never minded—they said you learned by asking questions, but Sarah repressed her curiosity as they trudged back up the hill. She wanted to ask what made him cough so violently he had to stop half a dozen times to catch his breath on the way to the Aunt Hill. The house was so named by her father because the four unmarried aunts lived in the white two-story atop the highest hill in Clarksburg with a bachelor uncle. Only two of the four aunts were still living, and now she knew Mahlon wasn't exactly a bachelor. She didn't know what he was. She kept her promise about not mentioning his wife to the aunts, but in the car on the way home she asked her mother.

"They haven't lived together for years."

"Did they have kids?"

"Yes, but they live with their mother. You ask too many questions. Don't bother your aunts about Uncle Mahlon's wife, you hear?"

Through the summer Sarah spent three days a week with Mahlon in his workshop. She fetched supplies and tools, watching everything he did, and always aware of the woman hiding behind the handkerchief on the wall. Garrett would have snickered over her big bazooms.

One August morning when Mahlon unlocked and opened the door to the studio, the heat nearly knocked Sarah flat. It swirled around her face in waves. Add a few flames and this could be the Hell Reverend Martin was always preaching about. Mahlon went to a slim drawer and withdrew a photograph taken in front of a factory she didn't recognize. It was in New Kensington, her uncle said.

"That's your grandfather on the right, and my brothers—your uncles—Thomas, Patrick, and Joe."

A dozen other men stood with them, some with arms thrown casually over the next fellow's shoulders. They all looked happy, joking, not fake-smiling for the camera.

Mahlon stared at the photo. "We were like family. Lived in the same neighborhood, drank a case or two of beer together every Friday night, moved together from factory to factory. We took pride in making the best damn glass in America. It's not like that anymore."

With a wistful look, he slid the picture away. From a lower cabinet she'd never seen him bother before, he withdrew a six-foot long metal pipe and laid it on the countertop. "You been a good little worker, lot better than I thought you'd be. Best apprentice I ever had."

She held back the silly grin threatening to pop across her face and kept her feet still. Her uncle didn't hold with giggling or wiggling of any kind.

"I work mostly with fused glass these days, as you've figured out, but I guess you earned the right to learn how to use a blowpipe. That is, if you still want to."

Did he have to ask?

Mahlon stripped to his white undershirt. "Came by late last night and fired up the biggest furnace and loaded it with batch. Even my big furnace is a pitiful thing compared to the factory's, but it's still hotter than hell in here and it's gonna be even hotter once the gate's opened.

You better not fuss or I'm taking you right home and you can forget about blowing glass."

"I won't."

He measured her with those coal-dark eyes. "I know you won't. Your first job is to open the gate of the furnace for me and once I move out of the way, shut it again."

Sarah pulled on heat-proof gloves and opened the furnace. With his blowpipe, her uncle extracted a gob of molten glass from a pint-sized container called the crucible. Heat swam visibly in the air. Sarah slammed the gate. Sweat trickled down her spine. She snatched her shirt collar from her skin.

Mahlon leaned the pipe against a wooden bench. He took a deep breath, his cheeks puffed up as if he were going to play a trumpet, and he exhaled into the pipe. The glass on the other end writhed like it was coming to life. A brilliant blue, it expanded into an ever larger ball, shimmering with light.

With muscled arms, Mahlon twirled the blowpipe round and round and blew some more. The gob on the end grew bigger, stretched thinner. He dipped it into the fire of a tiny furnace he called the glory hole. When he began to blow again, the mass shimmered in a magical state, neither liquid nor solid. To Sarah, it seemed as if Mahlon danced with delicately timed steps—blowing, twirling, dipping—moving to music only he could hear, the rhythms flowing naturally through his limbs. At the end of their dance together, man and glass, the pipe gave birth to a cobalt ball. Her uncle's breath, the kiss of life.

Sarah handed him a wet paddle and he flattened the bottom of the vase while she steadied the blowpipe. Using tongs, he broke the glass free and attached it to a punty rod. He used tongs and paddles to open up the lip of the vase. Then it was ready for the annealing oven. Even though she was only her uncle's helper, she felt his power flowing in her veins. She had witnessed secrets passed through the generations of her family, father to son, father to son, always father to son. Until now.

It had been a beautiful dance, but when it ended, her uncle coughed longer and harder than ever before. Afterwards, he grabbed a Stroh's from a little refrigerator and downed it in two gulps.

"Helps put out the fire," he said. He drank another on the slow trek back to the Aunt Hill.

August ended with a promise Sarah could continue her apprenticeship the next summer. A promise Mahlon couldn't keep. In February her uncle died.

Back at the Aunt Hill after the funeral, Livvie stood in front of the picture of autumn trees, displayed now beside the spring trees Sarah had first admired. On this occasion, Livvie abandoned her apron, but not her tissue. She dabbed her eyes, while the bones of the fingers on her other hand dug into Sarah's shoulder. "That awful white lung. It killed our papa, too, and my brother Joseph."

"Papa claimed it was the price you paid for the privilege of working with glass," Katherine said.

Livvie sniffed. "Some privilege."

"Papa thought so."

Livvie hugged her elbows close. "I'm glad the Heimbachs are through with glass."

The aunts walked their argument into the kitchen where the rest of the family gathered around neighbors' offerings of food. Sarah, alone for a moment, stretched her fingers up to touch the garnet foliage, remembering how the frit sifted through the screen to form the tree. When she closed her eyes, she could hear echoes of her uncle's music as he blew on the pipe. The sound thrummed through her veins.

One

DECEMBER 5, 1969

The trouble started the night Cal Caruso told Sarah he intended to give up his draft deferment—which was certifiably crazy. Sarah's head slumped against his shoulder, her first-ever beer sitting almost untouched on the sticky table before her in a puddle of condensation. She felt a little paranoid because the beer wasn't legal. She wouldn't be eighteen for two more weeks even though her first semester of college was nearly over.

Cal tried to tickle her neck, but she smacked his hand away. "Tell me you're not really going to do this."

The grin disappeared. "I told you if my draft number came up, I was going. The lottery's fair, except for deferments. Why should someone like me get out of going to Nam because my parents can afford to pay for college or because I play basketball on scholarship? The system dumps on guys who are poor. It's un-American."

Something in her throat shattered as he spoke. Cal's clothes and wavy dark hair were as neat as if he were cast in *Father Knows Best*. She couldn't picture him in fatigues like those boys she saw on the nightly news. Grim-faced boys who knew about Claymores, flak jackets, toes lost to jungle rot, resupply choppers that hadn't come, body bags. Something was terribly wrong with her, or he wouldn't be so ready to hold an M-16 in his arms instead of her.

"I've heard of guys cutting off a toe to get out of going, and here you are—tossing aside a perfectly legitimate reason to stay home. You can't really want to kill people you don't even know."

His eyes flickered with what might have been uncertainty, then hardened again. "*Want* has nothing to do with it. It's duty, the price of freedom. My father did his part, my grandfather did his, now it's my turn."

"But it isn't even fighting for our country. It's someone else's."

In high school, Sarah had been a goody-two-shoes—as her senior year crush phrased it—so she had never been inside The Sub before. The hangout had taken on mythic proportions in her imagination, but now she could see it didn't amount to much: a refurbished double-wide trailer converted into a bar with dim lighting and small Formica-topped tables, most scratched with initials. The one beside them displayed a crude drawing of male private parts gouged into the surface. Cigarette smoke snaked its way into her hair, clothes, eyes and lungs.

Cal finished off his Stroh's. A memory of Uncle Mahlon drinking the same brand the summer before he died surfaced in Sarah's mind. She pushed the thought away, along with the word *died*. That wasn't going to happen. Not to Cal.

"Come on now, drink up," Cal said. "It's not that bad, is it?"

It was that bad. Bitter and yeasty. Still, she took another sip, part of a self-prescribed cure, something to push past long-held antipathy toward alcohol. Every guy who downed a beer wasn't going to turn into her father. Under the influence, he was capable of being the most fun guy at the party or of displaying embarrassing sentimentality. Or with the slightest provocation, equally capable of flaying the skin from her brother's legs. She took another sip, grimaced slightly.

"Good, now hand it over." Cal's eyes never left hers as he slipped the Stroh's from her hand. His lips sensuously puckered around the lip of the bottle, his eyes still grinning, right at her. She felt the blush creep up her neck as if he were making love to her in front of God and everybody. They shared the rest of the bottle, arguing back and forth.

As he continued to make his case, she held out little hope of changing his mind. Cal ordered them both a second beer. "Maybe it will taste better to you in a mug."

"Yes, a glass." She still loved everything about glass, but her mother nixed her ambitions to follow in her uncle's footsteps: *No way, you want to die young like my father and brother, is that what you want? You'll send me to an early grave if anything happens to you, you know that, don't you?* The union representative had been amused when she showed up at the factory after high school: *Honey, nice little girl like you don't want to work on the floor. How about a job in our office filing papers?* So what else could Sarah do? She enrolled in college and majored in political science and journalism and liked her courses well enough.

The waitress returned with their drinks. Sarah drew her thumb through the condensation on the mug. An "l." She added a "C" and an "a" in front and grinned at him. She felt shitty-goofy-stupid but couldn't help herself. Cal made her crazy.

Light from the overhead fixture streamed through the mug, illuminating little bubbles that swam up through the amber liquid as though they were living creatures surfacing for air. Of course, that made no sense. They *were* air. This beer did taste better than the first and while she drank, she and Cal debated the state of the world. She thought Americans needed to do more to help starving Africans. He didn't believe in welfare of any kind, but when absolutely necessary he thought aid should go to your neighbors first. He believed in the administration's domino theory, that if one country toppled to Communism, it would start a chain reaction; she didn't. He thought draft dodgers in Canada were cowards; she thought they were smart, maybe even heroes for standing up against an unjust war.

He challenged her. "So if I go, you won't care whether I come back or not because in your eyes I'll be some coward who went to fight instead of going to Canada?"

"No, stupid, that's not what I said." By this time, a third beer—she didn't remember ordering one—began to ease the sharp edges from her words. She felt floaty as if the edges were also being erased from the table where they sat, from the buzz of the crowd, from the corners of her mind. A blast of cool air hit her waist. She tucked her shirt tail back into her bell-bottoms.

"I know you aren't going to write any more editorials against the war when I'm over there fighting."

"I'll write even better ones and get the damn war ended."

Cal pulled her closer and kissed her forehead. "Let's not argue for once."

She didn't want to. This was the fourth time she'd fallen in love with him. The first was in fifth grade. Even then, Cal Caruso was a charmer with wavy dark hair and blue eyes framed by black eyelashes so long PTA moms would shake their heads with envy. Wasted on a guy, they claimed. His smile, backed by a row of perfect white teeth, lit up the classroom. On Monday he sent Sarah a three-line note, "I like Cal, I don't like Cal, Check one." No fool, she checked the first line. In the next note passed across the aisle, he asked her to go steady.

She told her mother, who laughed. "And where exactly are you going?" Sarah stormed from the kitchen and shut herself in her bedroom. Of course her mother couldn't understand love—she was married to Sarah's father.

On Tuesday, Cal brought her a sappy poem: Roses are red, violets are blue, Cal's heart is all for you. They sneaked into the cloak room during lunch and took bites out of each other's sandwiches. Their hands trembled when they touched. Wednesday he brought her the blossoming branch of a Kwanzan cherry, pink powder puffs that tickled her nose. She could feel her heart blooming within, as fluffy as the flowers. On Thursday, Cal passed Sarah another note. They were no longer going steady. As of today, he was going with her best friend Rachel. Palm down on her desk and fingertips splayed upward, Rachel showed off an orange plastic ring Cal won after inserting many pennies in a gumball machine. Sarah wanted to pull Rachel's black braids until her eyeballs popped out.

In eighth grade Sarah's first kiss had come from Cal. Not a real kiss, she didn't suppose. Only on her elbow after he chased her around the playground basketball court until she fell and hurt herself. Real enough, though, that she thought of it every time he beaned her with a paper wad in class. Real enough to make her mope for days after he asked someone else to the spring sock hop.

In tenth grade they double-dated for two months. At the Coffee House they danced to "Back in My Arms Again." While watching *The Trouble With Angels,* they got Milk Duds and popcorn stuck in their teeth. Halfway through, they held hands. *The Bible* movie wasn't the sort of subject you held hands through anyway, but when Adam and Eve frolicked through the Garden, Sarah thought she'd die. The director could have used fig leaves, for goodness sake, instead of confronting audiences with all that nakedness. She and Cal scrunched into the far corners of the padded burgundy seats. It took half an hour of joking with friends at Twin Oaks Pizza before they could look at each other again. They argued while Sarah picked pepperoni off her slice. Cal and Jimmy Watson believed in the creation story exactly as it was written; she and Paula Jackman believed it was only a story. "I suppose you think the Virgin Mary story is a myth too," Cal countered. In fact, Sarah thought it likely.

Their religious differences caused distress at home too. He was Catholic; she was Methodist. "I hope you don't get too serious about him. For heaven's sake, they don't believe in birth control," her mother whispered after their fourth date, fingers spread over her mouth as if dirt might escape. It was the only time she ever mentioned contraceptives in Sarah's presence. Sarah dragged her fingers over her eyelids and down her cheeks in disbelief. It wasn't like they were getting married. And after all, her mother's relatives were Catholic. Why make such a big deal out it?

Then Cal's family moved to Charlotte, North Carolina, and after a few letters, their friendship faded like a flower pressed between the pages of a book.

The fourth time she fell in love with him happened in the Fairmont State College newspaper office at a meeting for freshman wannabe reporters. As soon as Cal saw her in the *Column's* office, he picked her up in a crushing bear hug and swung her around. "I *knew* there was a reason I came to FSC."

Her words flew out while her feet circled through space. "Yeah, right. I imagine a basketball scholarship had something to do with it."

"Partly." He planted a big, boisterous kiss right on her lips. "Only partly. I wanted to come home."

They had been inseparable ever since. Because FSC's entertainment options consisted of watching television in the dorm lounge or, alternatively, watching mold grow in the showers, every Friday he loaded his duffel bag and her suitcase into his Ford and drove the twenty-five miles to Clarksburg, where Sarah spent weekends with her parents and Cal stayed with his aunt. Assumptions were made. His childless aunt gave her a teapot, a family heirloom. Hinted more would come at the wedding. Evenings, they watched TV, studied, or took in a movie.

Never before had they gone to a bar, but the lottery was already changing this to that, shifting a routine from here to there. As Sarah drank her beers, an awareness settled into her consciousness. The Army made boys into men. Unless it maimed or killed them. In any case, the Cal who came home wasn't going to be the same boy who left. She had to stop him.

Cal put a quarter in the jukebox. As Smith crooned "Baby It's You," he tugged Sarah from her chair. At five-ten, she towered over many guys, but Cal stood six-three. He folded her close against a mossy green sweater, long arms wrapped around her waist. His scent—cedar with undertones of smoke and spice—left her slightly dizzy.

He drew back, both hands cradling her face. "God, you're beautiful."

She knew she wasn't—her nose, too long; her hair, too curly; her frame, too tall and thin; a gangly creature with pale freckled skin and gnawed-on cuticles—but she liked hearing him say it. The only possible answer was a kiss. As she ducked her head against his shoulder, her nose brushed the five-o'clock shadow on the underside of his chin, sending tingles down the insides of her thighs. She longed to slide around the dance floor, warm and entwined like this forever. If only Vietnam would go back to being a country no one had ever heard of.

By the time the song ended, they weren't dancing anymore. They swayed, bodies melded together. Sarah was certain everyone in the room could see what was happening, but she no longer cared. He couldn't leave. He couldn't be that stupid. Her shirt pulled loose from her jeans again, and Cal reached down to tuck it in, his hand resting on the bare flesh of her hip, and then she was swallowing him whole—lips, arms, legs, drinking him in through every pore. She felt so alive, as if her blood, a lazy river before, had turned into a flood sweeping her away. She hoped he had protection.

A tiny neuron fired a warning: *stupid girl, you're headed for trouble.* She couldn't listen.

Word of the sexual revolution had reached Fairmont State College. Whispers wound their way through the dorm. If anyone went to the college clinic or to any pharmacy in town to get birth control, they would call your parents. Sarah wasn't sure who "they" were, but she imagined the Dean of Women or the College President picking up the phone. One girl drove to a town twenty miles away to buy contraceptive foam, but Sarah didn't have a car, much less the nerve to walk into a pharmacy to make such a purchase. She didn't think she'd know how to use it anyway. She wasn't even exactly sure how a tampon worked. She hoped Cal's father talked to him about condoms, but being Catholic, maybe not. She couldn't ask. Couldn't bring herself to even think of the word "sex" in conjunction with what they felt. Such a dirty word, banned from television, polite living rooms, and schools. Recently, though, it had crept into magazines. She remembered an article in *Reader's Digest* praising girls who gave in to their feelings in relationships. The author—a male—said those girls were more honest than teases who held back. Maybe the world was changing.

Besides, no one else had ever called her beautiful—no, it was more than that, made her *feel* beautiful. When the song ended, they stood still, the palms of their hands pressed together, the bridge of her nose tucked under his chin. She ached in ways she knew no name for.

When he suggested they go somewhere else, she was ready. He drove to a friend's apartment, vacant for the night, and slipped a flat cellophane-wrapped packet from his wallet.

"Don't worry," he said, "I won't let anything happen to you."

Two

Dec. 6, 1969

Sarah sat at her desk, penciling in the proper position of a pig's liver while she waited for Cal to call. She smiled as she remembered the previous night. Three precious hours. Once, in a novel, she had read about foreigners who offered up bloodied sheets as evidence of deflowering, but there was no blood, no pain, only a little discomfort. Afterward, he whispered into her neck, wrapped her hair around his finger. When he rearranged a leg, she flowed with him like water. How many times had he told her he loved her? Ten? Twenty? Later, as he spooned against her back, she felt as if she would explode from the sensation of his arm draped beneath her breasts. Her body was a prism infused with light. Rainbows bounced off the walls and ceiling around her. Several times she was certain the boundaries skin created between her and Cal would dissolve and their cells would fuse together like melted glass.

When one o'clock came, she reluctantly reminded him they'd better go. She'd already missed the curfew her parents insisted upon. She peered into the bathroom mirror of this borrowed apartment. A guy's apartment with crust around the faucet, toothpaste splashes on the mirror, and a spider family residing around rusting chrome pipes. Her hair looked the same but different, still copper-colored but refusing to be reined in, spooling away in gazillions of tangled long curls. She attacked it with a brush.

"Stop worrying with it," Cal said.

She frowned and tried to drag a brush through it again. "Looks awful."

He stopped her hand and massaged his fingers into her scalp. "It looks like the ribbons my mom ties on presents—you know, the kind you curl with scissors. Happy hair. Giggly, wiggly hair."

He tickled her neck.

"Ha, ha." She swatted his fingers away, pretending to be annoyed. They headed for the car, breath misting from their mouths in gray cones. In the car they couldn't keep their hands off each other. She couldn't imagine how long it would take to say good night, to pull herself away from him in a drawn out tug-of-war.

Then, as she and Cal hopped up the steps to the porch, out came her father, Nelson Stevens, putter pants riding two inches below his belly, her father, who never got up when she came in, yet there he stood, milky-eyed and whiskey-scented.

"Do you know what time it is, young lady?"

She didn't die, though she wanted to.

Cal extended his hand. "Good to see you, sir."

They shook, but she felt her father looked at her wild hair and burned face and saw the bloodied sheet (though there'd been no blood). She thought he surely could smell the coupling of their bodies.

She realized she had been daydreaming for over half an hour and made an effort to resume diagramming the chambers of a pig heart, but the smell of Cal's sweat, his cedar-scented aftershave, kept distracting her, kept reminding her of the night before. She wore him in every pore, and so put off her morning shower. Every time she inhaled she could feel his skin pressed against hers.

By eleven, she crossed her legs at the knee and again at the ankles, rocking back and forth, trying to read her notes. Perhaps he'd gone to mass with his aunt. Sarah gave in and showered, hoping it would help her concentrate on the distinguishing characteristics of arthropods. Dr. Jeter's final was known to be a killer.

Running a washcloth over her own naked body only made Sarah more obsessed with thoughts of Cal. To hell with Dr. Jeter's pig. She would rather study Cal's latissimus dorsi and trapezius, his adductors and abductors, his extensors and flexors, his gluteus maximus. She wanted her fingers to memorize every mole, every ripple. Above all, she wanted to know the interior of Cal Caruso's heart. In which chamber did he store his love for her?

Foster, leash clenched in his teeth, nudged her leg. She scratched between his ears.

"Can't do it, little buddy. Not right now." Cal might call while she was outside. The dog was twenty-three pounds of devotion covered in black and white fur. If he had four legs, he might have weighed twenty-five. Foster was the best thing she'd ever gotten free. She carried him downstairs, opened the kitchen door, and let him lope into the backyard. She watched the dog, smiling to herself. She was reliving the moment when, rolling on top of her, Cal took both her hands in his, stretched them over their heads—

"You ready to go?" her father asked.

"Go?" She only half heard him, couldn't think what he meant, still remembering how with palms pressed together over their heads, Cal lowered his lips to hers in the gentlest kiss and for the second time—

"To the Heimbachs'."

The rattle of car keys against the yellow countertop pulled her back to the kitchen. Visiting the aunts had been a weekend tradition for as long as Sarah could remember. She hesitated, knowing how her aunts looked forward to an update on her college experiences. She hated to disappoint them.

"I need to study for finals. They'll understand."

"You okay, honey?" Her mother pushed a tangle of curls away from Sarah's forehead, fingers lingering, a clumsy show of affection designed, Sarah suspected, to disguise checking her temperature. Her mother didn't want to admit Sarah was old enough to check her own temperature should the need arise. Sarah and Garrett were late-in-life babies. When children hadn't come right away, everyone assumed it was too late for Johanna, but at thirty eight she surprised everyone, herself included, by conceiving Sarah. Garrett followed eleven months after.

"Yeah, I'm fine, why?"

Johanna's eyebrows scrunched together and brackets formed on either side of her mouth, a worried look that both comforted and annoyed Sarah. "You seem a little distracted and flushed."

"Just her usual ditzy self," Garrett said.

Her brother didn't deserve a response. Anything she said would only encourage him. Sarah watched them leave, her mother leaning heavily on the railing to support her weight. Her mother had been model-gorgeous with the kind of legs that graced hosiery ads when Sarah started grade school, but by the time she reached junior high, her mother had mushroomed to nearly 300 pounds. Sarah still couldn't get used to it. The more her father drank, the more her mother ate. Or vice versa—who knew for sure? Her mother was perennially dieting—and failing—because she gorged on sweets.

The family drove off. Sarah studied and fidgeted. The family came home again and the early hours of the afternoon ticked away. Ticked and ticked. Tocked and tocked. So, so slowly.

At four o'clock the phone rang. She thudded down the steps to get there first.

Her mother's words carried from the living room. "That girl sounds like an elephant."

At the sound of the voice on the other end, Sarah's legs turned to water. She sank into the love seat, able to retrieve her breath but not her heart, which descended into her stomach like a stone. It was only Rachel, home for the weekend from the university.

"I'm sick of studying," Rachel said. "Want to get some pizza from Twin Oaks?"

Sarah would give anything to get out of her room, to escape from phylum nomenclature, away from the pompous vocabulary of her psychology text, away from the pencil skid marks in her British literature notebook, evidence her professor's mincing monotone had lullabied her once again. She imagined the aroma of double cheese pizza—the scent of fresh baked crust and oregano-rich tomato sauce. For a moment, she flirted with the idea of a confession—and who better than her best friend since grade school? Sarah longed to share her feelings with someone—anyone—but the last person she could ever tell was Rachel. Rachel would marry in white tulle and satin, and until Rachel marched down the aisle of the First Presbyterian Church beside her man in that long white gown, he wouldn't get to second base. Guaranteed.

"Can't," Sarah said. "I'll probably have to pull an all-nighter for my biology final tomorrow." True, but if it had been Cal she'd have grabbed her coat.

She hardly touched her mother's eggplant parmesan. Each bite stuck in her throat. Why hadn't he called? Not even her mother's Apricot Delight, a gelatin concoction she was perfecting for a *Ladies Home Journal* contest, slid down easily.

For the first time, Sarah was forced to hitch a ride back to campus with her neighbor Jimmy and roomie Paula.

"Where's Cal?" Jimmy asked.

"Studying." Where was Cal? She wished she knew.

Monday morning she thought she saw him coming into the cafeteria, but when she raised her hand to wave, whoever it was turned and walked out. Monday afternoon, following the worst exam she'd ever taken in her life—how could anyone remember all those phylums and species?—the Resident Assistant called her to the phone in the second floor hallway.

"Listen, Sarah, the thing is, I don't think we should see each other again," Cal said. "I signed the papers this morning. Right after Christmas I leave for boot camp. I care about you—but what happened shouldn't have—it was all wrong—and I'm sorry."

"But—"

"This is how it has to be."

No, there were all kinds of ways it could be. Any way but this. Surely there were coherent arguments to be made, salient points in favor of other plans, other schemes. He could tell the Army recruiter he'd made a mistake. Tear up the enlistment forms. They were both writers—they could write to each other. She could fly over and visit him, though the thought of jungle snakes and bugs made her shudder.

"Why?" Her voice sounded thin to her own ears, not the demand for an answer she intended.

"It just is." A few seconds of silence. "Listen, you take care of yourself."

He hung up, leaving her with the dial tone droning in her ear and a metallic taste in her mouth. The specter of the family curse loomed: four unmarried aunts. Her own mother narrowly escaped her sisters' fate, marrying at an age when everyone had all but given up hope for her. Once at a birthday party, Sarah's best friend Rachel claimed whoever ate the last piece of cake would be an Old Maid. Superstitious nonsense—but Sarah never ate the last piece of any cake, just in case. Even though she knew better, a part of her still clung to belief in magic. In potions that could make her lovable. In kisses that would change fathers into sober judges, toads into princes, transformative kisses that led to happily-ever-afters. But where was the magic to make that March 31 lottery drawing go away?

Barely comprehending the questions in front of her, she sat through exams while she conjured up a list of all the things she should have said. Over the next few days, she realized Cal was avoiding her, timing his visits to the newsroom when he knew she wouldn't be there. She stumbled through the last week on campus. One afternoon when the dorm hallway was empty, she picked up the shared phone and dialed Cal's number, her eyes closing against the exquisite pain of hearing him say hello. She waited, suspending breath until he said it one more time, then hung up. Afterwards she chastised herself for her weakness. As foolish as sticking needles into herself.

The next day she did it again. And the next, again. Then finals week was over, and Cal, she knew, was on his way home to North Carolina.

Christmas vacation withered into an agony of explanations, everyone wanting to know where Cal was, why he enlisted, why they broke up. Each question stabbed her, but she was determined no one would see through her façade of indifference. Especially not her brother when he suggested Cal must have been really desperate.

"Why's that?" their father asked.

"Guy was willing to enlist to get as far away from Sarah as possible."

She supposed Garrett really thought he was funny. "Maybe you should enlist. You'd finally have to grow up."

In blue paper with smiling white snowmen, she wrapped the sweater she'd bought for Cal. She planned to give it to her brother even though it would be too big for him. Garrett was stocky, but not tall. She tucked the receipt in the box so he could exchange it. She almost cried when she parted the scissors and ripped the sharp edge across red ribbon—happy, giggly, wiggly ribbon—to make it curl. Almost cried, but she tightened her jaw and ripped the next strand twice as hard.

When the new semester started, she petitioned to take extra hours. Keeping her mind occupied was the only therapy she knew. One thing for sure: she didn't want anything to do with men. Not now. Not ever.

Probably not ever.

Three

MAY 15, 1970

With an art history term paper due Wednesday, Sarah tried to immerse herself in note-taking, but the people on the bus distracted her. The woman sitting next to her reeked from consuming oodles of ramps, those onions that grew wild throughout the hills in May. Equally annoying, the man behind Sarah kept kicking her seat, and two children nearby squabbled over a box of crayons. If she ever had children—which she seriously doubted—she would not ignore them while they irritated everyone else around.

Brakes squealed, and the Greyhound's door wheezed open once again. Two people got off, and diesel fumes entered. She looked up momentarily from her book on West Virginia art glass, pen poised over a note card. A coal tipple stood on the left side of the road, emerging from the earth like a giant version of the Erector set her brother Garrett had played with as a boy.

The little girl put down her crayons and rose up to her knees on the crackled surface of the green seat. "Look, it's a dirty bum."

Her brother scrambled up beside her, snickering with his nose pressed against the window. "It's Pop Bottle Pete."

Their mother looked up from her ladies' magazine. "Hush, now. You mustn't make fun of people less fortunate than you."

Sarah winced, then craned her neck to follow the children's pointing fingers. Sure enough, there was Pete, trundling alongside the highway with his shopping buggy, navy watch cap pulled over his bald spot. He wore a ratty-looking Army jacket despite the mildness of the day. His lips moved under a bushy mustache. Talking to himself. Everyone in the surrounding counties knew Pete as the fellow who roamed the highways collecting bottles, which he redeemed for pennies. All sorts of rumors circulated about him. He was wealthy but had no use for money. An ex-con who couldn't get a job. A murderer. A homeless guy who slept under bridges. The last might be true if he ran short of cash. Usually, though, he slept in cheap motels. Sarah never admitted to anyone she knew Pete, let alone that they were cousins.

The doors closed and the bus chugged up the hill toward Clarksburg, away from Pete. On the left, explosives had ripped away the entire hillside so bulldozers and bucket wheel excavators could harvest the black rocks within. The barren landscape and sheered-off cliffs resembled the desolate terrain of an alien planet. A few discouraged weeds were the only green in sight. She could forget about the strip mines until she rode one of the two-lanes in or out of town. Then the shock of their ugliness made her ache all over again.

As the driver shifted gears to climb the last hill before the city limits, the engine groaned. They passed Adamston Flat Glass and Rolland/Lafayette, both long gray rectangles with boarded up windows. During Sarah's childhood, twenty-six glass factories operated in the Clarksburg area, making everything from windows and tableware to mirrors and optical glass. Now less than a handful remained. No glassblowers. Only a few holdouts—men like Uncle Mahlon—kept the craft alive in small artisan workshops.

When the bus arrived at the Stealey Bridge, Sarah got out and walked half a mile home. The sidewalks had exploded after winter freeze and thaw cycles. The city didn't have money to fix them, so weeds sprouted in the cracks. All the older neighborhoods were drying up, with the closing of one after another of the glass plants. She detoured up Durwood Drive, past the white two-story where Cal's aunt lived. Not because she expected to see him. But walking by the house tore the scab off, something she'd never been able to resist, even as a child. He'd been "in country" several months. The *Columns* staff had received four postcards. Not a word to her personally. Once, she replied to his postcard with news about the staff. Signed the letter "Love, Sarah." He didn't respond. Instead, a few weeks later she found another one of those damned postcards thumb-tacked to the staff bulletin board.

Further up Durwood, she passed the modest brick house where Cal had grown up. In junior high they played H.O.R.S.E. and Around the World in the driveway. The memories made her want to run home, fold into a fetal position on her bed, and never go out into the world again. Five months had passed, and she still hurt and hated herself for it.

Shifting the suitcase to her other hand, she marched the last three blocks and up the final alley to her family's one-and-a-half-story Sears catalog home. Rita Watson was taking down the wash from the shared clothesline strung between their homes, the flab in her arms waggling as she tugged on a sheet. More than neighbors, the Watsons were like family to the Stevenses. They mowed each other's lawns, took vacations together, and helped raise each other's children.

"Jimmy sure brought home a lot of laundry." Rita always spoke with a bit of a hoot, her pitch see-sawing into up-notes at unexpected times, so that even her complaints came across as good natured. "Didn't know that boy had so many clothes."

"Look at you—already done with his laundry and I'm not even in the door."

"No wonder with all them classes you're taking. Wisht he took half as much interest in school as you do."

"Jimmy'll study more when he figures out what he wants to do."

"Better hurry up about it. I'm not paying for college on no six-year plan. Your mom's in there working her tail off for you. Been cleaning all day, cooking, making a cake. Be sure and tell her how good the lawn looks. She was out here first thing this morning pulling crabgrass and chickweed."

Her mother's irises pushed purple beards above sword-like foliage. The yard did look good. Sarah opened the back door and Foster, tail thumping brick-patterned linoleum, whined and nosed into her thighs. Sarah scratched his head. "Hey there, little buddy."

A friendly competition between vanilla and chocolate scents filled the kitchen as her mother slapped icing on an éclair cake. She stopped long enough to plant a kiss on Sarah's cheek. "Dog's been waiting at the door the last half hour. The way he knows when you're supposed to get here, you'd think he could tell time." She gestured with the knife to the countertop. "Your favorite cake—gotta fatten you up even if this meal will spoil my diet."

What diet? Her mother dipped a spoon into the icing and popped it into her mouth.

"I'm fat enough."

"Don't eat enough to keep a bird alive. We're having macaroni and cheese, green beans, and gelatin salad with miniature marshmallows, oranges, walnuts, and pineapple."

"Yum." Well, not really, but she humored her mother's gelatin experiments.

"And hot dogs."

Sarah wrinkled her nose. "Yuk." As if she would eat ground-up guts. Her mother would never accept that a child of hers was vegetarian.

"Heard from Cal?" Johanna asked.

"No, why would I?" Couldn't anybody get it? They had broken up. Finis. Splitsville. Kaputt.

"Saw his aunt in Kroger's, said he was getting along all right. Asked the family to send him socks, if you can imagine. He says they can't keep them dry over there and boys got toes rotting off. Stand up straight. I don't know what's gotten into you, hunching over like an old woman."

Sarah straightened her spine while her mother continued. "I think the military ought to supply enough socks for our boys to keep their feet dry, don't you? We pay such high taxes they could at least buy them enough socks."

"Saw Pete."

"No kidding. Where?"

Little clinks signaled her father's approach. Nelson rounded the corner from the living room, glass in hand, remnants of Crown Royal Canadian glistening over ice cubes. This time of year Nelson wasn't often home so early. He stayed at the office until eight or nine, cranking out tax returns for delinquent filers.

He sucked on his cigarette, sputtered out a cough, and hitched up his pants with his free hand. He was a gone-ass, pants always one inhale away from falling down. "So Pete's back in town."

"On the road out near Adamston Glass," Sarah said. "Looked like he was having quite a conversation with himself."

Her father refilled his glass and flicked ashes into the sink. "It's a shame."

Turning her back on them, Johanna resumed icing the cake. "Might be a shame, but I hope he doesn't come 'round here. Last time, he didn't leave till near midnight. He forgets some people have to work in the morning. Not to mention, he bummed cigarettes all night long."

Nelson took a long swallow. "I feel sorry for him."

The folds of fat on her mother's neck quivered with aggravation. "First words out of his mouth, 'Can I bum a cigarette?' Not even a decent 'Hello, how you doing?' Just 'Can I bum a cigarette?'"

"God only knows what nightmares he carries around from Korea." Her father sympathized because he fought in World War II.

Johanna whirled around and punctuated her words with little stabs of the butter knife, aimed toward Nelson, who eased away. "That man carried around nightmares long before he went overseas. Long before, and you know it."

"We can afford to give a veteran a few cigarettes is all I'm saying."

"I don't like him coming around. Gives me the creeps." The last words she muffled with her fingers.

Her father refilled his drink and sloshed the whiskey through the ice cubes. They tinkled against the glass. "So don't open the door next time."

She grunted. "Right, we'll all hide in the closet."

"Your irises look pretty, Mom." Sarah escaped to her bedroom.

The next morning Sarah pushed her dog along the jogging trail at the Veterans' Park in a stroller bought for $2.50 at Goodwill. A bald fellow, dewlapped jaw dragging against his corduroy jacket, nearly dropped the bag of bread crumbs he was tossing geeseward. She had grown accustomed to stares and head shakes since she'd rescued Foster from the pound in high school. On her first day as a volunteer, she was horrified to learn they were going to euthanize him. She remembered the steel in her mother's voice: "If you keep him, your days of volunteering at the shelter are over." Easy decision. She'd changed her summer service project to Head Start.

A thick layer of soggy leaves clotted together and slowed Sarah's progress. The two-mile trail snaked with the curves of the West Fork River through Veterans' Park. Halfway through the circuit Sarah slouched on a concrete bench, reading *Clarissa* for Dr. Pudsell's Early Novel class. The dog stretched out in the stroller, muzzle resting between his paws, watching the geese waddle down the embankment toward the river. Heavy rains had swelled the West Fork into a muddy mess. When a squirrel scampered through the canopy of an oak, Foster sat up and edged his paws over the front of the stroller. He whined.

"Stay," Sarah commanded. The dog whined again, nostrils quivering, then eased once more onto the blue-checked padding.

The reading was slow-going today. Her mind kept wandering over the differences in the way men and women used words. What had Cal meant, for example, when he said he loved her? Not the same thing she meant, obviously. She still thought about him all the time. Tried to understand what had gone wrong. He must have thought her body was ugly or she didn't know how to do it right.

Sarah found herself in the same situation as Lovelace's young woman in *Clarissa*. Seduced and abandoned. Who would want her, another man's cast-off? It galled her to know her father was right. "No man will buy the cow when the milk's free"—he'd said it numerous times while watching movies. Well, she thought, if a man doesn't want me after making love to me, I don't want him anyway.

But she did. She did.

When Sarah finished the next chapter, she stood up and brushed away a little sand clinging to her jeans. She lifted Foster out of the stroller. They set off on another circuit around the park. With a lopsided gait, the dog bounded alongside while she jogged, pushing the empty stroller in front of her.

"You're feeling frisky today, aren't you?" Must be the effect of cool spring air. If he ever missed his back leg, Sarah couldn't tell. The only difference between Foster and a four-legged dog was he tired more easily.

A sandy-haired guy about Sarah's age jogged by and lifted one hand in greeting. He was not quite handsome—too ruddy from exertion—but she liked his upturned nose and wiry build. The only others she passed on the second circuit were a gaggle of geese and a pair of young lovers, walking hand-in-hand in the self-absorbed manner of two people who mean the whole world to each other. Sarah trained her eyes on the river so she wouldn't have to watch.

She scooped the little dog into the stroller. "You're pooped, aren't you, pal?" Near the end of the third circuit, a squirrel scampered across the trail toward the riverbank. Before Sarah could stop him, Foster sprung out in pursuit. The squirrel skittered up a pine with the dog only a foot behind. Foster jumped at the tree, front nails scraping the bark. She ordered the dog to come. He ignored her.

The squirrel, high enough now to feel secure, taunted the dog with its chittering. Foster leapt again. This time his solitary hind leg came down on mud grown soft with rain. Though she could see what was going to happen, Sarah didn't have time to react. The embankment crumbled away, and the dog tumbled into the muddy waters of the West Fork.

She ran toward the river's edge, leash dangling from her hands. The dog paddled furiously along the bank, but the current erased every effort. Ears back, Foster's eyes widened with fear.

"Hold on, little buddy, I'm coming." She dug her heels into the mud and edged her way down the bank. Her tennis shoes skidded. She crouched so she wouldn't pitch forward and instead fell onto her butt. She pushed up, leaving one hand anchored in the muck to steady herself on the last few steps. She was vaguely aware of the fetid smell of the river, of the engine-like rumble of water churning by. Would she even be able to stand? She raised one foot and tentatively placed it into the brown water.

A male voice came from behind—"Look out." Gray sweatpants cleared the bank behind her, leaping into the water with a mighty splash. The man seized the dog and lifted him out of the knee-high water. As he turned around, struggling to keep his balance in the current, Sarah recognized the sandy-haired jogger who had waved earlier. He heaved the dog onto the embankment. Foster looked small and pitiful, fur plastered against his body. Sarah grabbed him and staggered, her feet sliding in mud. She clawed her way to solid ground. As soon as she let Foster go, he shook off, flinging drops of cold, dirty water all over her and the jogger, who had scrambled up the bank behind her.

"What a fine thank you, you little rat." She wrapped her arms around Foster's shivering body again, ignoring the musty odor. "What's the matter with you?" she asked the dog. "You could've drowned."

Foster's rescuer wiped mucky hands on sodden sweatpants. His shoes were ruined. She should have been the one to jump in. Why was she always so slow to respond in emergencies?

"I can't thank you enough," she said.

"No problem."

"I don't know what got into him today. He's usually so tuckered out after one lap around the park he snoozes the rest of the day."

"You can never tell what animals are going to do. What happened to his leg?"

"Don't know. He was like that when I got him from the shelter." Foster shivered, but their hero stood steady as a stone. "You must be freezing," she said. "I live around the corner if you want to come home with me. My brother probably has some dry clothes you could wear." She could borrow money from her mother to pay for the shoes.

He took two steps backwards as he spoke. "I'd better get on home before I start to stink like a dead fish. You take care of your old dog." He turned and jogged toward the parking lot.

She stared after him. "Wait—what's your name?"

His truck roared to life, drowning her words, and he was gone.

In the mudroom shower, he rotated his body so the hot spray struck first his abdomen and then his back. He let the water course over his head again and raked wet hair away from his face. Lava soap and hot water chafed life back into his body and washed away the smell of the river. Lord, that river was cold. As the shower warmed his muscles, he cursed himself as a fool. He should have gone home with her, dripping wet or not.

While he shampooed his hair, he replayed the first time he'd seen her almost six months ago on campus. An afternoon rain had been peppering the sidewalk. He could still almost feel the damp bricks of the administration building as he flattened himself under the eaves, waiting for the parking ticket office to reopen after lunch. Damned nuisance, but if he didn't pay those fines his credits would be held up. He would earn few enough of them as it was, and would have to withstand his father's anger and his mother's disappointment. He didn't want to make it any worse.

Wet students dodged past the few girls who'd toted umbrellas to class. Everyone hustled except one couple who moved as if they had nowhere to go, ignoring the rain. The girl was lanky with shoulder length hair. She bent to remove suede loafers and tucked them under a navy sweatshirt. A good decision. An attempt to save what obviously were expensive shoes. He could tell she wasn't country. A town girl with class, but not a snob. Natural and down-to-earth.

He'd seen the guy before in the gym shooting hoops and heard his friends holler out his name. Cal. A tall fellow, tall enough to have snagged an athletic scholarship.

Cal started tickling the girl.

"Stop." She swatted at him with one hand, holding the shoes in place with the other.

He fingered his way up her ribs into her arm pits, the girl squirming and giggling all the while. She tried to break away but he stayed right with her. They didn't even notice him pressed up against the eaves.

She screeched at Cal to stop, but you could tell she was enjoying every minute of it. Rain splattered the sidewalk.

"Make me," he said.

What she did next was a surprise. Instead of trying to run away, she turned toward him, raindrops trailing down her face and soaking her hair. Her shoes tumbled out of her shirt and clattered to the ground. Placing both palms on his cheeks, she drew his face down, oblivious to students scurrying past. Eyes wide open, nose to nose with him, she sucked his lower lip into her mouth and gently chewed. The guy's smile faded and he pulled her close. All steamy seriousness now. Plastered together, lips, chests, pelvises, thighs, everything wet. Her hair slowly transformed into a wild bush of curls.

Then she stomped on his foot, pushed him away, picked up her shoes, and scampered down the sidewalk on legs as long and lean as a deer's. She moved with the sureness of a girl who was loved.

In front of the North Hall now, drenched shoes dangling from two fingers over her shoulder, she turned and taunted him. "I can make you do anything."

Half a year later, the boy could still see her grin, could still taste her lips, still grew hard at the memory. The river odors were gone now, but he stood under the shower a few minutes longer and beat off. He should have gone home with her. Sarah. He'd found out her name by asking around. He should have gone home with Sarah and not worried about soiling the fancy house he imagined as hers.

No one had ever kissed him with such abandon. Not even Anita. After three years of dating, her kisses were barely less chaste than his mother's.

A scene of the girl at the park looped through his brain as he stepped across the concrete block floor. He remembered the exact angle of her legs as they eased down the river bank, how she wrapped herself around the mutt, face buried in his wet fur, how love seemed to stream out of her in fierce, almost visible rays.

He toweled off, the terry cloth scratching his shoulder blades, and he replayed Sarah's kiss again. He could almost feel her chewing his lower lip. Almost. He decided. Time to ditch Anita.

Cutting through the B.S.
Evil begets evil

By Sarah Stevens
Editorial Editor

May 10, 1970

Times were bad enough when the United States sent its soldiers into the midst of a civil war and they ended up annihilating a whole village.

The young men who wiped out the civilians of My Lai became confused, unable to tell friend from foe, in a land where the old man offering you water today might set the booby trap that kills your best buddy tomorrow. War is corrupting. It can turn even the most decent young men into killing machines. No one knows for sure how many old men, women, and children died at My Lai. Estimates range between 300-500. It's easy for Americans to brush off their deaths. We don't know the names of the dead.

Early this month, American soldiers invaded Cambodia, a neutral country. Another indefensible act. Across this country people have made it clear they want troops withdrawn from Southeast Asia. For two years, President Nixon has promised to get us out of this morass. Instead, we are enmeshed deeper than ever in the quagmire.

This week the war came home. Evil walked onto a campus of a small university in Ohio less than 200 miles from here. The National Guard, as ordered by Ohio Governor James Rhodes, marched against Kent State students protesting the invasion of Cambodia. These soldiers shot and killed four innocent civilians. This time, because they are Americans, we know their names. The deaths of Allison Krause, Jeff Miller, Sandy Scheuer, and Bill Shroeder will not be so easy to brush off. Two were not even protestors. Merely bystanders.

Some claim the Guardsmen were scared. Perhaps they were. But eyewitness accounts leave little doubt: guardsmen were in no danger. They fired from distances of 300 to 400 feet. One of their leaders gave the order to fire on protesters armed with nothing more than rocks.

Kent State students were exercising their constitutional right to assemble and their right to free speech. More than that, they exercised their responsibility to protest an unjust escalation of the war. They didn't deserve death by firing squad. Maybe they deserve medals of valor instead.

President Nixon was correct when he said in his televised address it was "not our power but our will and character that is being tested." Our character has been tested, and we have failed.

Four

MAY 17, 1970

Sarah bent her head down to whisper a kiss onto Katherine's forehead, her lips brushing against hair as white and wispy as a dandelion gone to seed. The furnishings of the Aunt Hill never changed. Uncle Mahlon's art glass on the living room wall, Aunt Maggie's afghan folded on the back of the sofa, and Uncle William's collection of carved elephants on the hunt board. Once, the Heimbachs numbered fourteen. Now only two still lived in the house, although the belongings of those who'd passed on remained as if the owners would soon return from an after-dinner stroll.

Katherine held Sarah at arm's length, eyes traveling up Sarah's body, coming to rest at last on her face. "You sure you been eating?"

"Yeah, the food's okay. They have eight different kinds of potatoes. Boiled, buttered—that's boiled with butter on top—parsleyed—that's boiled with butter and parsley on top—potatoes lyonnaise—that's boiled with onions and broth."

Katherine's laugh was kitten-soft. "Very creative. Do they serve meat with those potatoes?"

"They do, but you know better." There were only four other vegetarians on campus, according to the cafeteria manager. She accommodated them with alternative sources of protein.

Sarah made her way to the kitchen, a room full of cheerful energy with white appliances and masonry walls painted fire engine red. From Livvie's cutting board, she swiped a quarter-round of carrot.

"Can I do anything to help?" Sarah didn't know why she asked; the answer was always no. Sarah flopped onto the lone white painted chair, its seat covered in cracked red oilcloth that snagged her slacks.

Livvie's knife snicked against the wooden cutting board. "Nope. Almost finished up here." Livvie dumped the carrots into a Dutch oven. "How's school going?"

College was wonderful, Sarah said, except for Ed Psych, taught by a professor who committed the double sins of being boring and pompous. Sarah explained she'd petitioned to take extra hours again—why not? After Cal's departure, she had no social life.

Her father bypassed everyone for the refrigerator and snagged a can of Michelob. It hissed as he popped the top.

Sarah squinted at him, thinking *Kind of early for that.*

Perhaps he read her expression because he stuck his thumb under the elastic waistband of his pants and hitched them up a notch above his paunch. "It's after noon somewhere in the world."

Her mother laughed, and Sarah bit her lower lip. His drinking wasn't the least bit funny. Her mother's mood shifted. She spoke with fingers splayed over her mouth. "Guess who Sarah saw out walking along on the Shinnston Road?"

Katherine's bird-like eyes snapped between Sarah and Johanna, divining the answer at once. "So Pete's back."

The announcement elicited a head shake and "tsk" from Livvie. The sisters exchanged looks pregnant with meanings Sarah couldn't fully decipher. Concern for Pete definitely flickered across Livvie's face. Resignation—they would have to take him in if he knocked on their door. And something more—shame? Was it shame because they couldn't do anything to help him, or more akin to the way Sarah shrank when she thought about anyone discovering Pop Bottle Pete was her cousin?

Garrett took his pepperoni roll into the living room along with the latest *Sports Illustrated.* Sarah followed and dug into her book satchel for a copy of the college newspaper.

"You hear from the University yet?" she asked.

"Got my room assignment this week," Garrett said. "Can't wait to get out of this place."

Him—and every other senior. So many ended up coming back after going away, but she knew she wouldn't be one of them.

Her father rubbed the bridge of his nose. "One of these days you'll appreciate life in Clarksburg. Heard yesterday a new bank is opening on Main. This old burg is ready to take off again."

Sure, and for every new business starting up, two more closed their doors. Her father liked to talk about the good old days, which, in Clarksburg's case, came during his early childhood. Between 1900 and 1910, Harrison County doubled its population, and by 1920 it nearly doubled again. Italian, Austrian, Belgian, British, Spanish, French, Polish, Hungarian, German, and Greek families found their way to the green-clad hills. When the glass boom ended, half the population drifted away. Only about 30,000 remained.

Sarah returned to the kitchen and laid the newspaper on the breakfast table. Her aunts seemed to get such a kick out of keeping up with her work, especially Katherine, who paid for Sarah's textbooks.

"I interviewed Gloria Steinem for the *Columns*," she said.

Katherine slid her reading glasses on. "Right on the front page! Good for you! I heard a famous feminist speak once in Pittsburgh. Harriot Stanton Blatch. Today, hardly anyone remembers her, but she was well-known in the suffrage movement."

Metal pinged as Livvie sorted through a drawer of kitchen tools. Tomatoey scents drifted into the breakfast room.

"What're you making?" Sarah asked. "Smells wonderful."

Livvie wiped her hands on a blue-checked apron. "Squirrel stew." She scraped the rest of the vegetables into the pot without looking up, but her lips trembled the tiniest fraction, enough to give her away.

Sarah burst out laughing. "It is not."

"Vegetable soup," Livvie admitted. Her thin frame quivered with laughter. "But I bet none of us has forgotten my squirrel stew."

"I'll never forget how you squealed, Sarah, when Livvie smacked the cleaver into those squirrels," Katherine said.

Sarah wouldn't either. Their purpled flesh lifted off the cutting board as if they were still alive, and nothing could convince five-year-old Sarah they weren't. She was equally sure they were the very same squirrel babies from Livvie's fairy tales. Weeks went by before Sarah would speak to Livvie again. At home she began hiding her meat under the table, behind books in the dining room, in her mother's potted dracaenas. When her parents threatened to make her eat the moldy morsels, she slipped the meat to Roosevelt under the table or stuffed her mouth full and excused herself to the bathroom, where she spit the wad into the commode. Her aversion to meat stayed with her to this day. The sight of a blood vessel in a chicken breast made her gag.

Her father drifted in, second beer in one hand, the *Columns* dangling from the other. "I see Ms. Steinem isn't all you wrote about."

Sarah knew what was coming. Her father had been furious when she participated in Vietnam Moratorium Day in October. West Virginia Secretary of State Jay Rockefeller's presence as speaker at the event in Fairmont wasn't enough to persuade her father of its legitimacy.

Nelson continued to read as he talked. "You shouldn't be so quick to jump on the war-protest bandwagon. What happened to those kids at Kent State could happen to you."

"There's something wrong when a government is killing its own people. We have every right to speak out against this invasion of Cambodia. A country that years ago declared itself neutral."

"No politics, you two," Johanna protested.

"We aren't there to hurt the Cambodians," her father said. "The President's trying to hold the line against the Communists."

Sarah rolled her eyes. "By killing college students?"

"Remember many of those Guardsmen are only kids too. They were scared and over-reacted. Anyway, you should be careful what you write. You could wind up on somebody's list."

"Joe McCarthy's dead—thank God."

Her father lowered the newspaper to peer at her through thick wire-rimmed lenses. "J. Edgar Hoover isn't."

"They don't really keep lists anymore at the FBI, do they? I mean, this *is* the United States. For Christ's sake, it isn't like I'm communicating with Soviets." She cursed because it would irritate him and because it felt good to let out the bad stuff festering inside. She cursed because it was the language she heard all day on campus, even from professors. Everyone was angry.

"I'm not shelling out a fortune to send you to college so you can learn to cuss."

Sarah took a perverse pleasure in his predictable reaction. She held his eyes a few seconds, then looked away. Weak. Damn, she was weak. Still couldn't stand up to him.

"I don't want to see you get hurt, sweetheart," he said. "Your written words may come back to haunt you later when you try to get a job."

Sarah knew he meant to protect her, yet she turned her face away.

"Johanna, how about getting me another beer?" he asked.

Geez. Her mother would do it, too. She belonged to a generation of women who waited on their husbands hand and foot. Sarah would be damned if she would ever cater to a man.

Aunt Livvie joined them at the table. "Katherine might have gotten on someone's list. She wanted to change things, like you, and got mixed up with the Socialists."

"Oh, Livvie," Katherine protested, "that was such a long time ago. Besides, it wasn't just me. Whole towns in West Virginia voted Socialist."

Sarah couldn't picture her aunt involved in anything more vexing than choosing between patent or plain leather. Katherine's closet bulged with shoes in every style and color. "How did you get involved with Socialists?"

"Through acquaintances. I can hardly remember now."

Livvie stirred the soup one last time before settling into a chair at the breakfast table. "Of course you do. It was 1912, soon after we moved to Clarksburg. I was 17, you were 19. Papa, Joe, Tony, and Katherine worked at the Lafayette Cooperative Glass Company in Adamston. The Socialists were a labor party. Coal miners, railroad men, and farmers. All the glass workers. For a time, they dominated local politics, especially in Adamston."

"This was before Clarksburg annexed it," Katherine said. "Back then, it had its own government."

Its own government? Adamston was an unimpressive neighborhood. Only two stop lights. What was there to govern?

Five

KATHERINE, MAY 1912

I stepped around my desk, enjoying the sound of my new black buttoned shoes clicking against the wood floor.

Breathless from running, Bitsy held out a lunchbox, still clutching the handles of two others. Her freckles stood out prominently after a week of summer sun. As the youngest of the Heimbachs, ten-year-old Bitsy delivered hot lunches to the Lafayette Glass plant. In the bottom of Papa's and Thomas's pails, Mama would have packed extra salt to replace what they lost in sweat. My brother Joe worked in the pits, too, but his oldest son was big enough to carry lunch now.

In a few weeks the plant would shut down for the summer. When school and the factory resumed, lunch delivery would fall back upon Livvie, who worked out of the house as a dress and hat designer.

I tucked a wayward strand of brown hair behind Bitsy's ear, and then took the pail and peeked inside. Leftover pot pie.

"Mama said she only had enough chicken-fried steak for Papa and Thomas," Bitsy said.

Suited me fine. "Better run along. They'll be waiting for you."

We left Pennsylvania to join the cooperative over a decade after it started in 1899. Papa was reluctant to leave the Pittsburgh area while his mentor Karl and his wife Magdalen were in poor health, but after their deaths in 1911 he was free to better his situation. Wages in the Pittsburgh area had steadily declined after the advent of cylinder-blowing machines, which eliminated the need for the most skilled workers. Lafayette Cooperative was formed by glass workers from Pittsburgh, Papa's friends. The original members weren't blowers, so skilled men like Papa were in demand. The cooperative resisted mechanization, keeping wages high.

My official title was receptionist/secretary, but I practically ran the whole plant. Even Thomas admitted it. "Place'd fall apart without you, Katherine," he said. "You've got more business sense than anybody." Then why couldn't they call me what I was—the office manager—and pay me accordingly?

At least the men accepted me at the plant. At the phone company in Pittsburgh, where I had worked previously, I was the first woman employee and the men made snide remarks about how I'd be better off doing the only thing women were born to do. If my brothers could have heard their language, somebody would have ended up with a broken nose, especially on Friday night when beer flowed freely. Papa, though, would have blamed me. Would have ordered me to cover up my ankles because they only brought out the worst in men. Never mind that everyone was wearing their skirts shorter. Why, even Mrs. Taft showed a little ankle. Papa could be so old-fashioned. Take the way he and the rest of the blowers resisted Lubbers cylinder-drawing machines. Everyone else could see the old way would soon be used as often as a rich man's outhouse once he installed indoor plumbing. Companies with the new machines paid lower wages. Change was inevitable. The only question: when. And I, for one, didn't think it would be long. On some level, Papa must have known it, too, because he set up our brother William as a grocer.

I sat down at my desk and adjusted the skirt of my blue dress. The bodice looked quite smart, with a white pin-tucked inset and black velvet lapels, a feminine version of a man's suit. Livvie designed it. She wasn't smart, not in the least, but she could sew like a dream. The book smarts in the family landed squarely in my lap. I finished lunch, and returned to the orders on my desk. One big shipment of plate glass to head out to Kansas, and another all the way to Sacramento. Those were places I dreamed of seeing, places growing by leaps and bounds, and thus the demand for window glass—all those new houses needed windows. I thought it would be grand to ride the railroad all the way to California and gaze upon the hotels and banks and mansions windowed with our glass. Meanwhile, there were raw materials to procure. I was excellent at figures, and before long, I tallied up the amount of silica, limestone, and sodium carbonate the orders would require. Mr. Rolland would check my figures—a formality. He never once found an error.

Orders finished, I pulled out the flyer hidden under my desk blotter. It was an announcement for a political rally that evening, and I was sure I would die if I didn't get to attend. I hid the paper because my father would never give permission to go, but I was determined to find a way. The Socialists trumpeted the right of every citizen to vote, no matter their race, gender, or beliefs. A cause more dear to my heart than any other. Not since we'd moved from Pittsburgh had I experienced the opportunity to join with people of a like mind. I missed those clandestine meetings of the suffragette club. (Papa forbade those, too.) And if these Socialists were going to secure the right to vote for me, then I was, somehow, some way, going to join. Over the past few years, the party had captured government seats across the tri-state area, including a few in Adamston. But 1912 was going to be their year. I could feel it when I gripped the flyer in my hands.

I felt faint from the heat as I walked into the center of the plant. I hoped to tell Papa goodbye before I left, but he and Thomas were holding a pipe and three-foot long glass cylinder over the swinghole, which was a brick furnace. This was the old way of making windows. Papa first blew out a huge cylinder of glass. Then after it was re-warmed, they flattened it into a sheet. They were at a critical juncture, not a good time to disturb them. Papa didn't like my wandering into the plant anyway, because the men were often shirtless. As if shirtless men could shock me, living as I did with all those brothers.

After dinner, I slipped out the side door—and ran smack into Mama returning to the house with a bucket of water.

"And where do you think you're going?" Mama said.

In Pittsburgh, Mama had attended suffragette meetings with me until Papa got suspicious, so I appealed to her affection for the cause. "A political rally, Mama. The Socialists want to give women the right to vote." I parroted everything written on the flyer, adding, "I have to go."

"Not by yourself you're not, and I can't go with you tonight. William has mending needs done before morning."

"I'm a grown woman, Mama. You can't tell me what to do."

She snorted. "Yes, I can. Take Livvie with you. There's safety in numbers."

Moments later, Livvie and I slipped past the familiar homes of neighbors, all glass workers at the Lafayette plant. We bolted past the cooperative grocery and the new social hall.

"Hurry up." I grabbed Livvie's arm and tugged her in the direction of the swinging bridge. "I don't want to miss a single word."

We tripped across the wooden planks, holding onto the ropes and wrinkling our noses at the odor. The likely cause was the deteriorating carcass of a two-foot long catfish washed up on the bank of the West Fork. In front of the factory, a dozen men were gathered, including our brothers Joe and Thomas. I should have known Joe would be there, since he and his growing family were renting a house in Adamston. Well, there was no hiding in such a small gathering, so I marched up and greeted them.

"What the devil are you two doing here?" Joe asked. The oldest of us, he sounded like Papa. Bossy. Even more so, now that he had children of his own.

"Same thing you are," I said. "I came to hear what the Socialists have to say."

"What for?" Joe asked. "It's not like you can vote."

"That's exactly why we are here," I said. "They are in favor of women's suffrage."

Livvie tucked her arm through mine and hugged me to her side. "That's right."

"Women have no—" Joe began, but a man with striking red hair climbed onto the back of a wagon and started to speak. Those assembled hushed. We moved closer to the front of the crowd. The speaker, dressed in the clothes of a working man, looked to be in his late twenties or early thirties..

"My name is Walter Boyles. Most of you know me, know my work. For those who don't"—I swear he looked right at me and Livvie—"I'm a carpenter, and I'm running for mayor as a member of the Socialist party." He threw his whole upper body into his gestures and he had this deep voice. You couldn't help but believe him. He was passionate about improvements he planned for Adamston. How workers should own their own factories (they already did own several), how they would build sewers and water works, how they would pave the streets. When I asked if he was in favor of women voting, he said, "Sure am. Especially if you're voting for me." He waited for the laughter to die down. "Even if I do get to be mayor, I don't think I can bring that one off for you. Wish I could, though, wish I could." After that, I would have done anything to help him get elected. Walter persuaded Joe to run for an open council seat too. What better way to accomplish his agenda than to pack the council with like-minded people?

During the next week, I passed out Socialist literature all over town, and since Joe was running for office, I didn't have to hide my activities from Papa. Wasn't I the lucky one when Ernest Rolland asked me to give Walter a tour of the plant! We became quite friendly and I organized a second rally and persuaded the Lafayette Factory Band to provide music. The band drew in a much bigger crowd for this rally.

The last week of June we celebrated the end of the "blast" and the closing of the plant for the summer. Everyone came from miles around to the factory-sponsored carnival. Livvie took first place in the cake competition with her twelve-egg angel food. The boys entered hand-ball contests and pigeon races, and I gave a rousing speech in support of Walter Boyles for mayor and Joe Heimbach for town council. Of course I threw in a pitch for women's suffrage. The band played and there was dancing and carrying on until the wee hours of the morning.

The Socialists swept the Adamston elections, and under Walter's leadership the town sold bonds, built the waterworks, and laid the first sewer lines. I like to think I played a small part in securing those civic improvements.

MAY 17, 1970

Livvie set a basket of yeast rolls on the table. "Sometimes you acted as if the new mayor was the second carpenter who could walk on water, Katherine, but even you have to admit he had little to do with it when we voted for the first time eight years later."

The America her aunts grew up in didn't even seem like the same place they lived in now, a world where the right of every citizen to vote, indoor plumbing, and asphalt streets were givens. A world in which no politician could win on a Socialist platform, even if he promised an endless supply of bathroom tissue to a town that had none.

Katherine removed her glasses. "True, and despite what he did accomplish, the next year, the grateful town threw the Socialists out of office."

"They raised taxes to pay the interest on the bonds—I suppose that caused the change of heart," Livvie said. "The People's Progressive or Citizen's Party, or something like that, won in 1913. In those days, new political parties sprung up every year like weeds."

"But men like Walter didn't come along every year," Katherine said.

Livvie regarded her sister. "You know, for a while there, I thought you two might get married. You danced with him almost all night at the carnival, but then you seemed to lose interest. I wonder what ever happened to Walter Boyles."

"I believe he married and had eight children. Died of a heart attack back in '64." Katherine's manner was offhand, but her lips quivered, a tiny spasm rippling through wrinkles. Sarah wondered if anyone else noticed.

"Six years ago," Livvie said. "I don't remember hearing that."

"Yes, I went to the funeral. His wife was very nice."

Livvie eyed her sister sharply. "You should have told me. I'd have gone with you."

"You were busy canning tomatoes and I thought it best not to bother you." Katherine's eyes flitted down, then sideways. Hunching over even more, her aunt laughed in a self-deprecating manner. "Anyway, I was never important enough to be on anyone's list. The soup must be ready. It smells divine."

As Sarah accepted her bowl, she peered at her aunt, trying to see beyond the hunched back and white hair to the young feminist who'd kept up with Boyles all those years. Sarah wondered if she'd be telling similar stories about Cal to her grandchildren some day. *Oh, I met his wife. Such a nice woman.*

Good Lord, she hoped not. She'd become a famous journalist and travel to Cambodia and Laos and expose what was happening on the front lines. She'd interview French President Georges Pompidou. She'd write about starving children in Biafra and awaken the world to their plight. She refused to die unmarried and unknown in a white house on top of Lowndes Hill.

"Why did Lafayette and so many other plants close?" Sarah asked.

"Big companies owned by out-of-state folks didn't try to control output the way local management and unions did," Katherine said. "They quit shutting down for the summer or when the market was glutted. When supply is greater than demand, prices fall. It forced smaller plants out of business."

After lunch, Sarah dried dishes while Livvie washed. They were alone in the kitchen.

Livvie rinsed a Currier and Ives plate. A horse-drawn sleigh crossed a covered bridge on its face, a design rendered in bright blue against a white background.

"You know," Livvie said, "when I was about your age, a young man disappointed me and I withdrew from all my friends for a while."

Livvie handed the plate to her.

The scene depicted an American past that seemed so distant, when girls like her aunts wore long skirts and carried fur-covered mufflers. Yet not so distant, after all. How strange to look at Livvie and Katherine now, with their colorless hair, stooped bodies, wrinkled hands and faces, and see the young women in love they once were. Girls with hair ribbons and dreams of being kissed. No different from her.

"One day," Livvie said, "I decided, enough of this moping about and I got past it. I expect that's what will happen with you as well, don't you?"

Sarah set down the dish towel with a sigh. No use pretending or making excuses with Livvie. "I expect it will."

Garrett drifted in from the living room, picked up the wet towel, and swatted Sarah's butt. He laughed when she slapped him. "I forgot you don't have padding back there like a normal girl."

When Sarah complained about his immaturity, Livvie suggested clowning was his way of relating to people, something he did to make people like him. Sarah remembered once, when her father's fingers began to fumble with his belt buckle, Garrett quipped, "What's a matter? Those second helpings catching up with you?" Her father let go of the buckle and cuffed Garrett's head—gently, jokingly—admonishing, "I think you're the one getting too big for your britches, Mister."

Maybe Garrett's attempts at humor were survival techniques. Like her own escapes to her room to read, taking Foster to the park, or pounding a basketball on pavement, something she hadn't done for far too long.

After she got home, she changed into cut-offs and jogged three blocks to the neighborhood playground, dribbling a basketball most of the way, the rhythms recalled from school games, her fingers remembering the give and take, the satisfaction derived from controlling the ball. She shot hoops for half an hour and then joined in a scrimmage, three to a side, with some neighborhood teens who showed up. The depression she had worn for months like a rain-soaked bathrobe began to ooze from her pores along with sweat. Suddenly the specter of endless hot afternoons holed up in her bedroom at home was more than she could bear.

The following week, Sarah signed up for summer school and checked off three more required courses, including her phys ed requirement—a course in basketball. She was in a hurry for real life to begin.

Six

SEPTEMBER 4, 1970

The first Friday in September, Sarah trailed into Room 125 of the Language Arts Building for second-year Spanish. The only one who seemed happy to be in the four o'clock class was Buddy Davoli. Everyone knew him. Noisy, friendly, football player Buddy. Buddy was a shaken-up can of cola. He exploded into LA 125, a Greek god (Sig Phi) with a Roman nose and the muscled body of Michelangelo's David. Gloom dissipated as he punched a fellow athlete in the arm, slapped hands with a frat brother, and chatted up a cheerleader-type with oversized eyes.

Sarah also noticed the sandy-haired guy sitting on her left. He seemed familiar, but she couldn't place him. On Friday the "Roy Glen Hardman" written on his notebook caught her eye. Roy Glen's impact was subtle, the soft scuffle of well-worn penny loafers, rather than the squeal of Buddy's rubber-soled athletic shoes. Sarah felt vaguely nervous around Buddy's energy, the way he couldn't sit still in a seat, instead rolling his pencil down the desk while the professor lectured. The way his quadriceps bulged and pushed against his jeans as he jiggled his legs.

Roy Glen's demeanor pleased her more, his form compact and at ease in loose jeans and clean tee-shirt. When she dropped a sheet of paper, the white rectangle escaping like a sigh, Roy Glen scooped it from the air before it could touch the dingy institutional linoleum.

She accepted the paper with a whispered thanks. He didn't smile, merely inclined his head in her direction. He held her gaze long enough for Sarah to admire the clean slope of a jaw line and green flecks in amber eyes. Eyes that would melt ice. A shock went through her.

"It's you," she said. The guy who'd rescued Foster from the West Fork River.

"It's me."

His voice was so deep and well-modulated, it made her acutely aware of the way hers began to pitch up and down. "I wanted to pay for your tennis shoes, but I didn't know how to find you again. I mean, my dog would have drowned if not for you."

He lifted one shoulder. "Don't worry about it. Those shoes were shot before they got soaked."

"Still, I never could repay you."

The seconds ticked by slowly as students struggled to remember enough Spanish to follow Dr. Quero's lecture and respond to her questions. Roy Glen, Sarah noticed, sat quietly without taking notes. Once, he caught her looking at him and half smiled. A merciful woman, Dr. Quero dismissed class five minutes early with a warning: oral quizzes would begin the next week.

Buddy boomed out Sarah's name as she gathered her books and purse. Her face got hot. He had been in her Early Novel class last semester, but they hadn't exchanged a single word. How had he remembered her name? "I'm trying to get up a study group. Claire," he pointed to the cheerleader type, "has agreed and I told her you copped the best grades in old Pudsell's class." He flashed perfect teeth, the smile of someone who usually got what he wanted, including braces when he was younger.

Although she was flattered he remembered her, Sarah wasn't sure she wanted to spend study time with Buddy. He didn't seem like the serious type.

"I'd like to join, too," Roy Glen said. "Gotta keep those grades up."

So on Mondays and Wednesdays, Sarah ended up in a padded booth at Rendition Drug Store with Buddy, Claire, and Roy Glen. After two sessions practicing conversational skills—endeavors made difficult because Buddy was distracted so easily—Roy Glen asked Sarah if she wanted to go to a dance at the Student Union Saturday night.

Sarah weighed her options quickly. Still no word from Cal, and the more she saw of Roy Glen, the more she liked his quiet, steady approach.

"Si, señor," she answered. She guessed Foster could get along without her for one weekend.

~~~

The common area of the Student Union was stuffy with so many bodies packed inside. To accommodate dancers, support staff had pushed tables and chairs in the snack area to the sides of the room. A four-piece band set up on a small platform at the long end of the room.

Sarah was confident she looked good in her new peach hot pants, which were nothing more than wide-legged shorts that hit mid-thigh. Her father fussed over her purchase. Said hot pants made a girl look cheap. But what did he know? He still thought only hookers wore skirts above the knee, but even the Nixon girls showed a little knee now and then.

Roy Glen wore a lake green oxford shirt, which she complimented as they stepped onto the dance floor. "Brings out the color of your eyes."

His feet shuffled to Chicago's "25 or 6 to 4," somewhat off beat, arms swinging stiffly, forehead furrowed as he worked far too hard at having fun. He apologized for not being much of a dancer. "Now put me in a fishing or hunting contest, I might win."

She loved his voice, so deep, yet flannel-soft. When they sat the next song out, Roy Glen was quiet, so much so, that even with the music playing and forty or fifty other couples dancing nearby, she felt awkward. To fill the void, Sarah confessed she almost never stayed on campus for the weekend. She complained about the late hour of the Spanish class and regaled him with descriptions of the characters she encountered on bus trips home. He nodded at all the right times, but when he didn't contribute anything for so long, she decided he was bored.

At last he spoke. "I could give you a ride home on Fridays."

Perhaps she'd misread him. "I can help pay for the gas."

"No need. I pass right by on my way to Deer Lick Road."

"What road?"

He repeated his address.

"Never heard of it." She wondered if deer actually licked the road.

"Not surprised—it's out in the boonies. About a half hour out-side Clarksburg."

The band eased into "Colour My World." For this number, one of the band members traded in his guitar for a saxophone. Very sensual. A nice touch. Roy Glen pulled Sarah to her feet and coped with the slow song by holding her in his arms and dragging his feet an inch or two left, then reversing course. His style had advantages. He never would bump into other couples or step on her feet.

When the song ended, he led her to one of the small round tables. "You seeing anyone?"

"No." In a moment of bravery, she offered this: "My boyfriend preferred Vietnam to me."

"Stupid choice."

"It's a stupid war."

He hesitated. A beat too long. "It is. Absolutely. Glad I drew a safe number in the lottery."

It dawned on her he meant to compliment her rather than criticize the war. She looked away, pretending to watch the dancers.

Her confession must have tripped a lever in Roy Glen. "Anita and me dated all through high school. She took it kind of hard last semester when I told her it was time for us to see other people."

Sarah leaned away from him. "Ouch, that must have hurt. She a student here?"

"No. Went to work at Krogers right out of high school. Begged my parents to let her work for them—they have a little general store—but they can't afford to hire anybody. They do everything themselves."

After the dance, Roy Glen and Sarah climbed a winding staircase to the roof of the Student Union, a flat concrete surface with a few benches scattered about. Deserted at this hour, the rooftop seemed enormous under an expanse of midnight sky. From there, they could see most of the campus: the two women's dormitories, the cafeteria, the Administration, Fine Arts, Gymnasium, and Language Arts buildings. The two of them leaned on the railing, absorbing the night. An occasional couple, their chatter and giggles drifting up like fragments of a dream, hastened toward the dorms after the dance. It was chilly this late in the evening.

Each star stood out in sharp counterpoint to the navy sky, untouched by the street lights far below. The apricot scent of roses drifted up from a circular bed, its perimeter distinctly outlined with tiny lights. A brighter spotlight illumined the "Welcome to Fairmont State College" sign planted in front of the flowers. It was so quiet Sarah could hear the bubbling of the fountain in the garden below.

Roy Glen faced Sarah and wrapped his hands around hers. "The best day of my life was when I was eleven years old, and I bagged my first deer."

Suppressing her feelings before they could pinch her face, she pushed the picture of Bambi dying out of her mind. He was proud of his accomplishment and had every reason to be.

"No rack on that bad boy, only velvet, but my dad slapped me on the back and told me I done good. He said my deer would have the most tender meat I'd ever tasted, and he was right."

Roy Glen poked fingers into her hair, which had kinked up from the humidity at the dance. "How about you? What's been the best day of your life so far?"

There was the night with Cal, a night that resulted in as much pain as joy and, in any case, was hardly the sort of thing she would share. Sarah flipped through memories: graduating fifth in her high school class, bringing Foster home from the pound, organizing a Christmas party for under-privileged kids, getting an A last semester from Dr. Pudsell (he rarely gave them). She chose an event from seventh grade. After a semester-long struggle, the boys' basketball coach at school agreed to let his team play the girls' church league. Sarah's team lost the first two encounters. In the second half of the third game, after the girls captured the lead, Cal elbowed her out of the way so he could get under the basket for two points. The ref missed it. When she got the ball back and went in for her own lay-up, she knifed her elbow into his chest and reclaimed the lead. Sometimes two wrongs could make a right.

"When we won the third game, we were on cloud nine," she said. "And the best part came afterwards. The school decided to sponsor a girls' team for the first time the next year." What she didn't confess was she'd only played on the team for one year in high school. Girls had to decide which game they wanted to play: basketball or boyfriends. Cal, she remembered, was so upset when the girls won, for three whole weeks he refused to shoot hoops with Rachel and her at the playground. What was he doing right now? She tried to picture him walking through a jungle, tried to conjure up his face, but all she managed to retrieve was the photograph she carried of him in her wallet, still, lifeless. And why try? He didn't want to be with her, and she was with someone who did.

"So you were queen of the courts," Roy Glen said.

Standing on one leg, she raked the back of one bare calf with the front of her sandal. "Well, maybe a princess." She was only the second-leading scorer on the team. Never the best at anything.

"I should have guessed you played basketball from your height and the way you move. It was my sport too."

She was somewhat surprised because he wasn't tall for a guy, standing nose to nose with her, but from the way he'd rescued Foster and even from the way he'd snatched up her falling paper in class, she knew he had quick reflexes.

He twirled strands of her hair around his fingers. "Once upon a time there was a princess with hair the color of a shiny new penny and she met a handsome—well, sort of okay-looking—prince at college. They whirled—well, you whirled—you look really sexy when you dance—and he sort of stumbled—around the dance floor until they grew dizzy and before she could stop him, he kissed her."

He bent his lips to hers, and she felt warmth percolating through her veins. Her nose filled with the scent of apricots, her ears with bubbling water, her mouth with the sweetness of Roy Glen's kiss.

He pulled back a little to look at her. "What do you think happened next?"

"Maybe they kissed again."

Sarah jerked on the handle of the front door of the dorm for the third time. She looked at her watch. Only two minutes after one, and Sarah's bad luck her wing's R.A. pulled lock-up duty this weekend. DeeDee was as flexible as a mop handle. Because of those two lousy minutes, she would have to spend Sunday through Saturday confined to her teensy room between six at night until six in the morning. Every R.A. except DeeDee checked outside before she locked up.

The white-columned porch was empty; the narrow road winding through campus, quiet. Night insects scratched in the rhododendrons lining the dorm foundation and the occasional car whooshed past the college on the main drag below, heard, not seen.

Roy Glen touched her shoulder. "Sorry, I didn't mean to get you campused."

She slumped onto the top step, head sinking to her knees, arms wrapped around her shins, annoyed by the stone, so cold against her bare thighs. "It's not your fault. I should've watched the time more carefully."

"Maybe there's a way out of this."

As if. "How's that?"

"Don't go in at all tonight. Wait until the dorm opens up in the morning."

Was "slut" tattooed on her forehead? What kind of girl did he think she was? "Sorry, I might kiss on first dates, but we're not spending the night together."

"You've got the wrong idea. I wasn't talking about taking you back to my apartment."

"Good thing, buster, but it's too cold to sit out here all night hiding in the shrubbery."

"There are other places we could go."

Sarah arched an eyebrow. "For instance?"

He took a key from his pocket. "Now wait—it's not what you think. I clean the gym as part of my work-study program. Lots of nights, I shoot hoops after I'm done. Campus cop won't will think anything of it. How about it?"

Now that was a game of one-on-one Sarah was willing to play. Even on a first date.

She stood up and swung her purse back onto her shoulder. "H.O.R.S.E. Loser coughs up a penny for every shot missed. Be prepared: I'm gonna whip your butt."

"You must be afraid I'll win. Make it a nickel."

That was one thing she wasn't afraid of. She could sink any shot he made. "You're on."

Seven

SEPTEMBER *16, 1970*

Sarah slurped the end of her cola through a straw at the Wednesday meeting of the Spanish study group. "Can you believe I have to go to some dumb Fall Fair at Prickett's Fort Thursday morning? That bonehead Dr. Jordan says it will count as a test grade."

Roy Glen looked up from his cheeseburger. "I'll go with you."

It was decent of him to offer. She was glad he didn't hold the 25 cents she'd taken off him in H.O.R.S.E. and Around the World against her. "Thought you had calculus at nine."

"I can skip." She frowned and was ready to protest, but he said, "No, really, I have a solid A."

By midmorning when they set out, it was already so warm they didn't need jackets. When she realized he wore the same green shirt she'd admired on their first date, she tried not to smile.

As soon as they stepped through the gates of the fort, she fell backwards through time. The fort was a living history museum, staffed by interpreters who wandered around in period dress explaining and demonstrating how settlers lived in the 1700s.

Fourteen log cabins lined the twelve-foot high stockade walls. This alternate world existed only a few miles from campus. One woman, wide-brimmed straw hat tied under her chin, stirred long, lumpy, strands of wool into a vat of dye. It held pokeweed berries to yield a red-purple shade, but settlers, she said, used many different plants and berries to color yarns. In the nearest cabin, a woman with a white kerchief tied around her head, demonstrated how wool was spun into strands. A child sat at her feet carding the yarn, and another woman wove the strands into fabric on a loom.

As Sarah and Roy Glen moved through the fort, they encountered a blacksmith, a basket weaver, and a woman tending an herb garden. When Roy Glen found the gunsmith assembling a muzzle-loader, he engaged the man in conversation. Sarah asked a few questions, pretending more interest than she felt to make herself shinier in Roy Glen's eyes. He showed no signs of moving on, so eventually she wandered off alone.

Soon she found the glassblower, a thinnish fellow with long red hair pulled back in a ponytail. He wore safety glasses, thick and unattractive enough to transform even Paul McCartney into a nerd. He introduced himself as Robin Leuliette. The blow pipe, he said, was authentic for the period, a mini-pipe, a quarter of an inch in diameter. Sarah remembered her huge uncle's blowpipe. Even at eleven, she could have easily handled this little gadget.

"The three main ingredients in glass are silica or sand, soda, and lime," Robin said. "The soda is added to lower the heating temperature of the sand and the lime is added as a stabilizer. Without it, the sand and soda would be water-soluble, so the glass wouldn't be much good." He showed her a container holding batch.

He explained his propane heater wasn't authentic for the period, and it was unusual for the fort to allow the glassblowing. She watched as he turned out a wavy-edged bowl. He told her the shade of green was determined by the iron content in the sand.

Sarah unloaded question after question about the glass pieces she'd grown up with. How did they make glass turn amethyst, amber, green, milky? Again, he said it was all about the additions. Nickel, carbon, manganese, and copper resulted in various colors.

An hour later, Roy Glen found her still talking to Robin. The bowl she'd watched him make was cooling off in an annealing oven, but others were on display.

She picked one up so Roy Glen could admire it. "Aren't these gorgeous?"

"Um hum."

Clearly he didn't see the same magic she did. He shifted his weight from foot to foot. "We gotta go. I got a two o'clock chemistry class I can't miss."

The bowls were $10 a piece, and even though it meant she'd have to go without spending money for the week, she decided to buy one. When they got to the parking lot, Roy Glen chastised her. "What're you going to do with that thing? It's not even perfect. The edges are lopsided."

She huffed. "It's not supposed to be uniform. It's unique, a work of art."

He held out his hand to stop her. "Okay, okay, I get it. It's like a muzzle loader. Every one is a little bit different. The barrel length and twist affect the speed and accuracy of the bullets. Takes skill to use one."

"Yeah, that's it." Not exactly, but she didn't know how to explain the way glass affected her. Part was Robin Leuliette's skill, and yet it was more than that. The pieces he created were like people. No two identical. Beautiful yet flawed. What the glassmaker did with his breath—it was like borrowing a bit of God's power.

True to his word, Roy Glen gave Sarah a ride home after Spanish class. Sarah could see her reflection in the green paint of his 1966 Ford truck. It looked spit-shined. Holding her suitcase with both hands, he laid it in the truck bed next to his. Once they were on the road, Roy Glen's reserve fell away. He said he hoped to die someday with a little more dignity than Jimi Hendrix, who had overdosed in London earlier in the week. "Choking on your own vomit—can you imagine?"

She couldn't. Disgusting. Not even her father stooped so low.

"You won't catch a good old country boy like Elvis acting so stupid," Roy Glen said.

"Probably not, but he doesn't look so good anymore. I hate the white jumpsuit."

Roy Glen agreed he should ditch it and go back to jeans.

They talked about how much they wished they could have gone to the anti-war rally at Valley Forge. "My dad would've shit a brick," Roy Glen said.

"Mine too," Sarah admitted, "but I'd give anything to go to a rally. Even lie to my folks about where I was." The air zinged with possibilities.

On Saturday night, they went to the movies. Roy Glen wore the same green oxford again. But the next week on the ride home, he sat on the driver's side as quiet as those first hours at the dance. She didn't know where his thoughts were, but they weren't inside the Ford with her. He made no plans to see her.

She wasn't about to sit home moping. She went to the Yellow Submarine with her roommate Paula Jackman Saturday night. Quickly they located a table of girls they knew from high school. She was half-way through her first beer when a waitress set a second mug beside her.

"Wait—I didn't order—" But the waitress trotted off with a tray of drinks.

"I did." Buddy Davoli pulled a chair up to her table.

She hadn't even finished her first beer. She counted carefully, an exercise in control. Proof she could have a couple and stop. Proof she was not her father and her children would never have to tiptoe around her.

"Are you trying to get me drunk?" she asked.

"Maybe. That might be the only way I'll convince you to go out with me."

"You're so full of shit."

Buddy grinned. "You don't know how I have looked forward to hearing you tell me that again. The last time was when I failed to properly conjugate some Spanish verb."

"That was every Spanish verb you ever tried to conjugate, and I haven't said that many cuss words in my entire life." She bantered with Buddy several minutes, enjoying harassing him in Spanish. He gave it right back in a pathetically humorous mixture of Spanish and English. He called her *"caliente pollo,"* which she deciphered as his attempt to call her a "hot chick," and he wanted her to "wrap her *piernas*" around him. Instead of her legs, she threatened to wrap her chair around his head if he didn't stop. He didn't mean it. It was Buddy's persona. Slightly obnoxious to all the girls in a friendly, joking way. He threw out similar comments to the other girls at the table as soon as she introduced him. As Sarah began her second beer, the one Buddy had bought, her skin tingled with the odd sensation someone was watching her. She scanned the room. At a table across the bar, deep in the shadows, Roy Glen sat alone. She waved and signaled he should come over, but he didn't. Well, he could be that way. He didn't own her because they'd gone out a couple of times. He downed his beer and left. She flashed her perkiest smile at Buddy, but felt like an actress faking a good time.

After Roy Glen and Sarah left Adamston, there was very little traffic on the road. A good thing about driving on Sundays—not so many coal trucks out. The afternoon was warm enough to roll her window down and let the wind toss her hair.

Sarah tried to make conversation. "You ready for Quero's test?"

"Yeah."

"I studied two hours this morning and listened to those tapes she recommended."

He didn't answer.

"Bridge Over Troubled Water" played on the radio while they passed the strip mines outside Shinnston. Next came a string of small homes painted in garish colors with laundry hung on lines in the side yards.

When "Venus" came on the radio, she tried again. "My Aunt Katherine fell and broke her hip. I stopped by the hospital this morning. My mother says broken hips can be deadly for old folks."

"Hmm."

Hmm—that was the best he could offer? What was wrong with him?

He down-shifted the Ford into third and whipped around a coal truck lumbering up the hill. Sarah closed her eyes, her foot pressing hard against the floorboard. Seconds before a semi coming the other way rounded the curve, Roy Glen jerked back into his own lane. Next weekend she would catch the bus.

Finally he broke the silence. "Saw you with Buddy last night."

"I wasn't with him. He dropped by our table to say hi. Why didn't you come over?"

When the silence between them stretched to several minutes, Sarah decided—enough. No more dates with weirdos. Then he said about the only thing he could have to change her mind.

"I stopped in for one beer because I wanted to see you, then I needed to head home. My grandfather's funeral was yesterday."

Appropriate condolences tumbled out, but the shock that something this important had happened and he hadn't told her muddled her brain. She reached for a way to understand him. "Were you close?"

His face, unreadable as granite. "PawPaw lived on the farm next to ours."

She took that as a yes. "Why didn't you say something Friday?"

"Showing emotion is weak."

"But you should feel emotion. He was your grandfather, for God's sake."

"I didn't say I didn't feel it. I try not to show emotion. There's a difference."

Sounded like a bad John Wayne movie to her. After a pause, she added, "I'd have come to the funeral home."

"You didn't know him."

But I know you. Though obviously she didn't. Not really. She wondered if anyone could ever know anyone else. Really know them.

They sat in silence again. On her right, a picked field of corn, the stalks already desiccated and brown, bent with the breeze. They passed cows chewing grass behind barbed wire fences and a flea market bustling with bargain-hunters in pick-up trucks.

Another five miles and she couldn't stand the silence any longer. "What about good emotions? Do you hide those too?"

"Especially those. People think you're nice, gives them an edge over you."

She didn't understand men. Any of them. The Ford idled noisily in front of her dorm. This time he didn't get out or offer to help with her suitcase. Roy Glen waited until she reached into the back for her weekender before he leaned out the window and asked if she was free the following Saturday afternoon. She hesitated, still standing on her toes to grab her gear. She heaved the case up and out. Maybe his grandfather's death had temporarily jumbled his balance. Maybe he was irrationally jealous of Buddy—and she could see why an onlooker might have thought she was flirting, because, okay, she had been, a little. Or maybe Roy Glen was plain weird. She'd never know which, if she didn't give him another chance.

Eight

OCTOBER 3, 1970

As they pulled into the parking area of the French Creek Game Farm, the sun poked its way through the mist. Roy Glen loved mornings like this, the sky shimmering all pearly gray, the air crisp with a hint of smoke from burning leaves. He reached for Sarah's hand—a thin, white hand, fragile as his mother's china cups. He tugged her toward the trail, fingers entwined with hers, conscious of those long, jean-clad legs, the way she changed gaits easily, loping along one minute, pausing to kick her tennis shoe at a rock, then cantering ahead the next. It was pure foolishness, but under his jacket, he'd worn his green shirt again, the one she said made his eyes mysterious.

Twenty yards ahead, a covey of quail waddled along the side of the trail in a straight line, mama first, followed by the chicks. He couldn't have picked a better start to their outing if he'd tried.

"Oh, look at the babies—they're so cute." Her voice was barely a whisper so she wouldn't scare the birds, but Roy Glen could hear her excitement in the little squeal of the last word.

Sarah stopped to read the sign describing the species. "What's the funny little thing on their heads flopping around?"

He knew she meant the crest. He told her the male's coloring was slightly darker than the female's. How you could identify their call "chi-ca-go," how it sounded when a covey of two hundred took to the air at once when they were startled, how the wildlife officers laid heavy wire around the enclosure to keep predators out. "Hear the radio? It keeps hawks away from them."

He showed her pheasant tails and turkey wattles, pointed out spotted elk and woodchucks half hidden in the woods. He led her to shallow concrete holding pens constantly flushed with running water. The pens were full of trout—rainbows, browns, goldens. "They're sorted by size and species so they can stock the rivers and lakes."

"Oh, I thought fish grew naturally in lakes."

"They do, but the hatcheries make sure there's a big supply. Trout need both shallows and deep pools to survive in the wild, and the water has to be crystal clear and cool. It helps if the bank provides some cover. Trees that overhang. Rocks. They love to hide near rocks." Okay, he was really showing off, but he couldn't wait to take her fishing, to teach her to look for the best spot in a river, a low gradient where the current wasn't too swift. He'd always been able to pull trout out of the water while fishermen around him cursed empty ice chests.

"I tie my own flies," he said.

"How do you catch them?"

Inside, he was laughing his ass off. "I don't, silly. I make them from hair and fur, thin synthetic fabric and yarns."

"I thought you used worms for bait."

"Not for trout."

"Maybe fishing's not so bad then. I couldn't stand the thought of pushing a worm on a hook. I used rubber gloves when we dissected them in biology." She shuddered.

Lord, she was so refreshingly different from his sister Sandy, who taught him how to get worms to leap half-fried out of the ground with an electrified screwdriver. Sandy dropped wigglers down his shirt and laughed when he screeched. Because his sister was four years older, it seemed he was always playing catch-up to prove which one of them was the better man. It was pleasant to be around a girl who knew how to act like one for a change. Sarah looked as translucent and delicate as Sandy was thick and tough. And yet Sarah wasn't weak—she was a tough competitor in basketball. She'd even legitimately beaten him in a couple of those games of H.O.R.S.E. They'd taken off their shoes and played barefoot. He showed off some of his better shots, but spent most of the night wondering what it would feel like to run his hands up the acre of thigh revealed by those wide-legged shorts. There was something almost gawky about the way she moved, something he'd noticed in other basketball players, the way their joints looked as if they could bend in any direction on a moment's notice. The loose limbs didn't mean a lack of coordination. He suspected she'd keep her balance no matter what direction she veered off.

They held hands, drifting along the park trails. A fence along the right side kept the animals in. Movement caught his eye, a slight shift in the light. He grabbed her arm and pointed beyond the meadow to the forest edge. This was what he wanted her to see, why he brought her to the game farm. A doe and her fawn stood munching on the leaves of a small tree. Roy Glen and Sarah watched for some time before sneaking closer. The doe and her baby ignored them. At the closest point, Roy Glen stopped, leaning into the fence. The mother looked up, huge eyes holding his gaze an instant before she and the baby darted off, white tails bobbing, the soft thuds of their hooves diminishing as they vanished into the woods. Watching Sarah's awe, Roy Glen felt as if he were seeing deer again for the first time. Now she would understand. This was who he was, what mattered to him.

"They're purely beautiful," he said. "It's a shame they'll never make it if they are released in the wild. No fear. They've lost their edge, their instincts for survival."

A small herd of buffalo, great shaggy beasts, snorted randomly as they grazed, breaking the silence. Roy Glen could smell their fur, their musk, their power. He wished he'd been around to see thousands of them thundering across the Great Plains.

As they walked down the path, he didn't have to talk much. He let the place talk for him. Leaves rustled. Tall grasses bent in the breeze. The light warmed to a wintery gold and lifted the chill from the morning. It was the kind of morning he loved to spend hunting and fishing. Cumulus clouds piled up like a snow bank in the western sky. The breeze would soon take them over the horizon, he thought. No rain today.

They approached the mountain lion's pen. The big cat was crouched atop a ten-foot high artificial breccia. Rangers tried to make the habitat look realistic, but Roy Glen could tell it was fake. For a moment, he watched the lion, who was, in turn, watching him without seeming to. A stand-off. Knowing it could go on all day, Roy Glen pulled Sarah forward. Satisfied he'd won, the lion leapt from the fake rock, its quivering muscles stretched to impossible lengths, every movement controlled. What a frigging athlete! Roy Glen would have given anything to be able to jump like that.

Sarah seemed to stop breathing, watching doe-eyed, as the lion padded with great indifference across the enclosure. "I'm not sure I'd like camping if those are out there."

"No animal around here's a match for a man with a gun."

With a jug of Lambrusco and pimento cheese sandwiches, they picnicked on a blanket shaded by sycamores.

Afterwards, he handed her a long, slim box, the kind jewelry came in.

She tried to hand it back. "I can't accept anything like this."

"Open it."

He counted on her curiosity getting the better of her. She tipped the lid back and burst out laughing. "I haven't seen one of these in years."

His shoulders shook, though his laughter was silent. "What'd you think was in there? Diamonds? Pearls?"

"The box was a setup."

He admitted it. "You should have seen your face when you tried to hand it back."

She stretched the elastic necklace over her head and, parting her lips, sunk her teeth into a pink candy lozenge until it cracked into her mouth.

Gently—because he knew if he moved too fast he would spook her—he pushed her back onto the blanket. He kissed her, long and slow. Tasted the wine in her mouth. Slid his hand up her side until his fingers rested along her ribs beneath her breast. Sweet little girl breasts. Not big old cow udders like his sister Sandy's but soft mounds like peach halves. Anita's were somewhere in between, but in three years, she'd never let him near them.

He teased Sarah's lips with his tongue. Definitely a better kisser than Anita.

He drew back and looked at Sarah, curly hair spilled like clover honey across the blanket. He couldn't help remembering the fearless kiss he'd witnessed while under the eaves. With him, she was holding something back. Sooner or later, he was going to pry that something loose. He drew a finger down her cheek, kissed each eyelid. He could hear his father's voice inside his head, reminding him to control himself. Enough for today.

He wanted to savor her innocence.

Nine

Just once, Sarah wished Rachel would experience a bad hair day. But no, her best friend looked perfect as always, in a simple black dress under a camel hair coat. Sarah escorted Rachel around, first to her parents and her brother, then to Aunt Livvie, and finally to the casket, where Katherine's hair floated like a white cloud on pink satin. Then they withdrew to chairs and Rachel chattered about her sorority, still unable to fathom Sarah's choice not to pledge.

Sarah had her reasons. Sororities and fraternities seemed like silly extensions of high school cliques. Irrelevant when the country was at war. But Sarah kept her real thoughts to herself. Always had. When she and Rachel became blood sisters as nine year olds, Rachel declared there could be no secrets between them. Sarah agreed, even though she knew she would never tell her friend about the empty quarts of Crown Royal or beatings her father inflicted on Garrett and the way she cowered in her room, crouched on the floor, hands pressed against her face, feeling she should do something to stop her father and at the same time flooded with relief she wasn't on the receiving end of the belt. Sometimes, if Garrett particularly pestered her, she even felt a sense of satisfaction, of justice delivered, a flash of dark glee, followed inevitably by shame. No one deserved to be beaten, and she loved her brother. Yet she did nothing to stop her father. Neither did her mother, though she would protest. It did no good. And then there was cousin Pete. One more skeleton in the closet—only he didn't even own a closet. And, of course, there was Cal. No, she could never tell Rachel these things. Sometimes she wished for a ton of sisters like her mother had so there would always be someone to share with.

Maybe Sarah's thoughts conjured Pete up, because moments later he edged his way through the door of Chapel B, followed by his sister Martha Rose. Passing him on the way out, Rachel's nose crinkled as if she smelled something unpleasant. She probably did. Pete wore the same old Army fatigues and boots, and he often smelled faintly like rotten potatoes. He was clean-shaven except for a bottle brush mustache, and his face appeared washed. Sarah wasn't worried Rachel would recognize Pete as the guy who harvested bottles from the roadside. No one ever looked at the faces of the homeless or mentally ill.

There were still things Sarah didn't understand about Uncle Mahlon. Sarah had only met his children, Pete and Martha Rose, when they showed up for Thanksgiving dinner five years after Mahlon died. Martha Rose, much younger than her brother—only a high school freshman then—arrived with a snooty attitude and a suitcase. She was petite with chestnut hair and hardened eyes. She stayed at the Aunt Hill several months until their mother recovered from a mysterious illness and could care for her again. Sarah pestered her mother with questions about these new-found cousins. Pete looked almost old enough be to Martha Rose's father. "If you must know, Mahlon and Ava were separated for eighteen years. Katherine talked them into reconciling. The union only lasted a few months, long enough to result in Martha Rose. A shame, but Katherine, especially, was so opposed to divorce." Sarah questioned why neither Pete nor Martha Rose was at Mahlon's funeral. "Your aunts couldn't track them down in time," her mother said. "They felt so bad, they vowed never to lose touch again." But when Sarah wanted to know what was wrong with Ava, her mother said it was none of her business. Which Sarah interpreted to mean whatever it was, it was so bad even a senior in high school wasn't old enough to hear about it. At the end of the school term, as suddenly as Martha Rose had appeared, she vanished. Back to Iowa or Michigan or wherever she came from. After that visit, Pete and Martha Rose showed up for Thanksgiving, and for a while afterwards, there would be Pop Bottle Pete sightings along the highway.

Pete dragged his palm across slicked-back hair, stopping at the bald spot in the rear. Sarah shivered with revulsion, followed by pity. Thick carpet muffled the thuds of his military-issue boots as he tromped up to Livvie by the casket. "I got the message you left at the hotel. How did it happen?"

Livvie took both his hands. "Pneumonia, took her fast."

Sarah calculated Martha Rose would be a high school senior now. Looked older as she hung around the guest register, arms folded across her chest.

The reality of Katherine's death was beginning to sink in as Sarah touched her cold, limp hand, yet it was hard to believe her aunt was really gone. Sarah still half-expected Katherine to sit up, affix her reading glasses, and ask the management to turn up the lights properly so she could finish reading Mary Stewart's *The Crystal Cave*. Sarah had tucked the novel, bookmark intact, under the pink satin quilt.

Pete stood with them a moment but became agitated as his eyes traveled the room. He mumbled something incomprehensible and began to pace. Sarah could only catch snippets as he passed by: "Devil… wrong, wrong, wrong …why don't you shut up."

Livvie tried to take his arm, but he shook her off. She teetered and nearly fell—might have if Sarah's father hadn't been close enough to steady her.

The room grew silent, except for Pete. He paced, stopped, scraped his nails across his scalp, pulled at hairs in his mustache. His eyes darted from side to side, leaving Sarah with the impression he was talking *to* someone, not to himself. Thank God this hadn't happened while Rachel was here. What on earth was wrong with him? Martha Rose trotted along beside Pete awhile and then returned to Livvie.

Martha Rose flashed a smile that didn't begin to reach her eyes. "It's the red flowers. Pete says red's the Devil's color. It might be best if you took them out of the room. If something upsets him, I go along."

Sarah's father and Garrett removed two predominantly red arrangements and plucked a few stray carnations and roses from mixed bouquets. The funeral director helped them find a storage room to stash the offending blooms.

Nelson came back and leaned close to Livvie's ear, but Sarah could still hear him. "We can all be thankful you chose pink roses for the main spray over the casket. Where does he get these notions?"

Livvie's mouth tightened. "No idea. I wonder if some cult's got aholt of him."

The following day, a lengthy mass at the Immaculate Conception Church was followed by a cemetery service where wind bit cheeks and reddened noses, causing Sarah to send up a prayer for the priest to speed things up. She wiggled her toes, trying to decide if there was any feeling left in them. At last the family gathered at the Aunt Hill. No one mentioned Pete's odd behavior at the funeral home. Sarah tried to bring it up while the women were reheating casseroles, but Livvie shushed her. "Never mind. Pete is what he is."

Slouched in Katherine's favorite chair, boots propped on the coffee table, Pete was knocking back a beer with Sarah's father, regaling him with facts about small engine repair. Two ordinary fellows, talking cars and football, excusing the occasional burp. Not bad manners, just good food.

Sarah stood in the living room, balancing a plate of corn pudding, green bean casserole, and yeast rolls in one hand. An outsider wouldn't even guess anything was wrong with Pete. Surely they could get him off the streets.

When her father got up from the couch, she took his place. "Pete, I understand you served in the Army. When did you get out?"

The bottlebrush mustache whisked his lip as he explained he was still serving.

Sarah didn't see how that was possible. She forked up some green beans. "So you didn't retire?"

"I'm on a mission for Lady Bird Johnson, helping her clean up the highways."

She almost choked. "But Lady Bird isn't First Lady anymore."

The mustache twitched. "I know, I'm not stupid. But where do you think President Nixon got the idea for the National Environmental Policy Act that set up reviews of big projects and developments? Who do you think thought up Earth Day?"

Earth Day hadn't created even a flicker of interest on the FSC campus, but she told Pete she'd read it was the brainstorm of some senator.

"Nah, that little lady from Texas started it all." He fired off statistics in a rapid monotone. "For every two miles of highway there are 32,000 pieces of litter, which is composed of 59 percent paper, 16 percent cans, 6 percent bottles, 6 percent plastics and 13 percent miscellaneous. Litter totals don't include cigarette butts, which are toxic and account for more litter than all the rest combined."

She was stunned. He was either totally devoted to a clean earth or crazy enough to be locked up. "How do you get along on a job that doesn't earn money?"

"I turn in bottles for deposits, and Lady Bird pays me. I get a check in the mail every month."

Maybe he meant his Army pension. Thank heavens he wasn't really her problem. She took her empty plate to the sink and rinsed it.

Livvie touched her arm. "I have a little something for you."

Sarah hadn't been in her aunt's bedroom for several years. It was unchanged. The morning glories and cabbage roses on the black enamel chest remained fresh as the day they were first painted. The Madonna—Sarah had almost forgotten about the little statue. She picked it up. She still loved the way it shone when light fell on it, as if it remembered the fire that forged it.

Livvie smiled. "As I recollect, you used to beg to take that home. My father made it for my mother. I like to think his love for her is imbedded in that glass, the way she seems to glow with goodness."

Sarah returned the statue to the chest. The Madonna suddenly seemed to represent everything Sarah wasn't. Beautiful, good, pure, loved.

Beside the statue was an ivory jewelry box. Livvie took out a cameo and rubbed her thumb along its gold filigreed edge. The piece was an elegant ivory profile carved into a blush pink background. A tiny diamond was set into a choker around the lady's neck. She pressed the brooch into Sarah's palm. "I want you to take this. Who knows when I might be called home?"

Sarah pulled her hands away as if she'd touched lightning. "You're going to be with us for a long time."

"Please, I want you to wear it and think of me. You'll hurt my feelings terribly if you don't take it."

With thanks, Sarah fumbled with the clasp and pinned it to her navy blazer. Since the others were downstairs, Sarah tried again to address her cousin's problems. "Pete seen a doctor recently?"

Livvie stiffened slightly. "Yes, I believe he has."

"What's wrong with him?"

Livvie sighed. "He's a troubled man. Medication's supposed to help. His mother was—" Livvie hesitated, obviously searching for the right word—"too high strung, and maybe it affected him."

The mother again. Ava was more than high strung or people

wouldn't tiptoe around her memory the way they did. "Why doesn't anyone want to talk about what happened at the funeral home? Someone needs to help him."

Livvie's hands fell to her side. "None of us knows what else to do, so we pretend everything's all right. That's the way most families deal with things they're ashamed of."

Sarah had the strangest feeling Aunt Livvie wasn't talking about Pete anymore. Her aunt was right. Sarah hadn't told anyone about what happened with Cal. She felt like a fraud. Would Livvie still want her to have the cameo if she knew?

"You seem sort of down today," Livvie said. "I can tell it's more than losing Katherine. Does it have something to do with your fella again?"

It was as if Livvie read her mind. Sarah couldn't quite forget Cal, especially because Roy Glen kept distancing himself from her. He wouldn't come to Katherine's funeral, even after she told him it would mean a lot to her. He didn't like to go anywhere requiring a suit, tie, or dress shoes. Sprucing up a little didn't seem like such a big sacrifice to her. She kept telling herself if he loved her he would have been there for her. She was overwhelmed by such a powerful need to be connected to someone. There was this ache, a longing, something she couldn't explain.

"I feel so alone sometimes," she told her aunt.

"We all have times in our lives when we feel that way. Never forget you have your family. My father didn't even have that comfort when he came to this country. Anton was only fourteen when he made the crossing."

Ten

OLDENBURG, GERMAN STATES, SPRING *1877*

One night when he was fourteen, Anton Heimbach lay in his narrow bed, wide awake though it was late. He could still smell the family's supper: pork with apples and sauerkraut. His fists clenched the binding of the quilt his mother had sewn for his birthday. His parents were arguing again. The same words, the same arguments, every night for two weeks. Didn't they realize he could hear every word? That sound carried from the kitchen to the children's bedrooms a few short steps away?

"We have to send him," his father said. "The Prussian Army is monstrous. By the time another birthday passes, it will be too late. You know that. They won't let him go."

His mother's voice was a wail. "But, Joseph, by himself?"

His parents acted as if the decision was all theirs. He didn't know what he wanted, but they should at least ask him. They should ask.

Joseph pounded the wooden kitchen table with his fist. "You think I want this? Who will take my place in the shop if not my son?"

His father was right. If Anton left, it would be the end of Heimbach Glass. How could he let him go, knowing that? Anton wasn't even sure exactly how many generations of Heimbachs had labored in that building, certainly four or five. The small glass house did all sorts of jobs from vases to windows to bottles. Whatever anyone needed. Years ago, half a dozen Heimbachs worked there, but the last generation had produced mostly girls. Anton supposed one of their employees would take over the shop from Uncle Helmut and his father when they got too old to work, but it would never be the same.

"He's just a boy, my little boy." His mother, weeping again.

Anton curled up into a tight ball under the quilt. If only he could remain "her little boy" for the rest of his life. Or at least for as far as he could foresee into the future. To gorge on her potato pancakes and her apple kuchen. To help her make cider in the fall and pick raspberries for jam in the summer.

The wooden floor in the kitchen creaked. His father was pacing again—away from the table where his mother sat with her embroidery. "No, Mama, you are wrong. He is a young man." Anton straightened out his legs and sat up to hear better. "A good worker. He has great skill."

The clomping stopped. Maybe his father turned to face her.

"I am proud of him. You should see the vase he made today. The color of moss shot through with gold as if streaks of sunlight settled into the glass. As good as any Helmut and I have made. He can forge his own way in America."

Anton leaned back onto the pillow. In the shop his father had only said, *Not bad. Should fetch a decent price.*

"We may never see him again," his mother said. Anton imagined her putting aside the tablecloth she was embroidering for Lynette's dowry. He pictured her raising a handkerchief to her face.

"And if the military gets a hold of him?" Although his father was generally a soft-spoken man, he got so riled up over politics he sprayed spittle. The clomping resumed. "Look at Helmut's boy Johann. Dead in the uprisings. Made to fight against the very people he should have been fighting for." His voice trailed off. Anton imagined his father turning toward the kitchen fire, stiff-spined, averting his eyes from his mother's tears.

"It cannot happen to our Anton," his father said. "He will go next month. I have decided. I got a letter from Karl Reinhardt today. He will take Anton into the window glass shop where he works in Pittsburgh."

There was a significant pause of words and boots. Maybe his father was taking pity on Mama, placing his hands on her shoulders. Some gesture of comfort.

His voice softened. "Besides, who knows? Maybe we'll get to America someday too."

Anton knew his father would win this debate, and on this night the plans seemed final. The weight of what that meant settled upon Anton's chest until he could hardly breathe, the air in the bedroom suddenly hot and close. Lynette planned to marry in July. His family would laugh and dance and eat fine cakes without him. The losses ahead mounted. He would not see any of his sisters wed. Not even little Gitte, the blue-eyed elf who was his pet. He would not witness the births of their babies or serve as godfather or speak to their husbands if they strayed or displayed foul dispositions and needed to be jerked back into line. His parents could die and he wouldn't even know. How long did it take for a letter to travel from Oldenburg to America? He would go on blowing glass, eating meals with people he didn't even know as though nothing happened. He was ready to cry until he remembered his father's words: *I am proud of him. He will forge his own way in America.*

He believed in his father. Now his father believed in him.

Inside a wooden trunk, his mother layered his baptismal record, clothes, candles, his grandfather's heirloom watch, eating utensils, enough food for the journey—potatoes, beans, rice, dried apples, sauerkraut, hardtack—and last, carefully wrapped in two layers of cotton handkerchiefs, a wind-up monkey that walked on metal legs, his favorite childhood toy. He heard the sharp intake of his mother's breath as she laid the monkey inside the trunk.

Joseph came in, coughed once, and without a word, handed him a rose vase, the first piece Anton had watched his father create. His mother stripped the quilt from his bed and handed it to him. Anton wound it around the vase. He laid it in the center of the trunk.

"You can use my blanket tonight," she said, "if you need one."

On the morning of May 5, 1877, he bid his sisters goodbye outside the house. When eight-year-old Gitte threw her arms around his legs, he pulled her braids one last time. "Be good for Mama, Elfkin." He saw she was barefoot, toes digging into the dirt. "Where's your shoes?" She shrugged. Tilted her head in that way of hers. Those dimples and that winsome smile would ensure she always got her way.

She handed him a piece of folded paper. "Don't look at it until you are on the ship." He promised, slipped it into the pocket of his trousers.

Freckle-faced Wilhelmena pressed a cloth-wrapped sweet cake into his hands for the journey. The eleven year old was the only one of the Heimbachs to inherit his mother's frizzy auburn hair and small upturned nose. He wondered if she would inherit his mother's talent for baking and the doughy softness of her body as well. He thanked her and set the cake in the wagon next to his trunk.

Elsa folded his hands around a soft oblong object. "Safe journey, little brother." She caressed her thumbs across his folded knuckles before releasing his hands. When he lifted his fingers, he saw the rabbit's foot she always carried for good luck.

"Look after Mama and Papa," he told her. "Soon you will be the oldest in the house." Elsa nodded. She was the most beautiful of his sisters, with thick chestnut braids wound over her ears. Even the Heimbach nose had been shortened enough to appear refined. He doubted she would be single long after Lynette married. The doctor's son mooned after Elsa obsessively.

Tall, willowy Lynette began weeping as she clung to him, and his father gently loosened her grasp.

She ran her hands down the sleeves of Anton's new coat. "You look a fine gentleman." Her handiwork was her best yet, the wool soft and supple, the tailoring precise.

"I bet there's not a seamstress in America can hold a candle to you," Anton said. He remembered cuddling in Lynette's lap as she told him a story about a clever bear that eluded a hunter. He must have been about five; his big sister, ten. She invented many such bedtime stories, but in a panic, he realized he couldn't remember any others. It suddenly seemed important that he could.

"Time to get a move on," his father said. Anton hopped into the wagon behind his parents, waving to Mrs. Ziegler, who was sweeping her porch, and the shoemaker on his way to work and Uncle Helmut and his wife, who came to send him off. It was a quiet ride to Bremen, everything having already been said. Only the creaking of wagon wheels and the occasional bird broke the silence. The wagon rolled past spring green pastures dotted with cows, patches of aromatic lavender and yellow daisies, villagers going about their daily chores.

His father lifted the trunk from the wagon and set it on the ground. In every direction, people hustled about. So many people. Half a dozen dockworkers loaded crates aboard. A young, poorly dressed woman struggled with her trunk alone until two deckhands stepped up to assist. With one hand balanced on a cane, a gray-haired fellow tried to help his frail wife up the incline to the ship. Horses neighed their impatience. Wagon wheels rumbled. A drunk swore repeatedly though Anton couldn't locate any person these curses were aimed at. Everywhere there was the dank smell of river and fish.

His mother cried as she embraced him. "My little boy! My little love!" She felt soft as down under the grip of his hands, and so small. He stood taller than she by several inches. Everyone said he was going to be as tall as Uncle Helmut. Maybe taller.

After a few moments, his father touched her arm and she stepped away. Joseph set his hands on Anton's shoulders.

"Write your mother as soon as you get there. She will be worried."

Anton nodded. He didn't trust his voice. His father embraced him quickly. Slapped his back twice. Drew away. Motioned to two deckhands.

With a mighty exhale, two crew men hefted the trunk to their shoulders and strode up the gangplank. Anton boarded the Rebecca alone, a skinny boy of fourteen whose legs and feet and hands had grown too fast, disproportionate with the rest of his body. Half boy, half man.

From the ship's deck, thick with passengers, Anton could see his mother dabbing at her face with a handkerchief. He imagined he could still see the tiny lavender daisies with yellow centers embroidered on the linen square, but of course, he could not. Already distance worked to compress his former life into memories.

He felt in his pocket for the piece of paper from Gitte. In pencil she had sketched Mama and Papa standing in the middle, with Lynette and Wilhelmena on one side and Elsa and herself on the other. Right in the center, kneeling on one knee between Mama and Papa, was Anton himself. He traced his finger over his father's long nose and then over his own. It was the only picture of his family he possessed. He folded it carefully and returned it to his pocket.

The *Rebecca* set sail up the Weser River. Anton held onto the scrap of paper and Elsa's rabbit's foot with one hand and waved with the other. His parents receded into ever smaller specks and finally disappeared from view. Hours later the *Rebecca* stopped in Bremerhaven and loaded on more passengers and cargo. Then the ship set off into the North Sea. Germany, the only home Anton had ever known, vanished too. Only sky and water and the cry of seagulls remained.

Eleven

NOVEMBER *1970*

Lean and tightly muscled, Roy Glen jumped off an outcropping of rock deep in the national forest, on the prowl for more firewood. He reminded Sarah of that mountain lion they'd seen, same ease of movement, same tawny eyes, same disdain. She crossed and uncrossed her arms, sat down on a bench fashioned from a split log, jumped up again. The thought of spiders creeping up her back made it impossible to relax. She was antsy because she had lied to her parents and said she was staying on campus, antsy because she had never been wilderness camping like this before—were there bears or mountain lions or snakes hiding under the mountain laurels and rhododendrons?—and even more nervous because she and Roy Glen had not yet made love. It seemed likely they might before the night was over.

In the ring of stones Roy Glen positioned two logs and teepeed an armful of smaller sticks on top. Then he cheated, pouring lighter fluid on the pile before throwing on a match. With an orange whoosh, flames jumped skyward.

Roy Glen tossed her a can of Beanee Weenee and a manual can opener. "First course."

She could easily eat around the meat. No big deal.

While the beans warmed, they sat on the log bench with knees touching. Roy Glen opened two Stroh's and handed her one. She leaned her torso left until her shoulder nudged his, then leaned away. "So what's your plan? Your dream if you could do anything you wanted?"

"If I was rich, I'd get me the biggest, baddest truck money can buy and hunt and fish all the time."

Sarah could understand the challenge of tracking an animal, how that could be a thrill. It was harder for her to understand the need to kill. At least he killed only for food. Other guys she knew killed for the sake of killing, keeping the rack of a deer or the tail of a squirrel as trophies and discarding the carcasses. That seemed vicious and disrespectful of life. She got up to stir the beans, stopping a moment to inhale their earthy smell. The fire shielded them against the cool November night. She zipped her parka closer to the neck and turned the collar up.

"Since you aren't Jay Rockefeller, what will you do?" Sarah said, naming the richest West Virginian she could think of.

"Finish college, I suppose, though it's a real drag. Afterward, I guess I'll work for some business. Something financial."

He didn't have to worry about Vietnam since he'd drawn a draft number over 300. He could work with her father, she thought. Become a partner in the CPA firm.

"The rest of my plan is easy," he said. "I'm going to get married and have a big family—at least nine or ten kids—"

Sarah cut in. "Why not an even dozen?"

"—and get some land out near my parents. We'll put a trailer on the land until I can build a big house, and we won't borrow any money from the bank. We'll save until I can do it. I'm serious."

She drew in her breath. *We.* He was assuming they would get married. It was what she wanted, wasn't it? To love and be loved, to have a family of her own? Sure, she also had dreams of interviewing French presidents and traveling to Africa, but no reason she couldn't have both.

"You know I love you." His words and kiss were soft, like prayers.

Joy filled every empty place inside her and drove away the ache, as she fed the words back to him. He slipped his tongue into her mouth, his hand inside her shirt. They stumbled toward the tent. She was vaguely aware of the musty smell of canvas while he pushed her catty-corner across the sleeping bags, fumbling, tugging, pulling shirts away until they were skin on skin. Her limbs stretched to full length in a joyous inhabiting of her body like a cat. She licked his neck and bare chest, inhaling the mixture of light male sweat and soap.

The sound of his jeans zippering open pulled her from the trance. She pushed him away. "Wait, shouldn't you use something?"

"What? You mean—no way. Ten kids, remember?"

She wanted kids, too, but not a herd. Maybe two or three—and not yet, but she didn't know how to stop what they'd started.

"What if I get—"

He kissed her lips to quiet her. "Shhh, don't worry. We'll get married, start those kids sooner rather than later, but nothing's going to happen."

It wasn't hard to let herself believe as she ran her hands over his lean shoulder blades and down the furrow at the center of his back while they moved together. Minutes later, he rolled off her with a sigh and they spooned together. She would have sworn even the soles of her feet, curled against Roy Glen's, sang with bliss. Yet in the corner of her mind, barely acknowledged, a smidgen of disappointment in sex itself registered. It didn't go anywhere, over almost before it began. She buried that thought, that small betrayal of the moment, relishing instead the ecstasy of skin on skin.

Roy Glen raised up on his elbows and kissed her nose, her forehead, her lips. "God, I love you," he whispered into her hair. Abruptly he jerked upright.

"Shit." He stared at the tent flap, his forearms stacked across his knees.

"What?" She bolted upright and drew her knees against her chest to hide her nakedness.

"You've done this before, haven't you?"

In the morning Roy Glen woke up first. Sarah looked so innocent, asleep with hair in disarray, but she wasn't. Not really. He was over his disappointment; he guessed he was—there wasn't anything he could do about it, now was there? Odd how in such a short time he could experience an incredible high (the kiss he'd wanted, nothing held back) and the huge letdown (realizing he wasn't her first). He figured it out because she didn't resist enough. Too easy. He supposed it was that Cal she dated last year, the one in Vietnam. Surely not Buddy—there was only one night he saw them together—but he wouldn't put it past Buddy to have tried. It made him sick to think of someone else touching her, but it was done and he should get over it. Anita, his girlfriend all through high school, never let him. She was pure. Since they'd split, he had taken out several girls he met at the Yellow Submarine, but none he wanted to take home.

Now he wasn't sure about Sarah, if she was the kind of girl he wanted to take home.

The sun glinted on the clear water of the Williams River, casting mirror images of the black cherry, mountain laurel, and oak lining its banks. Leaves flamed the steep mountainsides, pressing in on both sides of the water with noisy oranges and glorious golds. There was nowhere else in the world he would rather be.

As Sarah walked toward him, the fallen leaves sounded like a fussy librarian shushing loud talkers. Shush. Shush. Shush. He hated libraries. All those musty books and stuffy old ladies guarding them. Why would anyone want to be in such a place when they could be out here instead? The moss green water glided by in a straight line as far as you could see. The far bank appeared to be about forty feet away, giving way almost immediately to the sharp tree-covered incline of the mountain. In hip-high waders, Roy Glen strode into the water.

"Watch me a few times. Then you can try," he called to Sarah on the bank. He whipped the line low upstream and let the current pull the fly downstream. As he reeled in the line and cast again, he remembered the way, zipped together in their sleeping bags, they made love for a second time. They stayed up late talking about their roommates' quirks. He shared an off-campus apartment with two other guys. Neither believed in doing dishes or tidying up the place. So once every couple of weeks, Roy Glen rode herd on them. He made one clean the bathroom while the other vacuumed. He tackled the worst mess—the kitchen—himself. They weren't friends. Just guys who shared rent. Sarah's roommate was even weirder than his, though Sarah seemed to like her well enough. Paula, the theater major who never went anywhere without a face full of make-up and clothes so loud they hurt his ears. He saw her flouncing around campus sometimes. Always made a big freaking deal out of waving to him. A real show pony.

He attached a fly—one he had made himself—to Sarah's rod and, standing behind her, guided her first cast. She didn't catch anything then, but on her second try, a flash of gold wiggled on the end of the line.

He couldn't believe her luck. "This spot's full of rainbows and browns, but goldens are rare. Take up the slack a little, keep it taut, not too taut, that's it. You got him."

She grinned as the fish shimmered like living sunshine on her rod. "Now what?"

"We take him off the line, ice him and go back for more." But when he held the line in close, she shrank away as if she was afraid, so he removed the trout for her and threw it into the ice chest.

"Don't hurt it," she said.

City girls—they could be weird. He explained that ice stunned the fish. Since the beans had burned to charcoal last night, all they'd eaten were brownies and some kind of dried fruit, nut, and cereal stuff she'd brought along. He was starving. They caught four rainbow, one brookie, and one golden, but the biggest fish of the day was three feet long. He helped her reel the torpedo-shape in. When it rested at last on the shore, they knelt beside the bony-plated body.

"What is this thing—the river's version of a knight in shining armor?" she asked.

Roy Glen pulled out his pocket knife. "Lake Sturgeon. We have to let it go."

"Why? It's huge, way bigger than you said they needed to be."

"Those rules were for trout. This sturgeon might be big, but it's still young. It'll grow almost twice as long. Might live to be 80."

"Jeesh. Like a person." She canted her neck and stared at the fish, eye to eye.

Roy Glen cut the line and lay the fish back in the water. For a split second, it lay still.

"It's dead." There was a squeal in her voice as if she were going to cry.

"Nah, it has to get over the shock of what's happened and realize it can swim again."

Sure enough, with a twist of its body, the sturgeon dove beneath the green waters of the Williams River.

"Thank goodness it's going to get a second chance," she said.

"For God's sake, Sarah, it's a fish."

"It looked wise. Like it might have messages about the origins of the universe."

He put his fingers on his temples and closed his eyes. "I'm getting a message from the sturgeon now. It says—it says—time to eat. I'm starved."

She smacked his fingers. "Okay, make fun, but I'm telling you that fish had amazing eyes."

Sarah built the fire and fried potatoes while Roy Glen cleaned the fish. He was careful to keep his back to her since she was clearly dismayed about having to kill them, though it was a shame. He wished she could observe his skill at filleting. He cut the heads off, too. Didn't want her freaking out again over amazing eyes.

He coated the fillets in cornmeal and fried them crisp in a cast iron skillet. "Hope you'll like them."

"I like fish sticks."

"You poor deprived girl. You are about to experience real food." He shoveled a hearty portion onto her paper plate.

Her eyes closed and she moaned over her first taste of trout. Soon, the last bite of white flakes savored, she licked even the grease and salt off her fingers. "Best meal I've ever had, best by far."

The girl did have some sense after all, even if she was squeamish. He was sure she'd get over it.

As they fished, Sarah fretted about his initial reaction to her not being a virgin. It hadn't occurred to her to lie to him. For all she knew, a guy could tell. And anyway, you couldn't expect to build a solid relationship on a lie. He seemed fine later when they made love again, and this morning as they fished. But when he sat up and said "shit," she felt so demeaned, so unwanted. Like shit. She wanted to get up, pull on her clothes, and run as far away as she could. But they made love again, and she thought he was okay with it now. She tried to put it out of her mind.

As they left the national forest late that afternoon, he asked her what she wanted to do when she graduated. It wasn't far away. She took heavy loads and CLEPPED a couple of courses, so even though it was technically only her second year of college, she would have amassed over three years of credits at the end of the next semester, spring term.

"Travel all over the world covering government and politics for the *Washington Post* or *Time* magazine," she said.

"So you don't want to get married and have kids?" Roy Glen asked.

"Of course I do." His question echoed her parents' concerns. In addition to journalism and political science, her father had forced her to major in education because teachers could always find jobs while writers were often poor and unemployed. As if she were ever going to teach. Her mother opposed journalism, too, wondering aloud how Sarah could manage a husband and children if she had to travel with her job. Sarah tried to block out everyone's worries, but the words gnawed at her. The world seemed to be telling her to choose—and as a girl, she didn't have many choices.

Her parents had been even less impressed with her first dream. She never forgot her uncle's studio, the art he created from dust. Vases so translucent she thought they would shatter if she touched them, yet they were much stronger than they looked.

"The only other thing I've ever wanted to do was make glass like my Uncle Mahlon."

"So make glass. You could do it in a home workshop and still have kids. My mother makes ceramics. She even sells her pieces at their store."

"I don't think there's a career in it. Even Uncle Mahlon only got to blow glass as a hobby in the end." Besides, her parents would have a fit because of the lung diseases you could get from glass work.

She didn't know many adults who got to follow every dream. But even if she chose to have a family first, maybe she could pursue her other goals. If she were lucky. If she didn't have ten children, because anyone who did, surely had no time for anything else.

Finally, they drove close enough to civilization to pull in a decent radio station. Immediately she sensed the announcer was soldiering on through tears, his voice splintering in odd places. The entire Marshall University football team, boosters, parents, and coaches, had fallen out of the sky the night before. Seventy-five people gone, incinerated, while Sarah and Roy Glen made love. The Marshall campus meandered along the Ohio River about 150 miles away. All those dreams vanished. How could you wrap your mind around the enormity of loss? She tried to imagine what their girlfriends, their parents, their best friends were feeling. She failed. They were too far away.

If she had never seen the campus, was it even real? Must be. Kids she'd gone all through school with, Randy Taylor and Debby Munsford, were students there.

No matter how she reached for it, she couldn't grasp the suffering, all those people who loved and would go on loving those boys long after their memorial services. (Would there be anything left of their bodies to bury?) She couldn't touch their grief. She felt the same way knowing how many thousands of boys had died in Vietnam. Numb. All those dreams turned to ash.

Twelve

DECEMBER *1970*

Sarah's mother dug through the cedar chest and located her Christmas sweater. "It won't hurt you to go somewhere without Roy Glen one night. Rachel's your oldest friend. Look how she came to Katherine's funeral."

The Sullivans hosted the open house, a dress-up affair, every year. Roy Glen refused to come. Parties didn't appeal to him. Sarah didn't want to go either, but she pulled on a rose wool mini skirt and jacket paired with a white blouse. She pinned Livvie's cameo to the jabot and made bets with herself. How long it would be until someone asked her who she was dating (two minutes—sooner than she'd expected) and how long until someone told her she looked too thin (five minutes—longer than expected) and how long it would take her father to find his way to the Sullivans' liquor cabinet (thirty seconds—she hit it right on the nose). She sent up a quick prayer that her father, warmed up with a highball before he left home, wouldn't get snockered and embarrass her. Two more drinks and his speech would slur softly. By the fourth, his eyes would glaze over. At five, he became unpredictable, sometimes contentious, sometimes maudlin, most often sleepy.

A professional decorator had recently redesigned the Sullivan home with antiques. Dark exotic woods with a few Asian accents. The Sullivans eschewed the current trend toward autumn colors in favor of red, black, and white. Rachel flipped a long tress of black hair over the shoulder of her cranberry dress with one hand and grabbed Sarah's wrist with the other. "You have to try the shrimp dip—it's marvelous. My mom got the recipe from a famous seafood house in Florida last winter."

Rachel always returned from Florida with a winter tan Sarah envied almost as much as the chance to see the beach. Rachel pulled her into the dining room where a sumptuous buffet was set up. In the corner stood their Christmas tree.

"Remember how much fun we used to have decorating the tree together when we were kids?" Rachel asked.

Sarah remembered it somewhat differently. The year the girls turned eleven, Mr. Sullivan clomped up and down a field for two hours before settling on the towering Fraser fir. "It's perfect, Dad," Rachel said as he tightened the bolts to hold it upright in the stand.

"It will be when I get done with it." He began measuring the branches and drilling holes in the trunk. He dragged a second tree, as big as the first, onto their porch. Measuring again, he sawed limbs off the spare tree and positioned new branches into the holes. He demonstrated how the girls were to hold the branches still while he wired them into place. "Lift it a little higher; no, a little more to the left, Sarah. Rachel, up a little more on your side." After two hours, Sarah's scratched arms ached, and the tree, more perfect than any found in nature, did not yet have an ornament on it.

Under this year's tree were stacks of presents, all carefully wrapped with creased edges and mitered corners. Most, she knew, were filled with matched outfits from expensive out-of-town boutiques. How jealous she had been of those perfectly coordinated sets! Made her grateful a pair of bell-bottoms and a tee-shirt would take a girl almost anywhere now.

An arm slid across Sarah's collarbone and hugged her from behind. "Sarah, sweetie, I see you're as sexy as ever." Rachel's father whooped with laughter.

Ah, yes, how long until Mike Sullivan poked gentle fun at the beanpole (eight minutes). In the background behind all the chatter and "White Christmas" playing on the stereo, Sarah could hear the phone ringing. "Paper still keeping you busy?" she asked. Hyper, frenzied, manic—these words would better describe Mike Sullivan's life as editor of the local paper.

"Yeah, worse than ever. Equipment's old, always breaking down. We're thinking about changing over to cold type. What do your professors have to say about it?"

"They say everyone will move away from hot type within five years." She explained why, but noticed his eyes roaming the room, lips parted to reveal clamped teeth. They ground together and released and ground again. Helen Sullivan called him to the phone.

Even though he was two rooms away, Sarah overheard his conversation. "Damn it, no, you can't put that on the front page. It's the holiday season. No one wants to read about body counts now. Page three, you hear me? And make it a brief, 18 point head." When he rejoined the party, he shook a couple of pastel antacids into his hand, a gesture she well remembered. Once she thought they were after-dinner mints so special and expensive only Mr. Sullivan was allowed to eat them. The phone rang again and Mike Sullivan cussed under his breath and strode off to answer it.

A little later Rachel's mother snapped a photo of Sarah and Rachel in front of the tree with her new Polaroid. In it, Rachel looked beautiful, a dark little pixie who only came up to Sarah's chin. The top of Sarah's head was lopped off.

Sarah's mother frowned over the picture. "Look how hunched over your shoulders are, Sarah. What's gotten into you? You didn't use to slump."

Did her mother not even notice she was so tall her face in the photo ended right above her eyes? She was a freaky giantess.

Sarah and Rachel took turns with the camera, presenting guests with instant photos. In the snapshot of Sarah's parents, Johanna held a plate loaded with appetizers and cookies, her elastic waist skirt stretched taut, emerald sweater gaping slightly in front around faux-pearl buttons, a dollop of shrimp dip smudged on the red nose of the reindeer whose job was to lead a sleigh across that ponderous chest. Johanna passed the photo to Nelson, his scotch and soda lowered momentarily as he gave the photo a cursory glance. "What am I supposed to do with this?" He bent down to set the photo on the coffee table. His drink sloshed out, splashing the photo, the table, the carpet. "Damn it, look what you made me do."

A flash of anger set Sarah's teeth on edge. Her mother hadn't done anything. It was his drinking. Always the drinking.

Johanna blotted the alcohol up with a tissue, apologizing. As she righted herself, the backward thrust of her shoulder blades popped the center button on her sweater, exposing her bra.

Sarah turned away, wishing she could evaporate into the wall.

She took herself off to the buffet, where Cal's aunt cornered her with concerns about his latest letters—how clipped they sounded, how rehearsed and false. "Have his letters to you sounded like this?"

"Excuse me, Mrs. Caruso," Rachel said. "I hate to barge in, but I need to borrow Sarah."

Rachel's room hadn't changed: a blush pink bedspread and drapes, ivory carpet and walls with a narrow wallpaper border of blush pink roses at the ceiling.

"How did you know I was dying to get out of there?" Sarah said.

"I know how it is. They won't leave you alone. When I broke up with Alex, it was 'Alex this,' and 'Alex that.' I wanted to scream. Speaking of break-ups, did you hear Toby Ellison and Kay Tollison split?"

Toby and Kay had gone to high school with them, and Kay pledged the same sorority as Rachel at the university so she and Kay were still good friends. "No! I thought they were getting married at the end of spring semester!"

"You can't tell a living soul, but Toby broke up with her because he found out she'd slept with this French exchange student last year. What on earth was Kay thinking? No guy wants damaged goods."

"No, of course not." Thank heaven Sarah had resisted sharing relationship woes with Rachel, had kept the damage hidden.

Rachel pulled her by the hand toward her bed. A box lay on the spread. "Anyway, I do have something I want to show you. I was cleaning out the closet yesterday and found this stuff. Recognize anything?"

Sarah sifted through the contents. From a plastic sleeve that once protected Mrs. Sullivan's plastic rain hat, Sarah fished out a carefully folded piece of paper. A code cracker for the secret messages she and Rachel used to write when they played spy. Underneath was a dictionary of hip terminology, like "daddy-o" and "pad," a remnant from the Cool Cats Club. A favorite Cherry Ames and a Nancy Drew, too treasured to pass along to younger cousins. And under those books were chunks of glittering glass—garnet, cobalt, emerald.

Sarah picked one up and smiled. "I think I still have some of these myself. We were so excited when we found them."

On their bikes, they had zigzagged the blacktop, faces reddening as they sucked air into burning lungs. Sarah remembered heaving her entire weight—all fifty-three pounds—against the pedals, yet halfway up Winding Way she was forced to dismount and push. A glint in the distance had caught her eye. The cache of jewels.

"Didn't we have the perfect childhood, Sarah? Don't you wish you could go back and do it all again?'

Sarah would as soon suffer hemorrhoids, but she smiled as if she agreed. She figured out her family wasn't quite like *Ozzie and Harriet*—or like the Sullivans—the year she turned eight, about the time they'd found those pieces of garnet and cobalt and emerald. When they searched for a box to store them, they uncovered a bottle of Crown Royal hidden in the basement. Rachel asked what it was. Pop, Sarah said. Same lie her parents told her. She didn't know what whiskey was. Only that something was wrong because it had to be hidden.

Like sleeping with Cal. Like sleeping with Roy Glen.

Sarah and Rachel had stored their uncut gems in an old Lincoln Logs box, until Rita Watson, who worked at Hazel Atlas, informed them they were only cullet—useless glass chips from the factory dump.

What, Sarah wondered, was Roy Glen doing while she relived her childhood? Probably fine-tuning his truck or rebuilding the engine of the '57 Chevy she'd never seen. Probably making plans to jettison his damaged goods. She wouldn't let herself wonder what Cal was doing. Four more months to go, his aunt said. Anything could happen in four months.

Thirteen

DECEMBER *1970*

A red-tailed hawk cruised the thermals overhead. Melted snows of the week before left the ground soggy. Sarah tugged Roy Glen to the other side of the hill to see remnants of a Civil War trench. It felt spooky walking along those ditches. As if she were disturbing the ghosts of soldiers who crouched there over a hundred years ago. Up here they felt like flesh and blood boys with names and mothers and sweethearts, boys whose bodies lay on the damp ground under her feet. She was pleased when Roy Glen spotted shot buried in the side of one trench. He rubbed it on his shirt tail and pocketed it.

She thought of another surprise for him, something she learned from Aunt Maggie. With a sharp rock, she poked at the exposed shale on a hillside until she uncovered a fossil of what looked like a giant centipede. Another souvenir of their outing.

Then he showed her things she hadn't noticed. A groundhog's burrow. Where the grass was crushed because deer bedded down there overnight. A hollow in an oak that raccoons called home.

They ate trail mix and shared a cola while standing on the ridge inspecting the town. All the little bunched-up houses puffing smoke into the air. Church spires. And in the distance, the boxy shapes of the Hazel Atlas Glass complex.

She noticed the attention Roy Glen paid to empty bottles and plastic wrappers. Every scrap went with them as they headed back. A sign of his character. A good ending to a perfect afternoon. It seemed like the right time to talk to him, even though the consequences of sex weren't something she wanted to talk about. If she mentioned birth control, she was assuming he wanted to be with her again, something she rarely could convince herself of. Yet this day was one of the rare ones when she felt sure he loved her. Almost sure. She rushed ahead before she could change her mind.

"Don't you think, maybe, we need to do something, you know, so we don't have a baby?"

His eyebrows scrunched together. "Why would you bring that up again? I told you before, it wouldn't be the same."

From his tone, she could tell he wanted to drop it, but she plunged ahead. "I don't think I could get an abortion, and I know I couldn't give a baby away for adoption."

"If anything happens, we'll get married. A little sooner than planned maybe, but so what? I hate school anyway. Don't worry about it." He set off down the hill, letting gravity pull him faster, faster, his boots thudding against the earth.

Sarah bounded after him. She supposed as long as they were getting married anyway, everything would turn out all right. Don't worry, he said. As if it were that easy. As they emerged from the woods, they were less than ten yards from Livvie's house. "I can't pass this close without stopping in," she said. "For a minute."

Roy Glen walked on, his back toward her. "You can if you want to. I'm going home."

At the foot of Livvie's steps, Sarah grabbed the railing. "Come on. We won't stay."

He turned halfway around. "No, I'm not kidding. I'm leaving."

"Fine." She could be stubborn too. If he wouldn't come, she would go by herself. He wasn't really going to leave her there, was he? She watched, half sick, as he drove off. Every time she thought she was beginning to wrap her mind around who he really was, he proved her wrong. He was edgeless, like the wind.

Livvie opened the door before Sarah could knock. "Was that your young man?"

Sarah admitted it was. "We argued."

Livvie took her into the kitchen where she was mending a loose hem, her chair pulled back slightly from the table, the lid of the tufted sewing basket ajar, revealing rainbows of spooled thread.

Molasses and spice permeated the air. "What smells yummy?" Sarah asked.

"Gingerbread. Should be cool enough to cut." Livvie ladled dollops of whipped cream on top and set the dishes on the breakfast table.

Livvie forked up a bite. "Too bad you had a fight."

"How does anyone know if it's really love?"

"I'm not the best person to ask. Try your mother."

That was a joke. Her folks were as romantic as wet socks. "I don't know how she stands it." Sarah mimicked her father's voice: "'Hey, Johanna, bring me another beer.'"

Livvie straightened her shoulders and set her fork down. "Your parents have a great love story. You knew Nelson gave up his family for Johanna, didn't you?"

Sarah shook her head. Her family hadn't been close to her father's parents, but she assumed it was nothing more than physical distance. They lived in Frederick, Maryland. No huge distance, now that she thought about it, though as a child, it seemed a journey of endless hours over fog-covered mountain roads.

"The Stevenses didn't want Nelson to marry your mother. They were university-educated folk and we Heimbachs were factory stiffs. And remember it was right after World War II. Mrs. Stevens hated all things German. Your father lost a brother in the Second War and your grandmother Stevens never got over it. Well, you wouldn't, would you, get over the loss of a child?"

"Of course not, but Heimbachs died for America in the First War, right?"

"Peter and then Thomas, though it took years for him to die in a VA hospital. Shell shock. Never the same after he came home. Never recognized anyone, not even his wife. William fought too. He was the only one who came home intact. The Heimbachs sacrificed as much for this country as anyone else. But all Mrs. Stevens could see was your mother's German name. And the Stevenses were teetotalers—a result of some relative who died from alcohol abuse. All the Heimbach men were well-known for their beer drinking. The only member of your father's family who came to their wedding was his grandfather, so your parents named Garrett after him."

Sarah digested this, then said, "But we did visit Grandma and Grandpa Stevens in Frederick."

"After you kids came along, the Stevenses softened and accepted the marriage, but your mother never could quite forgive them."

Maryland trips were up one day and back the next—and they always stayed in a motel. Which suited her fine because her grandparents' house smelled of arthritis rub, and sheets draped all the furniture. The depth of her father's love was a revelation. The only time she'd ever seen him with tears in his eyes was at Grandmother Stevens's funeral. Yet he chose her mother over his parents. Hard to connect that kind of love with where they ended up.

Sarah speculated aloud about whether she and Roy Glen belonged together.

"My mother knew," Livvie said. "From the beginning she knew Papa was the one."

Fourteen

FALL 1879

Adelisa Gustel Swartzbauer was not quite sixteen when she met the man she would marry. One morning she stepped briskly down Liberty Street, her warm breath steaming into the cold air. She gathered her shawl tightly around her shoulders and tilted her chin skyward toward the spire of St. Philomena's German Catholic Church. It was so tall it reached into the clouds. The most beautiful buildings man created were always dedicated to God. She believed that was true even amidst the filth and bustle of Pittsburgh in 1878. Such a disgusting city. So many people. So many smells. A mixture of sewage, smoke, chemicals, and animal dung assaulted Adelisa as she made her way down the street. She could hear the distant rumble of a train approaching from Johnstown, the clumping of hooves against dirt as horse-drawn carriages transported the city's more fortunate citizens to church, the whistle of a boat plowing through the gray fog that hung over the Monongahela to her right.

She tugged at the heavy oak door of St. Philomena's. The cold metal handle stung her already frozen hands. Inside the foyer, she skimmed her fingers over the small basin of holy water, then blew on them before they turned into icicles. She strode down the center aisle of the nave, her black leather boots scuffling against the stone floor. Sounds echoed against the high ceiling, soft sounds that mingled with the sighs of her gown and underskirts and the murmurs of worshippers assembling for ten o'clock mass. Adelisa sat in her favorite pew, the one she sat in every Sunday, across the aisle from a skinny boy who looked about her age. He, too, attended mass alone. Every week she smiled at him. Every week he blushed and looked away. That only made her smile more. It was the Devil in her, she knew. Her mother always teased her, "Dimple in the chin, Devil within," and there was no denying that dimple.

She positioned her black lace scarf more securely on her head and knelt on the bench below to pray, crinolines biting into her knees. Every week she prayed for her widowed mother, four sisters and three brothers, the family left behind in Berchtesgaden with little enough to eat or clothes to wear.

When Adelisa had first proposed coming to America, her mother shook her head. "Fourteen and all alone. *Schnapsidee.*" Crazy idea.

Adelisa was fearless. "I want to see what all the fuss is about, this America place. Everyone says you can make your own fortune there. They say everyone becomes rich."

Her mother continued basting the facing onto a collar. She cut apart discarded draperies from the house where she did laundry. With great care, she was fashioning the pieces into dresses for her daughters. "There are more important things than being rich. Think how hard they will work you. They might not call you an indentured servant anymore, but that's what you will be. What if they mistreat you?"

Such arguments had no effect on Adelisa. She wasn't afraid of work. What could you call her life now but hard work? She got up before dawn to make bread with her mother, took care of her brothers and sisters during the day while she sewed collars and sleeves for a local shop, getting paid by the piece. If the Godwins treated her badly, she would run away. Simple as that. Mr. and Mrs. Salathiel Godwin of Pittsburgh, Pennsylvania, advertised for a German girl to do light housekeeping and help take care of their three children. They would pay her passage in return for three years of service.

And now, 461 days later, she knew the Godwin children were not so bad. No worse than her own brothers and sisters to look after. The housekeeping was easier than at home; the house, less crowded. They lived in a two-story rambling white house with gingerbread trim along the eaves and over the front porch. In the rear stood a private two-seat privy for the family; another single-seater for the servants.

Learning English was the hard part of her new job. At first Mrs. Godwin was exasperated when Adelisa couldn't understand her, but gradually Adelisa learned the rhythms of the household, the slow, slow dance of daily life. When to wake the children, when to feed them, when to put them to bed. How they should dress, how they should behave. What to clean while the children napped. How much bourbon to pour into a short glass tumbler for Mr. Godwin when he came home from work. How long it took him to drink it, after which he would spend exactly five minutes with the children before he ate supper with his wife in the dining room.

Twice during morning mass, Adelisa caught the eye of the skinny boy, the last time as he returned from taking the sacraments, his lips twitching upward almost imperceptibly as he looked away. His nose was a bit severe, his face thin but handsome. In over a year, he had never acknowledged her.

Time, she decided, to take matters into her own hands.

Anton Heimbach saw his mother's face mirrored in Adelisa's high cheekbones, and the blue of his youngest sister Gitte's eyes laughed back at him from Adelisa's face. But though she was pretty, for him, it was love at first sound. The ecstasy of hearing his mother tongue spoken by this young girl with caramel-colored hair. He had been afraid to speak to her, but after she introduced herself, he could hardly stop asking her questions. Anything to keep her talking. Since arriving in Pennsylvania two years earlier, he had rarely found the opportunity to speak German with a girl his own age.

He walked Adelisa home from church, though the Godwins' neighborhood was in the opposite direction from where he stayed. Fallen leaves, orange and amber, crackled as they passed under a cluster of maples. If he narrowed his vision to shut out the smoke-belching factories across the road to his left, the earthy smell of the leaves could make him believe he was back in Oldenburg. The illusion burst when a tugboat moaned in the distance.

He inquired about the people she worked for. "Are they kind?"

She took off her shawl and tilted her face toward the sun. "Not so bad. Mr. Godwin is an importer. Not home much. Goes to his club. Mrs. Godwin demands much because she is important in society. Every day the ladies call on her about charity. I have to make the children behave properly when introduced and then keep them out of the way afterwards."

With her little black boots, she kicked the leaves that littered the road. Skipped a little, child-like. "And you? What is your work?"

He told her about Bakewell Glass. "One of the best glass houses in America. I make vases and bowls and glassware for the table." That was the glamorous part. He didn't mention sweeping floors and hauling off broken bits of glass that inevitably accumulated. He didn't tell her the factory was hot as hell in summer and freezing in winter because all the heat rose out of the stacks.

"There are hundreds of glass factories near Pittsburgh because everything you need is right here," he said. "Rivers, railroads, natural gas, and pure sand. So I will always be able to find a job." He glanced to see if she was properly impressed, and when she smiled encouragement, he continued. "My father arranged for me to finish my apprenticeship with a friend from Germany, Karl Reinhardt. We made windows at O'Hara Glass when I first came, but switched over to Bakewell this year. This is good. Tableware is more fun to make."

"You've been here for how long?"

"Since I was fourteen. Two years. I live with Karl and his wife Magdalen. Karl knows almost as much about glass as my father. He is a fine craftsman. A perfectionist." He realized the term might sound critical and hurried to explain. "You have to be, to be any good. And Magdalen likes to give advice as much as my mother does, whether anyone asks for it or not, so you have to get used to her."

"I think all mothers must be the same," Adelisa said. "Always telling you what is proper, what is not. Usually whatever it is you are doing—is not." They laughed. Then her smile faded. "I miss Mama. I wonder all the time what she is doing. If she still makes strudel for my sisters' birthdays. Oh, what I would give for a bite! And I worry my sisters are growing up so much their faces are like strangers."

Anton knew what she meant. Already, he had a nephew he hadn't met. Probably would never meet. "Maybe you would like to come after mass next Sunday? Karl and Magdalen meet with friends in the beer garden and dance and eat and sing the afternoon away. I know she would bring some of her apple kuchen if I told her a nice German girl was missing home."

After she agreed, he didn't even notice how many miles he walked to get back to the Monogahela Incline, which he rode up Mt. Washington, for once not even noticing the view of the city. He almost floated home to Coal Hill.

When Anton inquired if Magdalen might make her trademark kuchen the next Sunday, she tossed her head and planted her hands on broad hips. "She tells you she misses strudel and you offer kuchen. What were you thinking, Anton? I can't make strudel? Of course, I make strudel." She waved her spatula in the air as she talked, then used it to scoot sausages around to brown in the cast iron skillet. "As good as her mother's, I think. We will take strudel and kuchen. Then she can decide for herself." Magdalen looked at him slyly. "She is pretty, this girl?"

Anton's tongue wouldn't work. He jammed his hands in his pockets and shifted his weight from one foot to another. Maybe this was not such a good idea.

"Of course she is pretty." Magdalen ran her fingers through his hair. "Get yourself a haircut this week. Pretty yourself up for her."

Anton excused himself and went to his room.

A small band—flugelhorn, trumpet, clarinet, baritone, and accordion—flung the strains of a bouncy polka into the beer garden adjoining the brewery. About twenty people sat on split-log benches under an arbor of defoliated grapevines clapping and stomping to the music. Others clustered around wooden tables and chairs, everyone over the age of twelve holding a mug of warm beer while a group of dancers tossed their feet in the air and executed the intricate turns and toe-heel steps of the polka. Adelisa marveled that this miracle, this homecoming, had been going on so close to St. Philomena's without her knowing. She clapped as the band finished their song, and took another bite of cake laden with apples, raisins, and nuts. Closed her eyes. Cinnamon and nutmeg, for sure, and she thought she detected a pinch of cloves. "The kuchen, Mrs. Reinhardt. The best ever. And the strudel is wonderful, just like Mama's. So light, so flaky. This is what they serve in heaven."

Magdalen beamed at Anton. "She is pretty, your friend." Anton looked away, pretending to study the dancers. Magdalen touched Adelisa's hair. "I like a young girl with the coiled braids. It is how a girl should wear her hair. I myself wore it that way once."

The band began a schuhplattler in three-quarter time. Adelisa stood, beckoning. "Come on, Anton. It looks like such fun."

His face reddened and he shook his head, his dancing experience limited to his sisters, so long ago he wasn't sure he remembered how.

"Go on," Magdalen encouraged. He shook his head more vigorously.

Karl stood up from the table and offered Adelisa his hand. "Young missy, it would be my pleasure."

Anton watched Adelisa rhythmically strike her thighs, her knees, and soles of her feet. He watched her stomp. He watched her skirt flute outward like a fine piece of glass. Laughter floated over the strains of the music. Only Anton was not laughing.

"You must practice dancing before next Sunday," Magdalen said. "Karl will help you. He is a good dancer, see?" She gestured with pride toward the little mustached man. To Anton, Karl looked a lot like his father, though not nearly as tall. Or maybe Karl and his father were the same height and it was Anton who had grown taller in relation. He couldn't be sure. Not even of what his father looked like. Or his mother and sisters. His memory of their faces was growing fuzzy though his longing for them was as strong as ever.

When the song ended, Karl took Adelisa around to several tables of his friends and introduced her. Anton followed with his eyes. She talked and smiled easily.

He sipped his beer. "What if she won't come back with me because I wouldn't dance?"

"Of course she will. She is having a good time, isn't she?" Magdalen grasped his chin and wiggled it. "Smile a little, old long face. You are more handsome when you smile."

Breathless, Adelisa sat down beside Anton. "I met some people who live near Berchtesgaden. Can you imagine? Small world. We must come back next week."

Magdalen winked at Anton. He ignored her and smiled at Adelisa, who chattered on and on about the couple who knew her cousins back home. Karl and Magdalen went off to dance.

Adelisa took a draft of beer, wiping the foam from her upper lip. "Magdalen has promised to bring me her recipe for kuchen. And Karl said he would teach me to do the landler. Get him to teach you too, and we can do it together."

The part about being together sounded good to Anton. He wasn't sure about the dancing.

Adelisa held the crystal goblet up to the window light while she polished it. She wondered if Anton made similar glassware. No wonder he loved his work if this was the result. She twirled the stem in her fingers.

A firm hand grasped hers and stilled the motion. Adelisa gasped and would have dropped the glass if the hand had not anchored hers so decisively. She turned her head to find Mr. Godwin's face very close to hers. He was standing so near she caught the scent of expensive pipe tobacco clinging to his suit. Even though it was a handsome face with a strong, square jaw line, she grew uncomfortable. Blinking, she took a step backwards.

He chuckled. "I won't bite, little girl." His voice was a rich baritone.

Adelisa could think of nothing to say. She set the goblet back on the mahogany buffet.

From a matching cabinet, he took a crystal decanter of wine and removed the top. He poured two glasses of rich burgundy liquid and handed one to her. He held his glass by the stem and swirled the liquid around, then clinked his glass against hers. "To your beautiful hands. They were made to hold crystal goblets, don't you think?" He sipped his wine.

She looked down at her hands, which were smooth despite all the hard work she did. She was flattered he noticed. She took pride in her skin. Rubbed her hands with butter before she went to bed—a tip from the Godwins' fat cook who supplied the butter. "They're rich," she said. "The likes of them'll never miss a little pinch of butter."

"Drink up, my dear, or I will be insulted and think you don't appreciate my taste."

She placed her lips on the goblet and took the smallest sip.

Mr. Godwin arched his eyebrows slightly, as if to say he didn't take anything he said too seriously, and neither should she. "It has exquisitely bold undertones of currants and black pepper, doesn't it? Imported from France." He was a handsome man with a muscled body that looked fine in his hand-tailored woolen suit. Everything about him spoke of power.

Adelisa could only compare wine to beer. It seemed quite acidic, but she felt it would be rude to say so. "It is lovely, sir."

He touched the braid wound over her left ear. "Do you ever let those down?"

She blinked again uncertainly. Giggled a little.

Silk rustled behind her. "Sal, could I speak to you for a moment?" Adelisa turned and perceived Mrs. Godwin's frown. "In the drawing room. Now, please."

He set his glass down. "Every good dog answers to the call of its master," he whispered to Adelisa conspiratorially. In a normal voice, he added, "Of course, Louisa."

Adelisa took her glass to the kitchen. The wine trickled like blood into the sink basin. When the goblet was spotless, she carried it back to the dining room and placed it on the mirrored tray where Mrs. Godwin displayed them. Shining. Pure. Full of light.

Late in the summer Adelisa met Anton after church with a glum face. Sweat plastered an escaped strand of hair against her neck, and wide damp circles spread under her arms. The Godwins, she said, were satisfied with her care of their children and house and pleased by her pious attendance at church. But Mrs. Godwin was dismayed when one of her hoity-toity society friends saw Adelisa leaving the beer garden last Sunday afternoon. Adelisa didn't know how she would endure the 119 days left of her servitude without her afternoons with Anton. He and the Reinhardts were now the closest thing to family.

"Mrs. Godwin—she was wearing one of those steel hoops underneath her skirt that made her dress sway as she walked—" stiff-legged, Adelisa demonstrated cartoonishly, "—she took me into the drawing room for a private chat. 'Only a woman of questionable morals would drink beer in such an establishment,' says she. 'And it is said they dance there and play loud music on the Sabbath.'" Adelisa pinched her nostrils to get the proper nasality and mimicked Mrs. Godwin: "'It's scandalous. Simply isn't done.'" She released her nose and scowled. "From now on, I have to come straight back after mass. No more friends. No more good times. No more Sunday afternoons off." She didn't tell Anton quite everything. According to Mrs. Godwin, her husband was disappointed in Adelisa's behavior. Remembering his admiration for her hands and hair, she was sorry to lose his good will.

Sweat trickled between her eyes. The heat gave her an excuse to wipe her face with a handkerchief and catch the tear escaping down her cheek. The hankie, a gift from Anton, was his mother's, a cotton square embroidered with yellow daisies. She knew it was a personal treasure, a reminder of home. On her birthday, he had given her another gift. A glass vase crafted in the palest pink, shaped like a lily with reflexed petals. The flower funneled into a narrow well that would hold water. She often filled it with flowers she and the children picked.

Anton walked slowly with her to the Godwins', dodging horse manure and skirting puddles. Not all the way to the door, in case her mistress would object. They lingered under the shade of a hickory. Another tear seeped out against her will. Anton withdrew her tear onto his own fingers, the first time he had touched her except when they were dancing. She ached from the sweetness. Such bitter sweetness.

Fifteen

JANUARY 1971

"No way," Sarah said. Roy Glen couldn't pick up the phone and pretend everything was all right. She could find another ride home from college now that her classes were over at noon.

"Come on, I'm sorry I left you there." His voice was smooth, placating. "I wouldn't have felt right showing up unannounced."

"Bull. You hurt Livvie's feelings." Sarah lowered her voice as DeeDee, her R.A., swished by in pink bunny slippers, and once again Sarah regretted the awkwardness of talking on such a public telephone.

"I looked like a field hand—dirty boots and all—I would have made a bad first impression."

"She saw you walk off and leave me—think that made a good first impression?"

"Come on, I said I was sorry. Two Left Feet is playing at the Sub, and I know how much you like them."

His voice pulled at her. She didn't know how she would stand it if she never heard it again. She was remembering the gold flecks in his eyes, how he smelled like soap. She gave in.

She was sorry when he was fifteen minutes late picking her up, blaming it on his carburetor. At the Yellow Submarine they ran into her neighbor Jimmy Watson with her roommate Paula.

Paula was intent on being herself. While the army of girls in the bar wore jeans and tee-shirts like uniforms, Paula made a statement in a long broomstick skirt and fisherman sandals with socks. Lots of gold bangle bracelets. Paula and Jimmy had done the next-to-impossible and kept their high school relationship going.

Jimmy pulled out a chair. "Sit with us." Sarah accepted, although as soon as she did, Roy Glen's face grew steely. She realized she had never met any of his friends—why? She introduced him to Jimmy.

Paula, he knew from campus.

"Still got all A's?" Jimmy asked. Sarah admitted she did, mostly. He turned to Roy Glen. "She was one of the smartest girls in our class. Always setting the curve."

Roy Glen offered an almost-smile as acknowledgement.

Sarah knew from Rita that Jimmy was considering dropping out. "How 'bout you Jimmy? Things going any better?"

"Much. I'm putting more effort into it. Whatever it takes to stay out of a factory job." He related the horrors of his summer stint at Hazel Atlas Glass. "I'm not kidding. It was 120 degrees in there and you couldn't even stop working to get a drink of water."

Paula laughed. "Look on the bright side. You lost twenty pounds."

"I'd rather be fat. Ever since, I've been hitting the books—"

"At least once a week," Paula said.

"Come on, now, I've improved. All B's and C's last semester."

Sarah envied Jimmy the chance to make glass, and here he was throwing it away. "I always thought it would be kind of neat to make glass."

Jimmy rolled his eyes. "You're talking about the old days. Nothing neat about assembly lines. When I told the boss I was quitting, he says to me, in the kind of somber voice you use at a funeral, 'If you do, son, we can never hire you back.' So I tell him, 'I certainly hope not.' You shoulda seen his face."

It was disappointing to hear one more negative vote about glass as a career.

Paula grew all aflutter about a play she'd seen at the University. She knew the director and hobnobbed with famous actors at the cast party. Not only her outfit, but her gestures sparkled. Her hands swept boldly in the air, her body swayed closer, then further away. A sea of motion.

Sarah tried to hear what Jimmy was saying to Roy Glen, but the jukebox was blasting Led Zeppelin. Whatever it was, Roy Glen responded in monosyllables, lips barely moving.

Paula waved to someone and set her bracelets to jangling. "Look who's coming. It'll be a real high school reunion."

Rachel and Mark—the fraternity president himself—joined them. Instantly Sarah felt on guard. Once any boy was around Rachel, he forgot all about Sarah. Every boy in high school had fallen in love with the dark-haired pixie.

"Oh, I can't keep it to myself anymore, can I tell?" Paula asked Jimmy. "We're engaged." She held out her left hand to show off a thin gold band set with a minuscule diamond.

Paula wouldn't have been able to lift her hand from the table if Jimmy's pocketbook could have matched his adoration. It was written all over him. The way his eyes followed her when she walked away. The way he opened doors, fetched her extra napkins, listened, really listened, to every word she said.

Sarah's roomie had more good news. Over the break, she'd won her first major part in a production, Nora in Ibsen's *A Doll's House*. It was a complicated role with a tremendous range of emotion and character development, a great opportunity.

"You've got to come see me." She rattled off performance dates.

"Sure, we'll—" Sarah began.

Roy Glen cut her off. "We'd like to, but I think we already have plans that weekend. We'll check and get back with you."

Paula and Rachel scuttled off to the ladies' room. Sarah didn't have to go, but a minute later, changed her mind. Her hair. Her terrible hair always needed a comb run through it. When she opened the outside door, both friends were inside stalls.

Rachel was telling Paula that Roy Glen was really cool. "I don't know how to describe it. Something about his eyes. Sexy, don't you think?"

"Yeah, he's sexy, especially his voice," said Paula, "but he isn't very friendly."

"He's different from Cal, that's for sure. I think he's the strong, silent type."

"No, he doesn't like us. I wave to him on campus and he does this flick thing with his chin. I've studied body language in theater classes, and I'm telling you he doesn't like us." Paula flushed the commode. "It's okay. I don't like him either. Something about him gives me the creeps."

Sarah eased the outer door closed and made a fast retreat to the table. Rachel, she thought, was right. While Cal had been as friendly and playful as a puppy, Roy Glen was as unknowable as a cat. And Rachel was right about something else—he was hot. Paula just didn't get him.

Roy Glen got Sarah alone in the car an hour later. "Let's not do that again."

"What?"

He turned the key and the engine burbled to life. "Sit down with other people."

His tires squealed as he pulled out of the parking lot in the famous '57 Chevy, finally on the road with a re-built engine. The car fishtailed on ice, the motor growling its intent to charge forward, weather be damned. The walls of Sarah's throat constricted until they almost touched each other. When the motor and tires finally defeated the ice, she released the edge of the seat and the door.

Her breath returned to normal. "What's wrong with you? They're my friends."

"I don't take you out to be with someone else. I want to be with you. I hardly talked to you all evening."

She couldn't help herself. She was flattered.

"Besides," he said, "I don't really like those girls. Your roommate wants to be the center of attention. She's not going to stay with that guy—Jimmy. I bet you ten bucks she'll give the ring back before they graduate. And Rachel—what a snot. She expects the guys to kiss her feet, and they probably fall all over themselves to do it. She and Mark deserve each other. He probably puts on a tux to relax. I don't know why you want to hang out with them."

Sarah scowled. "I grew up with them, and they're my friends." But another part of her was singing in the dark: *He likes me better than Rachel. He likes me better than Rachel.*

Sixteen

FEBRUARY-APRIL 1971

For the next two months, Sarah saw Roy Glen nearly every day on campus. He walked her to classes, holding her hand. He asked for her help to prepare for English and political science tests. In return, he tutored her for the one math class required for her degree.

On the weekend when it was supposed to be her choice of activities, he asked if it would be all right if they went to a gun show. She agreed. He arrived a half hour late. She didn't want to make a big deal out of it. It was only one time. She wasn't perfect—so how could she expect him to be? The gun show chilled her, all that killing power gathered inside the Armory. She'd been in the Armory before to basketball games and concerts, but its true purpose dawned on her during the gun show. The National Guard—soldiers—met there every month and trained. The war on the other side of the globe suddenly seemed closer. As soon as Roy Glen checked out the rifles, she persuaded him to leave.

The week after, he arrived forty minutes late to take her to a drag race. He barely acknowledged her parents. Refused to make eye contact. The muscles in his jaws twitched. Her parents' eyes accused him even though they didn't say anything. His anger was so palpable that Sarah stifled her complaints. She couldn't explain the dark energy he possessed, but she knew it was there because of the force it exerted on her. A gravitational pull. It stopped her from walking away, though she knew she should.

At the raceway she sat alone in the bleachers while Roy Glen tinkered with his car down on the strip. Three middle-aged women clustered below her in quilted jackets. "Check out that guy," the thick brunette said. The others obediently looked at Roy Glen. The mousy one with an overbite waved her hand over her face. "Definitely hot. I'd let him play with my engine." The brunette responded, "Your engine ain't been handled for so long it's overheating just looking at that fellow." That set off a round of snickering.

Sarah was disgusted by their checking out someone young enough to be their son. Still, the guy they noticed out of all the others belonged to her.

Minutes ticked by slowly, race by race. Men, women, and even the children sitting around her yelled and clapped. She clapped wildly too when she thought Roy Glen won his race, but afterward, he was sullen. He'd miscalculated how fast he should have gone in the trial heats and was disqualified. Though he tried to explain handicaps and trials, none of it made sense to her. Why didn't the fastest car win? Period.

Sarah looked out her bedroom window. Nothing. He was an hour and fifteen minutes late. What if he didn't come at all? The asshole. Jerk. She tasted blood and realized she'd been sucking in her lower lip and dragging it against her upper teeth. She visualized him standing in front of her, weight mostly on his back leg, as he offered some excuse. She reared back and slugged him with all her power. The vision seemed so real her knuckles hurt.

But what if his car had skidded off the road and smashed into a tree? His parents would call her the next day and she would rush to the hospital. She scoffed at herself. If he were in an accident, he wouldn't enlist his parents' help in contacting her. He'd never even taken her to meet them.

At twenty after nine, Sarah's father knocked on her door. "You're not going."

She jumped to her feet. "Yes, I am."

"If he respected you, he'd be on time. He could at least call."

The nerve. If her father had respected his own family, he never would have dragged them through years of alcoholic misery. "Maybe he is somewhere he couldn't call. His car probably broke down."

He stared at her as if he couldn't believe she was that stupid. "Every weekend, Sarah? He can't even put on a decent shirt. Shows up in an undershirt. Real classy."

Leave it to her father to make her feel worse than she already did. As if she hadn't noticed Roy Glen never tried to look nice anymore.

"He's from the country."

"Even country boys have shirts."

"You can't stop me from going." She waited for him to say as long as he was paying her tuition she would do what he said—the whole spiel—but he didn't.

"I'm not going to stop you, but you should stop yourself." He closed her bedroom door.

Silently she cursed Roy Glen. She stood at her bedroom window, willing his Chevy to appear. Foster nudged his cold, damp nose against her leg as if commiserating. She sank to the floor and buried her face in his fur. "You're my pal, aren't you, old boy?" The dog rolled on his back and made pig-like snuffles while she scratched his belly.

By the time Roy Glen arrived at nine-thirty, she was nauseated. She ran past her father without a goodbye and slammed the car door. "You're late."

"Didn't have on a watch."

Why didn't he? Because he didn't care. She would tell him it was over. But then there would be two boys she had slept with. Where would it end? With three? Four? Six? No one was ever going to marry damaged goods.

From the glove compartment, he pulled out a long rectangle wrapped in aluminum foil and dropped it into her lap.

"What?" she asked.

"Open it."

She didn't want to.

"Come on, open it."

She slid her index finger under the edge of the foil. A Road Runner PEZ dispenser.

"Your favorite cartoon, right?"

She couldn't help it. She laughed.

April, the month Cal was due to return to the states, came and went. Sarah wouldn't have given it much more than a passing thought except her mother brought home news he planned to finish college in North Carolina near his parents. Good. Sarah wouldn't run into him. By summer's end, the buzz from the beauty parlor was that Cal's parents were distraught by the changes in him. Shrapnel lodged in his patella left him with a limp and considerable pain. A drinking and drug problem, too—self-medicating, his aunt hypothesized.

"A crying shame," Sarah's mother said while they were making a salad. "He was such a fine young man."

Sarah gritted her teeth and quartered a tomato. Would her mother still be full of praise if she knew the way he'd treated her? Nam messed up Cal's life—her life, too, in a way. She pressed too hard and the knife sliced into her cuticle. "Fuck a damn duck."

Her mother's mouth fell open. "Sarah Beth!"

Sarah shocked herself somewhat, too. It wasn't a word she'd ever said aloud. She brought her finger to her mouth and tasted blood. Her mother eyed her with sidelong glances and didn't say another word. She looked at Sarah as if she didn't know who she was—and she didn't anymore. Not really.

Seventeen

LATE NOVEMBER 1971

Sarah looked out the window as Roy Glen drove through the countryside, taking in the sofas on people's front porches, the quantity of rusted cars set up on blocks in the front yards. It had taken over a year, but she was going to see where he grew up, going to meet the parents. Quite possibly the grandparents of her baby. The past two weeks she'd been hungrier than she'd ever been in her life. She'd eat and minutes later run to the bathroom and hang over the commode. Almost certainly, she was pregnant but didn't want to tell Roy Glen until she knew for sure.

Late November depressed her. All those denuded trees, black limbs jabbing upward against a glaringly white sky. The long expanses of dormant meadows, not a speck of green anywhere. A monotonous painting in shades of taupe and gray.

They drove in silence until a sign caught her eye. "Raccoon Run. What a cool name! Do raccoons run across the road here?"

"A run is a stream, a creek." He pronounced it crick. "Lots of roads out here are named after the creeks they follow."

So many names included the word lick. When he explained they were salt deposits and hunters favored these spots because animals visited them regularly, she knew she was moving into an unknown world. In her universe, lick was what you did to a lollipop or what the teacher did to bad children.

"What're your favorite names for boys?" Roy Glen asked.

"The dozen we're going to have?" The first might be coming sooner than he thought.

"Six. The rest'll be girls."

She hoped he was as eager to be a father when faced with the reality. It was a relief to hear him still talking about having kids. They rattled off boys' names for five minutes, agreeing on none.

Moments later, Roy Glen turned onto a small wooden bridge. The car bumped and clacked across the boards. In the twilight, a modest white ranch-style home stood on one side of the road, its rear defended by a steep hill and several small concrete block outbuildings. A one-story was unusual for West Virginia. Because of the hills, most homes packed as much vertical space as possible onto the foundation. The Hardmans took advantage of a large flat plot in the valley. On the other side of the road stood a barn sided by a pasture and a rusted-out truck. They drove straight ahead into a large concrete block garage.

Roy Glen hopped out and raised the hood. "Something's wrong with this engine. Hear that?"

"Hear what?"

"It's missing." He tinkered inside with a wrench. "I installed Canfield aluminum heads and dual overhead cams." Sarah didn't know what he was talking about, but "hmmmed" as if she did. Roy Glen knew more about engines than she knew about political systems, and that was saying something since she was finishing up her last courses toward her degree. Every little clink and tink meant something to him.

"Gotta keep this old beast ready to out-run the cops," he said.

"What for?"

He looked at her as if she were stupid. "To outrun the cops. In case I get caught speeding."

She'd never even considered that course of action. If she got caught, she would pull over and say, Yes, sir, sorry, sir, it won't happen again, sir. "Isn't that dangerous?"

"Not in this car. She'll stop on a dime. How about getting in on the driver's side and revving it up for me?"

So there they were—finally at his parents—and they hadn't left the garage. She could barely hear him, his words swallowed by the engine's roar.

"Again."

She pushed the accelerator halfway to the floor and then let up. Metal clanked as he searched for the right tool. She could see an inch or two of his body leaning over the engine through the crack where the hood hinged.

"Again."

This pattern continued for some minutes. Sarah looked over her shoulder when the screen door of the house banged shut. His parents must have despaired of his bringing her in to meet them. Here they came, the hem of his mother's shapeless dress fluttering as she walked, revealing stockings rolled beneath her knees. She moved with deliberate steps, her ankles swollen over the sides of orthopedic shoes. His father, a stout man with high-waisted pants and long-sleeved oxford shirt, seemed to slow his pace to stay beside her.

"I guess Roy Glen is too shy to bring you in. I'm his mother Ellen." She adjusted the hairnet that compressed a roll of dark hair along her neck and smiled nervously. Sarah reached out a blue-cold hand to shake Ellen's.

"And I'm Frank," the father said. "We've heard so much about you. You're a pretty one, all right."

Sarah shook his hand too.

"You'd best come inside," Ellen said. "It's a right chill wind blowing up." She pulled her cardigan tighter across a large bosom.

Roy Glen still hadn't said a word, so she followed them to the house. In the doorway stood a stockier female version of Roy Glen—she could outwrestle him any day—his older sister Sandy. She led the way through the kitchen, which smelled of raw milk and yellowed linoleum. Strange, Sarah thought, how much it smelled like her Grandmother Stevens's house, a slightly stale odor that clings to a home when all the furnishings and way of life have been handed down through the generations like the holiday china. Sandy steered her into the living room and turned off the TV set.

"We were about to have dessert," Ellen said. "Peach cobbler." Sarah accepted the bowl of tender biscuit dough baked over golden fruit, and after tasting it, pronounced it delicious.

"Ellen and Sandy canned those peaches themselves," Frank said.

Ellen couldn't believe Sarah had never made a cobbler before and hustled to the kitchen to get an index card to write down the recipe for her. As if Sarah was ever going to make a cobbler. Trail mix and slicing carrots, celery, and apples were the extent of her kitchen repertoire. But his mother was sweet to go to the trouble to copy the recipe. What was taking Roy Glen so long anyway? In the silence Sarah concentrated on the clinking of spoons in the stoneware bowls and the thrum of a heater kicking on somewhere in the bowels of the house. When the spoons stilled, Sandy collected the dishes.

Sarah searched for something about the house to compliment. Not the serviceable orange and gold plaid couches and chairs. They were plain ugly, no two ways about it. Beside the couch stood an elaborate grandfather clock with a tiny deer poised in front of the dial. She suspected it moved about when the clock chimed the hour.

"Your grandfather clock is exceptionally beautiful," she said.

Sandy told Sarah the story of her trip to Germany, of her search for family heritage documents, of shipping the clock home as a gift for her parents. Silence brewed again when she finished. The clock ticked off the seconds more noticeably than before, it seemed to Sarah. She tried again. She gestured toward the spooky glass eyes staring down from oak-paneled walls. Huge horns curved back from small white ears. "Is that a Rocky Mountain sheep?"

A prize brought back by his own father from a trip out West, Frank said. He himself never left the state. Saw no need to. Frank's eyes lit up. "Do you like to hunt?"

She knew better than to confess she could barely stand to watch the death throes of a spider or roach. "I've never tried."

Frank stood. "I want to show you something." Sarah followed him out the back door toward one of the outbuildings against the hillside. She prepared herself to praise the bow and arrow or gun rack she supposed he wanted to show her.

He pushed open a door. "Sandy bagged two deer this year, a doe and a six-point buck, and Roy Glen shot a five-point."

Sandy not only could out-wrestle Roy Glen, she out-hunted him too. Through the dark a strong, vaguely familiar odor crept up Sarah's nose.

"This is our ice house." Frank fumbled for the light cord. A single hundred-watt bulb emitted garish light as it swung over the center of the concrete block room. The edges remained in shadow.

"Lookee here, this one Sandy got with a bow this morning." He pointed with pride at his daughter's catch. "You like venison? I'm going to finish butchering her tomorrow, and I'd be glad to send some home with you by way of Roy Glen."

Sarah wanted to admit she had never eaten venison, in fact, she ate no meat at all, but the words stuck in her throat, her eyes fixed on the headless deer suspended from the ceiling by a rope, its skin stripped away to reveal red twists of muscles. She wheeled away from the carcass and stumbled back outside. Any chance of making a good first impression on her future in-laws vanished into the grass with the peach cobbler. And now could there be any doubt it was her future father-in-law's loafers she was splashing with peach flecks? He kindly touched her shoulder and asked if she was all right. At least she thought that's what he said. She could hardly hear anything over her own retching.

With pen and legal pad on her lap, Sarah worked on an editorial about the efficacy of drug treatment programs. Across the living room, Johanna spooned a sundae into her mouth. The smell of overripe bananas made Sarah queasy. She planned to tell her mother first, if she could get her alone, and then let her mother break the news to her father. Didn't anyone else feel the tension crackling in the air? Apparently not. Her mother spit on a tissue and tried to wipe chocolate syrup off her sweater, and her father gulped his pop. Only Foster sensed the exploding particles inside Sarah. He whined and nosed her knee.

Sarah saw her chance when her father went next door to solicit Rex Watson's opinion about what television brand they should buy to replace the hunk of junk that required an occasional whack on the side to dispel the static. Then the phone rang in the den, and her mother went to answer it. Sarah sighed, from relief or regret, or some mixture of the two.

Johanna returned, all smiles. "It's Cal Caruso for you. I always did like that boy."

He was only two years too late with that call. "Tell him to fuck off."

Her mother's face hardened. "You tell him yourself."

Sarah pulled the paper closer to her nose and marked up her rough draft, slashing between "al" and "right" and adding an extra "l." She crossed out the last sentence and drew an arrow to move the third sentence up a line. Sarah's obstinance forced Johanna to return to the phone. As soon as she was out of sight, Sarah wadded up the editorial. It sucked. She couldn't write. Her mother's laughter drifted in and occasionally a word or two of conversation. Sarah straightened out the crinkled paper and resumed editing.

After a time, her mother returned with news. Cal was undergoing therapy on his leg. "He gave me his number to give to you. He'll be in town visiting his aunt until Sunday." She slid a note across the coffee table.

Ignoring it, Sarah trained her eyes on the editorial. Her mother started to walk away. Sarah couldn't let her.

Sarah set the editorial down. "Mom, there's something I have to tell you."

Eighteen

JANUARY 1972

A sewer line should never be pitched less than one-eighth inch to the foot; a quarter-inch is preferred. Although this crucial fact keeps life flowing along smoothly, it was nothing Sarah had learned in college. She found out from Roy Glen soon after they married. It was a fact the crew setting up Sarah and Roy Glen's new mobile home—the euphemism he used instead of trailer—failed to properly consider.

Sarah pressed the lever down. First there was a gurgle. Then a groaning from the bowels of the plumbing. Water filled the avocado bowl and reached the rim, bringing toilet paper with it. She jiggled the handle. Still the water rushed through the pipes. She squealed as it splashed on the pristine harvest gold linoleum. She shoved a towel at the base of the commode. She squealed louder.

"Honey, will you come here?"

"What?"

He sounded annoyed, but for God's sake he was only watching a re-run of *Hee Haw* on her parents' hand-me-down black and white. It wasn't as if he was going to lose the plotline. She ran the dozen steps to the living room, trying to convey urgency in her voice. "The commode is overflowing."

He slid his legs off the couch and moved past her with speed learned on the basketball court. He reached under the toilet and twisted the valve. "Jesus H. Christ. Why didn't you turn off the water?"

Sarah hunched her shoulders. "I didn't know how."

He shook his head. "Don't you know anything?"

She knew the roots of political science extended all the way back to Homer, Thucydides, Plato, and Aristotle. She knew William Randolph Hearst started the largest newspaper chain in the United States during the Age of Yellow Journalism. She knew the lead paragraph of a news story should be one sentence, preferably under 35 words. And she knew she was exactly two months pregnant today, two days after their ceremony with the justice of the peace. But she only knew three things about toilets. You used them, you flushed them, and you swished disinfectant around with a brush weekly to clean them.

Roy Glen peeled off wet socks, gingerly skirting the puddle. "Open the window over there. Air it out a little. I'm going outside to adjust the level of the trailer a bit."

She didn't mean to—it was baby hormones talking because she was tougher than this—but she sniffled the whole time she mopped. Why didn't she know anything important? Roy Glen knew everything. Not to pour grease down the sink because it would clog the drain. How to refill the windshield washer in the car. How to build steps and a deck for the mobile home. How to hook up the washer and dryer. How to tell if a fuse was blown. How to light the pilot light on the furnace when the wind blew it out.

He was right. She didn't know anything, but she was determined to learn. She would be a good wife if it killed her. She would make up for her mistakes. For not saving herself until after marriage. For not being more insistent about birth control. Somehow, some way, she should have figured out what to do. She couldn't help feeling this marriage shouldn't have happened. Not this way. How would she ever know if he loved her enough to marry her if she hadn't been pregnant? She pushed those thoughts away. They could make this work. They had to. A baby was coming, and already mother love enveloped everything else, caused her to dig her fingernails into her palms when she thought of any harm coming to her little butterbean.

Roy Glen insisted he could get a job on his own, turning down offers of help. After his interview at Hazel Atlas, he swaggered through the front door. "Piece of cake. I don't need favors from anyone."

Sarah didn't tell Roy Glen the truth. Her neighbor Rita Watson said it was impossible to get on at the factory unless you knew someone, and Rita knew everybody. She'd worked there forever, so she talked to the foreman on Roy Glen's behalf. Neither did Roy Glen know about the letter of recommendation her father had written for him. Hazel Atlas was one of Nelson's clients, so his word carried some weight. Sarah remembered how passionate Uncle Mahlon felt about working with glass, how much it thrilled her too during her brief apprentice-ship. She hoped Roy Glen would find the same pleasure, though she worried he might despise it as Jimmy Watson had.

She wrung out the wet towels and piled them in the new washer. Also avocado. In the kitchen, she stirred milk, cocoa, and sugar in a pan on the gas stove. When Roy Glen came in from leveling the trailer, he would be cold. She pulled the curtains open wider because the walnut paneling darkened the rooms.

While she waited for the milk to heat, she unpacked boxes of books, arranging them carefully on the shelves. Textbooks at the bot-tom; fiction next; dictionary, thesaurus, Bible, and Roy Glen's reference books on plumbing, carpentry, and home repair at eye level for easy access. She became so involved she didn't notice the milk boiling over until she smelled scorching. Damn—she couldn't do anything right.

By the time she cleaned it up, Roy Glen was pulling off his boots. "Whoo—cold out there." He rubbed his hands together.

The cocoa was still drinkable. She poured a cup to warm his hands.

"Mmm, exactly what I needed." He finished in two big gulps and pulled her into his lap. "Know what else would warm me up?"

She had a pretty good idea. For the first time in weeks, she felt optimistic. It would all work out. All it took was love.

Roy Glen could smell the sour milk as Sarah rinsed out his ther-mos at nearly one in the morning. He'd been lucky enough to clock an hour's overtime. He slouched in a kitchen chair, his back sore, head achy, feet cramped. Foster whined pitifully. Roy Glen's hand crept down to scratch his head. "Sorry old dog."

In the beginning, Roy Glen thought his job would get easier, that his body would adjust, but now he wasn't sure. Three weeks gone by, and every night, his muscles complained louder than the night before. He'd baled hay, cleaned barns and chicken coops, hoed his family's garden, and helped his father roof their house. He was used to hard work, but this was different. The repetitiveness of the tasks forced him to use the same muscles over and over with no chance to change posi-tions or stretch. He untied his boots and tossed them carelessly toward the mat beside the front door. One careened on its side.

Sarah set a plate of macaroni with tomatoes and cheese and a bowl of salad in front of him and poured a tall glass of sweet tea. His mother—only half jokingly?—suggested his wife was trying to kill him with all the sugar, but he liked it that way. While he ate, Sarah walked over and righted his boots. Lined them up perfectly, like bowling pins, side by side facing the door. God, she couldn't leave anything alone.

"How was work today?"

"Same as every other day." She was always trying to get him to tell her what he did at the factory, but there was nothing to tell. It was boring. He couldn't understand her fascination with glass. It was a paycheck. Nothing more.

"Did you make something pretty?"

"Avocado ashtrays. You want me to swipe one for your folks?"

"No, thank you anyway."

He knew what she'd say. He was only messing with her. "I brought home a set of glasses. Foreman took a set for himself and told the rest of us to do the same. You can haul them out of the truck in the morning." The foreman hadn't told them that, exactly, but the men watched him take a case, so they followed his lead. Sarah, he knew, would consider it stealing instead of understanding certain perks came with the job.

"Good. We could use some."

"Cartoons on them. Bugs Bunny, Donald Duck, and guess who else?"

"Who?"

"Road Runner, your favorite. I pulled three for you."

She reached her arms around his chest from behind and nuzzled his neck. "You're so sweet."

"Good dinner." He was glad she'd cut some ham into his macaroni. Plain cooking suited him fine, but she seemed to like trying new reci-pes. He suspected she was working her way through the *Better Homes and Gardens Cookbook*. He didn't mind. Most dishes were pretty tasty.

She sat down catty-corner to him. "I wish you worked day shift, so we could eat dinner together."

He wasn't even going to answer that. Night shift paid better and right now they needed all the money he could make, what with a baby on the way and paying his parents back for the loan on the mobile home. He speared a cucumber disc with his fork.

"Mom got a stroller for the baby today," she said.

He lowered the fork. "We can take care of ourselves. We aren't some charity case."

"It's not charity, it's a present for the baby."

Her family already had given them a vacuum cleaner, melamine dishes, stainless tableware, and sheets. "Tell her to take it back."

"Can't—she got it with green stamps."

He dropped it, but he was pissed. Her parents didn't think he could support her. They offered money for her tuition and books too, but he wasn't about to let her take it. She was his responsibility now. "Saturday we're going over to the farm. I want to work on the car."

"Okay, I'll take my typewriter and work on lesson plans."

Roy Glen couldn't see why she wanted to finish college anyway. She was going to be big as a cow by the time she started student teaching in late spring. Why did she want to parade around in front of teenagers like that? It wasn't like she was ever going to have to work.

He still thought about that guy Cal and what he'd done with Sarah, but a man didn't run away from responsibilities. Nosiree bob, he did the right thing and married her. And it wasn't so bad. She waited up for him every night, prepared a hot meal, kept the house and laundry clean. Most of all, he loved watching her walk away from him—like she was now to fetch the pitcher of tea. He loved those long legs, the natural sway of her hips.

There had been some strange surprises though. He'd never known a vegetarian before, so he'd been shocked to find out he'd married one. It wasn't a big problem since she fixed meat for him. A little weird to think he hadn't noticed this before.

And then there was her little habit of straightening up. Like what she did to his boots. Freaky. Book edges aligned on shelves, magazines on the coffee table stacked square. If he tossed *TV Guide* down any old place, within minutes she lined it up with the others, edges turned exactly perpendicular to the table. A strange habit, but he guessed he could live with it. Better a neat freak for a wife than a slob like his college roommates.

And she was nervous. Always biting her cuticles or twisting her wedding rings—didn't even know she was doing it unless he pointed it out.

And her wanting to visit with her parents and aunts every Sunday afternoon—what was that about? A grown woman shouldn't be so dependent. But his mother said a woman naturally wanted to be close to her mother when she was in a family way. So on Sundays, Sarah dropped him off at the farm and drove in to town to visit. He put up with it because his mother said he should, but he didn't like it. Her parents were a bad influence, trying to get her to live beyond her means. Besides, they didn't like him. It wasn't what they said. It was the way they looked at him. Like he wasn't good enough. They told him to call them Mom and Dad or Johanna and Nelson, whatever he felt comfortable with, but he didn't. He couldn't make himself call them anything.

Then Sarah set a bowl of peach cobbler in front of him. Cinnamon and nutmeg drifted up and chased away every negative thought.

"Your mother's recipe," she said.

He smiled. Being married wasn't so bad. At least there was sex every night, and now there was peach cobbler too.

In the fifth month of her pregnancy, Sarah fell asleep over a pile of tests, the essays still ungraded. At 11:15 she roused herself to heat Roy Glen's bean soup and cornbread. When he got home shortly afterward, she put his food on the table and left him alone. "Sorry, I gotta lay down before I fall down." She was so tired, and 6 a.m. and the bell for morning classes would come all too soon.

When he came to bed, he turned out the light and reached for her.

Jesus, not again, she thought. Not tonight.

It was the same every night. He rolled on top of her, kissed her once or twice, pumped a few minutes, rolled off, and went to sleep. Being enfolded in Roy Glen's arms satisfied her in a way sex did not. Just as she would sense there was something more, something she could almost touch, it was over. This time, she couldn't even rouse herself to pretend interest. When he finished, he sat up and turned the bedside lamp on. The butterbean fluttered. Disturbed by their lovemaking? With an effort, she raised her arms and held her softly rounded belly, humming inside her head, *Hush little baby, don't say a word.*

Through half-lidded eyes, she experienced a moment of sleepy pleasure watching Roy Glen's torso gleam in the incandescent light. His back was beautiful, lean and muscled, tapering from shoulder to waist. As he pulled on briefs and jeans, her eyes flashed open.

"Where you going?"

He yanked on a tee. "Out."

"Where?"

He kept his back toward her. "Drinking with the guys. Some of them were going to have a few beers at the Down and Under. A birthday. I said I'd stop in later if I could."

She could feel his eyes move down the length of her body, then rise to her face, where they moved across one cheek to the other, down to her lips, finally coming to rest on her swelling abdomen, his face expressionless. "You know, I always wanted to marry a virgin."

Her face burned as if he had slapped her. Cal stood between them so vividly she could smell his aftershave. Her stomach churned and she knew she was going to be sick. From the bathroom, head hung over the toilet, she could hear the truck roar to life. It was the fourth time that day she'd thrown up. Morning sickness was supposed to stop after three months. No one told the butterbean.

She went to bed and sobbed. At some level below words, she couldn't help feeling he was right to despise her. Experience was a good thing to have when seeking any job except wife. All this time, she thought he'd meant it when he said he couldn't wait to get married and have kids. When she'd told her mother she was pregnant, her mother told her there were alternatives to ruining her life, hinting at abortion or adoption. A child needs two loving parents, her mother said. Sarah silenced her mother with a hardening of the eyes. Sarah had never wanted anything in her life as much as she wanted this baby. Maybe her mother was right. Roy Glen didn't love Sarah or the baby, but her mother was wrong about one thing. There was enough love in Sarah to make up for anything lacking in Roy Glen. This baby would be adored. Already was.

Roy Glen came home after three.

In the morning Sarah felt as if she'd been stomped by elephants. Her thoughts shifted to her classroom, where she was succeeding, even while she failed at marriage. With students, her height was an advantage. Made her appear older, more in charge. While she fixed her hair, she thought about how much she liked little Verlene's can-do attitude and the readiness of Henry to answer any question. The students were mastering the material, and Sarah's supervising professor heaped praise on her lesson plans. Think of the degree as an insurance policy, her father said. Even if she never used it, it was there to fall back on. She could see the sense of that, though some days she could barely drag herself out of bed and drive twenty miles to the high school where she did her student teaching.

Whenever Roy Glen got home, no matter what time, he wanted sex. Evey time he was on top of her now, the mantra *I can never be what he wants* bounced through her mind like a trapped bird hurling itself against a window pane. By June, the circles deepened beneath her eyes; her complexion either wan from morning sickness or ruddy from heat, no in betweens. Afternoons in the trailer grew unbearably hot. The dark paneling closed in on Sarah.

In July, eight months pregnant, she finished her last courses in summer school and graduated with honors. Her parents gave her a $150 check as a gift and said to buy an air conditioner.

Roy Glen tore up the check. She cried. "You're never here in the day time. I can't breathe. It's all this extra weight and the heat." She took one look at his unsympathetic face and wailed, "Oh, you don't understand."

How could he? Her in-ie belly button had long since surrendered to pressure and became an out-ie. For the first time in her life, real breasts poked from her chest. Getting up and down from a chair required major effort. And something had happened to her sense of balance. She wobbled like a duck. She could never be too far away from the bathroom because of her bladder's demands. She felt as if she were inhabiting a stranger's body. To be more accurate, a stranger was inhabiting her body. She called her mother, who did understand.

Johanna understood the rest, too. How love was growing in Sarah's belly and pressed so hard against her heart it burned. Her mother was a different person to her now, one who had carted her around for nine months, full of love.

The next day her parents bought a new air conditioner for themselves and brought their old one over and installed it in the window. Immediately Sarah turned it on high, sprawled out on the couch, and felt the sweat on her forehead evaporate in the manufactured breeze. Roy Glen's lips thinned when he came home from work and saw it.

For two days he refused to speak to her.

At one of her final office visits, Dr. Jorgansen said it was time to discuss breast feeding.

"I think I want to," Sarah said.

He smiled paternally. "Most women don't anymore. Too inconvenient."

"Sweetie," her mother patted her hand, "imagine having to feed the baby at your in-laws' house. Having to—" fingers spread across her mouth, blurring her words—"expose your chest."

Sarah guessed that would be awkward, supposed they knew best. They were more experienced in these matters.

A week past her due date, she looked as if she'd swallowed a basketball. She spilled flour on the countertop. She sobbed. A sock fell from the laundry basket. She sobbed. She sobbed when she looked into the mirror. She saw herself through Roy Glen's eyes. Damaged goods.

Once again Roy Glen scanned the dark interior of the Down and Under. He'd run into Anita there a month ago, and he came back once or twice a week to see if she would show. He knew he shouldn't have, but he only wanted to see if she would come back. Nothing would happen even if she did.

She had been with Wally Roswell. Short fellow with solid arms and a smashed-in nose. Wrestler in high school. Nursing one beer after another, Roy Glen had stared openly at Anita and she knew it. Showed off for his benefit, rubbing her nose into Wally's neck on slow songs, working her hips seductively on fast numbers, and through it all, her eyes flicked Roy Glen's way to see if he was watching. He was—why hide it? On her way back from the ladies' room, she passed by him at the bar. Didn't say a word. Dropped a cigarette butt into his beer. He wondered when she'd started smoking.

Anita looked good. She wore her hair straight and halfway down her back instead of teased out all over her head. Filled out more, too. C cups, he guessed. Real, not padding. They jiggled when she walked.

From his sophomore year in high school until the end of his first semester of college, he'd escorted Anita to every decent movie and held her hand. A sensible hand, back then, with close-clipped nails. Sometimes her fingertips were stained greenish brown from pinching suckers off tomatoes or from picking beans. Now she wore red paint on those nails. He remembered making circles with his thumb in her palm, arousing himself until he was in such agony he couldn't even have told anyone what was on the screen. Alone in bed afterward, he worked on himself, careful to catch the mess in tissues so his mother wouldn't find the stains. Once he overshot and his mother found a wayward smear. The next night his father shuffled into Roy Glen's bedroom in house slippers. His mother was too delicate to speak of such things, his father said, and rightly so. A good woman wouldn't. "You see, Roy Glen, it's all a matter of self control. If you treat every girl as your mother or your sister, you won't go wrong." He talked about the Thing and how it was capable of defiling women and destroying marriages. The Bible, he conceded, had lots of begetting. They begat and begat and begat, as God intended. "But for God's sake, Roy Glen, keep the Damn Thing in your pants. A man has to exercise self control, son."

Roy Glen struggled for control, but no matter how he tried, the Damn Thing still squirmed at the sight of a jean-clad butt. The more he tried to shut off all thoughts of girls' bodies, the more his eyes strained to see the outline of nipples under tee-shirts. By the time he started college, he gave up. First he gave up church. Then he put pressure on Anita to move beyond kisses, and when she resisted, he gave up on her, too. Something in Sarah—her child-like body joined to what he'd thought was a woman's hunger—made him hope he could finally control the Damn Thing. Rope it down with marriage and kids. So far, it had worked.

Sooner or later, he figured Anita would turn up again at the Down and Under. He wanted a chance to talk. To know if she was happy. He wasn't sure why it mattered, but it did.

Right after midnight she sashayed in with an old high school chum, Wendy. Built like a fire plug, that one. He never could understand why a pretty girl like Anita hung out with such a heifer. In the mirrored wall behind the bar, he watched Anita and Wendy drink their beers. Anita strutted over and slid onto the stool beside him. He kept his cool. Didn't acknowledge her.

"Where's your wife?"

He shrugged. "Home, I guess. Where's your boyfriend?"

"Wally's not my boyfriend. We broke up."

He tilted his head her way. A question.

"I broke up because I want you."

The word "want" traveled from his ears straight to the Damn Thing. Bypassed his brain altogether. He knew he should get up and walk away, but the Thing was possessed by a life all its own. A force to be reckoned with. An insistent little bastard. It anchored him to the barstool.

"You shouldn't have broken up with him."

She slapped him, and he grabbed her hand, twisted her arm a little. Her eyes watered but he didn't let go. When she quit struggling, he linked his fingers through hers and they felt as if they belonged there. The clasp of her hand pulled him right back to high school again.

She raised her chin and her eyes held his. He'd always loved her eyes—almost black. "I couldn't do this if I was still with him," she said.

"I can't leave my wife." Not with a baby coming—he didn't have to say it. She would have heard.

"I didn't ask you to."

Not exactly, but what she meant was a decent person didn't cheat. He told himself that he would have walked away from anyone else—but if he walked away from Anita, he'd spend the rest of his life wondering.

Besides, Sarah had Cal, and Anita was finally offering him what should have been his. Sarah never needed to know. Just one time.

A single streetlamp lit the parking lot as he guided Anita to the truck. Where in God's name would he take her? She deserved better than the inside of the truck her first time. He was certain she could feel his hand burning where it rested against the soft cotton blouse at her waist.

When the engine burbled to life, she suggested going to the field behind the gym. "Remember how we used to walk under the trees there after your games?"

Thoughts of getting his hands on the prize pushed everything else away. While he drove, she rested her hand on the inside of his thigh. Killing him. He couldn't even make words come out of his mouth. After what seemed like an endless drive—but could only have been ten minutes—he turned into the empty parking lot and pulled behind the gym.

The slam of her door sounded so final. They were really going to do this. All along, he kept expecting her to back out, to say no, she couldn't, but here she was, smelling faintly like nutmeg, the way he remembered, pulling him against her, devouring his face, the concrete blocks of the gym supporting her shoulders. He moaned and fumbled with buttons on her blouse and shoved her bra out of the way, and his hands trembled over her soft flesh. It felt the way he'd dreamed, night after miserable night. She tugged on his zipper and when she touched him, it was all over.

All over her hand and the front of her jeans.

She kind of laughed, pulled his lower lip into her mouth, a last kiss before she said to the top of his head, buried now in her shoulder. "It's okay. I'll take it as a compliment."

He broke away, leaning against the brick wall, his face turned away from her. Didn't say anything—what could he say? This wasn't how he'd pictured it. He never could control the Damn Thing. What was the matter with him?

She fumbled in her purse with her clean hand, tissued off the ejaculate, and tossed the whole mess in a dumpster a few yards away. Without bothering to button her blouse, she grabbed his arm. "Come on—we were headed to the field when we got distracted."

He let her tug him onto the grass and followed her some distance up the hill, only three-quarters of a deep gold moon to see by. On the crest, Anita flopped down and patted the ground beside her. "Come sit."

He did what she said. Still couldn't look at her. What a performance. What a loser. What could she possibly think of him now? He hardly listened, his mind pinned to his failure, while she talked about waitressing, how she liked chatting with customers in the Barn, how she got good tips because she remembered to ask about sick children and new jobs. She plied him with questions about his job, shaking his arm, until he finally had to respond.

"Can't get used to doing the same thing, hour after hour."

"So change jobs."

"Can't, got responsibilities."

She was quiet for a while after that. They listened to crickets singing night music, and gradually his heart stopped pounding. He felt almost normal-like, for a loser. Anita tucked a long hank of brown hair behind her ear and leaned back on her elbows. "Kind of surprised you never came back to church."

He shrugged, didn't feel like explaining.

"After you broke up with me, I'd sit in the back pew every Sunday and watch the sunlight coming through those double doors—the door would open and the sun would be so bright once you looked into it, you couldn't even make out the usher's face. I'd sit there and watch for you and sometimes I'd think it was you coming in but it always turned out to be someone else. Tommy Butler or Wally Roswell."

"Wasn't me."

"I know. Why'd you break up with me, Roy Glen?"

He didn't think she would like the answer. He could feel himself coming to life again and thought this time could be different. He pushed her down onto the grass and slowly removed her clothes. He wanted to feel her completely naked. This time he would claim what belonged to him. She would see his equipment worked fine, thank you very much.

When he finished, he rolled over on his back and stared up at the pinpricks of light piercing the black sky. Claws scraped softly on bark—probably raccoons foraging for dinner. A car—sounded like a Volkswagen in need of a new alternator—passed by on the road below. He didn't bother to look to see if he was right. He could smell crushed grass and sour clover and could feel the tickle of little insects against his back. As sweat evaporated, his skin felt cool even though the night was humid. She was still holding his hand, but he didn't feel like he was in high school anymore.

"Who was it?" he asked.

"Who was what?"

"Who was your first?"

She let go of his hand. "Wally, it was Wally Roswell. What did you think—I was going to sit around waiting on you to change your mind and come back to me?"

"No, I didn't think that." But he guessed he had, a little.

He went back to the Down and Under the next night, but Anita wasn't there. Wendy was.

"She said to tell you she doesn't want to see you again. It was a mistake."

He'd known that when they'd done it the first time. His wife was ready to pop out a kid. That hadn't stopped him.

"She said don't try to call her."

"I won't."

Wendy parked her thick body on the barstool beside him. "Really?"

After two beers chased by tequila shooters, he was impressed by Wendy's sturdiness. Kept up with him, beer after beer. Nice thick hair, too. He took her to the truck and fell on top without preamble. No love talk. Just good old sticky, sweaty humping like pigs. She turned out to be the first girl he had who really enjoyed it.

Anita would find out. That was okay, too. A message of his own.

The next night his daughter was born.

Nineteen

August 1972

The center of gravity shifted when the nurse handed Mandy over to Sarah half an hour after her birth. Accommodating from the beginning, the baby arrived in the middle of the night, so her father could be there to witness the event. Mandy clutched a tiny fist around Sarah's finger with an amazing intensity that mirrored the fierceness Sarah felt for her. When Sarah gave Mandy her first bottle, the baby grasped a hank of Sarah's hair that tumbled across her tightly bound breasts. Sarah had agreed to bottle feeding, but now she was tempted to rip the bindings off and feed the butterbean herself. Why was nature's way so bad? Her desire to breastfeed was physical, innate, hard-wired into her, something she hadn't anticipated. One more sign something was wrong with her.

She hid something else from everyone. When Doc Jorgansen asked her what she planned to do about birth control, she wasn't sure. Roy Glen, when she'd brought it up, said to let nature take its course. But she wanted to cherish this child before adding any more to their family. Besides, how could they squeeze more kids into their tiny trailer? The living room was the only option for another bed. The doctor's suggestion of an IUD seemed the perfect answer.

"Can my husband tell it's there?" Realizing how that sounded, she amended her question. "I mean, will it bother him?"

"Trust me, he'll never feel a thing. There's a little string up there and that's it."

Sarah was surprised to learn that the union of two people into a new one was no less miraculous for having been repeated billions of times. When they took the baby home, Roy Glen nestled next to mother and child on the couch. "See the way her first two toes web together—like mine."

Sarah showed him a baby picture Roy Glen's mother had given her. "If you didn't know this was you instead of Mandy, you could hardly tell the difference."

"Yes, I could. Her lips are shaped like yours. Her kiss will be as sweet as her mother's."

It was the nicest thing to say, and she remembered why she loved him.

Sarah was awed by every detail of her baby—tiny flakes of fingernails, long sprouts of dark hair that refused to gel into a kewpie curl, rosebud-soft skin. She felt sorry for other mothers burdened by babies with faces misshapen by the birth canal, babies with harsh red skin. Somewhere within her brain, a shred of rationality whispered all mothers felt this way, but she shushed it. Her parents, if possible, seemed even more enamored with the baby than Sarah, distressed if more than a day went by without seeing Mandy.

The intensity of Sarah's emotions, the savage urge to protect and nurture this child, frightened her. She woke up several times a night to make sure the baby was breathing. One night she fell back to sleep after one of these checks. In her dream, she heard the front door open, then footsteps into Mandy's room. Sarah tiptoed down the hallway. An intruder leaned over the crib. She flew to the kitchen and boiled water to throw on him—no, that wouldn't do—took too long. She grabbed the chef's knife from the cutlery drawer and ran back toward the bedroom. The intruder—she couldn't see him distinctly, a faceless dark shape—was coming out with Mandy in his arms. Suddenly the baby appeared back in her crib and Sarah hacked at the dark man. She hacked and hacked and woke up panting.

Crawling from bed, she tiptoed into the baby's room where Mandy slept peacefully, legs hunched under her belly like an inchworm. Sarah slipped through the darkness to twist the front door knob. Locked. She felt foolish.

She washed stinky messes off Mandy's bottom and rubbed baby lotion into the soft folds of fat and kissed them. She giggled when the baby expelled gas. Her baby's body was beautiful, every inch, every crease of it. Each day brought discovery. Mandy's first smile, the first time she reached for the yarn doll Roy Glen's sister made for her, the way she stared at lights. Achievements duly recorded in the pink satin baby book. Historical events. More important than the lineage of English monarchs or incursions into Laos—those things that seemed important in college.

Roy Glen arrived home with gifts every week. A giant giraffe twice as big as Mandy. A royal blue toolbox with a red hammer, yellow screwdriver, and green wrench so—when she got big enough—she would be able to work on cars with him. A plastic fishing pole with a magnet on the end to catch primary-colored fish.

The best gift of all: late evenings with the guys stopped. When Mandy woke up for her midnight feeding, Roy Glen huddled beside them. Once or twice he even held the bottle.

1972-3

Sarah and Roy Glen's mobile home was parked six miles outside town on land his parents deeded over to him. The five acres of rolling hills were studded with hollies, hickories, birches, pines, and a glorious weeping willow that sucked dry the tail end of a stream. Roy Glen dragged stones from the creek to form a campfire near the trailer where they roasted hot dogs and marshmallows together. They crouched around it and talked long after dark on weekends. Once on a warm September evening, they made love on a blanket by the fire after they put Mandy to bed. Many a fall afternoon while Mandy napped, Sarah sat in a webbed lawn chair on their deck reading romance novels from the library. She gazed at the hillside where trees showed off garish colors like Spanish dancers. Anticipating the spring to come, she tucked crisp brown daffodil bulbs into the ground near the deck.

Then trees dropped their leaves and the world grew monochromatic, even the sky a dreary suffocating gray. In late November the snow came, blanketing the hills and roads, trapping Sarah in the trailer. She had no close neighbors. No signs of humans at all on bad days when the roads were impassable without chains. From Thanksgiving until the end of April, there were days and even weeks where she was confined to the trailer with the baby. Roy Glen could get off their hill in the truck, but the Chevy fishtailed on the lightest dusting of snow. He loaded the trunk with sandbags, which helped, but he still didn't like her driving the Chevy in winter because salt and cinders ruined the paint.

Her parents gave them a new color television for Christmas, a gift that helped lift her isolation. She involved herself in other people's lives, even if they were only daytime soap characters. She talked to her mother daily on the phone. Still, she missed seeing Rachel and Paula, missed hearing Rita's honky voice, and above all, missed regular visits with her mother and Livvie. When the daffodils popped up in early March, she filled with hope that her long days alone would soon end.

By late April when Roy Glen surveyed their property, only hollies and pines were fully green. By then, the daffodils, for the most part, had shriveled into brown husks, but dogwoods and redbuds dotted the tree line with color.

They had been married over a year and were saving to build their dream house. For months they pored over house plan books, preferring the spacious closets of one design, the hip roof of another, until Roy Glen finally drew up plans himself, incorporating the best features from each. He circled and criss-crossed the land twice with Sarah traipsing behind, eight-month-old Mandy draped around her neck and waist, plump as a little bear.

At last Roy Glen knelt on the crest of a knoll. "This is where we'll build."

Sarah squatted beside him, envisioning the house sketched on graph paper. In her mind the mud room off the garage, the kitchen breakfast bar, and the master bedroom with its own bath took shape as if they were already real. Roy Glen measured the foundation and drove four stakes into the ground to mark the corners. He pulled Mandy from Sarah's arms and carried her to one corner of the future house. "Right here will be your bed, Peanut. And when you look out your window—" he arced his wrist in the air—"you'll be able to watch your pony."

Sarah hugged them, her perfect family.

Roy Glen grabbed her hand. "I want to show you something."

She followed him across the creek and over the hill. They passed through woods with the occasional bloom of mauve phlox and trillium along the edges. A cabin in the middle of a meadow appeared on the horizon.

"My grandparents' house."

"How did they get supplies in and out?" No way a vehicle could drive in from their trailer.

"PawPaw drove his truck in from the other side of the hill."

As they got closer, Sarah could make out the faint traces of a track leading to the house.

"The entrance is off a dirt road out near Rt. 50. Hard to find unless you know where to look. They lived out here all alone when my dad was growing up and they had all they needed. Water, wood, fish, deer, berries, nuts, and a vegetable garden. If this country ever falls apart, this is where we're coming."

What was he talking about, fall apart? The United States wasn't going to fall apart.

"I've got plenty of guns and ammunition, so I can defend us."

"Against what?"

"Whatever happens. We'll be safe."

Instead of feeling safer, she felt vaguely apprehensive, at a loss to understand him once again. She let the setting wash her misgivings away, this meadow with the beginnings of spring wildflowers under a wide blue sky. "What were they like, your grandparents?"

"Good God-fearing people who stayed pretty much to themselves. Married at 16. Celebrated their 62nd anniversary and MeMaw passed away the next day. Keeled over out of the blue. PawPaw died a few months later."

She remembered Roy Glen hadn't even told her about that loss until after the funeral. Maybe staying to yourself was an inherited trait, like green eyes. The steps looked precarious, with rotted boards, so Sarah and Mandy stayed outside, but Roy Glen skirted the bad boards and opened the door. By shifting her position across what used to be the yard, Sarah could see the one-room building still had a few pieces of furniture. A table. A sagging bed. An ancient stove. Would have been mighty cozy with kids cluttering up the place too. And she thought the trailer was cramped!

As they hiked back to the trailer, Sarah tried to believe in the dream house, but there was a catch, a hold on these plans, because Roy Glen didn't borrow money. They had bought the trailer with a loan from his parents, which he paid back in eight months and declared it was the only loan he'd ever accept.

Sarah practiced economy. Washed out and reused plastic sandwich bags from Roy Glen's lunch. Little plastic tents dotted her countertop while they dried. She winced over the look of concern her parents exchanged when they saw nine upturned bags covering every inch of counter space.

She grew vegetables from seed and dug out a garden for tomatoes and peppers. Wild strawberries, raspberries, and blackberries rambled across the hillsides in succession once the weather warmed up. Sarah also planted rhubarb, and of these gifts from the earth she made jams and pies and cobblers. She darned socks. Bought the new generic products with black and white labels on supermarket shelves. Sewed most of Mandy's clothes. Melted leftover soap scraps together to make a new bar or shaved bits into the washing machine to conserve detergent. And when Sarah got tired of all the economy, she unfurled the floor plans, pictured the breakfast bar, and doubled her frugality.

One weekend Roy Glen dug a root cellar in the hill behind their trailer to store the foods she canned. Then his truck began to fail. He replaced belts and plugs and cleaned the carburetor, forestalling the inevitable. He bought a new truck, another Ford, this time with a capped bed, and there went their savings. They started over.

"Come on, it's Janie's birthday," Roy Glen's co-worker Bobby said. "You can't be that pussy-whipped."

Janie pouted, folding her arms. "At least have one little drink with me."

Roy Glen felt the Thing twitching as he eyed those arms. They made kind of a ledge to support the weight of Janie's full breasts. She was a secretary in the plant, someone he knew only in passing, but she was definitely coming on to him, something Sarah never did anymore. Sarah was all about the kid. Mandy this and Mandy that. But his decision didn't have anything to do with Sarah and the kid. Not really. It was about heat. It was about the chase.

"Guess one drink wouldn't hurt."

"It won't hurt at all. Promise."

And it didn't. Hurt at all.

That was the first night after Mandy's birth he had come home late, the first time he wasn't working overtime. He was back in the game.

Twenty

NOVEMBER *1973*

When Sarah opened her eyes Thanksgiving morning, the initial flicker of uncertainty from not being in her own bed gave way to contentment. She and Mandy slept at her mother's so Sarah could help with the big meal—the excuse Sarah gave Roy Glen. Why should she spend the day alone while Roy Glen went hunting at four in the morning? Afterward, he planned to work a late afternoon shift for double overtime.

Sarah and her mother finished sweet potato and green bean casseroles by eleven for the celebration at the Heimbachs'. The bluest of skies beckoned, only faint wisps of cirrus swirling overhead. Sarah bundled fifteen-month old Mandy into a bonnet and coat hand-sewn by Aunt Livvie, popped her into her stroller, and ambled through the old neighborhood. She passed Rachel's house, where four cars arched like an eyebrow along the circular drive. Pumpkins, a scarecrow, and sheaves of wheat guarded the front door. The pumpkins—artfully arranged to appear random—varied in height. The Sullivans' home was atypical for the neighborhood, the only brick house in a sea of clapboard, the only house on an acre lot. All the other homes were so close together if you spit out the window it would land in your neighbor's kitchen.

Sarah trundled down the sidewalk, taking care not to jolt the baby over curbs. After one particularly rough section of cracked cement, she peered into the stroller to check Mandy. The honk of a horn caused Sarah to jerk upright. She recognized the old Ford at once. Cal parked along the curb a few yards ahead and hopped out, the stiffness in his left leg, a slight drag, noticeable as he approached.

"Sarah, long time, no see."

His body had filled out since she last saw him. A man's body, with a thicker neck than she remembered and fuller cheeks. The eyes were as blue as ever, but dulled, boyish mischief left behind in some jungle swamp. Civility demanded some kind of response, and with every silent second, words grew harder to find.

"How you doing?" she managed at last.

He admired Mandy—of course, who wouldn't?—commenting on her perfect little mouth. He was back in college, majoring in physical education with a minor in journalism. "Lost the basketball scholarship—the leg." He looked down ruefully. "But the GI bill and my folks are paying my way." They chatted about the initial surgery on his leg and the subsequent therapy, his classes, how happy she was to be a mother. She tried not to look too directly into his eyes. Tried to suppress the bitterness that rose in her throat when she remembered his last phone call.

She cringed every time she heard a motor, fearing it would be Roy Glen passing by, even though she knew he'd stay in the woods until time for his afternoon shift. But someone who knew Roy Glen might see them and report that she was talking to a guy.

"You know," Cal said, "I always thought you and I—one day we'd—you and I—well—"

She could feel the blood drain from her face. Thank God he left the thought unfinished. She'd thought so too. Once upon a time.

CHRISTMAS 1973

He couldn't do it. He knew he said he would, but he just couldn't. He looked around at the pile of crushed wrapping paper, the scattered new toys—Raggedy Ann, a Big Wheel, a cash register that dinged every time Mandy opened the drawer, which she did every five seconds. (It was only cute the first thirty times.) Roy Glen loved Mandy, he did, and pretending Santa had eaten the cookies and left toys had been fun, but he was going to scream if that cash register dinged one more time. He didn't know where he was going to spend the afternoon, but it wasn't at the Heimbach house. Sarah would pitch a fit, but he couldn't face the endless dings of the cash register. He couldn't face her aunt's endless display of food on fancy china, the father-in-law's endless and silent disapproval, or the mother-in-law's endless attempts to get Roy Glen to talk. Roy Glen didn't know where he was going to spend the day, but it wasn't with the in-laws. He had to get free.

When the phone rang, Sarah was leaning over the Big Wheel to push Mandy across the living room into the kitchen. Roy Glen answered. It was the mother-in-law herself, her greeting an absolute song of Christmas cheer. He depressed the button to hang up and quickly released it.

"Today?" he said. "You've got to be kidding." He pretended to listen. Sarah twisted her head around and mouthed, *Who is it?* He shook his head at her and pretended to listen, made sure a frown creased his face. "Okay, if it's really an emergency, of course I'll be there." He hung up.

Her tone sounded a warning that she was going to be exactly as pissed as he thought she'd be. "You'll be where?"

"That was my foreman. The guy who was supposed to work my area today is in the hospital with pneumonia. I'm going to have to take his place."

She shot upright. "Today? You promised—Christmas Eve with your family, Christmas Day with mine."

"Honey, you heard the man." Actually, she hadn't, but he could convince her she had. "It's an emergency."

"I can't believe this. The first Christmas Mandy knows what's going on and you're going to miss it."

He packed a little anger into his own voice. "What can I do? I can hardly afford to lose my job. They need people they can depend on." He changed his tone to pleading, a bit of a whine. "You think I want to spend Christmas Day in that blasted factory?"

Her face softened with concern. "Of course not."

He had her now. Guilt was written all over her for selfishly worrying about herself when she should have been thinking about him.

The phone rang. He moved quickly. "I'll get it. Maybe it's Jack again."

It wouldn't be. It would be her mother, and with a little luck he could convince her she'd reached a wrong number a few minutes earlier.

He looked around the narrow smoke-hazed room. Besides the bartender, only three other guys occupied seats. Two leaned their elbows on the counter, silently watching the football game on the TV mounted on the wall at the end of the bar. The third stared straight ahead at the bottles lined up like bowling pins on mirror-backed shelves. Bunch of losers, all three. But he couldn't be picky.

It had been harder than he'd thought to find a place to hang out Christmas Day. Pool hall was closed. The Down and Under, closed. Even the Pink Pony had no lights on. But good old Oliver's was his salvation. Dump like this never shut down. It'd still be serving when Hell froze over. And it damn near had today. Colder than a witch's tit outside. Nearly as cold inside.

He ordered a Stroh's and a tequila shooter. "Turn the heat up a little, Bud."

"Can't," the barkeep said. "This is the best I can get out of that bitch of a heater. Usually so many bodies in here of a night, it don't matter."

Yeah. Body heat. The best kind. He'd sure like to happen onto some strange. He took a long drink from the bottle. Screwing Sarah was about as exciting as clipping your toenails. He watched the game even though he hated football. Always had. Better than sitting with the in-laws. Right about now, Sarah was explaining how he'd been called out to work. Her mother was probably making some cheerful noise of acceptance while her father sat in stony silence. Her dad wouldn't believe it. Not for a minute. Maybe he was watching this very same game. Unless they'd already called him in to carve the turkey. Roy Glen checked his watch. Too early. Definitely watching the game.

Roy Glen finished his shooter and ordered another set. Thinking about all he was missing—the chatter, the china, the ca-ching of the cash register—he could happily sit here doing shooters all afternoon.

Then Wendy walked in.

1974

On Thursday, Roy Glen came home on time, so Sarah tried to forget he'd been late every other night that week. She wanted to talk. Mandy's teething, bowel movements, and vocabulary, fascinating as they were, no longer occupied every waking moment of Sarah's day. If she didn't experience adult conversation with someone soon, she might explode.

She fetched him another glass of tea. "Nixon's going to have to release those tapes. Congress isn't gonna let him get by with claiming executive privilege forever."

His mouth curled up on one side. "These green beans taste like cardboard. Can't you learn to season them?"

She passed him salt and pepper. "Did you hear the Watergate burglars were paid off with money laundered in Mexico?" She snorted. "I can't believe he expects to get by with this crap even if he is president."

"I mean season them with a little salt pork."

"That stuff isn't good for you. Nothing but fat."

"Ask me if I care. I work all day while you sit home on your butt. The least you could do is fix beans the way I like them."

His words sucked all the air from her lungs. Because she did sit home on her butt all too often through the winter. What choice did she have? Someone had to watch Mandy. It wasn't like Sarah did nothing. She cooked, cleaned, did laundry, and was teaching Mandy her colors, numbers and alphabet.

Roy Glen scraped the beans into the trash. "I can't eat this crap." He handed her the plate.

She slammed his dirty dish onto the counter and filled the sink with water.

One Saturday morning in late August, Sarah canned tomatoes while Roy Glen slept. She traded stories for Mandy's promise to stay back from the kitchen, away from all things hot and harmful. Through the steam, she did her best to recreate the magic Aunt Livvie used to spin. Elves scampering through the tree canopy, fairies playing tricks, witches terrorizing all the good little creatures of the forest. Sarah boiled jars and lids, scalded and removed skins, cored, quartered, salted, packed, sealed, and water-bathed. By noon 48 quarts of tomatoes covered her counter and table. Her hair kinked like crazy from the humidity, but she smiled at her accomplishment. Two-year-old Mandy trotted off to use her potty chair by herself, something else that made Sarah proud.

Raking fingers across his scalp, Roy Glen emerged from the bedroom. "How about making yourself useful and fixing me some meatloaf. I have a hankering for a meatloaf sandwich."

She pushed back a damp tendril of hair from her cheek and continued to wipe down the jars with a clean towel. A man who came home drunk at 3 a.m. didn't have a right to hanker for anything. "Don't have any ground beef thawed."

"Why don't we make a little run to Krogers then? You've been spending too much on groceries. Make a list of everything you need this week and you won't have to go out again."

Great. She would need menus for the week and time to check every ingredient. And her one little outing on her own into the world would be wiped out.

"By the way, I don't want you picking up anything else from my parents' store. They can't offer the same discounts the big stores do."

"Won't their feelings be hurt?" They always seemed so happy to see her and Mandy.

"This is about financial management, not feelings."

Right. What would he know about feelings?

Mandy came back from pottying. "Me want merk, Mommy."

"Okay, squirt. Just a minute." She picked up the last jar and wiped it down.

Roy Glen opened the refrigerator and took out a gallon jug of milk. "I'll do it. I worked overtime yesterday, but I can still take care of the kid, and it's okay, because you're Daddy's little pumpkin, aren't you, sweetheart?"

Mandy nodded happily and accepted her cup.

Overtime, my ass. "Since when did they start serving Wild Turkey at the factory?"

His eyes cut over to her. "One drink to wet my whistle before I came home. You sure can bitch over nothing."

Kneeling to arrange the jars in the bottom of the pantry, she didn't bother to respond.

Roy Glen poured a glass of milk for himself and nudged Foster out of the way with his foot. "That dog stinks."

"Does not. Had a bath last week."

"He's getting too old. Old dogs always stink. We should put him out of his misery."

Through clenched teeth: "I'll give him another bath."

Before they went for groceries, Roy Glen stopped at a discount store. The heavy glass door was already whooshing shut behind him as Sarah finished unhooking Mandy from her car seat. Once inside, she took Mandy to look for new slacks.

Sarah tugged a tee-shirt over Mandy's head. "I'm going to cut off your merk if you don't quit growing so fast, Peanut."

"Un-uh. Me love merk."

"You must have grown two inches in the last two months. Pretty soon you'll be bigger than Jack's beanstalk."

As she pulled on matching slacks, Sarah noticed a rash on Mandy's waist. "What's this?"

"It's scatchy."

Sarah frowned. "You mean itchy. Remind me to put some calamine lotion on it when we get home." Sarah turned her daughter around to face the mirror to see the blue-flowered shirt with plain slacks dyed to match. "What do you think?"

"No, purpoo."

Of course she wanted purple, Sarah thought. If Mandy got her way, everything she owned would be purple. Sarah suggested buying both outfits.

Mandy nodded, bobbing ponytails tied with fat purple yarn. "Purpoo."

They bought Mandy's outfits, then found Roy Glen in the men's clothing department. An orange tag gleamed from the sweater in his hands: CLEARANCE $4.99. Roy Glen peeled it off. He tramped over to sporting goods without acknowledging Sarah as she trailed behind him. Behind him, beneath him, she thought—those were her places in life. What on earth was he doing? He stuck the tag on a fishing pole.

"Are you crazy? You're going to get caught." She knew he had learned to scrimp from his parents, who made very little money at their general store during the Depression. They were forced to extend credit to neighbors or know they weren't eating. Although the Hardmans were frugal to a fault, they were honest as far as she knew. She doubted they would approve of what he was doing.

"Shut up." He stomped toward the register.

Sarah and Mandy waited outside the big plate glass doors and watched from the sidewalk. The line moved slowly. First a college-aged woman returned a bedspread. The manager came to approve the transaction. Next a price tag was missing. Again the clerk signaled the manager.

Finally Roy Glen reached the register. When he plunked the pole down, Sarah held her breath. The clerk examined the clearance tag, frowning. Sarah closed her eyes. Fear settled like a stone in her stomach. When she opened her eyes, it was over. Roy Glen marched past her, fishing pole slung over his shoulder.

She ran to catch up. "I don't know how you could have done that."

He ignored her and addressed Mandy instead. "Your mommy is so naïve." He flicked his chin toward Sarah. "Your problem is you're spoiled. Never had to work for anything in your life. Never held a job, never had to worry about making ends meet. I'm trying to get the most for my money."

"It's one thing to hunt for bargains, but another—"

"A national chain can afford a little loss. You watch, few months from now, they'll cut the price on this pole anyway. Probably be less than what I paid."

Sarah stared out the side window, teeth clamped together. Who was this guy? Not the same man she thought she'd married.

She stayed two steps ahead of him in the grocery store and avoided speaking to him. He put back the brand of dog food she always bought for Foster and tossed a cheaper one in the cart. "You don't even try to compare brands."

She slung the bag he chose back onto the bottom shelf and restored the one she'd chosen to the cart. "I do compare. This one has meat as the first ingredient. Your brand is nothing but meat by-products and corn meal."

The muscles in Roy Glen's jaw were jumping. "He's a dog, for God's sake. He doesn't know the difference."

"I know the difference." Besides, Foster wasn't just a dog. He was an old friend.

After they unloaded groceries, they went to visit his parents, a Saturday ritual. Through her mother-in-law's kitchen window, she watched Roy Glen amble off toward the creek, the new fishing pole in one hand, Mandy's little hand in the other. She looked so cute with her own little pole slung over one shoulder. Sarah stayed behind to help Ellen make supper, privately stewing over the shoplifting, the late nights, the change in Roy Glen's attitude. Saturdays between noon and dinner were the only times she could count on seeing him. Not that she really saw him then. He disappeared into the garage or went hunting or fishing.

The way he talked to her was bad enough, but she always felt as if she deserved it. She couldn't forget she wasn't what he wanted. The shoplifting, though, crossed a line. It was no example for Mandy.

They returned home after supper, and she read *Goodnight Moon* aloud to Mandy, kissed her, and turned on the nightlight. Her feet padded down the hallway to the bedroom. As she changed into a nightgown, Roy Glen came in behind her and kissed her neck.

She shook him off. "We need to talk."

"Later."

"Now."

He pushed her onto the bed. It was useless. He didn't take no for an answer. A sense of loss enveloped her. Minutes later he rolled over and out of bed. He pulled on jeans.

"We have to talk."

He adjusted his pockets. "What about?"

"Why did you steal that stuff today in front of Mandy?"

Gold flecks in his eyes glittered in the low light. "I didn't steal, I switched prices."

"Same thing. Why would you do it?"

He raised his chin. "Because I can."

For several moments, they faced each other in silence, and Sarah couldn't bring herself to break it. So many things were unspoken. His drinking, the amount of overtime he worked—was it really overtime or was he going out God-knew-where all night? There was the word *sex*, which they never spoke aloud. There were unmentionable body parts. There was the word *love*, which they had said to each other, but not in a long while. Sorrow weighed down her tongue.

He went to the kitchen and grabbed his keys.

She followed, arms limp at her sides. "Don't go. We need to talk."

"Nothing to talk about." He turned away, muscles sleek and taut as a big cat's. He was so beautiful when he moved she couldn't help but love him. He was such a bastard she couldn't help but hate him.

"Talk to me."

He acted as if she hadn't spoken. She grabbed a glass from the counter and hurled it at his head. He ducked and it shattered against the wood paneling. "God damn it, talk to me."

He stared at her with empty eyes, the pupils pinholes. "That was really stupid. Now you have a mess to clean up." His voice was matter-of-fact, that same deep voice she'd fallen in love with. She despised its control now, when she wanted passion. A little anger. Something, anything to show he gave a damn.

He shut the door behind him. Sarah began to pick up the shards. Her heel came down on a shiny sliver. She pulled the glass out. Crossing the kitchen to get some paper towels, she left a red trail. One by one, she picked up the pieces from the Road Runner glass. If he thought he could break her with meanness, he was wrong. She could live with anyone. She could do it for Mandy. One day at a time.

When she finished cleaning up, she slipped into Mandy's room. Her daughter slept on, thumb in mouth, favorite blankie clutched in her other hand. She coughed in her sleep, a rasping sound from deep in her chest, and her eyes blinked open. Her fingers curled around Sarah's hand. Mandy fell back asleep instantly, if, indeed, she'd ever truly been awake. She coughed again, and her breathing sounded labored. Sarah went to her room and grabbed a blanket and her pillow. She folded her long legs into the small empty space at the bottom of the twin bed. Throughout the night she kept one hand against Mandy's back to feel her breath going in and out.

She couldn't shake the feeling something was wrong with her child, a feeling even more important than knowing something was wrong with her marriage.

Twenty-One

SPRING 1974

Watching Rita Watson's fat blue-jeaned butt jiggle around the track while she munched an apple depressed Roy Glen. Everyone in the factory knew her story. One day when Rita was eight, she had skipped along barefoot to Hazel Atlas with her father's lunch. They were short of help, so the foreman sent her home for shoes and put her to work. She was so short she had to stand on a box to wipe down the wares as they came off the line. Fifty years later, here she was, still slaving at the same job.

A dozen buildings sandwiched between a run-down neighborhood on the town's fringe and the four-lane, Hazel Atlas was the largest producer of tumblers and pressed glassware in the world. Whooptee shit.

Roy Glen took another hit of sweet pungent weed. A good long toke to ease the pain of contemplating fifty years at this crappy job. The three to eleven shift wasn't bad—it brought in an extra five cents an hour—and he didn't mind working holidays when his salary doubled to fourteen an hour. It was the work itself he hated. Standing on concrete floors in 120 degree heat in summer. Freezing his ass off in winter because all the heat went out the stacks. You couldn't even stop to get a drink of water or take a piss. Every two hours a relief worker spelled you ten minutes. You humped every second of those two hours to keep up with the machines. Yanking molds off on the fly to change up designs: ice teas, on-the-rocks, ash trays, candy dishes. The glass dropped automatically from overhead tubes and you'd better have the molds ready. You didn't dare let your mind wander.

Everywhere he turned, some old-timer was chewing and spitting. Said tobacco kept the glass dust out of their lungs. Chaw on the floor, chaw in their beards, chaw drooling from the corners of their mouths. Sometimes they missed the floor and spit on your boots.

College was a waste and he felt no desire to go back, though Sarah was nagging him about it. Said if he didn't like his job, he needed to learn to do something else. Said she could work while he finished school—yeah, right. As if he was the kind of guy who'd let his wife support him. Still, he couldn't imagine doing this for as long as Rita Watson. Weed was all that kept him sane. In two years of college, he somehow missed the marijuana revolution. Thank God it had found him now.

He held his doobie behind a pant leg as a tanker full of sand pulled into the lot. He was careful to hide it from Rita and her crew too. Didn't want Sarah's neighbor carrying tales to her folks.

Bobby snickered. "Whatcha hiding it for, buddy boy? You think those guys don't partake of a little now and then?"

"How would you know?"

"Who you think sells it to them?"

He probably did, for all Roy Glen knew, but why take chances? This job might bore him to tears, but he'd have a hard time finding another that paid as well in this dead-end town. Bobby was a little too careless about his habit for Roy Glen's taste, but then he didn't have a wife and a kid to feed.

Bobby must have guessed the direction of Roy Glen's thoughts. "How's Sarah?"

He shrugged. "Okay, I guess." Bobby always asked about Sarah. So what if he'd taken her to some dance another lifetime ago? And just because Bobby'd seen her talking to that guy Cal Thanksgiving Day didn't mean a damn thing. They were on a public street and the baby was with her, for chrissakes. Bobby had a big mouth. Didn't know when to keep it shut.

"What do you say we hit Oliver's after the shift, have a few drinks?" Bobby nudged Roy Glen in the ribs and wiggled his eyebrows. "Check out the females. It's ladies' night, buddy boy."

"Yeah, maybe." While Bobby rambled about a skinny girl he'd picked up in Oliver's the week before, Roy Glen was remembering slow dancing with a redhead in the Club Down and Under, testing out the spring of her behind, when he spotted Rachel and that fraternity boy of hers across the room. Even now, he flinched, remembering those hate-filled eyes. At least none of Sarah's friends would be likely to set foot in a dump like Oliver's. Not even her brother, who had seen him out in other bars. Obviously, Garrett had the good sense to keep it to himself.

Roy Glen took a deep drag, pinched his fingers over the burnt end, and pocketed the roach for later. He exhaled a cloud of smoke that looked like the exhaust coming from another tanker, which was rolling out toward the highway, having dropped its load in the silos beside the batch house.

The trouble was, Bobby thought he was some kind of Latin god. Judging by all the action he got—or said he got—women thought so, too. They must like his black hair, the Roman nose. Or maybe that wasn't what they liked at all. Maybe he was hung like a stallion. Roy Glen didn't know or care to know. He liked working the bars alone. He told women things with his eyes and they answered by jutting their breasts out a little further or cocking a hip to one side, sending sidelong glances his way while talking to their girlfriends. Same as saying the present conversation didn't matter a damn.

Still, Bobby was Roy Glen's supplier. It wouldn't pay to piss him off. And playing around at Oliver's would postpone going home.

With a major effort, he controlled the muscles in his jaw when Sarah greeted him. Same words every night. *Hi honey, how was your day, that's too bad, Mandy did this or that today.*

Sleep-disheveled and clad in a pink nightshirt, his wife leaned over him and set a plate of meatloaf and mashed potatoes on the yellow tablecloth, centering it precisely between the fork on one side and the knife and spoon on the other. She apologized because the food might be dry from holding it in the oven so long. Why didn't she come out and say it was 2:30, kind of late to be getting in? Why was she up anyhow?

"Yeah, I put in some overtime."

"Good," she said, "we can put the extra money toward the house."

The dream house. She never let him forget. The potatoes had crusted over, but he didn't care. He needed something in his stomach besides tequila and beer.

Down the hallway Mandy coughed. Explained why Sarah was awake.

"I took Mandy to the doctor's today," Sarah said. "He said she probably had a respiratory infection and put her on penicillin."

One thing in Sarah's favor was that she was a good mother. Sometimes he watched them together. Once when Mandy cuddled on Sarah's lap, Sarah closed her eyes, pressing the child into her, one hand against the side of Mandy's head, the other around her back. When Sarah opened her eyes this light was glowing, not only in her eyes, but all over, like you could see love coming off her in waves, and he felt like someone pinged his ribs.

The mashed potatoes nearly stuck in his throat as he tried to picture Sarah behaving the way Bobby described tonight. Absolutely impossible.

He and Bobby were sitting at a table next to the bar. It was so dark Roy Glen could barely make out Bobby's pock-marked face. Or maybe the four tequila shooters he'd done between beers had something to do with it. He wished the bartender would wipe their table off. His left hand kept sticking to it when he exposed it so the females would notice: no ring. The band's lousy imitation of Led Zeppelin only enticed one couple to the dance floor. Roy Glen only half-listened to Bobby bragging about his latest pick-up. A raven-haired woman with large breasts and an ass as round as two ripe melons stood next to the bar, laughing with an overweight redhead. It was so obvious she wasn't really interested in her friend. She was putting on a show. Wanting to get laid. He could smell her lust ten yards away.

"After the dance, see, we went parking," Bobby said. "So, there we were, in the back seat. And then we started making out, buddy boy, and let me tell you—" Bobby's voice rose in exuberance and he slapped his palm against the sticky table "—that girl was an animal, she was a fucking animal."

Roy Glen's full attention swung back to Bobby. The asshole was talking about Sarah, snicker-snorting in that silly way some people can't help when they've been smoking too much. What kind of moron tells a man something like that about his wife? And it couldn't be Sarah he was talking about. She was the least sexed woman on earth. She did the deed with all the same enthusiasm she mustered for doing a load of laundry. Hell, she made the bed with more enthusiasm than she displayed for any act she ever performed in it. Proved Bobby was ninety percent mouth, ten percent action, as Roy Glen suspected.

"So did you stick it to my wife?" Roy Glen kept his voice emotionless.

Bobby blinked. In a moment: "Hell, no." When Roy Glen didn't look away, he added, "Of course not."

Roy Glen let his eyes move slowly from Bobby's eyes, down to his chin, creep up to his forehead, then crawl across one cheek, then the other, without saying a word.

Bobby blinked again and threw back another shot of tequila. He laughed nervously. Roy Glen would have been surprised by any other reaction. Bobby stumbled all over himself, trying to cover his confusion. "You're a lucky man, that's all I'm saying, buddy boy. Am I right? Admit it."

Roy Glen didn't know what Bobby expected. Bedroom stories about him and Sarah? More like bored-room stories. You could tell Bobby'd never been married.

Roy Glen's chair scraped against the floor as he got up. "Yeah, sure, I'm a lucky man to be sitting in this dumpy bar with you." The band slowed the tempo down with a little Dylan. "Lay, Lady, Lay." Oh, yeah, he was waiting for a belly-grinder. As he passed the bartender, Roy Glen picked up a book of matches, black with gold lettering. Classy. Only thing classy about this dump. He tucked the matches in his jeans pocket. He only took them home if he scored, and tonight was a sure thing.

He approached the melon-butt, brushed his arm against her leg as if attempting to pass behind her, mumbled an excuse, stopped, his thigh pressed against hers. "Care to dance?"

While Roy Glen ate, Sarah returned to bed, her face toward the wall. He undressed quickly and rolled her over toward him, pulled her nightshirt up, and pushed his groin into her.

Melon-butt was a good lay, as horny as he'd expected. He had squeezed fistfuls of her breasts as he sat on her. She bucked hard against him, crying out as she came. And then he'd taken her again, ramming into that lush behind. Damn, if she hadn't come again.

His wife, on the other hand, barely woke up. Where was the animal Bobby talked about? He wanted some of that. Thing is, what if Bobby was right? Sarah claimed she'd only been with one guy. That

Cal. Roy Glen could never forget watching them kiss. Cal made the rounds in the bars these days. He supposed the fellow was good looking enough, but he had one hell of a drinking problem. Always stoned. What had she been like with him? What if it was only her husband who couldn't make her come? He had been convinced she didn't even know what an orgasm was. Now he wasn't sure. He rammed harder, Bobby's words repeating in his mind as he moved: She was a fucking animal. But it was no tiger beneath him now. More like a rabbit. He grunted with his release and rolled off Sarah. He couldn't imagine fifty years of fucking Sarah any more than he could imagine being one of the old-timers spitting chaw at the factory fifty years from now.

His wife crawled across his body. The last thing he heard before sleep was water crashing into the bathroom sink and Mandy coughing. The latter probably meant Sarah wouldn't come back to bed the rest of the night.

The next day while he showered for work, he couldn't stop thinking about Bobby's story. He toweled off roughly and dressed in the company uniform. As he tied on his steel-toed boots, he kept imagining her with Bobby. She didn't look like an animal, not as she poured milk into his thermos. She looked like a housewife and mother. Normal.

"Someone I work with knows you," he said. "Went to high school with you."

Sarah tucked a peanut butter sandwich into a re-used plastic bag. "Yeah? Who?"

"Bobby Marchio. Says he knows you real well."

She blinked and handed him his lunch kit. "Not really. We had a class or two together."

"He says you dated."

"We only went out once, a double date to a dance."

Her eyes flicked away. Was she lying? "Yeah? Well, he sure remembers it like it was yesterday."

She shook her head and stared right at him. "Really? I can't imagine why. Have a nice day and drive carefully."

She pecked him on the cheek, the way a wife should. He didn't believe Bobby Marchio, not really. He was bullshitting, like he did at the clubs. He didn't get half the action he claimed.

A monsoon was roiling in Sarah's gut. What had Bobby Marchio told Roy Glen? Bobby was the worst thing to happen to Sarah her senior year. Her neighbor, Jimmy Watson, told her Bobby didn't want to ask her out because she was a goody-two-shoes. She was crushed. When the girl Bobby first asked to a school dance accepted a date with someone else, Bobby asked Sarah. She decided to forget she was second choice. Not only did they dance and laugh all night, but she got her first kiss during a slow song. She sent up a big Thank-You-God. Now she wouldn't be the only girl in America to graduate high school unkissed (except for one game of spin-the-bottle in grade school, which didn't count, and the time Cal kissed her scraped arm, which didn't count either).

After the dance Jimmy drove out a country road and parked. He and Paula began to make out. In the back seat Bobby's kiss, so tender at the dance, transformed. His teeth gnashed against her enamel ferociously. She thought surely Jimmy and Paula could hear his teeth grinding. To her, the noise was deafening. She peeked at them to see if they noticed, but they were preoccupied. Was this gnashing normal? She had no idea. She wanted to lose the goody-two-shoes label, so she let him go on kissing her. In the car on the way home, she ran her tongue over her teeth to see if they were permanently damaged. At home, she checked them in a mirror. Her lips felt bruised, brutalized.

A few days later Jimmy told her any further dates with Bobby were out of the question. Jimmy eyed her with disgust. "He said you were an animal. What were you thinking?"

She was so stunned she couldn't answer.

Twenty-Two

SUMMER 1974

Sarah suspected Roy Glen had stolen the amber ashtray on the kitchen table from Hazel Atlas, though he said not. Most nights he tossed matchbooks into it. The latest was another shiny black square with a gold Oliver's logo in a typeface she recognized from her journalism training as Mistral. Very classy. The ashtray held matchbooks from every bar in town. Holiday Inn. Ramada. Down and Under. The Hole in the Wall.

"If we don't have enough money for me to buy a new pair of tennis shoes, why can you always find plenty to waste in these bars?" she asked.

He pulled on his beard. It looked scraggly, as if someone doodled on his face. "I earn it. If I spend a little on a drink now and then, that's my business."

Sarah studied him, the afternoon light casting harsh shadows on his face. "Are you with other women? Is that why you come home so late?"

He didn't blink. "I think you'd be grateful for the long hours I work to take care of you and Mandy. That's what it's all about. You and Mandy. What else do you want from me? I like to have a drink with the guys afterward."

He walked over to the bookcase and pushed a few volumes around until he found the Bible and laid his hand on it. "I swear, no other women. Now do you feel better?"

She did, though only a little. Drinking she understood. She grew up around it. Her husband used her body almost every night no matter what time he came in, so surely he must not be getting it elsewhere. But she wished if he had to drink, he would do it at home the way her father did.

"Why do you bring home matches? You don't smoke."

He scratched his ear. "They're free. Besides, you never know when you'll need a match. The pilot light goes out on the stove, you reach for one of these." He picked up a packet for emphasis and tossed it back in the pile. He gave her a look that said she was stupid for not figuring it out. "Keeps you from buying them at the grocery store. You spend enough as it is."

Free or not, Sarah didn't like them sitting on her kitchen table, but she let it drop. She felt powerless to change him, and the only alternative was to leave, a thought that pinned her to a chair with fear. She would have to admit she'd failed at the most important endeavor of her life: making a family. And what would she do without Roy Glen's health insurance? Mandy was always going to the doctor's for one thing or another. A rash, a cold, a cough. So Sarah closed her eyes to the matchbooks and pinched her nostrils against the feral odors Roy Glen wore like an invisible cloak when he finally crawled into bed.

After he left for work, she took out the photo album and flipped through to her favorite shot. A rear view of Roy Glen loping along beside Mandy, fishing poles slung over their shoulders. And another: Mandy serving her daddy a heart-shaped cake from her Easy-Bake oven. And Roy Glen lying on the couch, Mandy suspended over his chest, delight painted on both their faces. The day Sarah snapped the photo, he said, *We can never get a divorce.*

Why? Though she knew what was coming, she wanted to hear him say it.

He wiggled Mandy in the air. *This is why. I will never let her go.*

At the time, his adoration pleased Sarah. Now it worried her. She would never let Mandy go either.

She put the album away and withdrew her new purchase from its hiding place: the Masters and Johnson sex manual. She needed to find out what was wrong with her. A few pages in, she encountered a new word: orgasm. And more words. Foreplay and premature ejaculation. Maybe the problem wasn't hers alone.

Change required a plan.

Roy Glen heard the front door open and close as he got out of the shower. Sarah, home from her mother's, no doubt. He wondered what she brought with her this time. It was always something. Tupperware filled with some crazy kind of Jello. A sweater her mother picked up on sale for Sarah. A Mrs. Beasley doll or new jeans for Mandy. Her folks still didn't think he could support his family.

While he was toweling off, Sarah came in the bathroom dressed in some kind of black lacy underwear with a little pink rosebud between the cups of the bra and his Thing leapt up immediately. She leaned into Roy Glen and slipped her tongue in his mouth and squeezed his butt.

What was this about? His brain didn't have time to dwell on it too much. Her hands climbed all over him and her breath was hot. He pushed her toward the bedroom, only as they approached the bed, she shoved him down and climbed on top. He felt like he'd dropped into some alien world as she gyrated, her breasts still encased in black lace, her panties unsnapped at the crotch—unsnapped! Several bar-flies he'd met liked sitting astride, but never in a million years had he thought of Sarah trying something like this. It was demeaning be-ing underneath a woman. He pushed her over on her back and took charge and ended things to his satisfaction.

His pleasure was short-lived. She was supposed to be a mother. His own had never worn any kind of underwear but white. Big sen-sible garments that hung unashamedly on the clothesline. She would never behave this way. And before he could stop it, a picture of Sarah kissing Cal, her hair all long and wet and wild, rose in his mind. Roy Glen wondered when Sarah bought this underwear and who taught her these new tricks. Maybe she picked up men in grocery stores. Maybe she was doing something to his babies. If she wasn't, she would have been pregnant again by now.

Roy Glen seized her shoulders. "Where'd you learn to act like that?"

Tears welled up in her eyes. He shoved her away from him and grabbed his pants. He knew he should—wished he could—say he didn't mean it, he was sorry, but he couldn't. He didn't have a clue what he wanted anymore.

After the first ten minutes, Mandy tired of fishing, but she was easy to entertain. Roy Glen squatted beside her and showed her a box turtle crawling along the creek bank. It had a pretty shell, forest green with sand-colored lines that formed pentagons, polygons, and rectangles.

"Where's its head?" Mandy asked.

"Inside the shell."

"Why?"

"He pulls it in when he gets scared. To protect himself."

Head cocked slightly to one side, she peered intently into the shell. "Widdle turtle, come out."

Mandy tickled Roy Glen and simultaneously almost brought tears to his eyes. For the first time in his life, he knew there was something he would die for. He'd never felt that way about his country, certainly not enough to go to Nam. In a religious fervor when he was twelve and joined the church, he might have felt inspired for a few weeks, but it hadn't lasted. Too many thou shalt not's. But Mandy's voice, so innocent and serious, those fat cheeks—she was worth his last breath.

Following Mandy's nap, Saturday afternoons belonged to the two of them. And days didn't get better than this one. Head cradled in his hands, Roy Glen lay back on the creek bank, breathing in the scent of moss and mud, his rod propped beside him in a bucket wedged between some rocks. If anything struck, he'd know it. Creek was up some. Early summer rains. Overcast. Good day for fishing. He'd pulled out a couple bluegill already. In a cherry tree across the creek, a mockingbird ran through its songs: cheep cheep, twerp twerp, purty, purty, purty, twitter. He closed his eyes. Heard Mandy offer the turtle a piece of grass.

"Good God, Roy Glen, you're supposed to be watching her. She could've drowned." Sarah smothered Mandy against her chest.

How did Sarah creep up on him like that? "I wasn't asleep."

"You were. You didn't even open your eyes when I walked up."

Maybe not, but he wasn't asleep. He'd have known if anything was happening to Mandy. He sat up and took his rod apart so he wouldn't have to look at his wife. "She's fine. You baby her too much."

"She is a baby."

"Two and then some isn't a baby."

"You don't get it. You have to keep your eyes on her all the time."

"Me and her were getting along fine. I would never let anything hurt her." Why was his wife here? This was supposed to be his time with Mandy. "Thought you were helping my mother pick strawberries for shortcake."

"We finished. Already made the shortcake and whipped the cream. Good thing too. No telling what might've happened if I hadn't come along."

"Nothing would've happened. We were having fun, weren't we, Peanut? Tell Mommy about the turtle."

Mandy squirmed to get down and tugged her mother toward the turtle. "The turtle hided his head 'cause he was scared."

Roy Glen thought the turtle had the right idea. Sometimes the world got too annoying.

"What scared him?" Sarah asked.

"Me and Daddy. We tried to feed him."

Sarah tugged Mandy's hand. "We gotta go now. Grandma said we're having an early dinner."

As Roy Glen gathered up their gear, he watched Sarah walk away, Mandy riding on her hip. They were so beautiful he ached. He would never do anything to hurt Mandy. But the turtle was yards away from where he and Mandy first saw it. Maybe he had fallen asleep. He vowed it would never happen again. He'd never forgive himself if she got hurt.

Twenty-Three

FALL AND WINTER 1974

"Why not?"

"Because I say so."

Sarah didn't know how to argue if Roy Glen wouldn't even explain his objections to Rachel and Paula coming out to visit. "That's not fair."

"I pay the bills, it's my house, and I'll decide who comes here."

Now she wished she hadn't told him about Rachel's call. She never dreamed he'd object. "What am I supposed to tell them?"

"That's your problem."

She lay awake most of the night, wondering if she could find the nerve to let them come. How would he know? Even as she asked herself the question, she knew she couldn't do it. Somehow he would know. He'd see it in her face. She wasn't afraid of him, exactly, but there was something in the coldness of his eyes, the way his muscles tensed. The next morning she called Rachel and said she was in bed with the flu. She coughed a few times and tried to sound sick. Rachel became so solicitous Sarah felt guilty.

Next Roy Glen didn't want her to go to the grocery store without him. Said he wanted to help pick out the food. On Mondays an hour before he left for work, he drove her and Mandy to Krogers. If she needed anything else during the week, she could tell him and he'd stop on the way home from work at Quik Mart.

As he pushed the buggy through Krogers, he told her he would prefer if she didn't go to her mother's so often either. Once a month was enough. "Gas is too expensive."

"Not that expensive." But the price had doubled over the past year. Since the OPEC embargo, she could only fill up every other day. Even and odd numbered license plates alternated. Lines of cars at the pumps linked bumper to bumper down an entire block like a train.

"Besides," he added, "the Chevy's getting too many miles on it. You about wore it out finishing your degree. It wasn't meant for running errands. It's a racing machine."

He hadn't been to a race since they married. It was hard to justify driving if you weren't going somewhere. She set a gallon of milk in the buggy. "Maybe we should trade it in for something practical. Something that uses less gas."

His eyes bored into her. "Why can't you understand I put my heart and soul into that machine? Besides, if you quit running around so much, maybe you'd get pregnant. Mandy needs a little brother or sister."

She pretended interest in the label on the fruit cocktail. The IUD was still her secret. "What's visiting my parents have to do with it?"

He snatched the can from her hand and chucked it into the buggy. "All I know is you should be pregnant again by now."

Much as she loved Mandy, she was glad another kid wasn't on the way. The trailer walls were closing in on her. Another kid would only make her feel more trapped inside a small box.

Over the next weeks, snow enveloped the world in silence, erasing even the tire tracks marking the way to their nearest neighbors. So Sarah turned on *General Hospital* and *Another World* and talked back to Phil Donahue. She chatted with Mandy and Foster too, but there were days when she thought she'd go crazy. The grocery store would have been a great adventure.

Her mother phoned. "Aunt Livvie's feeling pretty low these days. She can't get used to living alone."

"I know."

"You might pay her a visit. I know she'd appreciate it."

Sarah wanted to scream: *I can't.* Instead, with great effort she controlled her voice. "Roy Glen won't let me drive if there's even a chance of snow." That blasted '57 Chevy was too precious.

"No snow predicted today."

It wasn't as if she set out to tell her mother. She didn't want to lay her problems on someone else, but the words flew out before she could tether them. "Roy Glen checks the mileage. He allows me enough for a visit to your house once a month, and even then he fusses."

The silence on the other end seemed to last forever. Finally her mother said, "I wish you'd have told me sooner. We thought it was us, that we'd done something wrong."

"No, it's not you." The last thing she wanted was to hurt her parents. "It's Roy Glen. I don't know what's gotten into him."

Half an hour later, her mother picked her up. On the drive Sarah worried someone would see her, someone would tell Roy Glen. They visited Livvie first.

"Stop," her mother said as they sat with Livvie in her kitchen. Sarah froze. "What?"

"You're biting your nails again."

Sarah looked at her cuticles, red and raw and ragged. She curled her fingers into her fists.

Later in the afternoon, as Sarah made the dinner salad, her mother poked her between the shoulder blades. "If you don't start standing up straight, you're going to be as hump-backed as Katherine was." Sarah tried to stand taller but felt like hunching in even more.

Garrett and his new girlfriend, Alisa, joined them for dinner. Six years older than Garrett, Alisa was divorced with a little boy, who was visiting his father that night. Sarah stared at Alisa more often than politeness allowed. Alisa was prettier than average with long auburn hair. She didn't look wounded or ruined or pitiful. She looked—normal.

Sarah couldn't stop talking, partly because she was starved for conversation and partly to cover up her father's stony disapproval of Garrett's girl. What did Alisa think of the new show, *Wheel of Fortune*? Sarah kind of liked it. Thank heavens Ford was sticking by his promise not to re-enter the Vietnam conflict. Last thing we needed was to escalate that mess again. And gasoline—why couldn't anyone stop OPEC from raising prices? What did they think of that new lady in Britain? Margaret Thatcher? About time a woman rose to the top.

Through Sarah's questions and Nelson's silence, Alisa remained charming and fielded intelligent answers.

After Garrett returned from taking Alisa home, Nelson started in. Why did his son want used when he could get fresh? Why would he want to take on another man's responsibilities? Why date a loser? When her father finished, without raising his voice, Garrett said he didn't give a damn if his father liked Alisa or not. He liked her and nothing else mattered. "Don't waste your time telling me as long as I live under your roof, I'll do what you say. I'm moving out. I've already signed a lease on an apartment."

After graduation, Garrett had landed a good job at an insurance firm, so it was time for him to venture out on his own, but the whole scene made Sarah sick.

Johanna drove Sarah and Mandy home. This became their weekly routine on her mother's day off. Sneaky, but Sarah didn't think Roy Glen could find out. The thought that he might sent her nails between her teeth.

At three in the morning, Mandy spewed cherry-flavored syrup all over Sarah's nightgown. Armed with another spoonful of antibiotic, Sarah tilted her daughter's chin upward, gently rubbing her throat until she swallowed. The maneuver resulted in tears and a temper tantrum that only worsened Mandy's breathing. Roy Glen wasn't home yet. That piece-of-shit was out drinking again. She knew it. She didn't allow herself to think about what else he might be doing. She settled Mandy back into the twin bed and curled in beside her. This cold was lingering far longer than it should.

Something was wrong. She knew it in the way all mothers know such things. The persistent coughing. The rashes. Try this ointment, the doctor said. A baking soda bath, her mother offered. Get you this ointment they put on cow udders—it works when nothing else does, Rita said. Her dad suggested a spoonful each of honey, water, and bourbon for the cough. But nothing worked.

Where the hell was Roy Glen? Why wasn't he ever home so she could discuss it with him? He didn't care about them—either of them—or he'd be here. Mandy settled back into a troubled sleep, her breathing labored and broken by periodic fits of coughing. An hour later, Sarah woke again, muscles sore from lying cramped and still in Mandy's bed. The bastard still wasn't home. She wished he was there so she could rake her fingernails down his face. She wished he was dead. It was the only decent excuse she could think of for his not being home at this hour, and she knew he wasn't dead. The bastard was drinking in some bar.

But he could be dead. His truck could have slid off the road and flipped, its roof caved in. He could have broken ribs or a cracked collarbone. A crushed spleen, a smashed forehead. Here she was wishing he was dead, and he might be. Tears slipped down her face. Mandy slept quietly now, so Sarah crept back to her own bed, her stomach twisted with guilt. Then she heard the crunch of his tires on the gravel. She looked at the clock. A quarter of five. Her hands knotted into fists. She pretended to be asleep when he came in, but he knew. She was sure he knew. The sheets vibrated with her anger. For once, he didn't insist on sex.

The next week he noticed tire tracks where the gravel thinned. Said they weren't his. Muscles jumped in his cheeks. "You having guys in while I'm at work?"

She felt faint. "No, of course not."

"Whose are they?"

"I don't know." Her mother's, but of course she couldn't admit it. "Your parents came over to see Mandy last week. Maybe the tracks belong to them." The Hardmans had visited. It was possible. He let it drop, but from then on, she had her mother park at the end of the drive and honk.

When she closed her eyes, she could see the jut of his jawline, held her breath as she remembered the way those muscles twitched.

Twenty-Four

FALL 1975

Mandy leaned forward on the couch, Raggedy Ann pressed between her chest and knees. "Mommy, I don't feel good." Mandy pointed to her chest. "Hurts here."

Her breath wheezed and whistled. Sarah kissed her forehead. No fever. Three rounds of antibiotics and still the child hacked. "Let's go see Dr. Jorgansen."

The waiting room was packed with patients of all ages because the doctor did it all. Delivered people from their mother's womb at the beginning of life and delivered them to the morgue at the end. In between, he made them feel better. Sarah pushed through the room, only vaguely aware of the smells of liniment, infant formula, oozing wounds, and germy old magazines with curled up corners.

As patiently as she could, Sarah explained to the fish-faced new receptionist behind the glass window she didn't have an appointment because it was an emergency. An emergency which, she thought, would be obvious to anyone with even a modicum of intelligence.

"I'll see if the doctor can work her in," fish-face said, "but he's really busy today."

Mandy wheezed and clutched at Raggedy Ann, eyes wild with fear. Each inhale seemed more desperate than the last. Her fingernails were lilac.

Sarah held Mandy toward the receptionist. "Listen to her. She can't breathe. He has to see her now."

Not waiting for the secretary to explain why it wasn't possible, Sarah stalked over to the door marked "Employees Only." Bull. It was only the door a nurse opened to escort you to an inner cubicle where patients waited all over again. She threw it open. She stalked to the nurses' station. The receptionist followed, protesting. A red-haired nurse Sarah recognized approached.

"It's okay," the nurse said to the receptionist. She whisked Mandy out of Sarah's arms and asked the receptionist to get Mandy's chart. "Let's go on back to a room, little lady. Come on, Mom."

The nurse sent for Dr. Jorgansen. He listened to Mandy's chest with a stethoscope, frowning. He barked instructions to the nurse, who left. He scanned her chart, flipping through the pages. "Third respiratory infection this year. I want to run some tests, but I think asthma is the problem. Linda is setting up a breathing treatment, if you'll come with me, we'll see if it's ready."

Dr. Jorgansen instructed Sarah to hold Mandy on her lap and lean her head toward the mist coming from the machine. In minutes, Mandy's wheezing noticeably lessened in intensity.

"We'll want a blood workup and a chest x-ray, Dr. Jorgansen was saying. Sarah tried to focus, close to collapsing with relief.

"Thank you, doctor. Thank you." She was teary eyed. Right then she would have willed over everything she owned to the man.

He smiled. "Glad we could help. I delivered this one. I'm going to give you a prescription, which I want her to take every day. Never miss a dose. And if her coloring ever shades to blue like this again, I want you to call an ambulance immediately. I suspect allergies are probably part of her problem."

"Oh, God, it's not the dog, is it?" She couldn't imagine having to get rid of Foster.

"Not likely. He's been around since she was born, hasn't he? More likely food or mold or even dust. We'll run some tests but we may never know what it is."

He asked the nurse to make an appointment for the next day. "Give Mrs. Hardman all the pamphlets we have so she can read them tonight."

When they left the doctor's office, Sarah drove straight to her mother's.

She carried Mandy through the familiar yellow kitchen, half afraid to put her down, as if a mother's arms warded off all danger. "You won't believe our little afternoon adventure. We spent the last two hours in the doctor's office."

Her mother turned off the oven. "What?"

Sarah's father came in from the living room. "Thought I heard you in here. What's wrong?"

Sarah pushed aside her daughter's bangs and kissed her forehead. "Mandy has asthma."

Nelson held out his arms. "Come to Grandpa, little sweetheart. How you feeling?"

Her mother's hands flew to her mouth. "Oh my God, all the coughing, of course."

Mandy pushed her lower lip out. "Nana, I been coughing bad."

They huddled together on the couch, Johanna on one side of Sarah and her father, who held Mandy on his lap, on the other. Johanna's weight depressed the cushions so deeply Sarah rolled downhill until she rested against her mother's comforting bulk.

Sarah pulled a half dozen pamphlets out of her purse. "Look at all the stuff the doctor gave me." She read the pamphlets aloud, pausing to ask her mother for clarification now and then.

"I'm not a nurse, you know, I only work in x-ray, so I don't know much more about this than you do."

No matter what her mother said, Sarah trusted her more than anyone else in the world. She was the rock. She'd managed to get Sarah and Garrett to adulthood without them being killed by some childhood disease and without them killing each other. No small feat.

Johanna patted Sarah's arm. "She's going to be fine. Your cousin Kenny had asthma and outgrew it." Sarah hadn't known, but then she had only met Kenny once.

It wasn't until they'd eaten a late dinner that Sarah thought to call Roy Glen at work. When she rang the factory, a receptionist offered to take a message. "Tell him Mandy is sick and we're staying at my mother's."

"Here's some news," her mother said. "Pete's back in town again. Staying with Livvie."

"Where's he been all this time?"

"Don't know. Didn't ask."

Pete drifted from town to town, as far as Sarah could tell, governed by rhythms and cycles known only to him. Just him and his shopping buggy and the highway. Perhaps his movements were dictated by inner voices. Sarah knew he heard them—he wasn't talking to himself but to someone or something else. His parents were dead now—Mahlon and the mysterious Ava—but at one time Pete's mother must have cradled him against those beautiful breasts, full of dreams for her son, the same kind of dreams Sarah cherished for Mandy. She must have ached watching his struggle.

That night Sarah lay beside her daughter in bed, listening for a long while to the labored rise and fall of her daughter's breath, ready to give her daughter her own breath if necessary. Her father drove to her trailer and brought back Foster. The dog lay at the foot of the bed as if he, too, wanted to keep watch.

"You spent a lot of money this month." This, on Tuesday at noon when Roy Glen examined the checkbook.

Mandy required daily medication. Also Dr. Jorgansen told Sarah to buy only fragrance- and dye-free detergents and tissues. The rashes, he thought, were from allergies, known triggers for asthma. So far, their intervention was working. Only one bad attack of wheezing following the doctor's visit, but fear gripped Sarah every time her daughter coughed in the night. Sarah's father took his cigarettes outside to avoid exposing Mandy to smoke. Her mother quit smoking completely, but unfortunately was putting on even more weight.

"All the extra money I spent was on Mandy's meds. What about you?"

He didn't answer.

Twenty-Five

Spring 1976

Sarah's mother finally persuaded Livvie to get her digestive complaints checked out, even made the appointment herself. "But I can't take her; I have to work," Johanna said. "Can you drive her?"

Sarah didn't even have to think about it. If Livvie needed her, she would be there. Aunt Maggie had been the only driver in the family. Not even Uncle Mahlon adapted to the age of the automobile. The Heimbachs rode streetcars or walked.

"You sure it's okay? Roy Glen won't get mad?"

"If he does, he'll have to get over it."

Roy Glen's parents agreed to watch Mandy at their store. In the morning, Sarah walked inside with Mandy, enjoying the way the wooden floor creaked like an old friend. The store was an eclectic mix of farmer's market and general store. You could buy everything from Slinkys and wooden puzzles to locally grown strawberries and headache tablets. Ordinarily, Sarah enjoyed browsing, but this time she left in a hurry, looking back only to notice how easily Ellen distracted Mandy by having her stack cans of tomatoes on a low shelf.

Sarah parked the Chevy in front of the Aunt Hill, and there on the porch Livvie waited in a navy pillbox hat and matching dress. And brown spike heels. Good Lord, Sarah swore to herself. She got out and yelled, "Stay there. I'm coming up."

She clutched the glass casserole filled with her mother's Orange Creamsicle gelatin and ran up the steps.

"You can't go in those shoes," she said as she reached the porch.

"What?" Livvie looked down at her feet. She laughed. "Oh, I didn't mean to put these on. I meant to put on my navy shoes."

And the heels were probably as high. "Let's go back inside, and

I'll help you find another pair." Like it or not, her aunt was not going down those stairs in spikes. Her pride would give way or she would end up in a body cast, and how stylish was that?

Sarah slapped cheese between buttered bread slices and put them in a frying pan. It seemed a strange role reversal, fixing food for her aunt while Livvie watched from the red oilcloth-covered chair. All through junior high, Sarah had walked to the Heimbachs' at lunchtime for homemade vegetable soup or egg salad on whole wheat. Livvie could make even canned soup seem gourmet.

Pete thumped down the stairs, his hair sprung out as if he'd been standing in front of a fan. A wrinkled plaid shirt flopped over dirt colored slacks. He wore socks, no shoes, and smelled as if he needed to change underwear.

"Where've you been?" he asked.

"Doctor's," Livvie said.

He grunted and moved behind Sarah. "What you fixing?"

Sarah smashed the toasted bread down with a spatula. "Grilled cheese. You want one?"

She fixed his sandwich while Livvie told Pete about her office visit. Dr. Jorgansen drew blood, but the test results wouldn't be back until the following week. He wrote Livvie a prescription he hoped would ease her stomach pain. He wanted her to get more tests done at the hospital, but she refused.

Pete took a few bites and washed them down with a cola. "You should do what he tells you." Toast crumbs jiggled in his mustache.

"That's what I told her."

"What good would it do?" Livvie said. "No matter how the doctor pokes and prods at me, I'm still going to die whenever the good Lord is ready."

Livvie stood firm against their arguments, and eventually they gave up.

Pete spooned out a second helping of gelatin, stirring up the sweet scent of mandarin oranges. "I'm looking for work. Heard of any jobs around here?"

He seemed normal at the moment, but Sarah remembered how he'd gone whacky over red flowers at the funeral home. "What kind of work you looking for?"

"Anything. I'm good at math, and I'm retired from the United States Army, you know, so I got experience."

True, but how much of his experience translated into civilian jobs? She wasn't sure. "I don't know of anything, but I'll let you know if I hear of any leads."

This seemed to be a good time to float her idea on the family. See how they took it. "I'm thinking about getting a job too."

"Are you now?" Livvie said. "Why?"

"Guess I'd feel more secure. That I could take care of Mandy if anything happened to Roy Glen." Or if she ever decided to leave him. And truth was, there was even more to it than that. No matter how much she loved her child, she was starved for adult conversation. For mental stimulation. For more connection to other people.

"I see. What will you do with Mandy?" Livvie asked.

"Haven't figured that out yet."

"My sister's started a nursery school," Pete said.

Livvie's laugh trilled across the table as she put her hand to her forehead. "Oh, that's right. Slipped my mind. I'd forget my head if wasn't attached."

"Really, Martha Rose started a business?" Sarah responded out of politeness. Martha Rose lived in Oklahoma or Iowa or somewhere out West. In the back of her mind, she also filed the puzzle of Livvie's memory lapse. It wasn't like her.

"Yep," Pete said. "She and her husband and kid—they got a kid now—bet you didn't know that. They moved here a few months ago, and she started this business. All the spots filled soon as it opened. I think she's going to do real good for herself."

Sarah barely knew Martha Rose, hadn't even known she was in Clarksburg—something else Livvie had forgotten? It wouldn't hurt to call. Get on a wait list. She reconsidered. What would she say? *Hi, remember me, your cousin who has never called you in your life before but I'm calling you now because I want something?* It would take courage—or gall—to contact Martha Rose.

Livvie's eyes closed and her head listed to the left. She jerked awake.

Sarah kissed Livvie's cheek. Her skin felt as dry and fragile as a winter leaf. "You'd better go ahead upstairs and take your nap. I'll clean up these dishes before I go."

She started to collect the spoons, but Pete took them from her hands. "Do I look helpless? I'll do them. You go pick up your little girl. Ask your dad if he knows of any math jobs. I'm good at math. And don't forget about me if you hear of anything. I'm not scared of hard work.

She was sure he wasn't, but she was scared for him. Florists and funeral homes were out. What job could guarantee no red flowers? And who knew what other triggers fired up Pete? She hoped he found work, but it wasn't her responsibility.

Livvie pushed her chair back from the table. "Come upstairs with me. There's a story I'd like to tell you about my mother. Heimbach women have always worked when they needed to. My mama wasn't always a nanny."

Twenty-Six

On the nine hundred and sixth day of her servitude—eight months into Mrs. Godwin's fourth pregnancy when she and the children went into confinement at her mother's home—Mr. Godwin crept into Adelisa's room after midnight, covering her mouth with kisses, ignoring her protests—*"Nein, bitte! Ich bin Jungfrau."* I am a virgin. He slid her nightgown above her waist. She slammed her palm against his nose. He drew his head back for an instant, his eyes like milk glass. His breath and pores reeked of bourbon, sickly-sweet.

Adelisa flailed at his chest, but she was no match for his power and determination. His bulk was twice her ninety pounds. Her nails raked stripes down his cheeks.

He slapped her with so much force her head bounced against the wall. The sweep of his arm knocked over the small table beside her bed. Glass shattered. She knew without seeing: it was the lily vase, Anton's gift to her. Godwin pinned her arms over her head easily with one hand. With the other, he ripped her nightgown down to expose her breasts. He bit her while she screamed and writhed. When she understood struggle was futile, she grew flaccid. As still and silent as a corpse. Her spirit broke from her body. It hovered, watching yet removed. Her senses severed, except for smell. Except for the sickly-sweet bourbon. While he pushed himself into her and tore her flesh, while pain seared her body, while he pumped and grunted like an animal, she was absent. Even when he finished and rolled off her, even when she was sure he was passed out, that it was over, she could not move.

She didn't know how much time passed afterwards—seconds, minutes, or an hour of impenetrable silence—before a pig-like snort he emitted in his sleep restored her senses. She slid out from under the dead weight of his arm and leg and stood up. Shards of pale pink glass impaled themselves in the soles of her left foot. She stifled a cry and sat back on the edge of the bed to pick out the pieces. She put shoes on first, then removed the torn nightgown and dressed.

Quietly she collected her few belongings: clothes, her mother's carved ebony rosary beads, a papier maché Kris Kringle she had brought from Germany.

She left behind a bloodied sheet.

She took only one thing with her that wasn't hers. A lantern. She thought of the cook's words: The likes of them will never miss a little bit of butter. They wouldn't miss a lantern either.

Sleet fell as she walked aimlessly through mostly empty streets. She didn't know where she was going, putting one foot in front of the other, vaguely aware she'd left the Godwins' neighborhood. The homes grew less fancy as she neared the business district. She was vaguely aware of the smell of hay and manure and knew she was near the stables. Soon she found herself in front of St. Philomena's. It hadn't been intentional, but standing in front of the great spire, she realized she had nowhere else to go. She banged on the door. The sexton answered, a raised eyebrow seeming to ask what on earth she wanted at this hour of the night.

"Could I speak with a sister?" She waited on a bench in the foyer, her mind racing through all the ways the night might not have happened. If only Mrs. Godwin had taken her along to Philadelphia on the train instead of leaving her behind to do the housekeeping. If only the cook and gardener had been awakened by her screams and come to rescue her. If only she hadn't smiled at Mr. Godwin one afternoon in the parlor and sipped his wine. Maybe she had brought this on herself. A punishment for the sin of pride in her hair and her smooth hands. If only there had been a lock on her door. If only, if only, she had stayed at home with her mother in Germany. She dropped her head to her knees and clasped her arms around them.

Impressions. Soft footfalls. A candle. Long hair hanging loose against a white nightdress. Alarmed eyes.

"I'm Sister Anne. You'd better come with me." The nun guided her back to their living quarters. Sister Anne bathed the worst of Adelisa's visible wounds with a cloth and ordered another sister to heat water for a bath. They seemed such tiny women in their white night dresses, much smaller than when clothed in habits and wimples, sweeping by in flocks at mass.

Adelisa tried to hide her body.

Sister Anne gestured for Adelisa to hand her clothing over. "Come on, we're all girls here." The nun passed the soiled items to another who whisked them from the room.

Adelisa scrubbed her skin with the coarse cloth and strong soap. Gradually she felt her muscles relax in the hot water. The sisters encouraged her to soak for as long as she wanted and kept the water hot. One combed her hair. No one had taken such care of her since she was a little girl. Another sister set a clean nightgown near the tub.

Sister Anne brought in iodine and a cloth. She inclined her bulbous nose in the direction of Adelisa's breast without really looking at it. "Nothing's filthier than a human bite." When Adelisa didn't take the bottle, the sister set it on the bench beside the nightgown.

"The iodine'll sting mightily, but you don't want an infection."

Adelisa dried herself and dabbed the iodine on the bite, sucking in breath. She dressed and sat down on the wooden bench. Pulled one foot up across her knee to examine the cuts. Groaned with pain shooting through body parts she couldn't even name. She dabbed iodine on the cuts and watched them turn violet. She would hate the color the rest of her life.

Sister Anne showed her to a small room, empty except for a bed and crude wooden chair. Aching with every movement, Adelisa eased onto the mattress. A sister entered with a cup of hot broth. "Drink this. You'll feel better."

Adelisa sipped. "Thank you for your kindness. You haven't even asked me what happened."

Sister Anne pulled the chair closer to the bed. "Any fool can see a beast attacked you, and it wasn't the sweet boy who sits across from you on Sundays." Adelisa looked up with surprise. "Oh, yes, I see you both, good children, here every Sunday, rain or shine. So I know who you are. God's children. If it will make you feel better to tell me, I will listen. If you don't, that will be quite fine too."

How could she tell a nun, a bride of Christ, about the dirty thing? It would be like throwing mud in her ears. It would defile the church walls.

"Nothing you can say will surprise me," Sister Anne said. "We've heard it all here at St. Philomena's. We know about thievery, incest, prostitution, murder, rape. You can tell me if you want to and know it will never leave these walls."

The sister laid her hand on Adelisa's brow. The touch, so gentle, so much like her mother's, broke her. Great sobs racked her body. Sister Anne folded Adelisa into her arms, rocking her back and forth, back and forth, murmuring, "There, there. There, now." Meaningless words, meaningless words. Full of comfort. Sister Anne prayed for her. The last thing Adelisa remembered before falling asleep was the sister touching her forehead and calling her "Lämmchen." It was what her mother called her when she tucked her into bed at night.

When Adelisa awoke, she found Sister Anne sitting beside her bed. The nun closed her Bible and smiled. "A good sleep is so rejuvenating, isn't it? One of God's many blessings. I expect you're hungry, and the noon meal has come and gone, but Sister Kate set something aside for you. I'll fetch it now."

Adelisa moved one part of her body at a time, ascertaining what hurt and what didn't. She explored her face with her hands. Her jaw felt unhinged, as if bones were scraping against each other. It ached even worse than the knot on the back of her head. Holding her head as still as possible, she got dressed. For three days the sisters fed her, prayed for her, and let her rest.

On the fourth day while she ate her lunch, Sister told her they found work for her. "It won't be easy, but you'll have a bed and something to eat." The position was doing laundry, cooking, and cleaning for a boarding house. "Mrs. Hilinski runs the establishment in a very poor neighborhood. Nothing like the fancy house you came from. But she is a member of our church for many years, and she will see to it no one bothers you."

Adelisa thanked her for her trouble. The sisters exuded so much kindness, she really didn't want to leave. She didn't want to face her life as a dirty girl. A defiled girl. Everyone would see what she was by looking at her face, shame emblazoned there as plain as the bruise on her cheek. "Couldn't I stay here with you? Become a sister?"

Sister Anne sighed. "What about the boy who loves you?"

Adelisa bit her lip. Did Anton love her? He never said so. But there was the way his eyes followed her across the beer garden. The respect of his touch when they danced. The gifts of his mother's handkerchief and the lily vase. Yes, he loved the girl she once was. But that girl was shattered into a million pieces. She lowered her eyes.

The sister rested her hand on Adelisa's sleeve. "Sometimes the greatest gift we can give someone is to allow them to take care of us."

Adelisa raised her chin. She was used to taking care of herself. Besides, Godwin had stolen whatever she might have given in return to Anton. "I can't tell him."

"You need time to pray about it. To heal. To learn God's will for you. If you feel the call, you will come back to us."

Adelisa shared her room with eight others, two to a bed. Still, the women had it better than the men who lived at Mrs. Hilinski's. In a room with four beds, eight men who worked night shift slept during days. At night the beds were occupied by nine day workers. Behind the lodging house was a weed-riddled alley with a central privy shared by twelve buildings backing up to it. When it rained, raw sewage poured through the streets. The stench was so powerful Adelisa covered her face with a cloth when she ventured outside.

The tenements abutted the railroad tracks. Regularly throughout the day, passing trains rattled the walls and floors and windows, what few windows there were. Coal-burning engines threw off gray grit that coated everything. It sifted its way down to her scalp and left a sandy feel in her mouth. When she blew her nose, she expelled coal dust onto the handkerchief.

During her first week of work, she scrubbed sheets and towels in a large vat of steaming water until her pale, smooth hands grew coarse. There was no butter to smooth on them. She only hoped the water was hot enough to kill the lice she saw leaping from the gray beard of one of the foundry workers as he ate his dinner.

She made huge pots of porridge twice a day, served the residents, and washed the sticky residue off the dishes and pans. For dinner she boiled up rice and beans or potatoes with chicken and cabbage. After dinner, she heated more water and scrubbed the pans—so many of them. Her hands were red prunes.

No matter how hard the work, she would rather be under Mrs.

Hilinski's roof than Mr. Godwin's. The residents might be poor, but they treated each other with respect. They were all working as hard as she was to stay alive.

Puzzled, Anton watched Adelisa lighting a prayer candle after mass, her head covered with a black lace cap, as it always was, inside the church. She had sat in a different pew, front row. Not once did she seek his eyes during the service. Never before had she lingered like this, behind everyone else. Was she angry with him? Had someone died? He waited in the back of the church for a long time and watched a nun approach Adelisa. They huddled together, whispering. Finally he went outside and skulked near the entrance, imagining all sorts of things that could have gone wrong. The bitter cold stung his cheeks. He stamped his feet to keep warm.

Some forty minutes later, Adelisa emerged under the great spire. He called out to her: "Wait!" When she didn't stop, he ran up behind her and touched her sleeve. She drew away, as if his fingers burned, and dashed off without speaking, eyes cast down. He thought—couldn't be sure, she turned her head away so quickly—a ghastly yellow-green bruise smudged her cheek.

Her rejection stung worse than he thought possible. Although Anton hadn't asked her, it was understood—at least, he thought it was—that they would marry as soon as her servitude was completed. The Reinhardts assumed it was so. The missus had already pledged her finest porcelain serving dish to him and Adelisa as a wedding gift. The one with bright pink flowers and mossy leaves. The sturdy double bed he slept in too. Magdalen Reinhardt scoffed when Anton protested it was too much.

"What need will I ever have of this extra bed?" she asked. "You're the only child I have." Her expression, so wistful.

Anton followed Adelisa as she hurried along the mucky streets. Past Jon Grier's Grocery. Past Hood's Importers of Fine Watches. Past Duff's Merchant College. Past a yellow mongrel that ignored Adelisa but snarled at him and nipped his trouser legs. She turned in a direction opposite of the Godwins' neighborhood, finally entering a doorway in a row of tenements. For some minutes he hung around outside, kicking at a piece of rotted wood, tossing pebbles at a frozen puddle to break the ice. He stopped a lad who came outside with a bucket of coal ashes and asked what was that building. "Boarding house," boy said. "If you need a room, best look somewhere's else. Old lady's house is full up—and then some."

Anton spent a miserable week brooding. He couldn't imagine what had happened, why Adelisa wouldn't talk to him. What had he done?

"Give her time," Magdalen advised. "Sometimes we girls are moody." Anton wanted to believe she was right, but he didn't think it was in Adelisa's nature to be sullen.

After mass, again Anton waited by the church doors while Adelisa lingered over the prayer candles. He couldn't think what to do. Finally he went up and lit a candle and knelt beside her.

She said nothing, but briefly met his eyes. Even in the half-light of the sanctuary, this close to her, he could see the trace of a bruise that blemished her right cheek. A light snow had fallen overnight, mostly melted now as they exited the church together. They walked in silence halfway down Liberty Street.

Each of Anton's words puffed visibly into the cold air. "What has happened?"

She scuffled along, black boots already damp. Her eyes darted away from him. "I left the Godwins. I really don't want to talk about it." She walked with shoulders hunched over, chin tucked against her chest. An old woman's walk.

"But why, when you were so close to being released?"

She plunged ahead of him, nearly losing her balance in the gray slush. "Please leave me alone."

The change in Adelisa's tone worried him, but the change in her eyes concerned him even more. He puzzled over it while he walked a little behind her in silence. He couldn't put into words what he saw there. Fear. Something broken and shriveled. He sensed her spirit, her words, even her body had withered.

He caught up to her and began to talk. Softly. He told her about his first spanking. When he was five, he rudely called his aunt fat. His story brought the ghost of a smile to Adelisa's lips.

Encouraged, he told her how his mother read Bible verses to him and his sisters every night after dinner. He told her about the picture his sister Gitte drew of their family, how he pressed it under heavy books and bricks to flatten the folds and how he made a wooden frame for it and cut a piece of plate glass to protect the front. "It's the only picture I have of my family," he said. "Only rich families in our town could afford to have photographs made. My father saved all his extra money to send me away."

"What a sad thing to save for." When she spoke again her voice was little more than a whisper. "We have lost everything in coming here."

"Not everything."

From the creases in her forehead and the biting of her lip, Anton knew Adelisa was more agitated than ever. Downtown Pittsburgh bustled with the usual people and noise. A train coughing up coal dust clacked down the tracks. Two little boys pelted a third with rocks. With the advent of spring, the blind street musician emerged from hibernation to play a mournful tune on his harmonica.

"Can't you tell me what it is?" he asked as they passed by Troth and Scott Boots and Shoes. "You know I would do anything for you." When she didn't answer, he tried again. "If it's money, I can lend you some and I'm sure Karl—"

Adelisa's shoulders began to shake. She covered her face with her hands. Great racking sobs heaved from her abdomen. For a stunned moment, Anton stood still. The street musician stilled his song. The sobs crescendoed until Anton, gathering his wits, pulled her close and held her face against his chest, muffling the cries. A team of horses trotted by pulling a carriage, the musician began playing again, the child being tormented with rocks cursed. People and sounds swirled around him, the world going on as before. It was the first time he had ever held her this close. He stroked her back lightly with his knuckles until she regained control.

It began to drizzle, and inwardly he faulted himself for not bringing an umbrella. He should have been ready to protect her. He leaned his head over hers as he led down the street, hand touching her waist. They took shelter under the awning of Patterson's Bazaar Stables, where they stood side by side, his cheek pressed into the top of her head, his arm about her shoulders. The odor of manure intensified with the rain. Adelisa began to talk, somewhat incoherently, the words flowing from her like a muddy river. When he understood she'd been raped, his fingers clenched into her shoulder. When he further comprehended a baby was coming, he drew her head into his chest, whether to smother her sobs or to comfort her, he couldn't have said.

He pulled away and slammed his fist into the side of a wooden wagon drawn up beside the stables. It startled the horses. Scraped his knuckles raw. He welcomed the pain as he clenched and unclenched his fist.

"Strutting around in his fancy clothes, pretending to be a gentleman. I should kill him." His words made her cry harder. With incredible effort, he contained his rage. It wasn't helping.

He held her close again and drew his thumb across her cheek. "We will marry. Now. Let's go back and find Father Francis before the next service." He took her arm and tried to lead her back the way they had come.

Adelisa pulled her arm free from him. "You'll never see me the way you did before. I'm ruined."

Anton captured her hands. "No, he is the filth, not you. Never you." He could see she wanted to believe him. For a moment, she seemed to try, then turned away again, shaking her head.

"No, you could never love the baby like one of your own." She dropped her head into her hands, crying. "I don't even think I can love it."

The rain came down harder now, soaking through their clothes. Mud coated the bottom of Adelisa's hem and splashed up Anton's trousers.

His muscles jerked with the need to smash something. Anything. Godwin was an animal. Anton couldn't let himself think about that. He wanted to say something to ease her pain, but he was only a glassblower. He knew nothing of pretty speeches. He grasped her by one shoulder. With his other hand, he forced her chin up, made her meet his eyes.

"We will name our baby Joseph."

She twisted her face away from him. He forced it back up again until their noses were almost touching. "After my father. Joseph Karl, after two of the best men in the world. There is nothing more to say. We will love him because the baby is innocent. He's done nothing wrong. Neither have you." He nodded his head once at her, insisting she acknowledge him. This time she did. He barely breathed a kiss onto her rain-soaked forehead.

Twenty-Seven

AUGUST 1976

To be loved as Adelisa was—Sarah couldn't even imagine what it must feel like. She couldn't imagine being attacked either, or coping with the hard labor Adelisa faced so bravely. If her grandmother managed to find work, surely Sarah, with her college education, could land some sort of job.

Because Roy Glen was too cheap to subscribe to the newspaper, Sarah got her mother and father to save theirs. While Roy Glen worked overtime Sunday, her mother drove them all to the Heimbachs', and Sarah searched the classifieds in the car. No teaching positions listed. Too close to the start of the term, she supposed.

She was thrilled to see the glass plant advertising an opening, even if it would mean working with Roy Glen. She inquired about it first.

"Sorry, honey," the receptionist said, "we don't have anything right now."

"But you advertised an opening."

"For a man. Only men work on the factory floor. They run the machines to make the glass. Takes physical stamina."

"I'm sure I could do it. I'm really strong." *I could outrun the boys on the basketball court,* she wanted to say, but it sounded foolish even in her own mind. She thought about mentioning Rita's name to see if that might get her the job. *Fool—Rita never managed to get one of the floor jobs for herself, and of course she would have if she could have. They paid much better.* No point in mentioning her father as their accountant either. He'd have a fit if he knew she'd applied for this job.

When Sarah called about an advertised reporting position, the managing editor wanted someone who could heave stacks of papers around. "We're a small operation and I'm looking for a man," he said. "One person has to handle both circulation and reporting."

She declared she was plenty strong enough to lift stacks of newspapers, but the guffaw traveling through the phone lines convinced her applying in person would be a waste of time. The secretarial jobs were limited to women with shorthand skills and office experience. She broadened her search to other factory jobs. Union Carbide. Ingersoll-Rand. Pittsburgh Plate Glass. She looked at house cleaning and lawn services. Anything was better than nothing, but she lacked the skill and experience for almost everything advertised.

The week school started, Sarah could hardly believe her good luck when she received a call asking her to teach at Hillside High School. The principal sounded desperate because the person they had hired took another job at the last minute.

As she agreed to interview, she felt an immediate lightening. A job meant independence, an ability to support herself and Mandy if she needed to. Good health insurance, even if something happened to Roy Glen. Even if she left him—an idea she allowed herself before pushing it from her mind. The principal wanted her to come in immediately.

Her excitement faded. "But I can't. I don't have a sitter."

"I'm the one who's in such a hurry, so bring your little girl along. I need to meet you and get your signature on this provisional contract."

An hour later she was dressed in a navy suit—her only suit, one she used to wear to church back in high school. While she drove into town, she thought about all the things she missed out on because Roy Glen didn't want her spending money on gas. Using the Chevy to take Mandy to Sunday School was out of the question. Sarah missed her old church family, missed the sacred tones of the organ and the hymns. She found herself singing them while she gardened. "Doxology." "In the Garden." "In Christ There is No East or West." She wanted Mandy to know what it meant to belong to a congregation. If she saved part of her paycheck, maybe she could buy a used car and they could afford gas. Many things would become possible—that's what she was thinking as she pulled into a visitor's parking place in front of the school.

Sarah found her way to the main office, holding tight to Mandy's hand. The school secretary seemed delighted to stop typing. "I was told to keep this pretty young lady here with me." She nodded toward Mandy. "Mr. Mirandi said you could go right in." Sarah knocked on the principal's door, opened it slightly, and edged her way in. The principal's balding pate made him look older than she thought he was. His face was round with smooth, boyish skin and he welcomed her with a smile that crinkled the corners of his eyes. Once she was seated across from him, she asked how he'd gotten her name.

"The funniest thing, I was getting some tax advice from my accountant and I mentioned what an awful day I'd had, how a social studies teacher was backing out of her contract at the last minute, and my accountant said he knew someone with a teaching degree and a political science major who might be interested in a job."

Her father. He'd practically saved her life. "Guess I'd better call and thank your accountant tonight." Better yet, there was a jar of rhubarb in the pantry. She'd make his favorite pie.

While the principal asked her the usual questions, she absorbed her surroundings a little at a time. The room smelled like furniture polish. Neat desktop: folders lay in a tidy stack, desk calendar, wire in-basket. Framed pictures: Mr. Mirandi shaking hands with the governor, University of Ohio diploma, framed collage of baseball cards. Photos of his kids lined up across a credenza.

Mr. Mirandi pulled on his ear. "One of the worst problems I have is finding last minute substitutes. You have a young child. Is that likely to interfere with your regular attendance?"

She had no idea how to answer honestly and still get the job. If he meant, would she put Mandy first, the answer was yes. "I'll certainly be here every day I possibly can."

At the end of the interview, he offered her the job and she asked if she could let him know the next day. She needed to make arrangements for Mandy before she committed.

"I wish I could give you time, but I've got to find a warm body. I told my wife I wasn't going home tonight without a signature on a contract."

She signed. Another opportunity like this wasn't going to come along.

After she put Mandy down for a nap, Sarah looked over her benefits package. Full health coverage of family members. Except for pre-existing conditions like Mandy's asthma. For those, coverage didn't begin until one year after the date of employment. She and Roy Glen would have to make it last one more year, one day at a time.

Pre-existing conditions. She could learn to hate those words.

She didn't have time to dwell on them. She called her cousin. Initial pleasantries passed easily though she could hear the "what's up?" in her cousin's voice.

"Uh, Martha Rose, I need a big favor. I have a job lined up and it starts Monday and I need somewhere safe and productive to leave Mandy. I've heard such good things about—" oh God, what was the name of her place?—"Hearts and Hands."

"We're full up already," Martha Rose said.

"Look, I'm desperate. I start teaching at Hillside High on Monday. Please?"

"The high school? Hold on a minute." Papers rattled in the background. "Um, here's the deal. Pete needs a job and there's a janitor's position over at Hillside. Put in a good word for him, and I'll make room for Mandy. How old is she?"

"Just turned four." She answered automatically, but her mind was hooked on putting in a good word for Pete. She remembered the way he whacked out over red flowers at Katherine's funeral. What on earth could she tell Mr. Mirandi—Pete'll be okay as long as you don't buy the secretaries red carnations for Valentine's Day?

"Look," Martha Rose said, "all you have to do is let him use you as a reference. You won't look like family—different last name. He can put down "friend" as relationship for both of us. They probably won't even call, but he'll need three references and your name on the form will help."

"I can go along with that." Then she had second thoughts. "But is he okay? I mean to be around students?"

"They let him out of the hospital, didn't they?"

Sarah hadn't known he'd been hospitalized. She bet Livvie knew. Another case where the family wasn't supposed to talk about it? Or did Livvie forget?

"He's on meds," Martha Rose said. "As long as he takes them, he should be fine. Pete needs someone to give him a chance. Livvie's making sure he's okay, and I'm gonna check on him regularly. But he needs a job. Sitting around twiddling his thumbs isn't good for him."

Sounded reasonable. How hard could it be to push a broom and wash chalkboards? He wouldn't have to interact with students. And he was a veteran. Sarah's father would say the country owed him a chance. She sealed the deal. Foster would be lonely without her and Mandy, but he'd have to get over it.

She was excited about this chance to use her education until she thought about telling Roy Glen. Her job would change their lives in major ways, and she sensed her working would throw him off-center. She felt like she'd swallowed a stone and couldn't sleep. When he came in drunk at 3:30 a.m.—so drunk he didn't even want sex— she lay very still, eyes closed. She put off telling him as long as she could. Finally when he got up for lunch Sunday, she couldn't delay any longer.

Even from several feet away, Sarah could smell his skin. Reminded her of vinegar. Or urine. His voice rose an octave higher than usual. "Are you crazy? I'm not going to let you go to work."

She held his gaze, not sure where her courage came from. "I've already accepted."

His face reddened. "What about Mandy? You forget about her?"

Sarah told him about the new nursery school her cousin had opened. "Mandy needs to interact with other kids. They have a certified kindergarten teacher on staff and a big outdoor play area." Sarah had been impressed by the swings and tricycles, all safely contained behind a chain link fence. She'd already given her cousin the first week's check.

Fists clenched tightly at his side, Roy Glen sprayed spittle as he paced between the kitchen and living room, shoving sandy hair away from his eyes. He looked ready to pounce on something. "I can't believe you did this without talking to me about it first. What were you thinking?"

"That we'd have a lot more money. That if anything happened to you, I could still take care of Mandy. That she will have my health insurance too. This asthma could get expensive." She would not give in to him, not this time. "Mandy and I both start school tomorrow."

On his way out, he slammed the door so hard the terrarium bounced off the kitchen table and shattered. Sarah swept up the pile of dirt and glass shards. The African violet that had thrived for so long in the cloistered environment lost a few leaves, but it would survive. She transplanted it into another pot.

The next morning, without disturbing Roy Glen, she fixed Mandy Apple Jacks and milk, and dressed her in matching clothes—a bit of a struggle since Mandy preferred combinations like red plaid paired with purple stripes. Sarah fed Foster and let him out to potty. When he returned, they set off for Hearts and Hands.

Sarah handed Martha Rose instructions for dealing with an asthma attack, should Mandy have one at school. The thought chilled her. She would never forgive herself if anything happened to her baby. "Thanks for making room for Mandy. I hope we'll get to know each other better since we'll be seeing each other every day."

"Me too. Maybe we can get our kids and husbands together for dinner sometime."

Not likely, as anti-social as Roy Glen was, but it was a nice thought. Martha Rose chomped gum while she talked, but when she held her mouth still, she was a pretty young woman. A blonde now, instead of brunette. Sarah could have passed her on the street and not recognized her.

At first, Mandy was fascinated by the array of toys, books, and playmates, but when Sarah said goodbye, she became hysterical.

"Mommmmmeee." The screeching reverberated from the concrete block walls. Mandy clung to Sarah as if she would never see her again.

Martha Rose told Sarah to detach Mandy decisively from her leg. "Don't look back. If you hesitate, she'll sense she can win and will keep on. They all act this way at first, but once you're gone, she'll settle in and play."

With her cousin's help, she pried herself free, at least from Mandy's hands, if not from guilt.

"Mandy," Martha Rose said. "Come and meet my daughter Chastity. She's younger than you." Sarah didn't think Mandy could hear over the screams.

On the way to Hillside High School, Sarah wondered if she was making a terrible mistake. In the main office, a secretary directed her to the cafeteria, where a general teachers' meeting would take place. She only knew two people who worked in the school: the principal, and her good friend Rachel Sullivan. At least, she thought Rachel was still her friend. She hadn't seen her—or any friend—for so long. She sidled into the room, sure she didn't belong. No one was going to like her.

The cafeteria filled up with teachers, noisily chattering about their summers. Sarah got in line behind a trickle of women pulling cinnamon buns off industrial-sized metal baking trays. After selecting one, she licked the sugary topping from her fingers and then found a napkin and coffee. She carried them to one of the formica-topped tables and dropped into a red plastic chair. Cheerleaders in shorts and tee-shirts were taping booster banners for football players to the walls.

Rachel arrived and Sarah waved her to the empty chair beside her, but before they could catch up, Mr. Mirandi asked for attention. Rubbing his hairless head, he asked for quiet again and the chatter subsided. He introduced new faculty members, including Sarah. "Mrs. Hardman will be taking over the newspaper this year, so give her all the help you can." His announcement came as a surprise. He hadn't mentioned anything about the newspaper in her brief interview. Being called Mrs. Hardman was a surprise too, one that sent the blood rushing to her head. It sounded like someone else. Her mother-in-law.

Mr. Mirandi delivered another surprise.

"We also have a new basketball coach and phys ed teacher, who couldn't be here today, but I'm sure you'll give him a hearty welcome when you see him next week. Cal Caruso is coming to us from the University of North Carolina."

Sarah's ribs squeezed together until she couldn't breathe. What brought him back to Clarksburg? She couldn't imagine having to work in the same building with him, and Roy Glen would have a fit if he found out.

After the faculty meeting, an attractive woman with short salt-and-pepper hair approached with her hand held out. "I'm Peg Fansler, social studies chair. Happy to have you aboard. We're going to meet in my room until we get this schedule mess taken care of, and then I'll show you your room and the books you'll be using."

They settled into desks in Peg's classroom. Rachel squeezed Sarah's hand. "Who could have guessed we would end up teaching at the same high school? I didn't even know you were coming here."

Sarah crossed her legs at the knees and again at the ankles. "Neither did I until a few days ago."

"I guess they were lucky to get anyone at this late date," Rachel said.

That was Sarah, a last resort.

"We were lucky to find Sarah," Peg said. "I checked her qualifications with Mr. Mirandi and they are excellent. She graduated magna cum laude and comes with strong recommendations from her professors." Gratitude filled Sarah and she felt a lessening of the inferiority that always festered in Rachel's presence.

Rachel flung her raven hair over her shoulder. "Well, isn't anyone going to notice?" She stuck out her hand, the fingers flayed slightly upward. A diamond with a circumference the size of an Apple Jack gleamed from her ring finger.

"So Mark finally asked," Lenitra said.

"What do you mean?" Rachel protested. "I finally said 'yes.'"

Peg hustled everyone into completing the class schedule. Sarah would be teaching five—two Early American History, two Modern American History, and one Political Systems. Newspaper was on her planning period. The department was changing to a quarter system using paperback texts, which meant the following nine weeks, Sarah would have all new students and new subjects. The administration was so boggled over the complicated scheduling they decided the department should manage it themselves. By the time an hour passed, Rachel, recipient of the best of everything since the day she was born, showed she hadn't lost her touch. She rejected student after student, until only 82 of Hillside's best remained. Sarah's class load was 126, similar to everyone else's.

When Sarah picked up Mandy, she was listening raptly to a storybook one of the teachers was reading. As soon as she saw her mother, she jumped up, sobbed bitterly, and demanded to be held.

"I know you won't believe this, but she made several friends and hasn't cried since you left," Martha Rose said. "She had fun."

"Did not." Big tears ran down Mandy's face. Sarah found a tissue and stemmed the flow.

"I wanna go home, Mommy."

When they got home, Sarah was surprised at what she didn't find. Foster. She expected him to be waiting at the door, wagging his tail, whining, slobbering all over her before bounding down the steps for a potty run. She called him, ducking her head into each room. Mandy followed behind imitating her. Sarah went back outside, bellowed his name again. No black and white furball strewn with seeds and ticks and other evidence of a romp appeared. It wasn't like him. Not like him at all. She went back inside and peered under the beds and in the closets. No dog. She pulled on jeans and boots and tromped past the hollies, waded through the blackberry brambles, hiked out to the willow by the creek, Mandy streeling along behind. She bit her cuticles. Caught herself. Stopped. Started again. Wherever he was, he would come home for dinner. Foster's interior clock was finely attuned to mealtimes.

She sank into the couch, a piece of cheap trailer furniture upholstered in gold velour. It had two stains, one from a melted blue crayon and another where Mandy had thrown up prune juice. She picked at them, as was her habit. But she had too much work to do to get ready for students and finally positioned the afghan to hide the blotches.

"Come see Mommy's grade book, Squirt."

Mandy examined the grade book and watched Sarah enter names on temporary rosters, then turned on Sesame Street and rummaged through the toy box for her Ernie puppet.

Dinnertime. Still no Foster. Sarah walked through the woods again, yelling his name. It was nearly dark when she crossed the creek and found the recently turned dirt on top of a knoll. A grave? It couldn't be, could it? Finally she called Roy Glen at work and left a message to call home.

On the first ring, she snatched up the phone. "Roy Glen, Foster's gone."

"I know."

"Where is he?"

A moment's silence. "I didn't want to leave a note, but this isn't easy over the phone either. He's gone, Sarah. He ran out in the road and got hit by an eighteen-wheeler."

She sank to her knees, vaguely aware of the twisted yarns of shag carpet digging into her skin. "Gone?"

"Yeah, I'm sorry. He took off after you."

Sarah snuffled. It was her fault. Foster missed her.

"Sorry, Sarah. You'd better reconsider this job. What if something happens to Mandy next? You think about it. I gotta go now, okay?"

Something clutched at her throat and traveled slowly to her gut. His story didn't feel right. Foster never ran out into the road. On three legs he didn't really run anyway, only sort of loped along. Had Roy Glen done something to Foster? No, he wouldn't have. And he wouldn't ever hurt Mandy—she didn't know why that thought even entered her head. He adored Mandy. She was his little fishing buddy.

Mandy dragged her blanket across the floor and stared at her. "Mommy, what's wrong? Where did Foster go?"

Sarah wiped tears from her face and pulled Mandy down onto her lap. "Baby, Foster isn't coming back. You know how I'm always telling you to look both ways before you cross the street? Foster didn't look and a truck hit him."

"But where is he now?"

"In heaven. Where good dogs go."

"I don't want him to go to heaven. I want him to come home."

"Me too, but he's going to be happy. He's running on all four legs now and there's no mean old ticks or fleas to bother him in heaven. No burrs tangled in his fur."

For the rest of the evening, Sarah went through the motions. Mandy's bath. Story time. After she tucked Mandy in, Sarah tried to read part of the history text. Gave up. Threw herself on the bed and buried her face in the pillow. "That poor old dog, poor old dog."

Drained, she fixed Roy Glen's dinner. At 12:30 he hadn't come in. She put his dinner in the refrigerator and left a note with questions about Foster: *Did you see it happen? When did it happen? Did he die right away? Where is he buried?*

In the morning, a reply scrawled by each question. *Yes. Right after you left. Yes. Beyond the creek.*

Right after she left. It didn't make sense. It wasn't as if she'd never left the dog alone before, never driven off in the car. It wasn't her fault, it wasn't, but was it Roy Glen's? Or simply an accident?

Two days later, Sarah stood at her classroom door, greeting students for the first time. She'd covered one wall with a map of Europe and posters of Roosevelt, Churchill, and Hitler. Beneath each, she taped a significant quotation from each man. For Franklin Roosevelt, she drew in red magic marker, "Democracy cannot succeed unless those who express their choice are prepared to choose wisely. The real safeguard of democracy, therefore, is education." For Churchill, she selected,

"A pessimist sees the difficulty in every opportunity; an optimist sees the opportunity in every difficulty." For Hitler, "Anyone who sees and paints a sky green and fields blue ought to be sterilized."

Despite staying up until after one in the morning reading the material—and Roy Glen still hadn't come home by the time she went to bed—she felt inadequately prepared to teach four new courses. And no matter what they called it, newspaper was a course. She would only be ahead of her students in reading by a few days. Still, she was so excited by the challenges ahead she could barely sleep.

Her voice quavered as she introduced herself and gathered personal information from her classes. "Before we start in on World War II, I would like to get to know you better. Tomorrow I want you to bring in a poster representing you. Your hobbies, your interests, your family, your friends." She held up a poster she'd made about herself. There was a picture of Mandy coloring with Foster by her feet, one of Sarah playing basketball in junior high, one of her clowning around with Rachel and Paula, a wrapper from a Snickers bar, and a magazine clipping of laundry detergent. "Because ever since Mandy was born, it seems all I get done is laundry," she explained. She included a Polaroid of the fused glass picture she'd helped her uncle make of autumn trees. She'd toyed with the idea of not including Roy Glen, but at last used a photo of him teaching Mandy to fish.

"Your presentation should last two to three minutes. Any questions?" she asked.

A lanky tow-headed boy in the back row raised his hand. Surreptitiously Sarah consulted her seating chart for his name. "Jeff?"

"What if we don't have any hobbies or interests?" His eyes gleamed with mischief and he watched her reaction closely.

"You'd better make some up or everyone will think you're the most boring guy at Hillside High." Everyone laughed, to her relief, and at that moment she knew she could do this. She squared her shoulders and stood tall and straight. She would keep her eye on Jeff Blogham. A bit too much challenge in his eyes. She would credit him with a good nature, though, because he laughed along with his classmates.

By the end of the week, each class plunged into the curriculum, from Kristallnacht to headlines, and Sarah's voice stopped jiggling like her mother's gelatin. A new routine developed at home with Mandy.

They played for the first hour after they got home, ate dinner, watched a half hour of television, and went through bedtime rituals, including story time. Then at 8:30 Sarah did school work until at least midnight. The 5:30 alarm seemed earlier every day.

She saw Roy Glen only as they rode to his parents' farm on Saturdays. Okay by her.

Friday night her mother called with Livvie's test results. Cancer. Livvie refused treatment. Right away, Sarah drove to the Heimbachs'.

Sitting beside Livvie at the kitchen table over cups of chamomile tea, Sarah choked back tears. "You should let the doctor try the chemotherapy. Cancer's not a death sentence anymore."

Livvie demurred cheerfully. "Life is a death sentence, sweetie, we just don't know exactly when we will die."

How could she smile so gently thinking about her own death? "With treatment you don't have to die. Not yet."

"The way I see it, I'm lucky. It won't be much longer until I join Mama and Papa and my brothers and sisters."

But what about us? Sarah wanted to say. *Don't you want to stay here with me and Mom and Daddy and Garrett?* It sounded selfish, so Sarah held her tongue, but she couldn't stop her fingers from twining through Livvie's, thinking wildly, irrationally, if she refused to let go of her aunt's hand, she wouldn't be able to die. "You can fight this."

"No, honey, I'm almost ready. The Lord will call me home when it's time. I must have a little more to do here yet."

Livvie rapped their clasped hands twice against the table as if delivering a verdict and let go of Sarah's fingers.

As the week wore on, Sarah replayed the scene over and over: her own fear, the acceptance on Livvie's face, the feel of Livvie's knuckles as they pulled away, the scent of chamomile and mint, slightly bitter, yet sweet woven through it all. Sometimes Sarah was angry that her aunt wouldn't fight. Mostly, she was amazed by Livvie's strength. If Livvie could face her own death with such courage, surely Sarah could summon the courage to face her own life. To meet challenges in her classroom. To stand up to Roy Glen.

At work, Cal turned out not to be a problem. He stayed in the gym at the opposite end of the building. They had different lunch shifts and arrived and left at different times.

Pete wasn't a problem either. She saw him most days, pushing a broom or shining the trophy cases. The balder he got, the thicker that bottle-brush mustache seemed, until his face began to remind Sarah of a walrus. They spoke in passing.

Mandy came around to the idea of nursery school, no longer crying in the mornings. One evening Mandy asked to borrow her grade book for a few minutes. Sarah agreed, warning her not to write in it. A while later, she heard Mandy talking in her bedroom. Sarah set down the papers she was grading, tiptoed down the hall, and peeked in. Mandy stood in front of her bed arranging three dolls. "Now, class, we are going to read a story." When she realized her mother was watching, she giggled. "I'm playing school, Mommy."

"What's on your tablet?"

Mandy held the yellow legal pad up. In big crooked letters was a roster with A's and F's after the names.

At one in the morning, Sarah stashed the last graded papers in her book bag and filled the tub with water. Lately, an odor clung to her. What was it? She grabbed her favorite lavender soap and scrubbed.

Twenty-Eight

OCTOBER 1976

The voice wasn't Sarah's—he knew that right away—but he'd heard it before. Slowly—to emphasize how cool he was though his heart was racing—he swiveled on the stool. She had brown eyes speckled gold, the color of a brook trout. He couldn't place where he'd seen her, but he liked what he saw curving out of the black tube top. She was short and blonde, but he bet the bush didn't match. Two-inch gold hoop earrings and a wedding band. Tight, tight jeans and high-heeled boots. A gold metal stretch belt encircled her waist, snake-like. A toy made for pleasure.

Red lips smiled. "You don't remember me, do you? I'm Sarah's cousin, Martha Rose."

The blood drained from his head, but not a flinch or a blink escaped. Mandy's day care teacher! He dropped Mandy off two weeks ago when Sarah was running late because of car trouble.

He licked his lips. "Look, I wouldn't do anything in the world to hurt Mandy. I hope you wouldn't either."

"Oh, relax, I won't tell, if you won't." She laid dark red fingernails on his arm, raked them slowly from his elbow to his wrist. "I don't want to hurt my little girl either, but here we are. Two grown-ups. This doesn't have anything to do with little girls."

When her cheeks dimpled with a smile, Roy Glen released the tension in his neck. Silly of him to worry. No way in hell Sarah was ever going to find out. She hadn't found out about the others. He rocked. He rolled. He was a goddamn super star with the babes.

"Any of those nuts for me?" She pointed at the bowl with one hand and squeezed his upper thigh with the other.

He answered with his eyes. Women always ate that look up, and Martha Rose wiggled her fingers even higher. "I like the unshaved look. Rugged."

He rubbed his cheeks and chin. "Getting ready for deer season."

She laughed. "I bet you're always ready."

The situation struck Roy Glen as way beyond cool. Doing it with Sarah's cousin and going home to Sarah and doing it again. No, his wife was just another stupid teacher. Not half as smart as she thought.

Twenty-Nine

NOVEMBER 1976

Sarah was groggy when Roy Glen woke her at three in the morning on the first day of deer season, but she stumbled into a bathrobe and slippers. In the kitchen she broke two eggs in a Teflon frying pan and watched through half-lidded eyes as the whites turned from clear goo into solids. She flipped them and kept the heat up until the yellows gelled, then slid each between two pieces of toast with a slice of American cheese.

She studied Roy Glen as he wolfed down the sandwiches. He looked like a homeless person, unshaven, shabbier than Pete on his worst days. He smelled as rotten as Pete, too, because he hadn't bathed for a week. Deer, Roy Glen claimed, could pick up the scent of soap and shampoo from half a mile away. He pulled a camouflage jacket over a tee-shirt with yellow-stained pits and a browned neckline.

Roy Glen and his uncles planned to take a twelve-year-old cousin on his first hunt. Earlier in the month, they'd constructed tree stands along well-used deer paths.

"Hope Pritch gets his buck today," Roy Glen said, "but deer always know when it's the first day of the season and they disappear. No matter how much you plan, ain't never easy."

Bits of toast crumbs and egg yolk dotted his beard. He tugged on a Caterpillar cap. "Mom and Dad will expect you and Mandy for dinner."

Sarah crept back into bed for two hours, and then spent the morning grading a backlog of papers while Mandy watched cartoons. In the afternoon she visited her mother and Livvie.

By the time Sarah arrived at her in-laws', it was already dark. She saw Roy Glen's truck in the drive and a sliver of light escaped from the cracked garage door. She grabbed the gelatin salad her mother foisted on her when she heard Mandy balked at eating vegetables. Some strange concoction with cabbage, carrots, spinach, and pineapple. Sugar-coated vegetables. Not such a good idea, but saying so would offend her mother.

Sarah guided Mandy with her free hand toward the garage and pushed open the side door. Immediately her senses were overwhelmed. Iron smell of blood. Male voices taunting. (*Come on, be a man.*) A boy's whine. (*No, I can't.*) Retching sounds. The picture she didn't think she would ever be able to erase from her mind: Roy Glen shoving a huge slab of liver—steam rising, the heat of life escaping into the cold November air—into his twelve-year-old cousin Pritch's mouth while the boy's father pinned his arms behind him.

Sarah swept Mandy up in her arms and ran back outside.

Half an hour later, Roy Glen came into the kitchen, freshly showered and smelling half decent for a change. His eyes moved over her face—left ear, right ear, chin, eyes—all while the muscles in his left cheek twitched.

"You had no business coming in here and telling his mother."

Sarah refused to look away though she could feel her lower lip tremble. Traitorous lip! "She was furious and took him home. I think that proves my point."

Roy Glen's parents took Mandy to the living room and turned the TV volume up.

"It's tradition. All Hardmans take a bite from the raw liver of their first deer. Even Sandy did it."

"It would be different if he chose to, but you forced him. He was gagging."

"For Chrissakes, he acted like a whining little sissy. Even his dad says so. When you don't understand what's going on, you ought to keep your opinions to yourself."

"I have a right to my own opinions."

"You didn't care about my opinion when you went and signed a contract with the school, did you? So why should anyone care about yours?"

Every argument led back to her job. If one of Mandy's toys was on the floor, it was because of Sarah's job. If she fell asleep on the couch and let his dinner burn—one time, for God's sake—it was because of her job. If she bought him the wrong brand of peanut butter, he blamed her job. If the car wouldn't start in the morning, it was her job's fault.

The meal with Roy Glen's family was difficult. Ellen broke the silence. "So how do you like your little school?"

Mandy happily told about the swing set, sandbox, toys, books, and new friends.

One corner of Roy Glen's mouth jumped. "She wouldn't need day care if her mommy stayed home where she belonged."

Mandy hurled herself out of her chair and onto Sarah's lap. "I miss you, Mommy. I want you to say home."

Her in-laws froze, creamed tomatoes halfway to their mouths. Sarah couldn't keep the bitterness from her voice. "Thanks, Roy Glen, that was really helpful."

"What? What'd I do? All I said was the kid needs her mother." He looked meaningfully at Mandy. "Looks like I'm right."

"What a four year old needs is to play with children her own age."

Again, Ellen tried to smooth things over. "Sounds like she's made new friends. Tell me about this little girl, Lollie. She sounds real nice. What kinds of things do you do together?"

Mandy sat up in Sarah's lap, sniffling, still clinging to her arm. "We play dress up with a box of clothes the teacher has. We are the mommies and put on high heels and go shopping. And we don't let Joey come with us because when daddies go shopping there's always a fight."

Her words hung in the air. Sarah looked at Roy Glen, who kept eating as if nothing important had occurred. Maybe he didn't even know it had.

Thirty

In the main entrance of HHS, Sarah stomped the snow off her shoes before proceeding down the hall. As she signed the office attendance register, Mr. Mirandi told her how much he appreciated the job she was doing with the school newspaper. She bounced down the hallway, shoulders thrown back, humming "Dancing Queen" under her breath and calling out greetings to students and colleagues.

In her own hallway, she halted. In front of her room, Pete leaned on a mop by her door. He was talking to Cal. She thought about turning around and finding someplace to hide until Cal was gone, but she supposed she would have to face him sometime.

Pete's voice carried all the way down the hall. "I maintained fuel and electrical equipment for the United States Army."

Cal reached out and shook Pete's hand. "Field artillery, rocket systems."

"Howdy, Sarah. I was telling Cal here I'm upset over the menu for today's lunch, and I'm going to have a talk with that cafeteria manager."

Cal cupped Pete's shoulder as if they were buddies.

Sarah looked from one to the other. "What about?"

Bug-eyed, Pete leaned toward her as if proximity would compel her to listen. She backed up against the wall and crossed her arms.

"They serve potatoes and carrots. Those are the Devil's foods. You shouldn't eat nothing grown underground. It's all dirty, touched by the Devil."

She ignored the smile on Cal's face. "They've been serving potatoes for years. It's what the kids like."

"They probably don't know how bad they are. Somebody better tell them."

Sarah closed her eyes and pictured those sweet ladies who worked in the cafeteria. *Go along with him*, his sister had said. "Why don't you hold off and let me do it? I know them pretty well and they'll listen to me."

"Good idea." He pushed his mop down the hallway about ten feet. A group of jean-clad students moved to one side to let Pete pass. Instead, he began to chat with them. Sarah hoped root vegetables weren't the topic. Pete wasn't acting crazy enough to be hospitalized again, but she wondered if he was taking his medication. She didn't feel comfortable asking him, but she would mention it to Martha Rose this afternoon when she picked up Mandy.

Cal dragged her into her classroom by the arm, took her books and tossed them onto the first empty chair. He hipped the door shut and collapsed into laughter. He leaned over, his hands on her shoulders, and drew her closer until their foreheads were almost touching. "I thought I'd seen some messed up dudes in Nam, but your cousin tops them all."

She had forgotten how tall Cal was. His was a great laugh, deep and clear as a bell. Sarah smiled up, and there were Cal's eyes, still Caribbean blue. Their eyes held a second too long, sending warm vibrations through her body. She drew back in confusion. Had he felt the same currents jumping between them? It was wrong. Way wrong. To hide her reaction, she organized the books and papers on her desk. She worried aloud that Pete would surely embarrass her, maybe even get her fired for vouching for him.

Perhaps Cal was nervous, too. In any case, he moved away. Her eyes were drawn to his left leg. The knee still didn't flex properly. "Was it worth it, Cal?" His eyes followed hers to his leg. "Are you sorry you went?"

He stared at his leg as if he didn't quite recognize it. "I'm sorry about the way a lot of things turned out, but I'm not sorry I went." His voice and eyes hardened. "I know you think the Age of Aquarius is ready to break out any day now, but it ain't gonna happen. It's a competition, Sarah. Always has been. For land, for resources, for friends who'll share their resources with you. I did my part to make sure the U.S. hung onto our share. We didn't win this time, but the guys on the ground over there—we gave it our best shot. And now no one gives a damn about us. That bozo in the White House even pardoned the draft dodgers."

"It's not true that no one gives a—that we don't care about the vets, but I think President Carter did the right thing. The boys who went to Canada followed their consciences, like you."

He blinked and changed the subject. "Look, I didn't come here to argue. I was waiting for you because Pete's sister—"

"Martha Rose. You met her at Thanksgiving dinner at my aunts'." Back when they were in love. Back when everyone assumed they would get married. They were in dangerous territory now. Her fingers twisted her wedding bands and she couldn't look at him. Pretended to search for something in her desk drawer. Brought out paper clips.

"Yeah, I remember." The laughter was gone from his eyes now. "I wanted to talk to you about Martha Rose. How well do you know her?"

Her eyebrows drew together. "Not well. Talked to her at a few family dinners. She moved back to town this year. Opened a day care center. She's keeping Mandy for me."

His eyes wandered around the room and were cold when they finally returned to her. "You can't trust her."

Sarah pressed him to explain, but the first bell rang and he limped out toward the gym. For a few minutes, she felt distracted, wondering what Cal was trying to tell her, but thirty-four students wiggling, giggling, and shoving their way into the classroom marshaled her thoughts.

After calling roll, she distributed handouts for group work on the beliefs of the Founding Fathers, secretly enjoying the pungent odor of purple mimeograph fluid rising from the paper. While she was giving examples of how they might fill in their charts, someone knocked on the classroom door. Orange hair, big freckles, rumpled plaid shirt hanging out over faded jeans—these were what Sarah absorbed in the first few seconds after the door opened. This Huck Finnish character ambled over in dirty work boots with a yellow schedule change card from the guidance office. Transfer from R. Sullivan to S. Hardman. Four weeks into the grading period, and the guidance office was changing Lee Price from Early American History to Founding Fathers. They probably had no idea the two classes used different texts, anymore than they knew R. Sullivan had 16 students—15 now—in her first period while S. Hardman now had 38. No one planned it that way, she could hear them saying. She tried to control her pique. It wasn't Lee's fault.

When the dismissal bell rang, Sarah tromped down the hall to Peg Fansler's room. "Look, Peg." Sarah held up the offending transfer slip. "I got another student in my first period. I'm out of desks. It's got to stop." She hoped her department chair could help.

Peg sighed. "I know. I took another one too."

"But why? It's the end of January. The kids have already missed the first month of the course." Sarah knew she was pointing out the obvious.

Students filed into the room. Peg gestured for her to move closer to her desk. "I know, but these kids will fail if they stay in Rachel's room and they don't deserve that. She's a good teacher, but so inflexible. Lee needs attention, but not in an obnoxious way. His mother deserted the family. Will you try with him for a week?"

A kid without a mom. It was the right thing to do, but she still felt like a sucker.

Thirty-One

FEBRUARY 1977

It wasn't Sarah's imagination. The radio this morning said it was the coldest winter on record. Sarah pulled on her nylon parka and boots and tugged a plum-colored snowsuit onto Mandy. They hiked up the hill. Roy Glen had disappeared earlier, despite the snow-covered highway. Supposedly, a Saturday visit to see his mother, but if it were true, he would have taken them with him. At the top of the highest hill on their property stood a chestnut tree, its limbs bare and brown. Sarah and Mandy turned around in front of it. Their boots made a trail of six-inch deep depressions, big ones and little ones, in the snow leading from the trailer to where they stood. Their breath steamed into the air. Sarah flung the aluminum saucer on the ground and invited Mandy to hop on in front of her. The first ride was sluggish on the carpet of snow. Twice they inched their way along, rocking the saucer back and forth until it freed itself from the clutches of the snow. After two more trips, the snow compacted into a smooth sheet and they flew down the hill, shrieking with laughter. The last time they carried the saucer to the top of the hill, Sarah stared at the tree line, where Foster was buried beneath the snow. Poor old dog. He'd never liked being cold. When they finished sledding, she and Mandy took dog treats up and laid them on his grave.

The phone was ringing when she got back to the house. Roy Glen's mother, Ellen, wanted to speak with Roy Glen.

"He's not here." Sarah's words came out clipped and cold because he'd lied to her and this woman raised the sneaky bastard.

"Could you run me in to see Dr. Turrain?" Ellen asked. "Frank's at work, and my left arm won't move. Not a bit. The tea kettle whistled and when I went to pick it up, I felt a little dizzy and then I couldn't make my arm move. I finally set the cup down and turned the kettle off with my right hand. It unnerved me some, I can tell you that."

Sarah's anger evaporated instantly. "Sit down. I'll be right there."

Sarah dialed 911 first, then Frank at the general store. Luckily, the gas station had installed chains on the Chevy two weeks ago—Lord, had Roy Glen been angry, said it would scratch the paint. The tics in his cheek jumped and his muscles tensed until she really was afraid he was going to hit her. But he hadn't. Getting off their hill was tricky, the back end fishtailing on ice. Once she got out on the main road, the car chugged along steadily. She drove as fast as she dared to her in-laws' farm with Mandy, the chains rumbling as they gripped the road.

"Ambulance is on the way," she told Ellen as she came through the back door into the kitchen. The gas floor furnace gave off blue light and wicked heat that smacked Sarah in the face. Her boots left sloshy footprints everywhere she stepped.

"Can't you take me to the doctor instead? I'll feel like I'm going to die if I ride in an ambulance. See? Just my arm." She tried to lift her sweatered arm but couldn't without help from her opposite hand.

Mandy keyed in on the word she'd only recently learned. "Foster died."

Oh, Lord, talk about dying was likely to upset Ellen. "Mandy," Sarah said, a warning in her voice. She studied Ellen for other signs of instability. Her mind seemed to be fine. No signs of disorder in the kitchen. Everything looked as tidy as ever, food stored out of sight, dishes drying in the drain basket, crumpled dish towel hanging on the oven door handle. Sarah knelt and turned down the floor furnace. What was it with older folks keeping a room stifling hot?

"Poor Foster," Ellen said. "I wondered why he didn't come over with you anymore."

"He died." Mandy tilted her head, eyes large and sorrowful. "We took dog treats to his grave this morning."

"When did this happen?" Ellen asked.

"The morning I started to work," Sarah said. "Guess he missed me and ran out into the road right after I left. I really feel bad about it."

"No, honey, Foster was over here with Roy Glen that morning. I remember because my boy sat right where you are now, all in a dither because you'd gotten a job. I reminded him I worked at the store, but it was like he didn't hear me. Foster lay right at his feet while he told us how Mandy was going to some kind of day care and strangers would be with her all day. To tell the truth, he sounded even more upset you were going to be around strangers."

Ellen had to be confused. In his note, Roy Glen clearly stated it happened in the morning right after Sarah left. Even after all these months she could remember exactly what he'd told her. He saw the truck hit Foster. An eighteen-wheeler. Another lie? What really happened to her dog? It sickened her, but right now, there were other problems to deal with. Ellen's memory and language processing were clearly functioning well, except for mixing things up about the dog. Sarah remembered a test she'd heard for strokes.

"Can you stick out your tongue?" she asked Ellen.

Ellen could. Mandy stuck hers out too.

"It's a pinched nerve or a frozen shoulder, don't you think?"

The way the arm dangled inertly seemed serious. "Maybe, but it's best to be sure."

Sarah could hear the ambulance clacking across the wooden bridge. Thank God. If it was a stroke, she'd heard immediate care was important.

She and Mandy drove behind the ambulance. They passed Frank going the other way. He u-turned and followed.

Two hours later doctors delivered a verdict. A small stroke. Her language center was unaffected, and she was already recovering use of the arm. They admitted her for at least an overnight stay.

Sarah took Mandy home. After missing her nap entirely, she was cranky all through dinner. Sarah put her to bed early. Still no sign of Roy Glen. She couldn't stop thinking about Foster. Why would Roy Glen lie about what happened to him? Could Ellen have been confused? She didn't sound confused. She sounded certain.

Mandy coughed off and on, and Sarah slept fitfully, waking at two, and again at three-thirty to check on her. When Roy Glen hadn't come home by noon Sunday, Sarah took Mandy to her mother's so she could visit Ellen at the hospital. The hurt on Ellen's face caused by Roy Glen's absence was replaced by concern when Sarah said she hadn't seen him to tell him about the stroke. Ellen sent Frank to check the emergency room and call the police station to see if there'd been an accident, things Sarah used to do before she wised up.

Around four a.m., Roy Glen crawled into bed, rolled her over and began kissing her. His breath smelled strongly of sour wine and of a woman's musk. An unmistakable smell like fish.

Sarah shoved him away. "Leave me alone, you bastard."

"Shut up." He grabbed her neck and forced his mouth onto hers. His beard scraped her face. She fought back the urge to vomit. He pinned one of her arms down and lifted her sleep shirt. She pushed at him with her free hand, but it was useless. Finally she lay limp as a rag doll. If she didn't think about it, it would be over soon. She turned her head and watched the clock. Two and a half minutes later, he rolled off. Premature ejaculation, she thought. She knew words for it now, but it was too late for words to help. From her side of the bed, she could still smell his sour breath.

"What really happened to Foster?" She asked even though she was pretty sure she knew.

"He ran after you the morning you started to work. I warned you going to work was a bad idea, but you wouldn't listen. Why? You ready to listen now?"

"Your mother told me a different story. She said Foster was with you that morning."

"When were you talking to my mother?"

"I asked you something first. What really happened to Foster?"

Roy Glen blinked once and scratched his nose, silent for some time, staring at the ceiling. "I shot him, okay? I didn't feel like taking care of some old dog while you were off gallivanting around. I'd never get a moment's peace with that mutt always whining to get in and out. Old as he was, I did that dog a favor. Now, why were you talking to my mother?"

She rolled toward the paneled wall, eyes filled with tears. Only rage held them back. She had known it was something like that ever since Ellen told her the dog had been with Roy Glen that morning. Why else would he have lied? She wished she could strangle him, wished she were strong enough, brave enough. She remembered his words, which felt more than ever like a threat: *You should reconsider this job. What if something happens to Mandy next?* Her job—her real job now, one she couldn't fail at—was keeping her little girl safe until she could get them away.

"Your mother's in the hospital. She had a stroke while you were out partying."

He jumped up and pulled on his jeans. "Christ, Sarah. Why the hell didn't you tell me? You can be really stupid sometimes."

She didn't answer. In an hour and a half, she had to get ready for school, but she wouldn't be able to sleep. Shoving her way past her husband, she went to the bathroom to shower. Semen oozed down her legs like pus. She heard keys clink, the door slamming, the motor burbling to life, tires crunching on gravel. Satisfied he was gone, she got a washcloth and a bar of soap and scrubbed her face and mouth until they hurt. Then she started on the rest of her body.

When she finished, she dressed and got started. She searched through the shoebox where Roy Glen kept important papers and found the passbook. Two hundred and fifty dollars. Five years of overtime and so little to show for it. Simply working double overtime shifts Christmas Day and New Year's should have made more than the amount in savings all by themselves. So what happened to the money? She filled a page of a yellow legal pad with things she needed to budget for. Food, gas, clothes, utilities. What would be left for rent?

On the way to her classroom, Sarah passed Rachel in the hallway. "When's the big day? My mom wanted to be sure she could get off work and the hospital's schedule is tight in June because everyone's taking vacations."

Rachel hugged her. "June 22. I couldn't get married without you and her there. She's been like a second mother to me."

The hug hurt. A long-sleeved sweater hid the bruises, big purple blooms Roy Glen probably wouldn't even remember making. Sarah imagined Rachel's expression if she were to find out Sarah was planning a divorce.

Thirty-Two

FEBRUARY 1977

"Mommy, are you paying attention?" Mandy pulled on her arm.

"I heard every word." A lie. Sarah's mind had wandered. She called to check on Roy Glen's mother every day, and each time Ellen said she was fine, and asked how Roy Glen was. The question let Sarah know he hadn't been to see his mother since she had left the hospital Tuesday. Each time Ellen asked, Sarah said he wasn't feeling well. Twice after work, she drove over to the Hardmans' with casseroles.

"You aren't listening good. I missed a word. Read aloud with me." They chanted the words to *Hop on Pop*.

It was nearly ten on Saturday morning when Roy Glen rolled out of bed and ambled into the living room. The sun was bright, the day and the roads clear, but flurries were predicted. Roy Glen wore jeans, dirty hunting jacket, and work boots. His fingers, callused from handling machinery, raked through his hair in an attempt to comb it. "I'm going out."

Sarah closed Mandy's book in surprise. She assumed they would visit his mother together. Over the past week, she had tried her best to act normal while she planned her next move. "What about your mother? I made vegetable lasagna to take over."

"I'll stop and see her later."

"Where you going?"

"I got business to take care of."

This easy dismissal burned her. In three strides she crossed the living room and confronted him in the kitchen. "I'm taking Mandy to my mother's so I won't be here when your mother calls and wants to know why you haven't come over. I've made excuses for you all week."

Roy Glen stopped at the door, his face twitching as if an insect had crawled across his cheek. "You and Mandy stay here."

The wood-paneled walls hummed with anxiety. From the hook by the door, Sarah lifted the keys to the Chevy. Her voice emerged a notch too loud. "No way. If you aren't taking us to your mother's, I'm going to visit mine."

With one hand wrapped around Sarah's fingers, Roy Glen tugged at the keys with the other. She struggled to hold on as he squeezed until the bones in her fingers felt as if they would snap. She relinquished the keys as tears of pain and frustration pooled in her eyes. Through it all, she was aware of Mandy, expressionless, eyes riveted on them.

"You're not going anywhere." He didn't yell. He almost never raised his voice. Sarah realized their marriage wasn't worth that much passion. "I'm taking the Chevy to be sure."

The pale winter sun seemed whiter, brighter to her. She sucked in her breath. A thin slice of time splintered off, a fragment she knew she would put under a microscope for years afterward, re-examining every detail. As Roy Glen opened the door to leave, the light froze his face in Sarah's memory like those glimpses you get in a disco when people and objects flash clear and stark against the black room. In that moment, she knew the unkempt man standing at her door was not her husband. He had nothing in common with the person she had fallen in love with. Maybe that man had always been a figment of her imagination.

Mandy's voice demanded recognition. "Bye, Daddy."

His eyes shifted toward her briefly. "Bye, Peanut." The door closed.

Apparently satisfied, Mandy trained brown eyes on Sarah. "Now can we go to Nana's, Mommy? Please?" The tilt of her head was a well-practiced tool of persuasion.

"Soon." If Sarah had to call her mother to come get them, she would.

Light streaked through the kitchen window, harsh and blindingly white, flooding the box of matches on the kitchen table. Sarah felt as if she were seeing them for the first time. Fahrenheit 357 Club. The Holiday Inn. The 25 and Over. Oliver's. Month by month, year by year, the pile had grown. She could read the story of their marriage in the colorful cardboard squares sporting fancy logos. She picked up a packet from Oliver's. She had never been there. Didn't even know where it was. She picked the whole box up, carried it outside, and dumped it in the metal trash can.

Back in the house, she rooted through the kitchen junk drawer, flicking aside rubber bands, half-full packets of lettuce and pansy seeds, a roll of breath mints, stapler, screwdriver, cylinder of kite string, and a packet of picture hangers until she found what she wanted: the spare key to Roy Glen's truck. She allowed herself a triumphant smile. He had forgotten it was there.

Mandy was printing her name down the center of the *TV Guide* in red crayon.

"Will you be real good by yourself if I go out to Daddy's truck for a few minutes?"

"When we going to Nana's?"

"In a minute."

"Why you going out there without a coat, Mommy? It's cold." As she faked a shiver, Mandy's brown pigtails danced and her eyes widened dramatically.

Sarah smiled at her daughter's theatrics. "I know. I need something from the truck. Be right back, ok?" Roy Glen had turned the truck so it faced the road, as was his custom. She and Mandy hadn't ridden in it for ages. As she unlocked the door, she could hear her mother's voice telling her a marriage had to be based on trust. But at some point, trust became foolish. This marriage wasn't going to last anyway. It was already dead and no one had buried it. She shivered as the wind whipped around her. Mandy was right. She should have put on a coat.

She slid into the passenger seat, careful to avoid stepping on the McDonalds trash, an assortment of tools and a few empty beer cans. She would begin with the glove compartment and work her way back to the capped bed. For one fear-frosted moment she was afraid to open it. Would he be able to tell she had rifled through his things? Didn't matter. She wasn't sure what she was looking for, but she would know when she saw it.

She opened the glove compartment and stopped breathing. Lying right on top—big and black and ugly as sin—was a handgun, squarish in design, all angles. Had he killed Foster with it? Or did he plan to kill someone? Her? Mandy? Sarah sat for what seemed like minutes staring at the gun, afraid to touch it, her mouth dry, but she had gotten into the truck to find out the truth. She had to see this through.

Next she found a baggie full of dried green stuff. Looked like dried grass. Marijuana? She opened the baggie and sniffed the contents: musty and pungent. Her eyes darted toward the road, sure an undercover cop would spring out of nowhere and arrest her for possession of a concealed weapon and drugs. She dumped it by the gun on the driver's seat. In the rear corner of the glove box, she found an unlabeled plastic vial full of white powder. Cocaine? Heroin? She knew jackshit about drugs, but she was sure the powder wasn't legal.

Under the canister was an envelope, which she turned over in her hands several times, examining the handwriting. A woman's round flourishes. She had written only Roy Glen's name on the front, so it had been hand-delivered or left where he would find it. Sarah pulled the sheets of paper out—three—and began to read: "Dear Roy Glen, As I write this letter, I am wanting you so bad. I think about us all the time." Sarah's hands shook. She had known, part of her had known, but she had never allowed herself to really acknowledge it. She flipped to the last page to see the signature. Martha Rose. There could only be one Martha Rose. Sarah wondered how long this had been going on. Before Mandy enrolled in day care at Hearts and Hands—or after?

The low rumble of a motor came from the highway below. She froze. Roy Glen coming back? No, a white station wagon. She waited until the diminishing rumble told her it was well on its way past their property before she continued to read. "Even though you haven't slept with your wife for years—" what a frigging lie—"what we're doing is wrong. Someone is going to get hurt. Probably all of us." She skimmed ahead. "Since Charlie found out, he has been acting crazy. He follows me. I have to be so careful now. Yesterday he held a gun to my head and threatened to kill me and you and disappear with Chastity. I don't think he'd really hurt me, but he might take off with Chastity. Although I want to be with you, I couldn't stand it if I lost my baby." Sarah read the letter again before she returned it to the envelope. Maybe Roy Glen carried the gun for self-defense. In case Martha Rose's husband cornered him. Cal must have known. This must have been what he was trying to tell her at school. Who else knew? Half the town? She wished she never had to show her face again.

The capped truck bed also had its shocks: two sets of clothes she had never seen before, cowboy boots, empty wine bottles, an air mattress and pillows. Three empty bottles of penicillin prescribed over a six-month period littered the truck bed. Sarah had to think about the meaning of those bottles. Did they have anything to do with the odor she couldn't scrub off?

The real shocker: a corrugated cardboard box labeled Campbell's Soup with a dozen baggies filled with what she could only assume was pot. He was selling.

She bolted to the trailer, buttoned Mandy into her parka, and had her halfway to the truck when she stopped. This was not the time to act stupid. She tugged her daughter's mittened hand back inside.

The discoveries in the truck delivered the final kick at the wall separating her from the truth, and when that wall shattered, the reality of her life lay before her. For a few seconds as she looked around the tiny kitchen and living room where she'd spent the past five years, she lost the ability to think. She sucked in her breath, could barely stand up. If they left now, what would happen to Mandy? She shook her head, as if to physically move past that *if.* She was leaving. She threw their clothes into garbage bags and tossed them into the back of the truck. Mandy's medicine and her favorite books and toys. Grade book and typewriter and textbooks and satchel of student papers. *Think, Sarah, think. What else do you need? Protect yourself. Protect your daughter.* From the shoebox in the bedroom closet where Roy Glen kept valuable papers, she grabbed the check book, bank book, and the titles to the truck and car and trailer. She didn't know where she stood legally, but she wanted some control over their assets.

Driving the truck for the first time intensified the feeling she was entering a foreign world. Compared to her car, the truck raised her up so high her entire perspective of the road changed. Unused to the vehicle's weight and feel, she drove slowly at first, hands shaky on the wheel. Her eyes darted from the berm to the double yellow lane dividers and back to the sky repeatedly. Flakes of snow drifted down, a ballet of white petals that twirled a few times and disappeared instantly as they kissed the windshield. Without mishap, she made it to her mother's driveway.

Johanna must have been watching from the window. She met them at the door, a half-eaten Snickers bar clutched in her hand. "What a nice surprise! What brings you here on a Saturday? I thought you'd be checking up on Roy Glen's mother. Can I make you some lunch? Cheese and crackers? Peanut butter sandwich? "

Sarah declined the food. Her stomach was churning from the morning's upheavals.

"Roy Glen has a cold, and he didn't want to expose his mother to the germs, so Mandy and I decided to come over here." The lie rolled off Sarah's tongue easily, smooth as glass. She glanced at Mandy, hoping she wouldn't contradict her, but after kissing her nana, she already was working the lever on the wooden M&M dispenser. Red, yellow, and green candies dropped into her hand.

"Sure hope you and Mandy don't get his cold. A bad one is going around. Everyone in the lab has it."

Sarah felt a twinge of guilt. Now her mother would worry about them.

"Where's your car?" Johanna asked. "I almost didn't know who it was when I saw the truck."

"Roy Glen's working on it." As her mother's brow furrowed, Sarah nearly slapped herself on the head. "Or rather, he needs to work on it. Some noise the engine is making."

"Be sure it's fixed before you drive it. Remember it carries precious cargo." She hugged Sarah with an over-padded arm and beamed meaningfully toward Mandy.

Besides Garrett's girlfriend Alisa, that "used" woman, that "loser," Sarah only knew of one divorced woman in Clarksburg. "Mom, how is Francesca Barberio getting along?"

Johanna looked at Mandy to make sure she was occupied with the candy dispenser. "She and the kids are having a hard time of it. One of the boys started rebelling after the—divorce." This last word whispered through fingers. "She sent him to live with Dick because she couldn't control him. At Lurleen's, I heard Francesca barely has enough money for food. Hasn't had her hair done in months. She never should have left him."

Sarah gritted her teeth. One thing she knew for sure: she would never let anyone take Mandy from her. Over her dead body.

"You feeling okay? You're not—" fingers over the mouth again— "pregnant are you?" Her eyes glittered with hope.

"God no." Sarah slipped into the bathroom and splashed cold water on her face. As she returned, she checked the time. Her mother's wall clock was shaped like a sunflower with a yellow center to match the Formica table and countertops. Sarah was amazed to find it was not quite noon. She felt as though she had already lived through several years this morning.

Her mother stirred potato soup in a large pot. "Feeling better? See if this needs more salt." She extended a spoon toward Sarah.

Sarah sucked the creamy mixture. "No more salt, maybe a pinch more pepper."

"Did you ever think about divorce back when Daddy used to get drunk and beat Garrett?" Sarah asked.

Johanna whirled around, brandishing her wooden spoon like a weapon. "You know what? It's time you forgave him. The trouble with you is you've never been able to see beyond the whiskey glass to the man your father really is."

"Sorry."

There was truth in what her mother said, but unless her mother could acknowledge the whiskey's effect, she couldn't see the man he really was either. Sarah closed her eyes and massaged her forehead.

Her mother hugged her. "Why don't you spend the night so I can take care of Mandy and you can get a good night's sleep."

Sarah's legs were weak with gratitude. She didn't know what she'd do without her mother's steady love. "I am feeling a little tired."

"You been working so hard at this new job, you've let yourself get run-down. Those kids probably bring all kind of germs to school and pass them on to you. You should wash your hands a lot." She stuck the spoon Sarah had licked right back in the soup.

"You'll get to visit with Garrett. He's coming for dinner. Alisa is out of town, a job interview, I think. Tonight's dessert is this new recipe I'm developing for a contest. The top prize is three hundred dollars. I poured strawberry Jello over chunks of Twinkies and after it gelled, I topped it off with sliced strawberries and whipped cream. I'd like to get your opinion. When I make it for the contest, I think I'll garnish it with a few chocolate-dipped berries. Should make a beautiful presentation, don't you think?"

She tried to muster enthusiasm. "Sounds like a winner."

Sarah decided to visit Livvie while Mandy napped. The sky was having a tantrum now, spitting flakes on vehicles and people indiscriminately. Nevertheless, she was getting the hang of driving a bigger vehicle. As she drove through town, she honked at Jimmy Watson, who was getting into his cruiser in front of the police station. Hard to get used to his being a police officer. He looked good in his uniform, as if he belonged in it. She eased off the gas a bit. Not that he was likely to stop her, but the stuff in the back end could get her arrested. Even if Jimmy was the Boy-Next-Door.

The crumbled concrete steps to Aunt Livvie's porch had fist-size chunks eaten away by ice storms and exploded by spring thaws. The old house, which had been immaculate when the sisters were younger, showed signs of exhaustion, much like Livvie herself. Nearly seventy-two, Livvie still stood as tall as Sarah but her skin hung loose, as if it had no underpinnings. Her aunt's eyes were cavernous, the cancer clearly progressing. Both Livvie and the house smelled sour. If impending death had a smell, Sarah suspected this was it.

Sarah put the gelatin dessert and spaghetti sauce her mother had sent into the refrigerator. When she came back, Livvie was easing herself onto the couch. Sarah adjusted a pillow behind Livvie's back and laid an afghan across her lap.

"What is it?" Livvie asked. "I can see something's wrong."

Sarah threw her hands up. "I don't know. Everything."

Her aunt chuckled softly and patted Sarah's hand. Livvie's skin was translucent as glass, revealing a network of ropey veins. "Now *everything* isn't wrong. You have a beautiful little girl and a wonderful job teaching school. I'm so proud of you."

Leave it to Livvie to remind Sarah of her blessings. She felt a little better already. Yet she dreaded telling her aunt about the divorce. As a Catholic, Livvie would surely be opposed. Even though her parents weren't Catholic, they were still going to go bonkers. Didn't matter. They all had to be told.

"What I mean is—" she took a deep breath "—I don't know if I can stay married anymore. Would you hate me if I got a divorce?"

"Don't be silly, I could never hate you, and I'm not even surprised."

Maybe Sarah hadn't hidden her problems as well as she thought. "My parents will have a fit."

"So you haven't told them?"

"They'll be so disappointed in me."

Her aunt squeezed her hand. "Can you imagine anything Mandy could say that would make you not love her?"

Nothing could ever breach that love. Did her mother really feel that way about her? Stupid to even question it. Of course she did. It was why she worried all the time. Why she was always shoving food at her.

"Lord knows, I disappointed my family and they still loved me," Livvie said.

Sarah couldn't imagine Livvie disappointing anyone. Her aunt was a paragon of virtue, the best there was.

"We Catholics don't approve of divorce for trivial reasons, but even our church allows it if the bonds in a marriage are truly broken, if there is a break in faithfulness. I think I know you well enough to say your reasons aren't trivial. You love your daughter so much you would stay in the marriage if you could. Am I right?"

Unable to speak, Sarah got up and pulled a tissue from the box her aunt kept on the top of the hi-fi console.

"Honey, whatever you decide to do, I will always love you. Your family will always love you."

Sarah sank back onto the couch beside Livvie. "But they will be so surprised. I haven't told them any of the trouble, and it's been going on for years. What if they don't believe me?"

"I suspect they've seen more than you think. Parents have a way of hearing what you haven't said."

Sarah laid her head against her aunt's thin-sweatered shoulder, their fingers interlaced. For a time, they sat cocooned in silence.

"There's something important I want you to have," Livvie said. "Grab a grocery bag from the kitchen first. Go upstairs to the sitting room and get in the bottom drawer of the vanity and take everything in it."

Uncle William had slept in the sitting room when he had been alive. Now, judging from toiletries and stationery arranged on the vanity and small desk, Livvie had used the space to get dressed in the morning and to handle correspondence. The only ornamentation in the room was a small faded print of the Crucifixion in a simple walnut frame. She realized it was a matching print to the one of the Assumption in Livvie's bedroom.

At first, when Sarah opened the bottom drawer, she was sure her aunt had made a mistake. It contained a stack of little books. Curious, she opened the top one. Not Livvie's spidery scrawl. The journal, dated August 1914, was written in a precise, almost calligraphic hand. Quickly Sarah dug down to the drawer's depths, withdrawing a book dated June 1909. She skimmed an entry about a family visit to the general store. Now Sarah understood what Livvie was giving her. The little journals contained the Heimbachs' story. But who had written it, if not Livvie? She dropped the books in the grocery bag and rejoined her aunt.

"Katherine would want you to have those journals. For years, she tried to get me to tell you and your mother this story, but I couldn't. I promised my mother I wouldn't tell anyone. But the truth is, I couldn't bear for anyone else to know. I was too ashamed. Once when I was a girl, I almost got married. I'm going to tell you a few things not even my sisters knew. The rest you'll have to learn from those journals."

Thirty-Three

I never was much of a student, as Sister Bernadette reminded me at least twice a week, so at fifteen I thought I might as well quit school. Make a little money and help the family out. I typed letters and filed papers, mostly for Mr. Curtin. It was Mr. Curtin who introduced me to Jay Vadeboncouer.

Jay was not what you'd call a handsome man. His nose and ears were a bit too large, his torso too long and thick to be in proportion with such short legs. His smile, though, was wide and genuine. He had big brown eyes, and they were always smiling at me. "You have the prettiest secretary in town," Jay told Mr. Curtin right in front of me. In my whole life, Jay was the only person who ever told me I was pretty. I guess I let it go to my head.

He worked for Atlantic Refining too, and did quite a bit of traveling for them. When he was in Pittsburgh, he took me to lunch, first with Mr. Curtin and others from the office, and later by myself. He complimented me often, said I reminded him of his sister. Once, he said my hair looked as soft as clouds and asked if he could touch it. "Certainly not," I said.

But much later he did touch it, and I let him kiss me. I'd never had a boy interested in me, so I was thrilled by his attention. He took me for rides in his car—a Ford. The first car I had ever gone for a spin in, and I guess I was as dizzy as a child.

One weekend he drove me and Katherine to Luna Park and we rode the roller coaster. We explored the Temple of Mystery, and of course we had to shoot the chutes, and watch the circus performers. Before we left, we had our picture taken together in the photo studio.

Mama and Papa never took to Jay. Having a car was "putting

on airs." He was Baptist and wouldn't drink beer with Papa and the older boys Sunday afternoon. "Doesn't try to fit in, does he?" Papa said after Jay left. "Besides, he's too old for you." Jay was twenty-five to my sixteen.

In October, Jay was leaving for Saudi Arabia. He didn't know how long he'd be gone. Several years at least, working for Atlantic. If the United States went to war, his mission would be very important, he said. He told me I was the most special girl he'd ever known and asked me to marry him. He gave me a beautiful pink cameo with a tiny diamond set in it as a token of our engagement. I hid it inside a sock in my dresser. Since my parents didn't approve of Jay, I invented excuses to rendezvous with him. A visit to a sick former schoolmate. A neighbor who needed some quilting squares. During our secret meetings, Jay and I made plans to elope before he was to sail for the Middle East. The trip over would be our honeymoon.

On the day we planned our escape, Mama insisted I deliver a pie to an invalid neighbor. I wrapped it in a towel—I remember gooey apples oozing through the lattice crust—and trudged off to Mrs. Amelung's house, resentful of every step. But when I breathed in the crisp air, I couldn't stay upset. Soon all the chores I did would be for Jay. My heart sang with that thought, and I began to relish the crunch of leaves beneath my feet. My eyes gathered in a store of tangerine and burgundy and gold to cherish. Next year I would experience no fall like this one. Only sand and heat. For a moment, the loss saddened me, but my mood rose again at the thought of Jay. I had seen plenty of colored leaves in my sixteen years, surely enough to last a lifetime.

I dreamed of traveling to far-off places and seeing strange things. Things I couldn't yet imagine. Men who wore turbans, Jay told me. Women who covered their faces. I would know what it was to be a wife, to sleep in the same bed as my beloved, to fix him eggs and sausage in the morning. And one day, if we were blessed by God, we would hear our son or daughter call out, "Mama, I had a bad dream. Can I sleep with you?" And we would tuck our child between us, safe and warm.

I anticipated the joys of marriage while I listened to Mrs. Amelung's recitation of aches and pains. In a hurry to be off, I was, but she asked me to feed her cat and to reach up in her pantry and bring down a box of candles, and since I was already there, couldn't I look for her gray woolen blanket—she thought it might be in the chest or else in the back of the closet. It was getting so cold now at night, she said. But I wasn't going to be cold any longer. Couldn't I stay a minute more and read the letter her sister had sent? Of course I could.

When I finished ministering to Mrs. Amelung, I sped home, light of heart and foot. Yeast rolls I had kneaded earlier were rising on baking sheets. Two chickens I had killed and cleaned in the morning roasted in the oven, and the potatoes were soaking in water. All I had to do was light a fire under them. Mama brought up three quarts of green beans to complete the supper. I wanted this dinner to be special, because it was the last we would have together for a long time, though no one else knew it.

Papa's blessing was the same as always, and the boys' manners no better than usual, all elbows and greed as they fought over drumsticks and breasts. Despite my best efforts to memorize each moment, to slow the ritual down, dinner rushed by in a flurry of passed bowls and clinking forks. Dinner had been a success, judging by the plates. Katherine's was the only one with a lot of food left, but she always used her fork more for pushing food around than for actually eating it.

After the boys and Mama and Papa excused themselves, Maggie and I collected the chipped blue stoneware dishes and washed them. Papa put his foot down and insisted Katherine couldn't leave the table until she cleaned her plate. He didn't care if she was eighteen. As long as she lived under his roof, she would take care of herself—she was wasting away.

But Papa was wrong. The minutes were ticking by and it was *my* life wasting away. Why couldn't Katherine hurry up?

I handed the clean dishes to twelve-year-old Maggie to dry. We put them away, and still Katherine dawdled at the table. Shouldn't she have to wash her own dishes if she was going to take all night? I couldn't stop grumbling.

Maggie, aware of my agitation, offered to finish. I ran upstairs and tidied my hair, rinsed my mouth, and pinched my cheeks for color. I took the letter, written days before, and laid it under my pillow. They would find it after Jay and I were on our way to New York.

I slipped away as if to take a walk in the yard. I flapped my hands at our husky Wolf, but he stayed by my side as I retrieved my bag, hidden in the shrubbery. I started down the road, Wolf at my side, to the place where Jay promised to rendezvous, far enough from the house no one would hear the motor. A half moon cast long shadows on the road. Though I often left in darkness to milk the cows, I had never gone away from home alone at night. It was quite chilly, and I snuggled into my coat, pulling it tighter about the neck, and settled down on top of my suitcase, using it as a sort of bench. I waited for Jay.

1977

Something terrible must have happened, Sarah decided. Jay died in an accident. Or got cancer. Surely he didn't stand her up.

"The rest of the story you'll have to get from Katherine's journals. I won't break my promise to my mother."

"That cameo?"

"Yes, it's the one I gave to you."

Livvie shifted her weight and winced, her eyes closing as if to shut out the pain. "Come and see me when you've finished reading. And after you're done, give your mother the journals. If Johanna hates me for—"

"She won't, she couldn't. Remember? Family loves you no matter what."

Sarah hoped it was true.

Thirty-Four

Alone in her room after her visit to Dr. Jorgansen, Sarah skimmed more journals. They painted a picture of early twentieth century life. Quite ordinary events. Katherine boasting about her grades in school, pranks the Heimbach boys played, a lot about a Mr. Wehner, who was apparently Katherine's boyfriend who accompanied her to Pirates' games. There was a solid description of their town, New Kensington, Pennsylvania, and Chambers Glass, where the Heimbach men worked. Several entries were devoted to the two youngest Heimbachs, who died in the 1909 diphtheria epidemic. It's not that the journals weren't interesting—they were, and Sarah would come back to them later—but what the devil did Livvie want her to find?

Sarah flipped through the pages randomly, frustrated, until in one of the books the name Vadeboncouer jumped out at her.

MAY 28, 1911

Patrick's wedding turned out to be quite respectable. Marie wore a lovely dark rose silk dress. Tony and Joe stood up for Patrick, and Tony's little Susan was the flower girl. Marie's two oldest sisters stood for her.

I sang a solo for the church service. Mr. Wehner and Sally Friesen said it was quite as good as the singing at the Pittsburgh theaters. Mr. Wehner said I missed my calling by not becoming a star in the musicals.

The party afterward was quite lively. My brothers Tony and Joe got together a band. Tony plays accordion; Joe, flute. Their friends from work filled in with other instruments. I danced often with Mr. Wehner.

Thank heavens it was a Saturday so that Livvie's friend, Mr. Vadeboncouer, did not repeat the scene he made at Patrick's engagement party. On that occasion, he would not drink because it was a Sunday, and ranted until the other men felt uncomfortable. Mr. V ignored Papa's opinion that he needed to relax a little. Livvie's beau is a Baptist. What do you make of that, Dear Diary?

There is a sad ending to the wedding: Patrick and Marie are moving to West Virginia. Better wages. Patrick says glass in Pittsburgh is going downhill and Papa should have moved on long ago. The more they mechanize, the lower the wages go for the workers.

Papa says he won't leave "Grandmother" Magdalen behind and she won't move because who would tend Karl's grave if not her? She has a point, but then I think, how long into the future is grave-tending supposed to go on? If forever, people could never move.

SEPTEMBER 4, 1911

I hope I have done the right thing. I was looking for a particular embroidered handkerchief this morning, and thinking that Livvie might accidentally have put it in her drawer, I was sorting through the hankies and stockings when I came across a letter.

It seemed so odd, a letter written in Livvie's own spidery hand, with "Dear Ones" on the envelope. I couldn't help myself. I read it.

I was amazed to learn my sister planned to elope with Mr. Vadeboncoeur. Not only that, she planned to go with him to Saudi Arabia and live among all those heathen. I am not ignorant of their strange practices. They pray to a different god called Allah and believe in Mohammed instead of Jesus. A man can take more than one wife. The dark-skinned men steal white women and force them to become slaves in harems. Can you imagine Livvie living in the midst of that, as sheltered as she is?

I hid the letter back in Livvie's drawer and went straight to Mama and Papa. They visited Mr. V. today in his rooms. Mama said Papa was pleasant but firm. If they want to marry, it must be after Mr. V. returns from Saudi Arabia. He does not know how long he will be gone, perhaps two years. Mama insisted Mr. V. must convert to Catholicism. Mr. V., Mama said, was equally adamant that he could not since his beliefs are strongly formed. In fact, he considered it his duty to spread the Baptist faith in Saudi Arabia if the opportunity arose. Livvie and he would raise their children as Baptists. Mama said if he didn't convert, there would be no children. Papa said he would be sitting with a shotgun near the place Mr. V. planned to meet Livvie tonight.

My poor sister is sitting out on the roadside in the dark waiting for a man who isn't coming. Mama says it is best this way. Livvie will think he backed out. She can be miserable about it for a while and then get over it. If Livvie thinks we kept him away, Mama says, Livvie will blame us and long for him. This way, it will really be over. I hope Mama is right.

OCTOBER 16, 1911

Livvie has confided nothing in me, but I hear her weeping after she thinks I have gone to sleep. She must have truly loved this man, else her tears would surely have dried up by now. Mama has invited Mr. Moran over to Sunday supper twice, but Livvie is absolutely listless in his presence. I asked Mr. Wehner discreetly if he can procure any other suitable friends.

NOVEMBER 27, 1911

Dear God! Livvie is expecting a child, and it is all my fault she is separated from the man who should, by now, be her husband. Mama and Papa blame themselves, but I know it is my burden alone to bear. They never would have known about the elopement if I had not read Livvie's letter. Why did I ever meddle?

Mama has been wonderful, not angry as I expected her to be. She held Livvie's head against her chest and rocked her as if she were a baby, the both of them crying, Mama the hardest. She told Livvie the truth about why Mr. V. didn't come. I wasn't eavesdropping outside the bedroom door. I only wanted to understand what was wrong with my sister. I was relieved when Mama didn't mention my part in events.

Papa is making discreet inquiries to see if he can obtain Mr. V.'s address to inform him of these circumstances. He is gone from Pennsylvania, but may not have sailed for the Middle East yet. Perhaps something can be done to set this right.

NOVEMBER 28, 1911

It seems Mr. V.'s devotion to Livvie was not as strong as hers to him. He wed before he set sail. A widow from their church, his parents said. They arranged the marriage because they didn't want their son to be alone so far from home. Now what?

November 29, 1911

Mama made an announcement today. She will raise Livvie's baby as her own. I don't know who will believe it—she will be forty nine when this child is born. I guess it happens sometimes, though. Livvie is to go into confinement immediately, and we are to invite no guests to the house. (What will everyone think after all these years of having more people traipse through on a daily basis than a train station?) We are to say Livvie has consumption and is too weak for company.

Mama made all of us promise never, ever to speak a word of the true origins of this child. She said if any of us did, we would burn in hell.

Later I overheard Mama giving Livvie her Madonna and her ebony rosary beads. She said there was a story that went with the Madonna, but Mama pulled the bedroom door shut and I couldn't hear the rest.

I have come to a decision of my own. I will take on the responsibilities of the child's father. It is my duty since it is my fault Livvie has no husband. This is my penance for my part in breaking my sister's heart. I will help to feed and clothe the child and pay for its education.

Though I doubt I would have ever married Mr. Wehner, he is bound to wonder when I avoid his company.

Thirty-Five

FEBRUARY 1977

The journals stripped away one more piece of Sarah's identity. Adelisa, who died before Sarah was born, was not her grandmother. Livvie was. The youngest Heimbach, of course, was Sarah's mother. Johanna. Dear God—what was her mother going to think about this?

Sarah reread Katherine's pledge. So that's why she never married.

Little moments over the years flooded back with newfound significance. Moments when Livvie's face grew unexpectedly distant and anguished. Sarah tried to imagine what it would be like to take care of Mandy, but never hear her child call her "Mama." Never be able to whip out photographs of her grandkids to grocery store clerks at the slightest encouragement, to glory in grandmotherhood the way her own mother did. And the shame Livvie must have felt over her pregnancy—Sarah understood that completely. She had been there—and how much worse for Livvie because the baby's father wasn't around to marry her.

Sarah was quiet during dinner, her mind bouncing between the journals and how she was going to tell her parents and brother she wanted a divorce. As soon as Mandy finished her dinner and skipped off to Rita's with a container of Twinkie gelatin, Sarah straightened her spine against the back of the kitchen chair and blurted it out.

Frowning, Johanna dampened her napkin with saliva and dabbed at a coffee stain on the yellow Formica table. "For heaven's sake, sweetie, things can't be that bad. All couples have little spats. You two need to talk to Reverend Morse. He's helped plenty of couples."

As if Roy Glen would be caught dead in a church or asking anyone for help. Sarah jumped up from the chair. It banged into the wall. "It's gone beyond that, Mom. Our stuff's in the truck, and we're not going back."

Johanna put the napkin down, all attention now, her eyes circling the table from Nelson, to Garrett, back to Sarah. "Calm down and tell us what's happened."

"For starters, I went to see Doc Jorgansen and Roy Glen gave me—" Her hand flew up to cover her mouth, her eyes averted. There was no way she could say gonorrhea. She settled for a disease.

Nelson slammed his palm on the table. Silverware jumped. Water sloshed in glasses. "That son of a bitch promised he'd straighten up."

Sarah couldn't believe what she was hearing. "You knew and didn't tell me?"

Johanna punched fists into her hips. "And you didn't tell me either?"

Nelson held his palms up helplessly. "I hoped everything would work out. Martha Rose's husband, Charlie, came to see me at the office. He threatened to kill Roy Glen if he didn't stop messing around with his wife."

"My niece did this?" Johanna interrupted.

Shaking his head, Nelson continued as if she hadn't spoken. "I don't know what Charlie thought I could do, but I talked to Roy Glen and he said he would stop, that he never wanted to hurt Sarah or Mandy. Obviously he lied."

Sarah couldn't help but feel doubly betrayed. Not only her husband, but her father kept secrets from her. She knew her father did it to protect her, but it bothered her, nonetheless.

"Sweetie, maybe you could still try counseling," Johanna said.

Garrett rolled his eyes. "Are you crazy? Martha Rose isn't the only one. I've seen him out with other women lots of times. About time you left him, Sarah."

Was there anyone she could ever trust again? Anyone who was open and honest? All this time everyone must have been feeling sorry for her, thinking what a fool she was. "Thanks a bunch for telling me."

Garrett couldn't meet her eyes. "I thought you probably knew."

"You could have told me—doesn't anyone ever tell me anything?" Johanna said. "Now, Sarah, I firmly believe people can change with the help of God. Roy Glen's made some really bad mistakes, but if you make him sleep on the couch for a while until—"

"Christ, Johanna—" Nelson shook his head again.

"Mom, he doesn't take no for an answer. He knew he had this—"

she stumbled over her words again—"disease, and he came home and forced—" She held her hands up in the air. Surely her mother wasn't going to make her spell it out. She wished she could crawl in a hole and disappear for a century or two.

Johanna pressed her hand tightly to her mouth, her eyes wide. "Oh, sweetie."

"He didn't even have the decency to tell me he was infected. I found the penicillin bottles this morning." Sarah realized she had been re-infecting him. No wonder he didn't get better.

"I can't go back there." The more she said it, the more she knew it was true. She steeled herself, waiting for her father to tell her she was a loser, that no man wanted used when he could get fresh.

Johanna's eyes narrowed. Her lower lip rolled in and she bit down on it. As it rolled back, she resembled a bulldog. She reached across the empty soup bowl and clamped her hand on top of Sarah's. "No, of course you can't, not if that's how he's going to treat you. What do you need? How can we help?"

Her father pushed his chair back and stood up. "What she needs is a damn lawyer. Ethan Hedgwick's the man."

Why had she been so afraid to tell them? Her father went straight to the telephone. He was right about what she needed, but lawyers cost money. Seconds later, Sarah could hear his voice coming from the den. "Ethan? We've got a problem here. One I think you can help us with."

Johanna began to gather the dirty dishes, and Sarah rose to help. Garrett pushed aside their efforts. "Sit still and let me do the dishes."

It was decent of him. Since he'd signed on with the Riley Insurance Agency, he had made a quantum leap forward in maturity. Maybe it was also his girlfriend's influence.

"Besides, you're liable to break something, and Dad will expect me to clean it up," he added.

Johanna put a cigarette in her mouth. She removed it to talk. "Don't look at me like that. I'm not going to light it. I just need to feel one between my lips. I suppose you were up at Livvie's so long today because you were telling her all about your divorce when you hadn't even told me." She put the cigarette back between her lips.

Was it possible her mother was jealous? "Actually, we talked more about her than about me. She told me some interesting stories. One of them I need to share with you."

"Believe me, I've heard all my sister's stories. Many times." She put down the cigarette and unwrapped a candy bar.

"Not this one." Her mother's world was about to undergo a seismic shift.

When Nelson came back to the kitchen, he handed Sarah a check for $200. "The retainer. He'll see you Monday a week, right after work, four o'clock sharp."

No words could adequately thank him, so she settled for kissing his cheek. He may have let her down dozens of times when she was growing up, but he sure was coming through for her now.

He squirmed under her hug. "Monday I'm going to bring home an application for a credit card. I'll co-sign, so it will get quick approval. Then I want you to make one small purchase and pay off the bill immediately. It's ridiculous for you not to have credit. You might need it in an emergency."

She thanked him. Now all she needed was a new day care arrangement for Mandy. "I can't stand the thought of Martha Rose getting her grubby hands anywhere near Mandy."

"The Methodist Church opened a day care center in the Sunday School wing last month. Mrs. Nicholas, your old Sunday School teacher, is running it. If you went to church like you should, you'd have known that."

That sounded ideal. Mrs. Nicholas was great with kids, and the church was a clean, safe environment. Maybe now that Roy Glen wouldn't be controlling her movements, she could start going again. Immediately she had second thoughts. She'd be too ashamed—the pregnancy, the divorce—everyone would judge her, just like her father. A loser.

"One more thing," Sarah said. "Whenever Roy Glen realizes the truck's missing, he's going to make a scene. He'll figure out where I am. He's dangerous. He's got a loaded gun, pot, and some kind of white powder—do you think it could be cocaine or heroin? Anyway, I don't want you all involved." Even as she said it, she knew it was stupid. They were involved as long as she was here, but where else could she go?

"I've got a baseball bat that might come in handy," Garrett offered.

"Don't be ridiculous," Johanna said.

Sarah was sorry her mother pooh-poohed his idea. A baseball bat sounded kind of good to her.

"I'll call up Rita Watson and we'll make sure Jimmy's around tonight," Johanna said. "We'll call him at the first sign of Roy Glen."

Yes, it was good to have a policeman for a friend. They could count on Jimmy.

Sarah and Garrett carried in all of her belongings. As Garrett heaved one garbage bag over each shoulder, he grumbled about their weight. "This better be good stuff, not trash in these bags." He left for his apartment soon after. Sarah was glad he was still visiting the folks once or twice a week. His company was transferring him to Philadelphia soon, and she would have hated for him to leave without making up.

Johanna carried her Strawberry Twinkie dessert to the table. "Who's ready for dessert?"

Sarah didn't feel like eating anything, but didn't have to heart to say so. She called everyone back to the table.

Now the family knew, and no one had disowned her. One problem dealt with. On to the journals. The person who was going to be most affected hadn't even read them yet. Before she went to bed, Sarah gave them to her mother. Like Aunt Livvie, Johanna was not much of a reader. When she wasn't at the hospital, she was too busy—cooking, sewing, doing laundry, gardening—to sit still. It took considerable effort to convince her she needed to read Katherine's journals right away. As Sarah lay in her old bed that night, she wondered if her mother had learned yet that Livvie was her mother. Wondered if, at first, she would feel deceived, betrayed, a little unhinged. Much the same as Sarah felt today.

In the end, it couldn't really matter. Livvie had always been her mother's mother in every way. Except in public.

By Sunday morning, to Sarah's surprise, Roy Glen still hadn't shown up. Maybe he had been too drunk when he'd come home. Or maybe he hadn't come home at all. Sarah was disappointed to learn her mother had only read a few of the early journals before falling asleep. She was anxious to discuss them. After breakfast, her parents insisted on taking Mandy to church with them.

"Sure you won't come?" Johanna said one last time.

But Livvie was expecting Sarah, so she drove back to the Aunt Hill. Livvie looked worse than the day before, more sallow and wasted as she sat at the kitchen table.

Livvie gazed into her coffee mug. "I'm sure you think I'm awful now."

"I feel as if you've given me an enormous gift. You've always felt like my grandmother, and now I learn you are. I only wish you'd have told us this years ago. Mom never suspected?"

Livvie's chin trembled. "I've never spoken of this part of my life, no matter how much it broke my heart." Her gnarled fingers twisted a handkerchief between them as if she were wringing out a washcloth. Sarah grasped Livvie's hands, her own eyes tearing up.

"Until Katherine died and I found the journals, I didn't know the part she played in my story with Jay. At first, I was hurt to discover how she betrayed me. Later, I was amazed to think how much she must have loved me. She devoted the rest of her life to making sure Johanna had everything she needed. And because they looked up to Katherine, Maggie and Bitsy followed her example. Bitsy was so shy, she probably never would have married anyway, but Maggie dated several men. She never seemed to love one enough to leave us. Katherine saved enough to send your mother to get her medical training as an x-ray technician and all my sisters chipped in to pay for her wedding."

One thing was clear to Sarah: families could take many forms. Katherine raised Johanna as if she were truly her father, providing for her all her life, and even providing for Sarah and Garrett. Sarah thought of all the books and shoes Katherine bought them, all the vacation trips paid for over the years. Sarah had appreciated Katherine, sure, but not enough. No one had ever understood the magnitude of her love. How blessed they had been!

"After—well, after—I wouldn't leave the house for the longest time," Livvie said. "Even when we moved to Clarksburg. I took up hat design and dressmaking because I could do them at home. Katherine dropped off the finished pieces and brought me new orders. Finally she persuaded me no one suspected a thing and I dealt directly with store managers. It was the perfect career because I could stay home with Johanna most of the time."

Sarah held her aunt's hand to her cheek. "What you have been through—it must have been awful."

"Not so bad. Everyone I loved has been close to me and I could watch you all grow up. I clung to this Bible verse: 'For I have learned, in whatsoever state I am, therewith to be content.'"

Sarah envied her. She yearned for the same peace and was determined to find it.

"We did travel quite a bit. We took your mother to the beach in the summer, and when she was through with her schooling, we went to Chicago and New York almost every year for the shows. Once we toured San Francisco and Napa Valley and another time drove down to Florida. We had such a good time, the five of us, sipping Brandy Alexanders and eating lobster tails. After your mother married, it was fun finding souvenirs to bring home for her and you kids. I hope Katherine got some satisfaction out of those trips. I feel terrible for the way my decisions hindered her life. John Wehner would have married her, you know. He wrote to her for many years. Maybe that Socialist fellow would have married her, too. I don't know."

Sarah remembered the story. Walter somebody. She supposed they would never know if he had proposed. "So you all moved to Clarksburg?"

"Oh, yes. Papa, Joe and Thomas were working at the Lafayette factory by 1912. The other boys wanted to make decorative glass, so they worked at one of the other plants. When your mama decided to marry a Methodist, Maggie and Bitsy threw a fit at first. But I insisted it wasn't right to interfere. Katherine took one look at my eyes—they must have been wild, I remember how I was shaking—and she told my sisters to leave Johanna alone. They backed down. Your mama and daddy raised you Methodist and that was all right with me. We all believe in the same God. Only the details differ. Help me up, now. I have a little something I want to give you."

Those familiar words echoed from years past. Sarah helped Livvie up the staircase. Livvie collapsed onto the bed, breathing heavily but insisting she was fine. "Honey, bring me the Madonna from the chest of drawers."

Not the Madonna. Not now. Sarah had stopped wanting it years ago. The little statue only reminded Sarah of her own shortcomings. Yet she walked over to the window where sunlight poured yellow through the blinds, illuminating the figurine on the black enameled chest. Livvie put her hands around Sarah's as she held the Madonna and drew her down onto the bed. Sarah kicked off her shoes and swung one foot up under her thigh, the other leg dangling off the side of the bed.

"You always asked for her, and I always said no. Today she is yours."

"No, Livvie, I couldn't take her. She belongs with you."

"You need her now. I'm going to tell you why Papa made her, and you'll understand." Livvie lay back on the pillow, her eyes closed. Sarah thought she'd fallen asleep and shifted her weight, thinking to tiptoe out, but Livvie's eyes fluttered open and she began her story.

Thirty-Six

Anton proved a patient man, waiting until Adelisa wanted to kiss him, to know him as a husband. Their love grew over the years, and the family increased by six more children after Joseph Karl. Anthony, Patrick, Peter, William, Thomas, and Katherine—and another was already on the way.

From Magdalen, Adelisa learned to make perfect bread, apple kuchen and Wiener Schnitzel. She was kind to her first child, Joseph, although she never was able to shower him with the same warmth that naturally flowed toward the other children. Anton kept the boy with him whenever possible and lavished attention on him. At least twice a week she took the children to visit with Magdalen, who spoiled their brood as if they were her own. Adelisa was sunny-natured and it rubbed off on her children.

Still, some nights as she began her prayers, Anton would see a tear on her cheek when she wasn't quick enough to wipe it away. He knew she was tormenting herself. Her pain ate at him like acid. As he watched his wife kneeling, so reverent, so sincere, fingering the carved ebony beads of her rosary, it came to him, this idea for the little statue. Adelisa revered the Blessed Mother. He would create a little statue so beautiful, so full of God's understanding and forgiveness and perfect love, it would erase the old scar completely.

At closing time, the men made end-of-the-day pieces by mixing leftover batches of glass. No one ever knew what they would look like, muddy blends or glorious swirls of rose into white. Men also did special projects off the clock.

The first step was to make a model for his statue. Anton took a glob of clay and began to sculpt, his long fingers pushing and smoothing and shaping the damp red earth. This was much harder than anything he'd attempted before. The refinement of the features required precision. For three weeks, he smashed partially formed models and started over. Anton's mentor, Karl Reinhardt, advised him on tools he might use on the clay and on modifications he might make to the composition. Week after week on Sunday afternoons, he tried and failed to sculpt the face he could see in his mind.

Nearly a year passed, when in desperation he asked the Virgin Mother herself to guide his hands. He poured out all the passion he felt for his wife. As his hands worked the clay, the Virgin's countenance gradually emerged, slender, elegant, serene. She stood nine inches tall in her flowing robes, the perfect shape he had envisioned all along. Her face was Adelisa's.

Two weeks later on a Sunday afternoon under pretense of going for a walk, Anton took Joseph, now ten and his apprentice, to a foundry near the glass plant. A friend used the model to make an iron mould, which would receive the molten glass.

The next week at the end of the day, a quantity of clear batch remained. Karl claimed it for Anton. The boards creaked as they crossed the planked floor. Anton handed the mould to Joseph. From the crucible of the furnace, Anton extracted molten glass. With a prayer, Anton puffed out his cheeks and blew the kiss of life into the little virgin. The glass flowed steadily from the pipe until the mould was full. Anton set the statue in the oven to anneal overnight.

To produce a translucent satin finish, he carefully sandblasted the glass, coughing as particulate scratched his throat, despite the bandana tied over his nose. When he finished, Joseph wiped the glass down and polished it.

Anton set the Madonna on the bench and stepped back to admire her. She was doe-eyed, with slightly upturned lips. Her expression calm, accepting. What began as little more than dust transformed into a thing of light and beauty. Surely, she had acquired a soul of her own! He fingered the satiny sheen of her long gown. Traced its gentle, flowing folds. At the very moment he stepped back to admire her from a more distant perspective, light streamed through the window. He drew in his breath. She glowed from the inside with a golden light, like his Adelisa, though parts of her remained in shadow. The penumbra only intensified her beauty, gave her depth, hinted at a woman's mystery.

The Madonna would be his love song, his perfect poem for Adelisa.

FEBRUARY 1977

"Now you can see. This Mary is so much more than a virgin. She's the mother, the one whose love is unconditional and pure. She holds all the mystery and magic of a woman. I'm giving this Madonna to you with the same message my father gave to my mother, and my mother passed along to me. Your family—and your God—see into your heart. We love you always, no matter what. If you go through with the divorce, let the Madonna remind you how much you are loved."

Sarah pulled away, feeling undeserving of this gift, of this love, but Livvie seized her arms. "When you look at her, I want you to remember how much I will always love you, whether I am still here or not. Promise me."

And Sarah did. She realized it would be wrong, hurtful even, not to accept this gift with her whole heart. Livvie's breaths grew slow and ragged. Sarah sat quietly holding her hand for a few minutes before leaning over to kiss her forehead. "Sleep well, Grandma," she said. "I will always love you, too." Livvie's chest heaved, and Sarah thought she saw tears in the corners of her eyes.

Thirty-Seven

FEBRUARY *1977*

Roy Glen vaguely processed Sarah's absence when he got in from a night at the Down and Under, but he was too stoned to give a flip. As afternoon sun and consciousness seeped in, the magnitude of the problem crashed into him. She'd not only taken the truck, but everything in it. She must have found the spare key. What else had she found? He told himself not to panic. She may have gotten mad and driven off, but that was probably all. No reason for her to look in the glove box or the back end. Why would she? She only wanted to see her parents, that over-dependency thing. She probably hadn't found any of his stuff.

But what if she had?

He parked down the street from her mother's house and waited. The longer he waited, the madder he got. What right did she have to take off with his truck? Ever since she had started this job, she thought she didn't have to listen to him. When he got her home, he was going to beat the crap out of her.

He rubbed his hands together to keep warm. Periodically he started the Chevy's motor to run the heater and take the chill off. Not too often. The neighbors might get suspicious.

At one point in the waiting, he remembered the letter in the glove box. He pounded his fist into the steering wheel. He tried to remember what it said. Enough, he was sure, to condemn him. If Sarah found the letter, he could kiss his marriage goodbye. And despite everything, he wasn't looking for change. He wasn't looking to lose his daughter.

For almost two hours, he sat there shifting his opinion, one minute deciding Sarah'd found his stash, the next sure she hadn't. The muscles in his face started to twitch. Happened a lot lately. He massaged his jaws to ease the spasms.

Before the truck cleared the crest of the hill, he recognized the sound of the motor. Sarah parked in front of her parents' house. He could tell she spotted the Chevy right away. He got out and stood on the sidewalk. Maybe he could figure out what she knew from how she acted. The truck door opened and she slid off the seat. They stood staring at each other for what seemed forever. She darted toward the house, taking the steps three at a time. No way to catch her, but if she thought she could slip away from him so easily, she had another thing coming. He'd break a window if he had to. He bounded up the front steps and rang the doorbell six or seven times. He lost count.

Finally she came back outside. He heard the lock click behind her. Why? Didn't want him in the house. Again, why? Where was Mandy? He sensed her parents watching from the windows. Well, let them watch. She was his wife, and he had a right to talk to her.

"Have you lost your mind? You can't take my truck and disappear. Get Mandy and your stuff. I'm taking you home."

She folded her arms across her chest. She seemed taller, somehow. "I'm filing for divorce."

His mouth went dry. "Whatever's wrong, we can work it out."

"I don't think we can."

"Till death do us part—remember? We both said it. I meant it, and I know you did, too."

"We also said stuff about being faithful."

So, she had read the letter. A wave of fury rushed over him. She had no business going through his things. With effort, he stayed calm though the muscles in his face were twitching again. "You can't walk out on me without talking about it. Not when our kid's involved. Think about Mandy."

"I am thinking about her. I don't want her around you."

His head felt as if it was going to explode. "No divorce. I'll take Mandy from you if you even think about it."

Her voice went all hysterical. "You can't. I have evidence. The penicillin bottles." She pulled an orange plastic bottle out of her jacket pocket and shook it in front of his nose.

He grabbed her hand and squeezed until the plastic cracked. She cried out as an edge cut into her palm. Served her right. His voice was low, even. "A bad cold. So what?"

"Stop lying—I went to the doctor—I know."

That wasn't good. And if she'd been in the truck bed, she'd found the rest of his stuff. "You go to a lawyer, you'll have a bigger fight on your hands than you can manage." He snatched the cracked bottle from her hand and flung it onto the porch. It rebounded slightly off the wood planks and settled near the front door.

"No judge is ever going to give you custody. You're sleeping with my cousin."

"I'll get Bobby Marchio to say you were a slut even back in high school. And I'll name Cal Caruso. Half dozen guys I work with will say they slept with you. All I gotta do is buy them a beer."

"Tell you what. You put them on and I'll bring on half the town. Seems everyone knew about your other women but me. We'll see who the court believes."

He knew her. She wasn't half as brave as she sounded. He knew exactly how to knock the wind out of her sails. "You weren't even a virgin when we married—do your parents know about that? Guy has a right to expect a woman to be pure."

To his surprise, her eyes remained hard. "My love was pure. That should have been enough."

He changed tactics. He loaded his voice with sincerity. She loved his voice, had told him so. "It is enough, it is. There's never been anyone else I cared about. You're the only one. The others were just about sex. I can't tell you how sorry I am. I never meant to hurt you. We can work this out, for Mandy's sake."

"Too late."

"Come on, I'm begging you, give me another chance. You know how much I love Mandy. She needs a father."

Sarah walked away to the other end of the porch and leaned against the railing. Funny thing was, watching her walk away reminded him of all the things he loved about her. The easy grace in her movements she was totally unaware of, the long, lean angles of her legs. That thick mop of hair. The way she played school with Mandy and her dolls. The effort she poured into learning to cook and garden.

She turned back toward him, and the uncertainty on her face gave him hope. Until her neighbor Jimmy Watson pulled up in his cruiser.

At the sight of Jimmy's cruiser, Sarah's spine collapsed at least an inch as the tension eased out of her bones. She felt safe now. Before Jimmy could get out of the car, Roy Glen vaulted over the porch railing, sprinted to his truck, and took off. The other set of truck keys—she had forgotten about them. Now she was stuck with the Chevy—and no keys. For a minute Jimmy stood on the sidewalk as if he were debating taking off after Roy Glen. Instead, he bounded up to the porch.

Jimmy lifted her hand and observed the blood. "He do this to you?"

She pulled her hand away, not about to make a fuss over a little cut. "It's nothing."

Jimmy dragged her inside and insisted on photographing the injury. He went back on the porch and photographed the plastic shards on the porch. He handed her the Polaroids. "You may need this as evidence."

She rolled her eyes. "Of what?"

"You always were a tough little girl. Remember the time you tried to leap over the Johnsons' picket fence and impaled your thigh on it? Your mother wouldn't even have known if I hadn't come over and asked how you were. Admitting you need help doesn't mean you're weak. You need anything, all you have to do is ask."

"How about waving a magic wand and getting me some keys for the Chevy?" She was teasing, but he said to consider it done. There were advantages to having a policeman as a friend.

That evening Sarah sat cross-legged on the couch, Mandy bucketed on her lap. While her father yelled at some basketball team on TV, Sarah told Mandy they weren't going to live with her daddy anymore.

"Who'll take me fishing?" Mandy asked. Sarah assured her she would take her any time she wanted to go.

Sarah's father, who as far as Sarah knew, had never fed ducks before in his life, took Mandy to the park. A helpful distraction. His sensitivity surprised Sarah. When they left, she was alone in the living room, TV blaring but unwatched. With Mandy absent from her lap, Sarah felt a yawning hole open up inside her. Had she done the right thing?

Her mother hollered from the kitchen, "Get in here and help me ice these sugar cookies."

She never made sugar cookies except for Christmas. Too much work, and treasured all the more because of the rarity. Sarah went jelly-soft as she realized her mother, as always, was using food to show love.

When they finished with the cookies, they went next door to Rita's to watch Snuffy, whose puppies were about to make their debut. Not even fist-sized, the first one emerged, a ball of wet fur with slits for eyes.

"Dibs on the biggest, baddest pup in the litter," Jimmy said.

Sarah didn't know how she was going to manage it since she didn't even have a house of her own right now, but one way or another, she was going to talk the Watsons out of one of those pups. Sarah heard her father's car in the driveway and went back to her mothers' house to bathe Mandy. Johanna stayed on at Rita's to watch the birthing.

After tucking Mandy into bed, Sarah worked on lesson plans. She slouched against the couch, stocking feet propped on the coffee table. Her father roved between the kitchen and living room to replenish his glass with Famous Grouse. She was nearly done when her father walked by—a sixth time? Seemed like it. He lurched in her direction, his torso between her and the table lamp, causing a shadow to fall over her paper. Though he towered over her, weaving and bobbing, she could still smell the scotch on his breath.

He set his drink down on the finished plan for Early American History. "What're you doing, anyway?"

Grimacing, she moved the drink onto the table, snatched the paper up and flicked the damp spot. "Hey, I put half an hour into writing that. I don't want to have to redo it."

His lips curled, his weight shifting from one leg to the other, clumsily retrieving his drink from the table. "You think you're pretty important, don't you?"

Sarah grew rigid. There was no reasoning with him when he got like this. "No."

"You think whatever you're writing there is important. It doesn't make a damn bit of difference."

"I'd rather not turn in a lesson plan with scotch rings, that's all."

"You know, there was a time when they wouldn't a let a divorced woman teach. There was a time everyone would have said you'd made your own bed and you had to lie in it."

Her face burned. Yes, and there was a time a married woman couldn't teach, a time when women couldn't vote and they were considered property of their fathers and husbands. No more. Her brain told her these things, but he'd punched a hole in her chest. She wrote

"Objective" at the top of the Political Systems lesson plan. She followed the word with a colon, refusing to look at her father. Keep writing and he'll go away, she told herself. He did, his butt dropping onto the other couch, where he promptly passed out. In the morning he wouldn't even remember the nastiness. But she would, and no matter how many times she told herself she could choose not to let it bother her, it still did.

Soon after she finished her lesson plans, her mother returned with news Snuffy had birthed three pups. Sarah handed her mother Katherine's last journal. "You don't have time to read them all, but at least read this one, starting where I bookmarked it. Before you go to sleep tonight. No excuses."

An hour later, Johanna found Sarah entering current events scores in her grade book. Her mother was pale. "This can't mean what I think it does." She had done the math. Figured out she was the baby and didn't want to believe it. "I feel so betrayed. Lied to my whole life."

Lied to, yes. Betrayed, no. Her family had acted to protect her and Livvie. Just as Sarah's father and brother hid things from Sarah to protect her. It wasn't betrayal at all. It was love. She understood now. It was up to Sarah to convince her mother how lucky she was, how lucky they all were, to have four Heimbach women as buffers between them and the world. Before Livvie died, she needed to know that her family knew her for who she was, and they still loved her.

Thirty-Eight

MARCH 1977

"Nervous, honey?" Hedgwick's receptionist was in her early thirties, smartly dressed with hair lacquered into a French twist.

"No, why?"

She raised her eyebrows and looked pointedly at Sarah's hands. Sarah realized she was biting her cuticles.

"Know how I stopped?"

"How?" Sarah asked.

"I wore a rubber band around my wrist, and every time I caught myself with my hand in my mouth, I snapped the rubber band hard. Sounds silly, but it worked."

It must have. The nails were perfect ovals with burgundy polish to match the office décor. After a short wait, Sarah was invited into the lawyer's private office. Ethan Hedgwick extended a hand from a French-cuffed shirt with gold cufflinks, two little golf clubs that crossed. The judge would require grounds for divorce, Hedgwick said. Proof of cruelty or desertion. West Virginia didn't yet have no-fault divorce, although other states were beginning to move in that direction.

She told him about the love letter, the gun, the marijuana, the white powder. He dismissed these with a wave of his hand. "I need evidence of his cruelty to you. Did he come home with lipstick on his collar?"

She shook her head. His clothes were so dark, who could tell?

"Smell perfume on him?"

No perfume. Only nasty smells. Again she shook her head. She sank deeper into the leather chair and scraped her fingers rhythmically over the fat brass nail trim. What did this man want from her?

He pointed to the trim. "Please stop that. What else can you tell me?"

She detailed the late nights, what her father and brother knew, but Hedgwick insisted family members weren't enough. "Will your friends testify they saw him out with other women?"

Sarah was not about to ask. Her middle finger caressed one of the brass beads on the chair. It was cool to the touch. She itched to rake her nails along the strip of metal bumps, to hear the thack-thack-thack again. Either that or flip this man the bird.

"Never hit you, shoved you?"

"No, but I have a photo of a cut hand." He wasn't impressed. She could only think of one more thing to offer. She made her voice as small as she felt. "He gave me VD."

Hedgwick pressed fingertips together and licked his lips. "Yes, that is cruel. A husband brings home a venereal disease—definitely physical abuse."

It was? She never thought of herself as abused. There were the nights she said no, when he insisted, the scent of other women all over him (and somewhere deeper than rational thought she had known). Was that abuse too? It was worse than perfume, but she couldn't tell Hedgwick this. The bruises on her arms. Was that abuse? Only sissies made a fuss over a bruise. She'd learned that on the playground with the boys. She was no sissy.

Penicillin bottles weren't enough to satisfy Hedgwick. At the end of her fifteen minutes, he commanded her to find a non-relative to testify Roy Glen spent time alone with another woman. Like an hour in a hotel room. When she left his office, all she wanted was a long, hot bath.

Rita refilled Sarah's mug with steaming coffee and passed it to the back seat. Sarah leaned against the door of Rita's Buick and stretched her legs out across the tan upholstery. She was cold and bored. They had been sitting in the parking lot of the Down and Under watching the door Roy Glen and Martha Rose had entered twenty minutes earlier. No action. This could go on for hours.

From the passenger side, Johanna held out her mug for a refill. Just then, the door to the club opened and out walked Roy Glen. Johanna slid down in the seat and a loud "Shit!" erupted as hot coffee hit Rita's pants leg. There was a scramble for tissues and considerable confusion, as they dealt with the spill and kept their eyes on Roy

Glen. He opened the back end of the truck and climbed inside. They couldn't see what he was doing. As he slid across the truck gate, he tucked something into his jacket pocket. He hopped down, strode to the bar's entrance, disappearing inside.

"What was that all about?" Rita said.

Drugs, Sarah thought. He was distributing in the bar.

A few minutes later both he and Martha Rose came out, got in the truck, and rode to another bar. The pattern repeated at this bar and two more after that.

After the last delivery—by now Sarah was certain that's what was going on—Roy Glen and Martha Rose crawled together into the back end of the capped truck bed. Hiding behind curtains she had sewn, Sarah thought bitterly.

"Action. Write this down," Rita told Sarah. "It's 2:12 p.m. Your lawyer wants facts, we'll give him facts. Yessiree bob."

When the truck began to rock, Rita snorted. "What a nasty place to do it." In an obvious attempt to distract Sarah, Johanna shared hospital gossip. The wife dying of cancer whose husband was bringing his new girlfriend along for the wife's radiation treatments. The girl from the neighborhood who fell off the high dive and landed on the cement and lived to tell about it. The young man mangled in a motorcycle wreck. Sarah barely listened, nauseated with humiliation. It was one thing to know her husband was messing around, another to actually have to witness it. She was the first to notice the rocking stopped. "Heads down."

Rita slumped in the seat and checked her watch. "She's messing around on her husband for *that*? Get this down, 2:19 p.m., rocking stops."

The back end of the truck opened with a metallic snap Sarah could hear inside the car, even with the windows closed against the cold. She wiped the condensation off the window so she could see what happened next. Roy Glen and Martha Rose settled onto the tailgate, legs dangling over the edge. Roy Glen lit a joint, took a hit, and passed it over to Martha Rose.

Johanna snorted. "Will you look at him? Too cheap to give her a cigarette of her own. Wish I had one right about now."

"It's pot, Mom."

"All them boys over to the factory smoke pot on their breaks," Rita said. "Several deal it right there in the canteen. That Bobby Marchio—he's the big supplier."

"Didn't you go out with him once, Sarah?"

Sarah wished she hadn't. "I'm pretty sure Roy Glen is dealing, too."

"You should report them to the police," her mother said to Rita. "Why don't you tell Jimmy?"

"Wouldn't want it to get around I'd snitched," Rita said. "Next thing you knowed, I'd be stuck on night shift."

"Let's go. I don't see how your lawyer can complain this time," Johanna said. "Not with all we have to give him."

Sarah yawned. "Oh, but he will. He'll lick his lips and say, 'More details, more details.'"

"Uuuugh." Rachel stormed into Sarah's classroom first thing in the morning, dressed in a pink bouclé suit.

Sarah turned from the blackboard. "What's wrong?"

Rachel threw her hands up in the air, and when she lowered them her shoulder bag slipped awkwardly down her arm, dangling from her elbow. "Everything. You have time to talk?"

Sarah set down the chalk. Notes on the board could wait. She had never seen Rachel this perturbed. Mark must have broken off the engagement.

Rachel slammed her purse on a student desk. "My dad is driving me crazy. The florist says he can't get enough calla lilies to decorate the altar. Some problem with a major supplier. He says he has to fill in with Easter lilies. He assures me they'll be beautiful, but I don't know. They seem so ordinary. And last night the caterer let us sample his hors d'oeuvres. They all had garlic or onions in them and my father went ballistic and threw him out."

Tears ran down her face openly now. Sarah handed her the box of tissues she kept for students. Rachel blotted her face. "Now we have to find a new caterer—and who else are we going to get? A Taste of Class does all the best weddings. Last week the invitations came back with a typo, so they are being re-printed. Nothing's going right."

None of this sounded catastrophic. "Stop crying. You have a bad case of bridal nerves, that's all. You still love Mark and he loves you, right?"

"Mark," she snorted. "He tells me to handle the details myself. He says the wedding's a woman's job. His job is to attend the bachelor party and drink champagne at the reception."

"It can't be that bad. Everything will work out fine on your wedding day. It will be beautiful—you'll be beautiful, as always—and you'll forget all these problems. You'll laugh about it later."

Rachel tucked her hair behind one ear. "I know, but it's so stressful. My father always takes over. I wanted a nice wedding, sure, but he makes such a production of everything. Look at this list he gave me." She pulled a paper from her purse. "Everything has to be perfect. We should have eloped like you."

Apparently Rachel had forgotten Sarah's prenuptial pregnancy, which made a big wedding out of the question. She always felt she missed out on something by eloping. Maybe if she and Roy Glen had actually made it to the altar together, they wouldn't be splitting up now. She wondered if Rachel knew. It was hard for Sarah to talk about, but the people she worked with would find out sooner or later.

"Roy Glen and I separated."

Rachel's hand flew to her face and then she touched Sarah's arm. "I'm so sorry, and here I've been going on and on. When did this happen?"

"A few weeks ago." It felt good to tell a friend. She should have done it sooner.

"What happened?"

Sarah had been dreading the question everyone was bound to ask. She decided to tell the truth. She was tired of lies. "He's seeing another woman, several actually."

Rachel pulled her into a hug. "I'm so sorry. I've seen him out and thought about telling you, but couldn't bring myself to. I mean, I didn't want to hurt you."

No wonder he didn't want her to go anywhere. Everyone had known but her. "Let's not talk about it. Too gloomy. Is there anything I can do to help you straighten out your wedding problems? Make some phone calls? Pick anything up?"

"You're sweet to offer, but no. This is something I have to get through. One more ordeal with my father."

Rachel, Sarah thought, had no idea what an ordeal with a father was. "You know, I was always jealous because your father was so cool, so involved in your life."

Rachel rolled her eyes. "I love him dearly, but he made my life a nightmare most of the time. I had to be the best at everything, win every prize, run for every office, pad my resume with every imaginable honor. Second best was never an option."

"I thought you liked being in the spotlight. You never complained."

"Neither did you."

Sarah blinked. "What do you mean?"

Rachel opened her mouth as if she were going to say something then closed it. "Never mind."

Sarah couldn't let go of that *neither did you*. Had Rachel known all along about the drinking? The beatings? Why hadn't she said anything? With a shock, the answer came to her: the same reason no one in the family talked about it. Alcoholism and cheating husbands were taboo subjects because they were likely to embarrass or hurt someone. The trouble was, silence hurt, too. It erected a barrier between family members, forced friends behind a fence. She'd never let Rachel, Paula, or even Roy Glen close enough to see the family's shame. Yet they'd all seen anyway.

Soon after word got around, Mr. Mirandi called her to his office. On the way through the hall, she thought she might throw up. Some area schools fired unmarried pregnant women. Suppose they found out somehow about the VD. Would they fire her? They couldn't fire you for getting a divorce, could they? No, of course not. She'd learned one of the guidance counselors was divorced. Still, as a first-year teacher, she had no job protection. She needed those health benefits. In six more months, insurance would kick in for Mandy. No more pre-existing conditions exclusions. Beg, cry—she would do whatever it took to keep this job. She knocked on the principal's door, tentatively at first, then more firmly.

"Have a seat." He gestured to the chair in front of his desk. He pulled his ear. "This is difficult for me."

Oh God. He *was* going to fire her. She held her breath.

He looked directly at her. "There's no way to pussyfoot around this, so I'm going to come out and say it. I heard you're getting a divorce, and while I don't know your exact circumstances, I know how important money usually is at a time like this."

Sarah controlled her expression.

"I wanted to make sure you understand the school board's personnel handbook, the policy on absences. If you miss a school day for a court hearing, your pay is docked. To avoid problems, I suggest you find some friendly colleagues to cover your classes while you need to be gone."

She fought back tears of relief.

"If you don't know anyone well enough to ask, I'll line someone up for you," he said.

Peg and Rachel would probably do it. She stood to leave.

He opened his door. "The last issue of the paper was excellent, Mrs. Hardman. I was surprised those kids could write so well—better than reporters for the city paper most of the time."

She thanked him. "They're great kids. The process of revision and publication really brings out their best."

"Pass my compliments on to the staff." With a courtly sweep of the arm, he gestured her through the door first.

Thirty-Nine

MARCH 1977

The black chest didn't look the same without the Madonna on top. Sarah set a vase with two dozen red roses in its place. They had arrived with a note from Roy Glen to please come home. She threw the note out and started to trash the flowers, but at the last moment decided Livvie might as well enjoy them. Sarah glanced over at the bed, where her mother was sponge-bathing Livvie. For the past two weeks, Johanna had slept in the bedroom next to Livvie's. Sarah still didn't know exactly what had passed between Livvie and her mother when they discussed the journals, but they clearly were at peace with each other.

"Can I do anything to help?" Sarah hoped her mother would say no. It wasn't at all like bathing Mandy.

"Thanks, Sarah, but I can handle it." Her mother wrung out a washcloth and matter-of-factly lifted Livvie's gown. Sarah looked away, not before noticing Livvie's eyes, directed upwards, either in agony or humiliation. It must be so hard to be reduced to dependence again. The dark rims, which underscored all Heimbach women's eyes, had turned deeper charcoal. Most of Livvie's flesh and muscle had already made an exit for the promised land, leaving behind bones and a thin layer of skin.

Sarah shuddered, seeing herself as an old woman. The same long nose, the high cheek bones. Even at twenty-five, the quarter moons under Sarah's eyes were darkening slightly. Lilac moons.

"How's Mandy?" her mother asked.

Sarah's mood brightened as she remembered her daughter's joy in discovering Nana had bought her a box of Apple Jacks. "Fine. She was already up watching cartoons with Dad when I left."

Sarah dusted the rooms upstairs until her mother called for assistance in making up the bed. Her mother pulled the used sheets gently out from under Livvie as Sarah lifted her easily. Even her bones seemed unsubstantial, light as leaves, already ghostlike, as the cancer ate away her marrow. Sarah clamped her lips together, concentrating on the job, her hands smoothing soft cotton under and over Livvie.

.Johanna held the basin firmly in front of her and marched toward the bathroom to empty it. Sarah wondered if she would ever be as capable and confident around sick people as her mother.

When they finished, they went downstairs to the kitchen. Johanna poured two cups of coffee and brought them to the table. "I know you're feeling bad about the divorce, but you and Mandy will be fine after it's all over. You can do anything you put your mind to. You're my girl."

It was good to have a cheerleader. "What's with the rubber band on your wrist, Mom?"

"Behavior therapy. I went to see Dr. Jorgansen because my feet were getting numb and he says I have diabetes. He put me on a strict diet, so no more Jello or cookies. Every time I want a sweet I'm supposed to pop the rubber band and before long I'll associate sweets with pain. I have to take pills too."

By the way, I have slowly been killing myself for years, Sarah thought. Her mother had to stick to the diet. Sarah didn't think she could stand another loss. Not her mother. Not on top of everything else. Her mother was her rock. Sarah remembered the receptionist's story about the rubber band and her nails. "Think the rubber band's working?"

"Too soon to tell, but I haven't scarfed down a cookie or piece of candy all week."

"Good for you. Tell you what, I'm going to get one and snap it every time I start to bite my nails, and you could get Daddy to pop one every time he wants a drink."

Her mother's face stiffened, and Sarah wished she'd kept her mouth shut. Now their moment of closeness would be spoiled. Silence descended on the table.

Johanna's mood shifted as she stared into her coffee cup. "You asked me a question awhile back, and I about bit your head off. I'm sorry. You asked if I ever thought about divorcing your father, and the answer is yes. When Garrett was about eleven years old, your father beat him so hard the marks were still there days later."

Sarah knew exactly which time she was talking about. The day after the beating the stripes on her brother's legs still showed beneath his shorts as they shot baskets in the backyard with Jimmy Watson and Rachel Sullivan.

"I told your father if he ever used his belt again for anything other than holding up his pants he was going to find new locks on the door when he got home from work. I bought the locks. I even went to a lawyer and brought home a separation agreement and laid it in front of him. He never wore pants with a belt again at home. Bought all those elastic waist slacks. Called them his putter pants."

So that's why the beatings stopped. If only her mother had taken a stand the first time it happened. Yet Sarah knew how easy it was to let something slide until it spun out of control. Wasn't that what she had done with Roy Glen? At least her mother finally made the demand, and amazingly, her father loved her mother enough to change his behavior. That was the difference between her father and her husband. Her father, she thought, was a rare exception. Most people didn't change.

What would happen if her mother demanded he stop drinking? Would he stop? Could he stop? The beatings weren't the only damage her father inflicted.

She touched her mother's hand. "You did a brave thing."

"It wasn't brave at all. I was terrified. I didn't know if I could support you two on my salary alone. Thank God I didn't have to. You don't have to worry. If you run into money trouble, you let us know."

"Thanks, Mom." Sarah sipped her coffee. She was thinking about Pete's family, remembering the beautiful picture Uncle Mahlon had fashioned of Pete's mother. Sarah smiled at the thought of how he'd hidden her breasts in the artwork with his handkerchief.

"What ever happened to Pete's mother Ava? What was wrong with her?"

Johanna wrinkled her nose. "It's sort of embarrassing, but I guess you're old enough to hear this. Ava was one of those nymphos—she'd go after anyone—delivery men, guys in the grocery store, even a priest. Your aunts were scandalized."

Sarah could imagine.

Johanna snapped the rubber band against her wrist. "Boy, I'd kill for a cookie right now. Anyway, Ava was committed to mental hospitals several times. Electric shock therapy finally helped some."

What would they call a man with an over-active sex drive? Stud? Womanizer? No one—not even Sarah—was suggesting Roy Glen needed to have his brain fried.

After her mother left for work, Sarah tidied up the rest of the house and sat on Livvie's bed. Livvie seemed improved since morning, bird-eyed and alert, her head propped up by two pillows. The pain medication Sarah's mother had administered clearly provided some relief.

Livvie eased up even taller in the bed. "I want you to do something for me."

If only there *were* something Sarah could do. She smoothed Livvie's hair away from her forehead. "Sure, what?"

"I want you to write out my will."

Sarah winced. "Don't talk like that. What I want is for you to get better."

"I'm ready to go, honey. It's all right. Bring a pen and some paper over here."

Sarah brought her aunt what she asked for but suggested she needed a lawyer.

"No, I'll keep it simple. When the nurse gets here, she can witness it. Take this down. I name Johanna Heimbach Stevens executor of my estate. I authorize her to pay all my bills. I don't have any debts, just utility payments."

Sarah wrote it down, then scratched out the last sentence. It sounded too conversational.

"Now, this next part is important. I bequeath my house and all the furnishings in it to Sarah Stevens Hardman."

Sarah couldn't continue. "Oh, no Livvie, that's too much."

"Fiddlesticks. Isn't worth half as much as you think. Old place is falling apart. Like me. You may live to regret the day you inherited it. But I figure it'll be a roof over your head and Mandy's, and you're going to need one. Besides, if you didn't come live here, this old house would be sold to strangers."

Sarah protested again, but Livvie said, "Don't argue. This is *my* will."

The idea of strangers in the house did make Sarah queasy. For the first time since she'd started the divorce proceedings, she began to form a picture of a happy future for herself and Mandy. She could take Mandy into the woods behind the house, the way Livvie used to take her. She would find scrapes on rocks and tell her daughter it was where a unicorn had sharpened its horn. They would find arrowheads, and somehow Sarah would dredge up those old stories of brave Indian girls Livvie used to tell.

"I don't know how to thank you."

"Stop crying now. I need for you to get this down. The rest of my estate is to be divided evenly between Johanna Heimbach Stevens, Garrett Stevens, and Pete Heimbach. I'm including Pete because he needs our help. Print my name and leave space above it for me to sign. How's that for simple? And no lawyer gets a dime."

Livvie squeezed Sarah's hand again, but her eyes closed. Sarah recopied the will neatly and left it on the bed. The retired nurse returned, a gray-skinned woman barely younger than Livvie.

Sarah closed the blinds to shut out the midday sun. She kissed Aunt Livvie's papery cheek. "I love you."

"I love you too, honey." Her voice was as scratchy as an old record.

When Sarah got back to her parents' house, even though she wasn't Catholic—or even a very good Methodist—she knelt in front of the statue, which now sat on her dresser. She whispered a prayer for Livvie, one she'd heard Livvie herself say many times: "Hail Mary, full of grace, the Lord is with Thee. Blessed art Thou among women and blessed is the fruit of Thy womb, Jesus. Holy Mary, Mother of God, pray for us sinners now and at the hour of our death. Amen."

She touched the Madonna gently with her fingers. The sun streamed through the window and the little statue burned with light.

Forty

Dear Garrett,

Little brother, you wouldn't believe my week. If I knew how much trouble the newspaper was going to be, I would have demanded extra pay instead of giving up my planning period to advise it.

In the April issue, one of my reporters quoted two new kids, a Puerto Rican brother and a sister, saying drug use was worse at Hillside than in the Pittsburgh school they transferred from. An hour after the paper came out, these kids charge into my room, claiming they were misquoted. The next day I get a note from my principal inviting me to a meeting with the parents of these kids and their lawyer. The principal says I have to document how I teach the class before the 9 a.m. meeting.

Sound like the day from hell? No? There's more. I pick Mandy up and she has a cold. At 1 a.m., she's wheezing in her bedroom—your old bedroom, actually. She tells me she feels like she's drowning. I give her asthma medicine, but it doesn't help, so Dad calls an ambulance. I'm so scared I can hardly breathe, either. I keep thinking, what if they don't get here in time? They came fast, thank God. EMTs administered oxygen and a shot. Between their intervention and breathing treatments at the hospital, they got her under control, but I can tell you I was petrified. It was 5 a.m. by the time we got out of there.

Dad cancelled his morning appointments and watched her a few hours so I could go to my 9 a.m. meeting.

The two lawyers did most of the talking. I apologized to the parents, but after an hour and a half, I got tired of going round and round. I said we could go on the intercom and let their kids publicly retract the statement or we could print another story in the next issue and let their children tell their side of the story. I warned them it might not be the best idea to drag it up again a month later. You know what finally made them happy? They wanted me to promise the paper wouldn't interview their kids again. Like I would let a staffer get within ten yards of them.

When you coming home? If you want to see Livvie, make it soon. She's going downhill fast. I stopped to see her this evening after work, but she was mostly asleep and I wasn't sure she knew who I was the few times she opened her eyes. Mom said she told you about Aunt Katherine's journals. What a shocker, huh?

How do you like Philly? The insurance business must be the right career for you or you wouldn't have gotten this promotion so fast. Guess you found a use for all those tired jokes you used to tell in high school about cannibals, dumb blondes, and Polacks. I'm sure they make great ice breakers with clients (if they aren't cannibals, blondes, or Polacks). I bet they'd be surprised to know what a jerk you were. Remember how you used to stand at the foot of the girls' staircase at school and look up the girls' skirts?

I know I don't write much. I think about you, though—every time I pass the basketball court and remember how many times I whipped your butt out there.

Love,
Sarah

CLARKSBURG, APRIL 20, 1977

Dear Mrs. Hardman:

I regret to inform you the insurance card you turned in for your daughter's emergency room visit on April 12, 1977, is no longer valid. Roy Glen Hardman dropped the policy, effective March 1, 1977.

The bill for services is $215. Please remit this amount by April 30.

Sincerely,
Mary Northwater, hospital billing services administrator

Clarksburg, April 26, 1977

Dear Bob,

I wanted you to know how concerned I am that my daughter, Sarah Hardman, sacrifices her planning period to advise the newspaper. State law says a school can't ask a teacher to teach on her planning period, and yet as her principal, you have. After the recent problems with the April issue, surely you can see the advantages of the school offering journalism as a regular class instead of students trailing in from study hall. This change would reduce the school's liability as well.

I mailed your tax forms in today. I am enclosing brochures on the tax-deferred annuity we discussed. It would effectively reduce your tax burden and increase your retirement savings.

Sincerely,
Nelson Stevens

Poem in Sarah Hardman's mailbox, April 25, 1977

"My Favorite Teacher"

She talked, and I interrupted.
She directed but I would only
Follow from a distance
Grudgingly.
She tried to teach me to listen.
I chose not to and she still
Wouldn't give up.
Finally I discovered the truth she was leading me toward all along:
Being strong doesn't mean having the loudest voice.

—Jeffrey Blogham, sophomore

APRIL 28, 1977

Dear Sis,

How is Mandy doing? She adjusted to not seeing her daddy? I don't think I can make it home any time soon. I haven't accrued any vacation days. Wish I could see Livvie, though. She was always good to us, better than most grandmothers I would guess.

Also, I am saving what little leave I have for July. Alisa and I are getting married. (I know. It's about time, since she gave up her job and moved to Philly with me.) Do you think it bothers Mom that Alisa is six years older than I am? We were wondering if you would let Mandy be the flower girl, as long as she hasn't adopted your habit of picking your nose. I'd hate to have her at the altar with her finger up her nose. Ryan is going to be ring bearer. (He calls me "Daddy" now.) The wedding won't be fancy, but I did agree to trade my over-alls for a suit and spit out my tobacckey and wear shoes. Just for the ceremony, not for the reception. Seriously, we would like family and a few close friends to be with us.

I am anxious to see Ryan and Mandy together again. He says he hates girls, but I keep telling him they are fun to play with. He says "Yuck." I get such a kick out of that kid. I've agreed to coach his tee-ball team this spring. We start practice next week. Me, a coach!

We paid a visit to the emergency room this month, too, though nothing as drastic as what you went through with Mandy. We were playing catch in the backyard and Ryan ran for the ball, fell and whumped his head on a tree stump. Five stitches.

Mom's Favorite Kid,
Garrett

NOTE HAND-DELIVERED TO RACHEL SULLIVAN, APRIL 30, 1977

Rachel,

I am sorry, but I won't accept another transfer from your class. I have forty students in my second period already. You only have twenty one. I taught Jeffrey Blogham the first three nine weeks, and found him very bright and personable. He is mischievous, but excels in small group work and oral presentations. I'm sure he will shine in your debate class. Please give him a chance.

Sarah

CLARKSBURG, *MAY 1, 1977*

Dear Mrs. Hardman:

If we do not receive payment for the emergency room visit of April 12, 1977, by the end of the month, we will turn the bill over to a collection agency.

Sincerely,
Mary Northwater, hospital billing services administrator

LETTER IN SARAH'S MAILBOX AT SCHOOL, *MAY 1, 1977*

Dear Sarah,

This is the hardest letter I ever had to write, but it is part of my AA recovery program, so I hope you'll give me a chance to say what I have to. I am sorrier than words can express for the way I treated you before I left for Vietnam. Please don't throw this away—hear me out.

First, I am sorry I slept with you outside of marriage. When I went to mass the next morning with my aunt, she encouraged me to confess, pointing out if I was going to put my life in danger in Nam, I might as well do it with a clean slate. Father Hainey assured me the only way the confession would count was if I was sincerely contrite. Contrite enough to not repeat my sin. How else could I do that except by not seeing you again? I wanted to, you can't imagine how much I wanted to, but I believed it would be wrong. I planned to tell you not to wait for me anyway. It didn't seem fair to ask you to—or worse yet, expect you to—when you were so opposed to my enlistment. I felt I had the right—and the responsibility—to enlist, but not to mess up your life too. I realize now I had already messed up your life. A more decent fellow would have taken you home, not kept ordering you beers. I knew exactly what I was doing, how easily you'd get tipsy since you'd never had a beer before. But one thing I learned in Vietnam is I am not a very decent fellow.

When I first came back, I thought maybe everything worked out the way it was supposed to. There you were, happily married. Then I saw your husband out with other women, including Martha Rose, and I knew you couldn't be happy. After I heard you were getting a divorce, I felt even worse. Maybe none of this would have happened if I'd been a more decent fellow.

I am going to a progressive Catholic Church now, and one lesson the priest delivered struck a chord with me. He says people can become Born Again Virgins. He made a believer of me. In my heart, Sarah, that is what you are. I would give anything if I could go back and undo that night. I hope you find happiness, because you deserve it.

Love,
Cal

Forty-One

MAY 1, 1977

"Stupid, stupid, stupid." Sarah sat in her car in the teachers' parking lot, banging her head against the steering wheel, Cal's letter held loosely in one hand. When she found the letter in her office mailbox first thing in the morning, saw who it was from, she fled to her car, knowing she couldn't read it in her classroom where a student or colleague might wander in. Cal was such an idiot. He could have at least told her why he wasn't going to see her again. Didn't it ever occur to him or to the priest how that goodbye-take-care-of-yourself phone call would make her feel? Unloved. Like a brown paper bag over the head wouldn't even begin to cover her defects. How could he have been so dense?

Her anger spent, she thought about what he'd said about going back and undoing that night. Thought about all that would change. How one thing led to another. Maybe she wouldn't have married Roy Glen. But then she wouldn't have Mandy. How could she ever wish to undo her child?

No, things did turn out the way they were supposed to, even if they hadn't turned out pretty. And a Born Again Virgin? A joke, a man talking, someone who hadn't undergone childbirth. She was a mother, and the only mother who might have been a virgin died about two millenniums ago. The only thing virginity was good for was giving it away. That didn't mean she thought sex was cheap. It wasn't. It mattered who you slept with. But all this hymen worship as if it were the only thing that counted—why couldn't men see there was more to a woman?

Not a decent fellow—Cal kept saying that. But he was, for God's sake. He was still one of the most decent guys she'd ever known. Even if he was a moron.

She looked at her watch. She didn't have time for this foolishness. Students would be at her door in three minutes. She blotted her eyes with a tissue and thanked the Lord the teachers parked in a lot separate from students. It would never do to let them see her weak. In the classroom she was fearless—a rock, a stone, as easy to move as a mountain. That's what she wanted them to think, anyway, though she'd never be as good at it as Rachel.

She sprinted toward Michelle, Hannah, Teddy and the others who would be waiting for her.

At the end of the day, she slipped a brief note into Cal's mailbox: "Good luck with your AA program. I hope you find happiness too. Sarah."

At three-thirty in the morning, the phone rang. Sarah was the first to stumble down the stairs and answer, but her mother and father, robed and slippered and sleep-disheveled, soon stood beside her in the den. They listened as she countered Roy Glen's threats.

"You can't take Mandy from me," she said.

"You've slept with half the guys in the factory."

"Ha—I don't even know them." She chose her words cautiously with her parents listening. Would they believe him?

"You can't prove they didn't."

"And you can't prove they did."

"I'm warning you, if you go through with the divorce, I'll ruin you. I'll take Mandy."

She hung up on him. Almost immediately the phone rang again. This time her father picked up.

"Listen, you sonofabitch, you call here again in the middle of the night, I'm going to find that truck you love so much and beat the crap out of it with a baseball bat. And then I'm coming after you. Leave my daughter alone."

He slammed the phone down. His hands were shaking, his face red. He looked like a man on the verge of a second heart attack.

Johanna rubbed his back. "Calm down. Think about your blood pressure." Over his shoulder, she shot angry looks at Sarah, as if this was her fault. She guessed it was. She was dumb enough to marry Roy Glen.

Her parents went back to bed. Sarah tiptoed in to check on Mandy. Still sleeping. The only member of the house whose heart wasn't pumping with anger. Sarah didn't know if anyone else went back to sleep. She only knew she didn't.

Sarah was helping first period students fill out worksheets on totalitarianism and fascism when a boy dressed in gym shorts and running shoes arrived at her door with a note stapled closed on all sides. The kid was out of breath. What on earth?

Sarah pried it open and looked for the signature. Cal. She went back to the top: "Come to cafeteria quick. Secretary will cover class. Pete's lost it."

She barely managed to turn the "shit" into a "shish" when she remembered all the eyes and ears trained on her. "Into groups, now, please. Finish the worksheets. Mrs. Thompson is on the way." The last words she hurled over her shoulder on the way out the door. Pete had been doing so well. What had gone wrong?

She heard the chaos before she saw it. Pete bellowing Bible verses, a chorus of angry, muttering, food service workers, and Mrs. Collins, the cafeteria manager whose voice carried over them all. "Don't you come in here and tell me how to run my lunchroom. No one tells me how to do my job, mister. I don't care how many Bible verses you scream at me, I ain't listening. Not to one word—do you hear me?"

Half the school could hear her, and several teachers in nearby rooms struggled to keep students in their classrooms. Kids loved a good fight, and from the sounds of it, this one was a doozy. Inside the food preparation area, Pete circled and preached, with the cafeteria manager right beside him.

Pete held his hands out in supplication. "Almighty Lord, cast down these sinners—"

"Who you calling sinners, Mr. High and Mighty?" Mrs. Collins took two steps for every one of Pete's, but she wasn't about to let him get ahead of her, in steps or words.

"—help them see the error of their ways."

Mrs. Collins veered away from Pete to avoid stepping on frozen French fries scattered across the floor, but she quickly moved back into orbit. "Error—what error? You got a lot of nerve."

Sarah joined Cal. The gym was next to the cafeteria, and the commotion had drawn his attention. "I tried to stop him, but it only made him angrier, so I sent for you."

There was nothing cute and walrus-like about Pete now. A red vein pulsed in his forehead. "Why, Lord, do they serve these children the Devil's foods—"

Mrs. Collins grabbed a broom and swatted at Pete's legs. "Devil's food! You're a few cards short of a deck. Get your crazy self out of my kitchen."

"—grown right in the Devil's garden, a harvest from the Devil's own backyard."

"Me and my girls are church-going folks. You got no right to come in here—"

Pete spotted another tray of fries behind workers clustered near the sink. With a sweep of his arm, the baking sheet clattered to the floor. "Cast out these demons!"

The women shrieked. Mr. Mirandi entered and pulled Mrs. Collins aside. "I don't think yelling back at Mr. Heimbach is going to help. I'll call the police."

Sarah couldn't let that happen. She planted herself directly in Pete's path and hoped he wouldn't run her down. She repeated his name until she got his attention. "I want you to come out to the parking lot with me. I have a surprise for you."

Everyone except Pete got quiet. No one asked why she, a first-year social studies teacher, was intervening.

Pete skirted by her and kept pacing, but his eyes narrowed. "What surprise, you gotta surprise, I don't know nothing about a surprise but they gotta get the Devils' food out of this kitchen."

She didn't know what surprise. She'd figure something out when they got there. She talked over the river of words streaming from his mouth. "It's about your mother, but wouldn't be a surprise if I told you."

He scraped his hand across his scalp and broke his pace. "I thought you were going to talk to them you were supposed to talk to them about the root vegetables—"

She remembered Martha Rose's advice to go along with him when he got this way. "We'll have to do something about it. Definitely. We will. But don't you want to see the surprise? It won't keep. We have to go right now. Your mother would want you to come with me."

He grasped his hair as if he wanted to pull what was left of it out and he began racing around the circumference of the room again. "My mother's dead, my mother died, she cut herself, the tub was full of bloody water, I saw it, I saw it all, and there were hundreds of them, women and children, shot to pieces and dumped into the ground, and then the gooks covered them up with dirt, buried them like they were nothing more than potatoes, threw dirt right on their faces, we should have stopped them, we should have."

Sarah shouted over his twisted thoughts. "Yes, I know, but there's something in my car you have to see."

No one was more surprised than Sarah when Pete let her lead him to the parking lot. Cal and Mr. Mirandi came along. To keep her safe, she supposed, if Pete went ballistic. What was she going to show him? She knew so little about his mother, the woman scorned as a nympho. Sarah had only seen one picture of Ava, the one Mahlon had made. That became her inspiration. She asked Mr. Mirandi if he had a pen and a slip of paper. He fished in his jacket and found both. As they neared her car, she scrawled out a barely legible I.O.U. It was the best she could do.

When they got to her car, she asked Pete to sit down in the passenger seat. He lowered his backside into the seat, work boots still on the pavement, his torso moving up and down to his knees, up and down. His words still flowed in the direction of the pavement, so she was forced to break in. She handed him the I.O.U. and knelt beside him. She told him about the art glass picture of his mother she'd seen in Mahlon's studio.

"This note is a promise. I am going to find that picture for you. I'm going to take you to Livvie's now. I'm sure it's in her house somewhere."

"My mother?" He looked at her for the first time since getting in the car. "My father made a picture of her?"

More gibberish followed, so Sarah talked over him again. "Yes, I saw it once, and he told me it was our secret, but now it's our secret, yours and mine. It's a beautiful picture, and we're going to find it. Let's take you home now."

"Be back shortly," Sarah said to Mr. Mirandi. "Mrs. Thompson will stay with my class?"

Mr. Mirandi nodded. "Come by my office when you get back."

Her life was falling apart, piece by piece. She took Pete to Livvie's and made sure he took his medicine. He'd probably missed it for days, Livvie being in no shape now to look after him. You'd think Martha Rose would have figured that out and looked in on him herself. What happened to checking on him regularly? Too busy hustling men in bars? (Okay, she was being bitchy, but she didn't care.) Livvie's nurse came in and Sarah enlisted her help in locating the phone number for Pete's doctor. He gave the nurse permission to give him a shot of something to make him sleep. Sarah called her mother to let her know what was going on.

On the drive back, she thought about something Cal told her once. Charity should begin in your own community. In college, she had been eager to write about starving Africans and veterans' benefits and social issues, but what had she ever *done* to help someone else? Very little, and the thought shamed her. She was Pete's family, too, yet she had allowed an elderly, dying woman and his back-stabbing sleaze of a sister assume all responsibility for him.

Sarah leaned forward, fingertips pressed into the edge of Mr. Mirandi's desk, and explained what little she understood of Pete's mental illness. "I think his time in Korea might have made him sick. He rambled a lot today about a mass grave. I'm asking you to give my cousin another chance."

Mr. Mirandi rubbed thick fingers across his bald head. "It'll depend on what a doctor says. I can't do it if he could become violent, but I'm a Korean vet myself. The years don't always chase those memories away." He flipped through his rolodex and called someone he knew at the VA hospital, arranging for a nurse and social worker to visit Pete. They would check his medication and set up an appointment for psychiatric evaluation. "Let's get him straightened out first, and if we can do that, he can come back to work. Now all I have to do is convince our cafeteria staff not to walk out the front door in protest."

Sarah didn't envy him that task. The rest of the day was so busy she barely had time to catch her breath. Only another teacher could understand how exhausting it was to be on stage all day, meeting the needs of thirty-some kids at once. No time for coffee breaks, bathroom trips, or phone calls—benefits other people took for granted.

Justin, the sports editor, said his story wouldn't be done on time because the track coach, who taught at the junior high, was never on campus. He had tried to reach the coach at home, but he hadn't returned the calls.

The owner of Pig-Out Barbecue called to cancel all future ads. In a story comparing three barbecue places in town, the reviewer listed prices of comparable items and Pig-Out's ran the highest. Never mind that the review praised their food.

When the last bell rang, Sarah closed her eyes and massaged her temples. The intercom crackled. Mr. Mirandi asked her to come to the office. During her planning period, two boys on her newspaper staff told the study hall teacher they were going to interview a car dealer about teens buying used cars. Instead they went to a convenience store and pulled two cases of beer off the back of a truck and threw them in their pick-up. They were underage. A crime of opportunity. The store's videotape captured them in the act. The proprietor recognized the starting linebacker on the football team. Budweisers, open and partially consumed, were in the boys' hands when officers arrested them in the linebacker's home.

Sarah listened wordlessly to Mr. Mirandi's recounting. At least he was calm. Not accusatory. In fact, he was the most sensible person she'd talked to all day. But even Mr. Mirandi might not be able to help her out of this mess. She wondered if her teacher's license could be jerked. It was ridiculous to set up newspaper class so kids were enrolled in study hall and showed up in her room whenever they felt like it. The best kids, the leaders, were there every day. The worst—well, now everyone knew what the worst ones did.

She went home and fixed dinner for Mandy and her father, too sick with worry to eat anything herself. Her mother was on afternoon shift again but left word a social worker had placed Pete in what they called a halfway house temporarily.

Cal phoned. The teachers' lounge was rocking with news of the beer heist. "You might want to contact the NEA. Get a lawyer to protect your rights." The last thing she wanted was another lawyer in her life. With all the problems at school, she could feel the chances for Mandy's health insurance draining away.

Forty-Two

MAY 1977

Now that the end was near, the private duty nurse withdrew to the kitchen to make coffee. The family kept vigil around Livvie's bed in a room lit only by two soft lamps, Sarah's mother on the right side of the bed, holding a cool cloth against Livvie's forehead; Martha Rose, clinging to Livvie's withered left hand, one leg anchored on the floor, the other dangling in the air, her mini-skirt riding up to expose curvy thighs and Sarah couldn't help thinking her cousin might have learned to keep her legs together a little better after all the trouble she caused—but she was family and they couldn't prevent her from being there, so Johanna said; Sarah, seething at her mother's side, full of shame in Martha Rose's presence (a woman Roy Glen preferred to her) and resentful of her intrusion at this moment, of having her attention pulled away from Livvie against her will; the men—Sarah's father and Pete—standing at some distance from the foot of the bed, shuffling their feet, awkward as men are at such times; and behind the men, the picture of the Assumption on the wall with Mary's placid smile and uplifted eyes; and they all prayed and waited for an end to Livvie's suffering. It had lasted too many months already.

They waited as the last of Livvie's life burned away. Sarah watched as her grandmother—and she had been closer than most who could claim that title in front of the world—expelled her last breath and joined her brothers and sisters on the other side. The last survivor of a generation of Heimbachs, thirteen children of an immigrant glass-blower and indentured servant, newcomers to this country with a dream of a better life for themselves and their children, a dream that perhaps was fulfilled. It was the end of her story.

Johanna touched Livvie's cheek. "She's one of the angels now."

Her mother was only partly right. Livvie—and Katherine and Maggie and Bitsy—had always been angels. Death couldn't change that.

Martha Rose began weeping again, her head lowered to Livvie's bosom. Sarah whirled on her heel and left the room. Where had Martha Rose been all the months Livvie was sick? Sarah found her way down to the kitchen.

The nurse handed her a cup of coffee. "She gone, sweetheart?"

Sarah sucked in her lips and closed her eyes in response. When she heard her cousin ask for a cup too, Sarah gritted her teeth and edged her way to the opposite side of the room.

"Wait, Sarah, there's something I want to say."

"We don't have anything to say to each other." Sarah passed through the archway into the living room.

Martha Rose darted forward and caught her arm. "Well, I do. I'm sorry, I was wrong. You've always had everything—good parents, good family—and you always acted like you were better than me. It pissed me off."

"Yeah? I'm sorry you're pissed. You want him, you're welcome to him."

Sarah's father loomed behind them. "Let it go, Martha Rose. This isn't the time or place."

Martha Rose let her hand fall away as she addressed Nelson. "But she needs to hear what I'm saying. I'm trying to apologize. I'm going to work things out with my husband." She turned to Sarah. "You should do the same."

As if Sarah needed advice from her. "You weren't the first other woman, but you will be the last. I'm done with him. Now, if you're finished, I need to pick up my daughter at Rita's."

Her father escorted her to the door.

"Thanks, Daddy." Impulsively, she kissed his cheek.

"Drive carefully, Princess."

Mr. Mirandi pulled on his ear and then studied his shoes as he recited words he'd clearly rehearsed. "Board policy says you can only claim bereavement leave for immediate family. Mother, father, brother, grandmother." He raised his eyes and his voice became conversational. "The school board will change the law next year, I think, to give us three days of personal leave to use however we see fit, but right now, it's immediate family or your pay is docked. I wanted to make sure you understood. I'm sorry."

Sarah was silent as she considered what she should do. She didn't want to betray secrets, but Livvie was dead.

"She is my immediate family, sir. My grandmother."

His head jerked back slightly.

"I can explain."

He looked her in the eyes. "No need, your word is good enough. Do you want to go home today? You're entitled."

She didn't. One thing about teaching was it kept the mind and body fully engaged. No sitting around and moping. She read announcements to her homeroom, collected last minute prom dues, led two discussions on medical experiments performed on twins during the Third Reich's rule, provided illustrations of excellent and weak thesis statements for term papers, double-checked the accuracy of the advertising manager's receipts before turning the money envelope in to the finance secretary, felt a girl's forehead and, indeed, it was hot, so she wrote a pass for her to sign out, drank a cola and ate cheese crackers while conducting a meeting with editors on the progress of the graduation issue of the newspaper, and proofread stories with the news staff on her planning period. After school she copied materials for the next day. There hadn't been one spare moment to dwell on Livvie all day. Alone in her bedroom that night, she finally wept for Livvie. And she wept for Katherine and Mahlon and Foster and the families of those Marshall boys who'd fallen out of the sky. She even wept for Roy Glen. For all those losses. All that lost love.

Livvie came to her in a dream. Sarah, still a child, stood on a chair by her aunt's side in the red and white kitchen. They were mixing gingerbread, and the kitchen was filled with fragrance. Molasses, ginger, cinnamon. "Would you promise me something?" Livvie asked. "Light prayer candles for me. Thirteen. One for each of my brothers and sisters so we'll be reunited in heaven."

The next afternoon before she picked up Mandy, Sarah walked up the granite steps to the Immaculate Conception, the church she had attended as a child so many times with her aunts. The path to the altar was shorter than Sarah remembered. Her footsteps sounded cold and lonely as they echoed off the domed ceiling. Incense lingered in the empty sanctuary. On the right side of the altar, exactly where Sarah remembered them, were tiers of candles set in gold, red, and blue glasses. About a third flickered, sending someone's prayers heavenward. She tucked a ten dollar bill into the honorarium box, grasped long wooden matches and lit votives, twelve of them, clustered together. She whispered their names, each uncle and aunt. The thirteenth she lit for Livvie and gave thanks for the blessing of her family. The Heimbachs were together now.

The next day they buried her grandmother.

The two-story white frame house sat at the top of the hill, same as always, but now it belonged to Sarah and Mandy. The earth pushed against the retaining wall in the front yard until it no longer stood upright but leaned toward the street at an ever sharper angle. One day the dirt would win its struggle, exerting force against the concrete until it collapsed into the street.

Mandy ran up the concrete steps, followed by Sarah and her mother. Nobody waited on the porch to greet them, but Sarah felt the ghosts of her aunts, benevolent presences in death as they were in life. She could swear she smelled ginger and cinnamon as she opened the door, even though she knew it was memory playing tricks on her.

Over the weekend Sarah and Mandy moved their few belongings to the Aunt Hill. Clothes and toys and books. Sarah decided to sleep in Mahlon's old room and put Mandy in Bitsy's. Both had wide windows to let in the light. She closed the door to Livvie's room, its emptiness too much to face.

Monday morning the phone rang before Sarah even had time to fix herself a cup of tea. Adrenaline surged as her mind ran through possible bad tidings that might merit such an early call: her father had had another heart attack, her mother or Garrett had wrecked on the way to work, Pete needed someone to bail him out of jail.

Her mother was trembly with news. "You'll never guess who came through x-ray early his morning."

"Who?"

"Martha Rose. Two cracked ribs, a black eye, and a concussion."

Geez—had her cousin's gun-waving husband snapped?

"Guess who Jimmy Watson arrested for assault?" Two beats of

silence. "Roy Glen."

Sarah swore softly into the phone.

"You barely got out in time, sweetie. Don't you go back to him, no matter what."

Her mother had nothing to worry about. She wouldn't have anyway, but now she knew how careful she had to be. She had sensed an increasing level of tension, an anger Roy Glen held barely beneath the surface. She had to do more to ensure he couldn't get to Mandy. Time to call on the Boy-Next-Door.

Jimmy Watson now lived in a one-room apartment two blocks from his mother Rita. The narrow three-story building's ancient crumbling bricks were periodically relieved from their monotony by wooden window frames painted a light mustard color. All the windows, Jimmy said, were painted shut, except one in the rear, which he'd pried open with a crowbar. A small air conditioner sat in it. The apartment's location suited Jimmy because he still ate most meals with his parents. Rita, however, had told him he was "growed up" and refused to do his laundry. Evidently she'd stuck to it, because two pair of jeans were thrown over the back of Jimmy's kitchen chair, a pile of rumpled tee-shirts fell in all directions, half-on, half-off the seat, and dirty socks and underwear lay on the floor beneath it. He shoveled the mess to the floor so Sarah could sit down.

"Ever hear of a laundry basket?" Sarah asked him.

He grinned. "Got one. It's full."

"Good thing the police department launders your uniforms."

He set a mug of coffee in front of her on a breakfast table she recognized from Rita's basement storage room. She inspected the rim of the mug and decided he did a better job with dishes than laundry.

"See you let your hair go natural," he said.

Self-consciously, she combed her fingers through the curls.

"Never did understand why you tried to straighten it on those big juice cans. A stupid girl thing, I guess. So, what's up?"

"How would you like to help an old friend?"

His eyes narrowed. "Keep talking."

She explained she wanted him to bust Roy Glen. "I don't want him to stay in jail, but I need to make sure he can't get custody of Mandy."

"You think he'll give up his supplier? That's the only way he won't do hard time if he has as much dope in his truck as you say."

Bobby Marchio was an old chum of Jimmy's. Maybe the best thing would be for Jimmy to find out for himself who the supplier was. "If you tell him he'll be locked away for months or even years—and remind him that means no sex—"

"None he'd want to have, anyway," Jimmy said.

"—he'll give up his supplier in a heartbeat. The important thing is to convince him staying out of trouble is part of the deal. He can't hurt Mandy or my folks or me and he can't commit perjury or any other crime or he goes straight to jail and doesn't get to pass Go."

"You're sure this stuff is in his truck?"

"Definitely."

"And he'll try to outrun me if he sees my lights on?"

"Guaranteed. He prides himself on outrunning cops."

"He won't this time. We'll be all over him like stink on shit." Jimmy's eyes narrowed again as he studied her. "I didn't think you had it in you to suggest something so dirty."

"Motherhood's a dirty business, Jimmy."

"I didn't mean it was wrong. Just surprising, turning in your husband. Not that he doesn't deserve it."

Jimmy had no idea. Sarah didn't share the nasty stories Roy Glen was threatening to use in court, the fake witnesses he said he'd parade in front of her mother and the judge. Roy Glen hadn't left her any choice but to play the game his way. When she was elbowed on the basketball court, she'd learned to elbow back. She remembered how.

Forty-Three

MAY 1977

Rain pelted the black umbrella as Sarah scurried from her car to the courthouse. If April showers bring mayflowers, what does the Mayflower bring? Now why, she wondered, would such a silly joke pop into her head at this moment? What mayflowers brought were memories of Livvie's stories about fairies using the green leaves as umbrellas, and as fragments of those stories floated through Sarah's mind, she knew Livvie's spirit walked with her, deep in her bones. She hurried by the statue of Stonewall Jackson riding his horse, her heels splattering dirty water onto her hose. She remembered sitting on the back of that statue with Roy Glen once when they were lovestruck and silly. Not all of their ride together had been bad. Once inside, she folded her umbrella, which dripped across the foyer.

Sarah sat on a wooden bench in the upstairs lobby, a somber space with high ceilings and marble floors. She tried to remove the muddy spots from her hose with a tissue. Hopeless. Little tissue flakes stuck to the wet spots. She crossed her legs at the knees and again at the ankles, awaiting her turn to see the Honorable Henry Miller. Judge Miller was familiar to her in the way of neighbors you know but never invited in for a cup of coffee or glass of lemonade. When she was a child, she could count on him to buy Girl Scout cookies and to smile and wave as he got into his car while she played hopscotch in front of his house.

In front of Sarah, a statue of Athena, blindfolded with scales in her hand, sat on a pedestal. Maybe there was a goddess who weighed the balance in relationships too. If it moved too far out of kilter, she would cast judgment. The two sides need not be equal, Sarah mused, for a relationship to work out to everyone's satisfaction. Sarah would give all her time, effort—even her life if it came to that—willingly to her child and expect little in return, except, perhaps, for love.

What happened between a man and a woman was more complex. She thought an equilibrium developed early between them, one person usually more needy than the other and willing to subjugate himself or herself. That balance shifted with births, deaths, new jobs, new friends—a little more give, a little less take, whatever it took to keep life humming along. Sometimes a woman merely took the place of the man's mother, giving her all, expecting little in return. Except, perhaps, for love.

Johanna and Rita joined Sarah on the padded bench to await the judge.

"McGarrett, Hawaii Five-O, reporting for duty." Rita's hoot echoed all through the hallway.

Rita was Rita. Nothing intimidated her, not even the austere courthouse, and that, Sarah found, was a comfort. Her right hand found its way to her left, seeking her rings, still surprised to find they weren't there. She'd pawned them to pay Mandy's hospital bills. Sarah dragged fingers across her eyes and rested her face in her hands.

Johanna stroked the top of her head. "It'll all be over soon."

The bailiff admitted them to the courtroom. It looked much as she'd expected from television, but the smell surprised her—like a library, like yellowed paper. The bailiff led them to oak chairs near the front, where Ethan Hedgwick stood talking to the judge. A few moments later he joined them.

"Your husband decided not to show, which means the divorce will not be contested," Hedgwick said.

Thanks to Jimmy. Unless Roy Glenn had made bail this morning, he was still sitting at the police station. Jimmy said he'd given up Bobby, Bobby gave up his supplier, and who knew where it would stop.

"You still have to convince the judge you have grounds to sue for divorce," Hedgwick said.

Sarah found the whole process barbaric. Maybe someday they would grant divorces without public airing of grievances.

Hedgwick asked her to tell the court why she was pursuing divorce on grounds of cruelty. Sarah told about the love letter from her cousin and how Roy Glen didn't come home at night.

"What other acts of cruelty has he committed?"

Sarah closed her eyes. Hedgwick said she had to do this. "He gave me a ve—"

Judge Miller cracked his gavel three times. "Enough. Mr. Hedgwick, there's no need to act like Perry Mason here."

Rita snickered. The judge looked at her sternly. She stopped.

Judge Miller looked directly at Sarah. "Do you still love your husband?"

At the beginning of the proceedings she had sworn an oath on a bible to tell the truth. She loved Roy Glen with a hate so strong she wanted to choke the life out of him. She loved him with a sorrow so intense if she let herself cry the first tear she might never stop.

She took a deep breath. "No, Your Honor."

"Divorce granted." Judge Miller also readily granted her request to restrict Roy Glen's visitation to supervision from his parents. Sarah wondered if he was this helpful to all wives seeking divorce, or if there were benefits to being his neighbor. She didn't care. Mandy was hers. Now Roy Glen couldn't take her away. The nightmare was over.

As they left the courthouse, Rita mentioned her nephew, Robin Leuliette, was demonstrating glass blowing at the arts and crafts fair in Grafton the following weekend. "You should come on out and see him. Bring Mandy. She'll have a good old time riding in the bumper cars and they usually set up a little train."

Leuliette. Why did Sarah know that name? After some searching, she retrieved a mental picture of a pony-tailed glassblower she'd seen years ago at Prickett's Fort. "I'd love to go. I've always wanted to work with glass, but the unions kept girls out."

"Be glad of that—you wouldn't have liked factory work anyhow. Now, what Robin's teaching is glass blowing. What you've always had your heart set on. He's taking names for a summer workshop now, and he don't care none whether you're a girl." She laughed wickedly. "Fact is, he likes girls."

"Maybe the Heimbachs aren't through with glass yet," Sarah said.

Johanna's face looked tortured. "Oh, Sarah, you can't mean it. You have a little girl to think of. Remember, it killed your grandfather and your Uncle Mahlon."

Rita dismissed these concerns with a wave of the hand. "It's not like the old days. Some of them pipes Robin's got is made of flexible tubes, stuff that doesn't transfer the heat up to the lungs so bad. And he's got vacuum cleaners and filters—suck those stray particles right out of the air. Let her give it a try."

Sarah felt a tickle run up her spine at the thought.

It took eighty-five minutes to end a marriage, counting driving time to and from the courthouse. Though Sarah felt a little dazed the rest of the day, she delivered directions, passed back papers, and checked homework as usual. After school Mr. Mirandi handed her a contract for the next school year. Sarah signed it immediately before he could change his mind.

Next year Mandy would have insurance. Only three months until pre-existing conditions didn't matter anymore. Hopefully, nothing would happen between now and then.

"Where's Mandy?" Sarah asked.

Mrs. Nicholas's startled eyes bounced around the church playroom as if she'd misplaced something. The former Sunday School teacher's eyes were telling Sarah things she didn't want to hear. She scanned the children clustered at a little table dressing a bear in a raincoat and rubber boots, those sitting in a line of chairs playing "train," and those sprawled on the floor around a picture book. She scanned again. The next seconds passed slowly. She felt disoriented. Dizzy. Oxygen-deprived. This couldn't be happening. Any second now, Mrs. Nicholas would tell her Mandy was in the bathroom, and Sarah would take a deep breath. Laugh at her own silly imaginings.

"Your husband said you'd patched things up, and Mandy practically threw herself on him, so I thought—" Mrs. Nicholas's arms fell to her sides.

He'd taken her. After all Sarah'd done to prevent this—arranged for his arrest, told Mrs. Nicholas only she or her parents could pick up Mandy. He slipped by all the safeguards and snatched her. This couldn't be happening, but it was. Her heart began to beat faster than a hummingbird's wings, and oxygen flooded her brain.

"Your phone."

Mrs. Nicholas stood still.

"Where's the phone?"

Jolted into action, Mrs. Nicholas pointed toward a closet-sized office. Sarah strode off, Mrs. Nicholas following, full of apology.

Later, Sarah thought. After she got Mandy back, she would listen and forgive. Right now, she needed Jimmy Watson.

"Go to your mother's and stay put," Jimmy said. "I'll check your trailer and then go talk to his parents. Everybody on the force will be out looking for him. Call you as soon as we know anything."

At the door, Mrs. Nicholas looked worried. "They left in such a hurry, Mandy forgot this." She pressed Mandy's inhaler into Sarah's hand.

Forty-Four

MAY 1977

Roy Glen couldn't remember exactly how they'd gotten to Paw-Paw's cabin, but here they were. His hands were sweaty, sticking to the stock of his Springfield. He remembered loading it with 30-0-6 cartridges, but didn't know where he'd put the box of ammo. Maybe he'd left it in the truck. The air inside the cabin hung thick with mildew.

Leaky roof needed fixing. A mattress, sagging and brown-stained, offered the only seat. Mandy plopped onto it. He lowered himself beside her, slinging the rifle across his lap, trying to figure out his next move.

Sarah would find the note he left in the trailer and she would come—he knew she would. Could he convince her to stay? Maybe. Mandy was with him, and Sarah loved the kid. More than she loved him, and God help him, sometimes he resented Mandy for it. He envied the way Sarah would throw herself into doing the Hokey Pokey as if she were four years old, too. Sarah and Mandy entered their own world, one he only skirted the edges of. They never invited him in.

Same way with Cal and that kiss. The world had blown by them in the rain and they never saw it. Sarah still didn't know what he'd witnessed. She never let him in. Maybe he never knocked. If that door had blown open, he might have laughed a little, and said, *You know the first time I saw you? It wasn't when I jumped in the river after the dog.*

Even the dog. She cared more about that smelly old mutt than him. Cried buckets over him, for God's sake.

Mandy tugged his arm. "Come on, Daddy, you said we were going fishing."

"In a minute, Peanut. Daddy needs to think."

She touched the barrel of his gun. "You going to hunt deer instead?"

The barrel was pointed right above her legs. If she stood, it would have pointed right at her. He flipped it away from her.

"What're you going to do with the gun?"

He wasn't sure. Why did the child ask such impossible questions? He felt threatened, and the Springfield might be the only thing between him and those who would strip away everything that mattered.

Wrinkling her nose, Mandy stood up and tugged harder. "Come on. It's stinky in here."

Through a fog, he looked at his grandparents' house. Once, it had been cozy. In his mind he could see MeMaw's red quilt on the bed, and a square oak table and chairs in the kitchen with blue enamelware cups and plates on top. "If we clean it up, it could be our secret clubhouse, yours and mine."

Mandy let go of his arm and hopped up to study the grayed wall boards. "And Mommy's."

"And Mommy's, if she wants to join."

"She will. We can't have a club without Mommy. But you have to get rid of the spiders and the stink. Could we paint the walls purple?"

"Any color you want."

Fishing forgotten, she was describing what they could put in the clubhouse. From time to time, coughing broke her chatter. Mandy debated which of her friends from day care she would invite to visit the club house. None, of course, could be invited. There was a lot he needed to do if they were going to live here. Find out if the well water was good and if the pump could be repaired. Buy seed—but he guessed he'd have to plow first. Meadow grass, sumac, and blackberry canes had reclaimed PawPaw's garden long ago. Sarah wasn't going to like his plan, but too bad. She would live here with them, or nowhere. She could choose. As MeMaw used to say, hard times is better than no times at all. One thing was certain. No one was going to find them back in this holler.

"Your nose is bleeding, Daddy."

Damn. He didn't need this now. He pulled a hankie from his jeans and applied pressure to his nostrils. He wished he could take another snort. Sharpen his mind.

"Can I put on play clothes and go outside?"

Play clothes? He didn't have any clothes for her except what was on her back. "Play in what you have on." His voice sounded weird and distant because he was pinching his nostrils.

"Mommy won't let me."

"Mommy isn't here now. Go ahead and play."

She hacked a few more times. "I'm thirsty."

Couldn't she leave him alone even for a minute? He couldn't think when his head felt like it was full of broken glass. There wasn't anything to drink or anything to drink out of. He should have planned better, would have if he'd had time.

"Daddy, didn't you hear me? I'm thirsty. My throat hurts."

"Damn it, I'm thinking. Give me a minute."

Mandy's cough scratched at his ears like sandpaper. Until now, he figured Sarah exaggerated how bad it was. One more nagging point about his being gone too often. "Where's your medicine?"

"There's one at school and—" hack—"one at home and Mommy keeps some"—hack—"in her purse."

Lot of good that was going to do. Maybe water would help. They'd have to walk back to the creek.

Sarah started to follow Jimmy's orders, but as she headed toward her mother's, she realized she couldn't sit and wait for someone else to find her baby. She turned her car around and sped toward her in-laws' house. The tires dipped into one bone-rattling pothole after another, but Sarah didn't dare slow down, not even while crossing the Hardmans' narrow bridge.

Ellen answered the door in a shapeless housedress. "Sarah! I'm so happy to see you and—" She looked around, surprise written on her face. "Where's Mandy?"

Sarah explained the afternoon's events. The welcome left Ellen's eyes. They were as responsive as the bighorn sheep's on the wall behind her. Cold and hard as glass. "You understand I can't take your side."

"I'm not asking you to. I'm asking you to help me find Mandy."

Ellen picked at the creases of skin around her elbows. "I don't know where he might have taken her."

Somehow, Sarah needed to make her understand they weren't adversaries. "You and Frank love her, and I trust you completely to take good care of her. That's why the divorce settlement says Roy Glen can see her, but only under your supervision. He's using cocaine, Ellen. You don't know what he might do."

"For heaven's sake, I know my son. He would never hurt her."

"Not if he's in his right mind, but he hasn't been himself lately. You know all the trouble he's been in. The arrest for possession and intent to distribute. The assault charges—"

"They were withdrawn."

"Not because the assault didn't happen. My cousin dropped the charges, but her hearing is permanently damaged, did you know that?"

Ellen's chin quivered. "He would never hurt Mandy."

"He shot Foster, he told me so, and he threatened to hurt Mandy if I didn't quit my job."

Ellen's eyes clouded with doubt. The grandfather clock ticked off the seconds loudly behind her. "He wouldn't do it. Not my boy."

"Mandy doesn't have her inhaler. If she has an attack, she could die."

"Let me call Frank. See what he thinks."

Hysteria rose in Sarah's throat as she thought of more precious seconds lost. "She's your only grandchild and she could die, what is there to think about, for God's sake?"

Ellen's voice swelled with hysteria equal to Sarah's. "You don't have to yell at me. I love her, too. The cabin. PawPaw's cabin. It's the only place I can think of where he might take her."

Sarah jumped to her feet. Of course. She should have thought of it herself. That ramshackle bunch of barely standing boards back in the hills. Hadn't he said it was where they'd go if the country fell apart? Sarah guessed he might go there when his little corner crashed and burned.

Ellen was right behind her on the way out the door.

At first, Mandy walked by Roy Glen's side on the way to the creek. By the time they were halfway there, her breaths grew so ragged Roy Glen laid his rifle down. He packed his hankie up his nostrils and carried her the rest of the way, huffing through his mouth. Beside the creek, he set her down and cupped his hands into a deep spot between two rocks and held the cool water out for her. She tried to sip but couldn't catch her breath long enough to drink. Water trickled through his fingers. With alarm, he took in her eyes, wide with fear, took in the bluish nails. Once, he'd heard a deer sucking air like this. Last breaths after an arrow pierced its lung.

Roy Glen pulled the hankie from his nostrils—the blood would have to flow. He scooped Mandy up and ran. He could call for help at the mobile home. Maybe there was even a spare inhaler Sarah hadn't taken. He followed the stream's path through the woods to the crest of the hill, where he skidded to a stop, boots digging into damp earth.

Below in the driveway sat a police car. Had they rescinded bail? Not likely. They'd turned him loose a few hours ago when his lawyer worked some kind of deal. Would Sarah have called the cops because he took Mandy? I mean, all he was doing was seeing his own kid. How could that be a crime? He could turn around, head for his truck on the other side of the hill. Drive Mandy to the hospital himself. One look at her bluing complexion changed his mind. He thundered down the hill, yelling as he went. He saw the officer, Glock gleaming in his hand, but didn't stop. It was that friend of Sarah's again. Jimmy.

"Asthma attack—she needs a hospital," Roy Glen managed to huff.

Jimmy holstered the weapon and opened the rear door of the cruiser. "I'll get you there. What the hell happened to you?"

Roy Glen remembered the nosebleed, how it must look, and mumbled something about falling. He climbed inside with Mandy as Sarah and his mother drove up, blocking the driveway. Sarah threw the car door open, motor still running, and sprinted to them. One look at Mandy, and she zipped open a compartment of her purse, whipped out an inhaler, placed it in Mandy's mouth and pumped. Sarah's arms wrapped around Mandy like a blanket, her lips pressed to the child's hair, her forehead, her ear. "You're going to be okay, baby. Breathe deep."

He hoped Sarah was right. He'd never been around during one of Mandy's attacks, never appreciated how frightening they were. Roy Glen realized he wouldn't have known what to do with an inhaler if he'd found one. He leaned forward and touched Mandy's cheek.

Sarah's eyes burned into him and he drew back. "I didn't know what to do when she got sick."

"If anything happens to her—"

She didn't have to finish the thought. Her eyes said it all. She would kill him herself. This wasn't the cowed little girl he'd married.

Jimmy backed up and pulled around Sarah's car onto the highway.

Roy Glen looked back at the driveway and the idling car. "What about my mother?"

"She'll figure it out," Sarah said.

Not long after they arrived in the emergency room, his mother, quite pale, found them clustered around Mandy's bed. One chubby nurse had packed Roy Glen's nose with rolls of gauze and handed him an ice pack to stop the bleeding. His voice sounded alien, as if it originated on another planet. At least the packing blocked that Listerine-spilled-over-shit odor of the hospital. He explained how his daughter's face was covered with a mask that delivered medication. How a nurse had hooked Mandy up to an IV with steroids. How different nurses and doctors came and went. All this had happened in the few minutes it took his mother to find a place to park and then locate them. Roy Glen had never felt so helpless in his life. (And his Springfield was no defense at all against this threat. Where was his rifle? For the life of him, he couldn't remember.) They were at the mercy of the staff. He hoped they knew what they were doing.

Sarah sent someone to X-ray for her mother and soon she, too, crowded into the cubicle. All three hundred pounds of her. Lord, the woman was as big as a mattress, but Sarah was glad she was there to run interference with the staff. Roy Glen's mother and Jimmy moved to the larger waiting area outside.

After what seemed forever, yet another doctor listened to Mandy's chest with a stethoscope and said she could go home. "But Mrs. Cottrill at the reception desk needs to speak to you first."

Sarah took charge of belongings and her mother took charge of Mandy. They all herded into the waiting area. A black and white sign identified the woman behind the desk as Mrs. Cottrill. "You needed to see me?" Sarah asked.

"Yes, Mrs. Hardman. Since you don't have insurance, I would appreciate your writing a check before—"

Roy Glen's mother interrupted. "Of course Mandy has insurance. Hazel Atlas has good insurance."

Sarah winced. "Actually, she doesn't have insurance. Roy Glen cancelled it."

His mother turned on him. "For God's sake, Roy Glen, what were you thinking?"

Sarah knew what he was thinking: he needed the money for drugs.

Johanna turned on Sarah. "For heaven's sake, why didn't you tell us? How did you pay the bill the last time?"

"Hocked my rings."

His mother's head dropped into her hands. "I could drop through this floor right now." The embarrassment only slowed her a few seconds, but by the time she whipped out her checkbook, Johanna was already inking in the name of the hospital on the top check in hers. They argued, each insisting on paying until Mrs. Cottrill suggested they split the bill, and that's what they did.

Roy Glen followed Sarah and Mandy into the parking lot. For a brief flash, Roy Glen imagined the three of them making the journey home together. But as Sarah took charge and made arrangements for Jimmy to drive his mother and him wherever they wanted to go, he knew it wasn't happening. Not in this lifetime.

In the cruiser's back seat, Roy Glen's mother took his hand. "I have some money saved up, my rainy day fund, and your father doesn't know a thing about it."

Strange things were happening to the women in his life. Since when did his mother hide money from his father?

She stared straight ahead, not looking at him while she talked, but Roy Glen didn't think she saw the traffic at all. Her eyes were focused on some future path only she could see. Her eyes were hard. Determined. "While we were in the waiting room, the nice officer here—he says he's an old friend of yours—offered to help."

Roy Glen would hardly call Jimmy his friend. Jimmy had arrested him. Jimmy was Sarah's friend.

"Your father doesn't believe in drug treatment programs. He says jail's the best place for you. But I think treatment might help, and I'm going to give Officer Watson the money to get you into the best program available."

"I don't have a drug problem, Mom."

"The boy I raised wouldn't beat people up or cancel his daughter's insurance if he didn't have a king-sized problem."

"I'm fine, I just like to relax once in a while."

Her voice became raspy. Bordered on hysteria. "You can't lie to me, I'm your mother. I diapered you, damn it, and you'll do as I say."

Forty-Five

MAY 1977

One drawer at a time, Sarah moved the black chest into Mahlon's room and reassembled it. She unwrapped the Madonna from layers of protective newspaper and stroked the satiny surface until a stinging pain almost made her drop it. Turning it over, she discovered a minute chip on the base. A drop of blood pooled on her index finger. She sucked it off and returned the Madonna to the chest, feeling that same squeeze in her chest she'd felt when her uncle had told her girls couldn't blow glass. That there was something wrong with her. Something wrong with all girls. She remembered her aunt's words: *Mary is so much more than a virgin.* Mary was the mother. Being a mother was the most important thing that ever happened to Sarah. But it's not all I am, she thought. She was *more*. More than virgin, wife, mother. Then she remembered the last thing her aunt said about Mary: she represented all the mystery and magic of a woman. That, Sarah could accept.

Light sifted through the window and illuminated the center of the figurine. The Bible, Sarah remembered, said the angel Gabriel sent a bright cloud to Mary, a stream of light, and she gave birth to the one who forgave us for our sins. Maybe that was another message of the statue. Forgiveness. The kind you have to give yourself. That was why people needed Jesus, because forgiving yourself was so damn hard. Sarah turned her face into the sunlight and let it warm her skin.

The phone rang. "We're coming over to get you," Rachel said.

"Who's we?"

"Me and Cal. We're taking you and Mandy out to dinner."

It was good to have friends, but she wanted to sit alone on the porch swing, watching the stars wink, after Mandy went to sleep. "Well, I don't know."

"You're not staying home and moping. You have an hour to get ready."

They went to Twin Oaks for pizza. The wooden legs of the chair scraped against the linoleum-tiled floor as Sarah pushed Mandy a little closer to the table. Nothing had changed since high school. Still smelled of fresh baked crusts, tomatoes, and oregano. Same juke box in the corner, its lighted glass curves inviting customers to play their favorites.

The hangout hadn't changed, but Sarah realized they had when Cal ordered a Coke. No more Stroh's for him. And because she didn't feel comfortable drinking one in front of him, she ordered a Coke too.

Sarah picked the pepperoni off her pizza and put them on Cal's plate.

He held a slice of pepperoni under her nose. "Doesn't it smell wonderful? This animal died for you, and only an ingrate wouldn't accept his offering. Someday, you'll die and be food for worms. It's a cycle that's meant to be."

Not a pleasant thought. Yet there was a lot of truth in what he'd said. Humans were animals. Why did we spend so much time denying it? He wiggled the slice in front of her. She closed her lips and teeth over it and snatched it away from him. The spices burned—in a good way—on her tongue. Though she didn't think she could make a habit of eating ground-up guts, if Livvie could chop off the head off a hen and pluck its feathers, surely Sarah could learn to eat one. She had conquered her antipathy toward alcohol. Mostly. She could do the same for meat. Once in a while. A few bites.

"You know," Cal said, "one of the nice things about getting older is you learn everything isn't as black and white as you once thought." He turned to Rachel. "Sarah and I used to fight all the time in college, has she ever told you about it? I was hard-headed. If she wrote about a person's right to determine what the end of his life was like, I would be a real jerk and tell her she wanted to play God."

Sarah placed Mandy's napkin on her lap. "You don't think so now?"

Cal washed down a bite of pizza with Coke. "I still don't like the idea, but sometimes doctors can go too far in preserving life."

"What changed your mind?" Rachel asked.

"My uncle died of Lou Gehrig's disease. He suffered terribly, more than he needed to, because doctors could extend his life but not in any state you'd want to live in. He couldn't talk or walk or even eat. They outfitted him with a feeding tube."

Sarah had moved the other way, from thinking any caring person would choose to end a family member's suffering to realizing how difficult it would be to withdraw treatment. At what moment could she have made that decision for Livvie? It was complicated.

Rachel withdrew a long, narrow sheet of paper from her purse. "Look at this list. I am so sick of my dad taking over this wedding. Ice sculptures in the shape of doves. Real doves to be released when we say our vows. They'll probably poop on my veil and I'll burst out laughing during the ceremony."

Mandy giggled. "She said 'poop,' Mommy."

Rachel apologized, but Sarah waved her off. Secretly, Sarah couldn't believe Rachel had actually said the word either. Good for her.

"Tear it up," Cal said.

To Sarah's surprise, Rachel howled and ripped it in half. "A big burden has been lifted off my shoulders. Whew. I feel giddy."

Rachel, Sarah was sure, would accept a new list from her father tomorrow.

Cal withdrew a paper from his jacket and ripped it in half. "My contract. I have decided not to teach or coach next year. I'm going to do what I've always wanted—write sports stories for a newspaper."

Sarah swallowed a half-chewed lump of pizza. "That's a pretty major decision to make so quickly."

"I've thought about it for months. Watching your kids interview this year made me realize how much I miss it. Already got my application in for reporting jobs."

As Cal drove down Bridgeport Hill, he asked Mandy if she could see the upside down champagne glass made by the twinkling lights of the town. Sarah smiled, remembering when her parents had first shown her the illusion. The illusion was pretty, but it was important to see the town the way it really was. The cracked sidewalks, the empty glass factories and storefronts mattered. Seeing them was the first step to making improvements.

Instead of going home, Cal stopped at the playground. He retrieved a basketball from the trunk. "Mandy can swing and I'll take on the two of you. A game of Around the World. It'll be like old times."

Rachel tucked her hair behind ear. "You mean like the time we whipped your butt in junior high?"

Those days, Sarah realized, were gone. Cal would never run the courts again. But he could play H.O.R.S.E. and Around the World. No matter what you lost, you built a life on what you had left.

Both she and Rachel were out of practice. It took a few minutes to warm up, to remember the feel of the ball arching toward the hoop.

"I'll be kind," Cal said. "Start you off with an easy one."

He laid in a shot from three feet out. Both Sarah and Rachel made it. He clumsily completed a lay-up, Cal who'd never been clumsy in his life. Sarah made it.

Rachel missed. Cal tried a show-off shot from center court. Missed. Now it was Sarah's turn. She hooked one in from under the left side of the basket, an old trademark of hers. Rachel missed, but Cal made it. Sarah missed the next shot, and it was Rachel's turn. She took a wide stance on the foul line, swung the ball between her legs, and heaved it toward the basket.

"No fair," Cal protested. "What a wussy shot."

"You have to make it," she said. "I can make this shot all night."

To Sarah, it seemed as if he didn't even half try. Probably offended his male pride. The game broke up with lots of laughing, and as he took them home, they argued over who really had the better team in junior high.

He dropped Rachel off first. At Livvie's, Sarah lingered at the door with him while Mandy ran inside to use the bathroom.

Cal leaned against the railing on the top step. "Why did you marry him, Sarah? I always thought it would be us."

They'd made so many mistakes—both of them. When she first contemplated divorce, she wanted to blame someone, something. Vietnam. Cal. Roy Glen. Her father. Her mother. Herself. But maybe it was no one's fault. Some matches were made in heaven. Some weren't. Maybe it was that simple.

She shrugged. "I loved him. At first."

"Remember what I wrote you about being a Born Again Virgin? I still believe that. I wish I could undo the harm I caused."

Even with him standing on the step below her, she could look straight into his eyes, those beautiful cerulean eyes. The shine was returning to them. Undo it? Any of it? Shoot, being this close to him still made her skin tingle, and how could you undo one thing without undoing everything that followed?

"I can't buy into this Born Again Virgin routine of yours, but I forgive you for everything if you promise never to bring it up again. It wasn't all your doing, anyhow. I thought I could keep you from enlisting."

He shuffled his feet. "So you want to have dinner with me? Or take in a movie? We could find one Mandy would like."

"Thanks, but I need to get myself back on solid ground right now." One thing she was sure of: she didn't want anything to do with men. Not now. Not ever.

Probably not ever.

A gargantuan task lay in front of her. She needed to search inside for the girl confident enough to beat the boys in basketball, the one who'd been brave enough to contemplate traveling alone to foreign countries to cover news, the one who dreamed of making glass. The one who believed in herself. Mandy deserved that mother.

She watched Cal going down the Heimbachs' steep concrete steps and called out for him to watch his step on the broken concrete, one of many repairs she needed to make.

Damn, his butt was cute.

Boxes stacked two deep lined the Heimbach living room, a narrow path remaining between them. Sarah piled on another carton. Threading her way through the rooms on her way to the attic, she paused to look through one of the rear windows facing the woods, where the maple and oak leaves were losing the golden shimmer of spring, moving daily toward the rich green of summer.

Cleaning out the house was sad, but also fun in an odd way. Sarah found a pillbox hat with little feathers tucked into one side in a round box in the attic. As soon as she touched it, she knew it was one Livvie had designed. Sarah didn't wear hats much, but she would wear this one. To church next Sunday. A promise she made herself.

In another box, she found Mahlon's picture of Pete's mother. She could fulfill her I.O.U. She ran her finger over the glass, awed by the way all the little pieces fused together to form a person's face. Not so different, she thought, from a person's insides. Lots of little pieces, broken bits accumulated over time. They formed a history and a personality, and the older you got, the more pieces there were to mesh together. Sometimes pieces refused to integrate, like Korea, for Pete—whatever he'd witnessed there, and maybe things he'd experienced with his mother, too.

Pete rented an apartment in the same building as Jimmy, who promised to keep an eye out for him at home. Sarah would do the same at work. Mr. Mirandi had sanctioned Pete's return to Hillside High, with orders to stay away from the cafeteria, and he was functioning well again.

Sarah labeled boxes for Goodwill, while her mother fixed a couple for delivery to Martha Rose. "I don't like the little slut either, but she should have some of the Heimbachs' things. After all, she was Mahlon's daughter, and Livvie practically raised her for a while."

Sarah looked at the vases and goblets in the china closet. All colors. All hand-blown. The pieces would bring a lot of money at auction, but she hated the thought of parting with any of them. The iridescent carnival glass bowl. A dozen goblets, each in different swirls of color. An amethyst glass plate with an edge that looked like lace. A tall asymmetrical vase in blue and silver. "What are we going to do with all the glass?"

Her mother wrapped a wooden candlestick in newspaper and set it in a box. "I assumed you'd want to keep them, the way you've always loved glass."

"But Livvie didn't leave them to me in the will, so they rightfully go with the estate. They have to be worth a lot of money."

"Some things are worth more than money. No way are they going to auction, and it would be a shame to split the pieces up. They stay in the cabinet, just as they are."

Sarah couldn't help it. Her eyes filled. She didn't know if she could bear to live with all that beauty. Would there come a day when she could pass those vases or the spring and autumn trees hanging on the wall and take them for granted?

Her mother wrapped the mate to the candlestick. "Come on, now. We have a lot of work to do to get ready for this sale."

Sarah cleaned out Livvie's jewelry box, separating pieces family members might want from costume jewelry for the yard sale. Slipped under the velvet lining was a photograph taken at Luna Park. Sarah recognized Livvie right away, but her hands trembled as she realized whose arm rested possessively along Livvie's shoulders. A man staking his claim. She studied the short, broad torso and smiling brown eyes and took the photo to her mother. Johanna's eyes watered as she held it.

"We could try to find him," Sarah said. He was probably dead, but her mother might have half brothers or sisters somewhere.

"No." But a minute later, "Maybe. I don't know. It would be such a shock to his family."

They didn't have to decide today. In the back of the jewelry box, Sarah found two small acorn cups joined in the middle

"What's that?" Mandy asked.

"A fairy telephone." Sarah marveled that Livvie had saved it all these years. Cradling it in her palm, Sarah remembered the story Livvie told the day they found it.

"Tell me," Mandy said.

Sarah did her best to tell the story of fairies who played in the woods of Lowndes Hill. A rattlesnake bit the baby fairy, Mithka, and she couldn't fly anymore, so a kind neighbor lady took her home to keep her safe. When Sarah finished, Mandy asked her why she looked so sad.

"Because I miss Aunt Livvie, honey." And because now she understood the source of the fairy mother who let someone else care for her child, loving her only from a distance.

"What happened to Mithka, the baby fairy, Mommy? Did she ever go back to the fairies?"

Sarah remembered the ending. A prince took Mithka to his glass castle in the woods and kept her safe. She could look out and see her beloved forest and all the fairies. It wouldn't do. Not for Mandy. "One day Mithka put her feet on the ground and began to walk and as soon as she did, she grew stronger and turned into a real live girl."

"That's boring. I want her to marry a prince."

"No way. She marries a real live man when she's thirty—"

"That's way too old!"

"Is not, but first she becomes an architect and builds a house right next to Miss Natalie's. And sometimes, she looks in the mirror and finds glitter on her face. Then she knows her mother has flown by and kissed her."

Mandy ran to the dresser and picked up the antique silver mirror. "There's glitter on my nose and my eyes and my cheeks and my mouth 'cause you kissed me a zillion times today." She put the mirror down. "I still want her to marry a prince."

Didn't every girl want a prince? Trouble was, there weren't any. Any more than there were fairy princesses. "Come on, glitter girl. We need to haul these boxes to the car."

As Sarah carried a box down the back stairs and into the kitchen, again she thought she smelled molasses and ginger. She whirled around, half expecting to see Livvie in her apron—the cherry-print one with a tissue tucked into the bib—ready to pop a pan into the oven. She could almost hear the clink of a whisk against a mixing bowl, almost feel her finger dipping into whipped cream and then it was all gone, leaving her as hollowed out as a dessert spoon.

Forty-Six

July 1977

Sarah sat cross-legged on the floor beside Mandy in her parents' living room in front of the television, their two dogs, Josephine and Napoleon, nosing into Sarah's armpits for attention. The neighbors, the Watsons, leaned back in the recliners. Sarah's parents cozied up on the couch with Jimmy Watson squeezed in on the end nearest Sarah. Two bowls of popcorn on the coffee table made the room smell like a movie theater. Sarah's former roomie, Paula Jackman, was making her television debut, a bit part in a new sitcom, *Three's Company*. All of Clarksburg was sitting in front of televisions tonight as excited as if she were their own daughter. Paula was going places, and Jimmy Watson was more anxious than everyone else put together. He alternated between half crazy laughter and biting his lip. Paula was leaving him behind, and it was a tribute to his character that he was still rooting for her success. With sudden foresight, Sarah could hear an older Jimmy mention the famous actress he'd dated, and his wife would search his eyes for regret, for traces of old love lingering despite the outward happiness of their lives.

Johanna crunched on a celery stick. "Heard Martha Rose went back to her husband."

"Again?" Sarah said.

"Bet it doesn't last." Nelson sipped his beer. "That fellow was born to be a doormat."

Sarah hoped her father's indictment didn't apply to her. She didn't want to be anyone's doormat ever again.

Ten months after Roy Glen killed Foster and disposed of his body, Sarah acquired Josephine from the Watsons. She was an adorable mixed breed with spaniel and poodle genes. Josephine carried on so when Sarah left for her glassmaking lessons, she realized the dog might be lonely. She brought home a scruffy terrier from the shelter and named him Napoleon. Watching the dogs relate opened Sarah's eyes.

Josephine, an outgoing dog, suddenly rolled over in submission. Napoleon took advantage, biting Josie's leg, stealing her food, mounting her at will, chasing her until she wheezed and collapsed.

The important thing Sarah learned was, before becoming part of a pack—and what else was a marriage?—you needed to know what kind of dog you were lying down with. You needed to be sure it was good natured and to snarl immediately if your leg was nipped. Allow the offense to pass even one time without rebuke and you've given permission for the Alpha to do it again—and again—and again— and he will bite harder until he finds your boundaries. He will corner you so you can't escape because without you, he has no power. It was never happening to her again. She couldn't blame Roy Glen. Things might have turned out differently if she had refused to go out the first time he showed up late. Such a small thing, but one thing led to another, and another.

Josie grew incapable of acting, her reactions delayed because she measured every response against Napoleon's approval, trying to decide if he was going to drag her across the floor by her tail. But even sweet little Josie, when pushed hard enough, eventually bared her teeth.

A hangnail on Sarah's index finger, one thirty-second of an inch, was driving her crazy. Her thumb itched to pick at the imperfection. She snapped the rubber band on her wrist.

Jimmy leaned down from his perch on the couch and touched the rubber band. "What's with this?"

She explained. He picked up one hand and inspected the nails. "Looking good. Must work. Guess who I saw walking the highway toward Shinnston today?"

Sarah drew in her breath, not wanting to believe it. "Pete?"

Jimmy nodded. "I checked on him after breakfast, and when he wasn't there, I went looking. I tried to persuade him to come back with me, but he wouldn't. Even as an officer of the law, I can't force him."

"So everything we did was for nothing. The job, the apartment, the medical care…" Sarah's voice trailed off, her thumb worrying the hangnail. Shit. She snapped the rubber band again.

"Not for nothing," Johanna said. "He knows he has a safe place to come home to. That's worth something."

Actually, it was worth quite a lot. Her mother set up automatic rent payments from Pete's invested inheritance. He could come home whenever he chose to. Sarah fished nail clippers out of the coffee table drawer and cut the tiny piece of skin from her finger.

"My nephew says you're doing real good with the glass lessons, best student he has. Rita winked at her. "I think he'd like to teach you about a whole lot more than glass."

Sarah felt the heat climb up her neck. "Don't be ridiculous! He would not."

Jimmy grimaced. "That is ridiculous, Mom. Robin's way too old for her."

Was he? Seven years didn't seem like an impossible breach. Robin was only thirty-three, but she hadn't really considered him as anything beyond her teacher.

"Quiet everyone," Rita said, in that sledgehammer voice of hers. "Show's coming on. This is going to be a hoot."

August 1977

Robin's workshop in nearby Grafton was housed in a refurbished warehouse, a brick building once used by the railroad. Sarah tightened the coated rubber band that held her hair away from her face. She wiped her hands down her blue-jeaned thighs and pulled on safety glasses and gloves.

The past two months of lessons—and fifteen years of waiting—all led to this moment. Sarah dipped the end of the mini-pipe into the crucible. When she withdrew the pipe, Robin slammed the furnace gate shut, his red pony-tail swinging to the side, a lop-sided grin on his long face. Sarah liked that grin. He was painfully thin, and no one was ever going to call him handsome, but he radiated kindness from every pore. A patient teacher. A good and gentle man.

"Ready?" he asked.

"I was born ready. Glass is in my genes."

She puffed out her cheeks and blew. Inside she could hear music. Jim Morrison, lighting her fire. She blew and twirled and dipped. As her arms searched for the right balance of surrender and control, she visualized Uncle Mahlon, could see his strong arms and feel the authority of his moves. She borrowed techniques from Robin. Before long, she found her own rhythm, her own techniques. She knew what to do because in her dreams she had blown glass since she was eleven years old. And at that moment, she knew exactly who she was.

Her breath and power flowed down to the molten mass. Slowly the bubble expanded into a globe resembling a large Winesap, glowing with light. A few minutes more and she'd break the glass off, open the lip, shape it with paddles and tongs. A vase for Mandy, the love of her life. Together, they would fill it with coneflowers and phlox from Livvie's garden. Sarah didn't think she could get much higher.

About the author and this book

Photo by Dave Terry

Donna Meredith is a freelance writer living in Tallahassee, Florida. Her articles have appeared in *Tallahassee* magazine, the *Southern Literary Review*, *Columbia School Press Review*, the *Tallahassee Democrat*, and the *Midwest Review*.

The Glass Madonna is her first novel. It won first place for unpublished women's fiction in 2009 in the Royal Palm Literary Awards, sponsored by the Florida Writers Association and was also runner up in the 2009 Gulf Coast novel writing contest. She also has won awards for her short stories and essays. From 2009-2010 she served as president of the Tallahassee Writers Association. Currently she coordinates the Seven Hills Literary Contest.

She taught English, journalism, and TV production in public high schools in West Virginia and Georgia until retirement. "I was blessed to work with so many fine young people over those years," she said.

Donna earned a BA in Education with a double major in English and journalism from Fairmont State College, an MS in journalism from West Virginia University, and an EdS in English from Nova Southeastern University. She also participated in fiction writing workshops at Florida State University. She resides in Tallahassee with her husband John and two Pomeranians.

"While the setting of *The Glass Madonna* is my hometown of Clarksburg, WV, the protagonist Sarah is not me, nor are the other characters meant to portray members of my family or my friends," Donna said. "The story attempts to delineate the changes in attitude and culture that occurred during the 1960s and 1970s. Though some members of my family worked in the glass industry generations ago and I admire those artisans who work with glass today, I never had any desire to do so myself. I used the glass union rules to illustrate one of many career paths closed to women. Through extensive research, I tried to accurately depict life in the the early 1900s in the Pittsburgh and Clarksburg area, yet the characters' stories are entirely invented. Like most fiction, this story pulls together fragments of reality and melds them into completely fabricated scenes for dramatic purposes."

For more information about Donna Meredith's books and writing, visit the author website: www.donnameredith.com.